Invisible

Tiffany,

Keep chasing your dreams,
they know the way.

Also by DelSheree Gladden

Escaping Fate Series
Escaping Fate
Soul Stone
Oracle Lost
(Coming Fall 2014)

Twin Souls Saga
Twin Souls
Shaxoa's Gift
Qaletaqa

The Destroyer Trilogy
Inquest
Secret of Betrayal
Darkening Chaos

SomeOne Wicked This Way Comes Series
Wicked Hunger
Wicked Power
(Coming 2014)
Wicked Glory
(Coming 2014)

The Aerling Series
Invisible
Intangible
Invincible
(Coming Fall 2014)

Invisible

Book One of
The Aerling Series

DelSheree Gladden

Createspace

Invisible
Book One of
The Aerling Series
Written by DelSheree Gladden

Copyright © DelSheree Gladden 2013
Cover Design DelSheree Gladden
And Hannah Jennifer
Published by DelSheree Gladden

ISBN-13: 978-1492967224
ISBN-10: 149296722X

For my husband, Ryan, for his support not only with my writing, but his support in everything I do no matter how crazy life gets.

Acknowledgements

I owe a big thank you to Apryl Baker for encouraging me to explore Wattpad and share my work with the amazing readers there. Apryl is always willing to share ideas and help other authors and I count myself lucky to have her as a friend.

I would also like to thank the fabulous Wattpad readers for embracing Mason and Olivia and falling in love with their story. If not for their enthusiasm, I would have likely let Invisible languish on my hard drive for a long time, not sure if anyone would be interested in a story about an invisible boy. Their encouragement and enthusiasm has pushed me to share Invisible with a wider audience.

As always, I need to thank my ever supportive writers group for their help and guidance. Thank you Linda, Angela, Apryl, Ann, Rachel, and Susan. You ladies are the best!

I also need to thank a wonderful reader named Hannah Jennifer. Her love for Invisible inspired her to design a fan cover for this book. I loved the design so much I asked her permission to build on her idea as I created the final cover. She was so gracious and allowed me to work with her design and come up with the cover you see now.

Finally, thank you to my husband, Ryan, for always being there for me no matter what.

CONTENTS

Chapter 1

Invisible

My best friend is *not* imaginary. He's not a ghost, either. And I'm pretty sure he isn't a hallucination. He's just Mason.

He is, however, invisible.

Zipping up my jeans as I stumble into my tennis shoes, I shuffle out of my room. By the time I reach the bathroom, I have both feet solidly in my shoes, even if the laces remain untied. One jiggle of the doorknob sets me to growling. Locked. My eyes dash to my sister, Evie's, door, only to find her making her way down the hall herself. Her hair is sticking up in all sorts of wild ways, so it's pretty safe to assume she hasn't seen the inside of the bathroom yet, either.

"Mason?" she asks, stifling a yawn.

"Who else?" I grouch.

Evie giggles. "You know, for someone who's invisible, he sure does worry a lot about how he looks."

My little sister was the first person in my family to admit Mason was real. My mom and dad passed off my new friend as typical five-year-old stuff. Mom thought it was cute when I asked for extra snacks to share with Mason. Dad didn't even hesitate when I asked if Mason could sleep in my room with me. Evie was only three when Mason first showed up, but she took to him right away. She thought it was great fun to watch him move things and make the cat fly. Really, he was just carrying the cat around in his arms, but since Evie can't see Mason, to her it looked like everything he touched could float.

I've always wondered why Mason's clothes disappear when he puts them on, but the cat never did. He can put something in his pocket and it vanishes, but if he just holds it, it floats. Mason doesn't know either. I think it must be something he's doing without realizing, but Mason disagrees. As far as he knows, that's just how it's meant to work. Since he's the invisible one and I'm not, it's hard to argue with him.

"Mason!" I yell as I pound on the door. "Hurry up!"

I hear a muffled response, that I'm sure was not an apology for hogging the bathroom. I sigh and reach for the key. My fingers brush along the door frame for the simple metal shaft that acts as a rather low-tech key. Finally finding it, I shove the key into the lock and poke around until the door finally opens. Evie stalks in dutifully.

Five seconds later, Mason howls as the shower water turns ice cold. Evie pops her head back out. "Did I get him?" she asks.

● ● ●

Evie can't hear Mason, either. Nobody but me can, not unless he's touching them. And even then, they have to have accepted his presence as reality in order to hear him. I don't know why that works, but it does. I learned a while ago to just accept the bizarreness that comes with Mason.

Laughing, I nod. "Yeah, you got him."

Evie jumps out of the doorway, and just in time. Mason stalks out soon after with a towel slung around his waist. His eyes fasten onto me. The snarly expression on his face doesn't faze me. "That was low, Olivia Lynn Mallory."

Ooh, he used my full name. I'm so *not* scared. "Quit hogging the bathroom."

"I was in the shower!" Mason snaps. "Naked!"

I try not to laugh. I fail. "It's not like she saw anything!"

Mason bristles. "So! It's the principle of the thing. I deserve some privacy!"

"You have all the privacy in the world," I laugh. "What you don't have is the bathroom to yourself."

Evie and I both push past him and grab for our toothbrushes. I'm the only one who can hear Mason muttering under his breath as he storms away, but Evie can imagine his response well enough and giggles along with me.

When our toothbrushes are both back in the holder, I turn to Evie and say, "Don't mention that to Dad, okay?"

"Wasn't planning on it," Evie says.

My little sister moves on to curling her hair as I fish around for my makeup. We may look alike with matching blonde hair and green eyes, but our tastes in hairstyles are vastly different. Evie's locks turn into gorgeous spirals while I spray on a leave in conditioner to get mine straight and frizz free. As we get ready, I can't help but think about how much my dad has changed when it comes to Mason.

He was the last one to admit Mason was real. I had been out in the backyard when I was about eight years old tossing a Frisbee back and forth with Mason. I'm not sure how long Dad stood there watching, trying to figure out how the Frisbee was stopping in midair and flinging itself back to me. It must have been long enough for him to see the implications. The good and the bad.

The good included Dad getting to have a son. Not that he didn't love his two daughters, but I think all dads want a son no matter what they say. There is something strangely fulfilling in playing catch—which is something Dad and Mason do on a regular basis now.

The bad had to do with Dad realizing that when I asked three years earlier if Mason could sleep in my room with me, and he had said yes, he hadn't just been playing pretend with me. Not that anyone worried about what Mason and I were doing at night at eight years old, but well…we wouldn't be eight forever. The spare bedroom got cleaned out the next day.

Now, eight years later, we're all sitting down at the breakfast table. Mom dishes out five rather than four plates of fried eggs and sliced cantaloupe like normal. Nobody bats an eye when it looks like a fork is spearing fruit pieces all by itself. This is totally normal for us, but we don't have people over for dinner very often.

"Evie, did you finish your algebra homework?" Mom asks.

"Yeah, Mason helped me with the last few problems."

Mom smiles at Mason—well in his general direction, anyway. "What about you two?" she asks Mason and I. "Did you finish your reports on *The Federalist Papers*?"

"Mason's is on your desk, and mine is in my backpack," I answer for the both of us.

You would think being invisible would get you out of homework. Not so. Once Mom quit freaking out about seeing Mason toss Evie in the air, she decided that if he was real he was going to be treated just like her other children. He is required to sit through all my classes and turn in assignments. The only difference is, Mom grades his homework instead of my teachers.

Dad looks up from his phone, where he was reading the morning's most urgent emails, and says, "I have a couple of clients coming over this evening for dinner."

Mason's body tenses in response to this news. I'm the only one who notices. I reach over to pat Mason's knee reassuringly, but he pulls away. Frowning at his response, I turn back to Dad.

"Mason, you're excused from dinner tonight."

That only causes him to become even more glum.

"Olivia, you're excused as well." Dad says, surprising both me and Mason. Dad hands over two crisp twenty dollar bills. "Have fun tonight, but please stay out of trouble."

Evie chuckles along with us at the memory of the incident Dad is referring to. We really didn't think anyone else would be at the driving range that late. Mason just wanted to hit a few balls. None of us realized the attendant could see what we were doing. Poor guy.

"Thanks, Dad. We'll be good. I promise." I take the cash and stuff it in my back pocket.

Evie screws her face up in annoyance. "Why can't I be excused too? Your dinner meetings are boring."

"Because little girls who ditch class don't get to go anywhere," Mom reminds her.

• • •

That sets Evie to scowling. It's just a good thing Mom and Dad didn't discover that the reason Evie skipped out on history was so she could make out with her boyfriend. At fourteen, Evie is not supposed to have a boyfriend. At seventeen, I've been allowed for a while now, but that doesn't mean Dad is all that keen on the idea. Luckily for him, I'm not all that social. I have Mason.

I drop my dishes off in the sink and tug on Evie's hair as I pass back by. "Come on, grouchy. We better get going or we'll be late. Mason…" I say, turning to ask him a question. My voice drops off as I see his backside retreating out of the kitchen without a word. Huh.

A few minutes later, Evie and I head for my grumbly, creaky Cherokee. My parents can afford better, but Dad is an insurance executive, and he knows all the statistics of teenager drivers by heart. Not to mention the premiums. I get a safe, but not very cool car. He gets peace of mind and decent rates. I pull my door open and find Mason in the passenger's seat, which is actually kind of weird. He usually tries to talk me into letting him drive.

Not sure what to make of that, I climb in and pull out of the driveway. The drive to school is only about fifteen minutes. It passes in silence. Another oddity. Mason is a total chatterbox on normal days. When I pull into a parking space, Evie hops out and heads for Aaron Chaplin, her not-so-secret boyfriend. Mason makes a move to leave, but I grab his arm before he can.

"Hey, what's with you this morning?"

Mason shakes me off and reaches for the door handle. I grab for him again, missing his arm, but snagging his hand instead. Mason stops trying to get away, but he doesn't look at me.

"Mason, what's wrong?"

For a moment, I don't think he's going to answer me, then, his eyes snap up to mine. "Stop treating me like a freak, Olivia."

The heat of his accusation startles me. So do his words. "What?"

"I'm tired of being *less* than everyone else," he snaps.

"Mason, what are you talking about?" The anger that flashes in his eyes is reflected in how he tosses my hand away from him.

He's really angry, I realize in shock. Mason never gets mad. Taking advantage of my surprise, he bails. He's out of the Cherokee and slamming the door shut before I can move. It takes some effort to come out of my stupor and follow him. My brain catches up with him along with my feet a few seconds later.

"Mason, wait," I say as I catch his arm. "Is this about this morning in the bathroom?"

● ● ●

4

He doesn't answer, but the way his shoulders bunch up is answer enough. "Don't do that again."

"I won't," I say quickly. "I was just playing around. I didn't mean to make you mad."

"Well, how would you like it if someone barged in on you in the shower?"

It takes me a few minutes answer. "But, she couldn't see you, Mason. I wouldn't have done it if she could."

"Exactly," he snaps.

Shaking my head, I try to make sense of his anger. "Are you mad about her turning the shower cold, or bursting in on you?"

"I was naked! As in no clothes on. I don't care that she can't see me. It's no different than if she could."

"Uh, yeah it is, Mason. I never would have sent Evie in if she could see you."

Mason's hands shove deep down into his jeans pockets. "I don't want it to be different," he growls.

Suddenly, things start making sense. Mason doesn't pull away when I step closer to him and take his hand in mine. He has always been so good natured about being who he is. He was always willing to play a part in a well devised practical joke. He loves freaking people out. Halloween is his favorite time of year. But there have been times when I wondered if any of it bothered him.

"It wasn't just this morning," Mason says more quietly. "It's dinner, too."

"We get a pass on a boring business dinner," I say, trying to sound chipper. "There's this movie…"

Mason interrupts, saying, "It's the reason behind everything, okay? No, I don't want to sit through a discussion about insurance premiums. I know Evie didn't see anything this morning. But both happened because I'm different."

I don't want to sound accusing, or obnoxious, but I don't get why this is all boiling to the surface right now. "Mason, what's going on? None of this kind of stuff has ever bothered you before."

"I know," he says with a sigh. "I love you and Evie and your parents, but…"

"But what?" I ask.

"Sometimes I get tired of being the guy nobody can see."

Whatever I might have said to that, it gets stuffed back down my throat as we're both ran into from behind. Mason catches me when I stumble, and

● ● ●

we both turn around to find the culprit. A tall, lanky girl with wispy brown hair and bright, red-framed glasses is stumbling back to her feet as well.

"I'm so sorry!" she gasps. "I'm totally lost. Can you tell me where the office is?"

"Uh, it's the first building on the right. It's not attached to the rest of the school."

"Thanks a bunch," she says with a laugh. A small shift in posture sends her bag sliding off her shoulder, which nearly sends the books in her arms scattering. It takes her a moment to get everything back under control. She clutches her belongings a little more tightly and looks back up, still smiling. "I've been wandering the halls for twenty minutes. Then someone told me to go back outside. I'm a mess."

At least I wasn't the one who said it. I glance at Mason sideways. The way he's trying not to laugh makes it even harder for me to keep a straight face. I turn back to the girl, who immediately sticks her hand out to me.

"I'm Robin Montgomery, by the way," she says happily.

"Olivia Mallory," I say as we shake hands.

Our hands part ways, and then she does something completely unexpected.

Robin sticks her hand out directly in front of Mason and says, "And you are?"

Stunned is not a strong enough word to describe the look on Mason's face. I'm pretty sure my jaw is sitting on my shoes.

My, "You can see him?" is compounded with Mason's, "You can see me?"

Robin's grin freezes. Her extended hand drops away slowly. She glances between us looking confused. "Uh, yeah."

"You can see me?" Mason repeats, clearly doubtful.

Hugging her books a little tighter, Robin shrugs. "Is this some kind of new kid trick? If it is, at least it's original. I've got plenty of experience with being the new kid, but I've never had anyone pretend I'm seeing things before."

"What do I look like?" Mason demands.

Robin shrugs, apparently willing to play along. "Okay, you've got reddish-gold hair that's longish, but not too long. You're eyes are blue, but super dark, and they have this awesome silver color right around the pupil. That's really neat! Do you wear special contacts?"

Neither of us answers, too surprised by her accuracy and detail.

Continuing, Robin says, "You're pretty tall, well taller than me, anyway. You look like you might play soccer...or maybe baseball, judging by your build. And you're totally hot, just in case you didn't already know that."

That last comment breaks Mason out of his stupor, bringing on a grin. "I like this girl. Can we keep her?"

"Does that mean I passed the test…or game? Whatever this thing was?" Robin asks.

"Yeah," I say, still a little shaken, "you passed."

Robin's giggle brings another smile to Mason's lips. He extends his hand again. "I'm Mason, by the way."

They shake hands, their eyes glued to each other in a way I find myself just a bit irritated by. The feeling only intensifies when Robin looks over at me and says, "Please tell me Mason isn't your boyfriend."

"Boyfriend?" I say, nearly laughing. "No, he's my …"

I struggle to find a word that explains what Mason is to me. Robin waits patiently for me to finish confirming Mason is single and up for grabs. Mason, oddly enough, has stopped ogling Robin, and is now staring at me rather intently. The sudden pressure to define Mason's role in my life makes me falter and stumble through a rather incoherent answer.

"Mason's my brother, well, kind of … I mean he's not really, but he's my, um, best friend. You know what I mean?"

"Uh, sure?" Robin says. No way she understood my rambling, but I think she gathered enough to determine Mason isn't my boyfriend, so she seems happy enough.

I glance over at Mason for help. The sadness echoed in his eyes startles me. He turns away to listen to whatever Robin is now saying, leaving me confused and hurt. Did I not give the right answer? I wasn't trying to hurt his feelings, but I've never had to explain Mason to anyone outside my family before. I think of him as my brother, but I know he's really not. I stand there feeling like a jerk as understanding hits me. Right after he confessed his frustration about being different, I have to point out that he is the odd man out in our family. Why didn't I just say he was my brother and leave it at that?

Robin's sudden gasp brings me out of my thoughts. I'm surprised to see her hands pawing at Mason's neck. I step forward, wondering what has her so worked up, but all I see is the weird birthmark Mason has always had. The trail of pigment that looks something like a meandering stream isn't your typical blotchy birthmark, but it's certainly not worth practically crawling up Mason's body to get a better look!

I step forward to get this strange girl off Mason, but she finally snaps her hands away and gapes at him.

"Oh my gosh! You weren't kidding, were you? You really were surprised I could see Mason!" she squeaks. "I had no idea! Why didn't you just tell me Mason is an Aerling?"

Chapter 2

Caretakers

The final bell rings as Olivia and I stare at Robin. We are both too stunned to react, but Robin jumps at the sound. "Oh my goodness! I am never going to make it to class today. Can we meet up at lunch? I don't know anyone else, and I have like a zillion questions to ask you! Where do you two usually sit? Oh never mind, I better run. I'll just look for you, okay? See you at lunch!"

She whirls away, nearly dropping her books again, and starts jogging toward the office. I'm still having trouble wrapping my head around Robin. The rambling monologue she just threw at us certainly didn't help. Olivia is the first to break the silence.

"Mason, what did she just call you?" Olivia asks.

I shake my head. I have a million questions, but I'm also terrified. I try to play it off as nothing, hoping Olivia won't notice my fear. "I think she said *Air-ling*. Maybe? Either that or she called me an earring."

Olivia smacks my arm. "She did not say earring."

The fact that the bell rang and we are both now tardy finally sinks in. We start toward our class, but that hardly means our minds are on school. Fear tried to hold my curiosity hostage, but it isn't strong enough. "What the heck was she talking about? And why could she see me?"

"I have no idea. She was beyond weird," Olivia says. She bites the corner of her lip. "I mean, she was nice, but strange."

"She said I was hot." I grin as Olivia rolls her eyes. "What? It's nice to know! No one has ever told me that before."

"That's because no one but me has ever seen you before," Olivia says as we approach the door to the classroom.

I smirk at her. "So are you saying I'm not hot?"

Her answering glare isn't very encouraging. "Really?" she snaps. "We just met the only other person who has ever been able to see you, and she seems to know something about what you are, and all you can think about is whether or not you're hot?"

"So? I'm curious. You know you're beautiful. Everyone thinks so. Guys stare at you all the time. I don't have the benefit of external validation of my appearance. I've got you, that's it. You've never said a word about my looks. So, yes, I'm curious. Am I attractive?"

Olivia shrugs, annoyed that I am not taking this as seriously as she is. "I don't know. I guess? I've never really thought about it, okay?"

Her hand reaches out for the door, but before she pushes it open, she turns around to glare at me. "When you decide to take this Robin chick seriously, let me know. Her seeing you may not be a good thing. Think about that," she snaps.

She yanks the door open and stalks to her desk. I follow at a more leisurely pace. In truth, Robin's words did freak me out. I think it's awesome that she can see me. Her having a name for me…there's a good chance Olivia is right. It could change things. One thing I know from experience is that change is *not* good.

Lately, living under a separate set of rules because of who I am has been getting to me, but I still wouldn't trade my life for anything. The idea of not being with Olivia, or Evie and their parents, scares me more than I care to admit. They are my whole world.

Slipping into an empty seat at the back of the room, my mind continues to whirl. For a long time, I am stuck thinking about the word *Aerling* and what that might mean. I try to contemplate the impact Robin might have on my life, but after a while I decide to give up because I know too little to figure anything out and I'm too scared to try. I resign myself to three more hours of confusion before I can ask Robin a few questions. In an effort to distract myself, my thoughts turn back to Olivia and the answers she gave today.

My eyes slip over to her. Quietly staring at the board, pretending to be interested in a lecture on the Napoleonic Wars, Olivia takes no notice of me. As I watch her, my jumbled thoughts slow. I wasn't kidding when I told her she was beautiful. Her strawberry blonde hair makes me think of summer days playing outside. Her lips are only a shade darker than her hair, and her dark green eyes border on evergreen.

What makes her even more attractive is that she doesn't seem to care. She's not one of those girls who doesn't understand how pretty she is or pretends not to know in order to tease. Olivia knows she's attractive, but she doesn't see why that matters. Guys hit on her and she shrugs them off without another thought. I wish I could shrug it off when guys hit on her that easily. Nothing irritates me more.

Having said that, I have perfected the art of pretending not to notice other guys' interest in her. Although, that ability is tested when Hayden Benton tugs on a strand of Olivia's hair in order to get her attention. The annoyed expression Olivia has been holding all class slips away as she turns to face a guy most girls would go all gooey-eyed over in a second. Something to do with his dark hair and equally dark eyes, not to mention the fact that he spends more time working out than studying. I don't get it.

Curiosity lifts Olivia's eyebrows as she comes face to face with Hayden's all-too-charming smile. Somehow he makes asking to borrow a pencil a seductive encounter. Not that Olivia seems to notice. She shrugs and hands him a spare pencil before turning her attention back to being irritated at me. Hayden keeps staring at the back of her head.

The whole encounter takes me back to the parking lot, to Olivia's answer to Robin's question. I guess I can understand being caught off guard when Robin abruptly asked about our relationship. She's never had to explain that to anyone before. I slump into a sulk as I remember her answer. Brother? Kind of? Best friend?

Are we best friends? Of course.

But her brother?

I am *not* her brother.

The bell rings and the class files out. Olivia ignores me, and I know she will continue to ignore me until I prove I'm ready to be serious. On principle, I'm not terribly fond of serious. Today is different. I'm not just being flippant. I'm afraid. I have no desire to start up another conversation about Robin right now. We step into the hall in silence. I'm prepared to spend the next three class periods the same way. Too bad other people aren't on the same page.

"Hey, Olivia!" Hayden calls out. "Wait up!"

Startled, Olivia turns around. "Yeah?"

Hayden trots up to her with another obnoxious smile. He slips a pencil out of his pocket and offers it up. "Thanks for letting me borrow this."

Olivia takes the pencil back with a shrug. "Sure, no problem."

For a moment, I worry that Hayden is about to attempt a full out conversation. The thought of standing here listening to his inane drivel has zero appeal. There is something about his dark hair and athletic build that I find offensive. Or maybe it's his casual ability to capture just about anyone's attention. Although, it might be the way his hand brushes Olivia's arm like it's nothing as he asks her a question about the lecture we just sat through.

Yeah, I'm pretty sure that's it.

Not interested in hanging around for Hayden's charm, I head for our next class. I'm surprised when I see Robin plow around a corner at breakneck speed. She catches sight of me just before knocking into a couple too busy making out as they walk to notice the collision. Their obliviousness doesn't keep Robin from getting her feet tangled and pitching forward.

Two quick steps brings me close enough to catch her elbow and save her from nose diving. Robin beams up at me…once she makes it back up to standing. "You okay?" I ask.

Laughing off the incident, Robin says, "I'm not normally this klutzy."

● ● ●

"Sure, sure."

"Really! It's just first day jitters. Not to mention the fact that this school is a maze! I can't find anything."

Feeling suddenly like taking a break, I lean against a row of lockers. "What exactly are you trying to find this time?"

"Room 217? I'm supposed to be taking AP English with Mrs. Hamilton."

"AP?" I ask.

Robin rolls her eyes. "Why do people always sound surprised when they find out I'm smart?"

It's hard not to laugh. "It might be the tripping and dropping things and bumping into people." I shrug jokingly. "Just a guess."

Her huff of irritation is downplayed by her smile. "Whatever," she says. Then she holds out a stack of books. "Can you hold this? I think my phone is buzzing at me."

"Uh, not to be unchivalrous, but I think the other students might find floating books to be a bit strange," I say, holding my hands up in apology. "Your class is around the corner to the right, though."

The blush that spreads though Robin's cheeks is kind of cute. "Sorry! I keep forgetting you're an Aerling, not a human. I'm such a mess today."

Robin does some shifting, and snatches her phone out of a side pocket on her backpack. She mumbles something about overprotective parents as she reads the text she just got. Thankfully, she doesn't notice that I have checked out of the conversation. What did she mean when she said I wasn't human? She's not serious, is she?

I mean, it's always been pretty obvious that I'm different, but I just figured it was some kind of genetic thing, or radiation, maybe even a super power. Not human? I never actually considered the possibility. The idea is somewhat disturbing, but at the same time, kind of cool. What if I'm like Superman?

"Anyway," Robin says, bursting into my thoughts, "thanks for helping me find my class. Where are you off to?"

It only takes me a moment to decide, my curiosity getting the better of my fear again. "Actually, I thought I might check out what an AP class is like. Mind if I join you?"

Robin beams at me again. "Not at all!"

We file through the door and Robin finds a seat next to the wall of windows. It's perfect because I can park myself on the sill and still be within "chatting" distance. Of course, Robin probably isn't familiar with my version of note passing, so I take a moment to explain before the teacher gets class started.

● ● ●

"If you pretend you're taking notes, I can read whatever you write from here."

Robin's eyes dart toward me for a brief second before settling forward as if I weren't there. She neatly places two sheets of loose leaf paper on the desk. I wonder why she has two. On one she writes, *Cool, I have tons of questions for you!* On the other she writes the date and *AP English.* I stifle a laugh when I realize she's actually taking real notes along with the fake ones. Robin is an interesting girl.

Mrs. Hamilton launches right into her lecture, not even bothering to take notice that she has a new student in her room. Robin doesn't seem put out. Instead, she turns her attention back to her papers. For me, she writes, *Do you remember how you came here?*

I shake my head. There wasn't any *coming* here. I've always been here. Robin sighs, clearly frustrated.

Why is that the one thing Aerlings can never remember? They remember everything else.

Her comment piques my interest. I do have a very good memory, eidetic even, but I can't remember everything. There are big sections of my early childhood that are nothing more than fragments, fragments that I don't really like to think about. Even now, I shy away from the bits of memory that try to surface. The flash of pain, the terror of a hand clamping down around my arm.

A nudge from Robin send images like that back into the recesses of my mind. I glance down at her notebook, eager for a new question. What she writes surprises me.

Tell me about your name.

If she were asking Olivia that same question, she would get a pretty basic answer, something like how Olivia comes from olive tree which is a symbol of peace in Latin, or that she was named after her maternal grandmother. I was surprised when I realized naming a child didn't hold the same significance in most families as it did in mine. In my first family, that is.

"When I was named, everyone in the family was gathered around me. Everyone placed one hand on me, and I remember feeling strange in this new place, but it was okay because I knew how much everyone loved me. I remember seeing my mom smiling at me. My dad was crying. It was the only time I ever saw him cry, except …"

My hands ball into fists as I try to ward off the image his face contorted in pain. Robin has been staring at the board, listening both to me and the teacher, but after a few minutes she glances over at me in concern. Afraid she'll start asking questions, I force myself to continue.

"My mom said each of my names would mean something. Each one was special, and would help me remember who I am," I say slowly, still trying to shake off the pain talking about this sparks. "My first name, Mason, meant I would be strong, physically and mentally, but more importantly, I would be the kind of person people could rely on. Someone who would stand up for what I knew was right."

Wow, Robin writes, *that's a lot to live up to.*

I laugh. "And that's only my first name!"

Robin smiles, barely stopping herself from giggling. *Tell me about the other two.*

Shaking my head, I say, "Maybe later. My turn."

I watch as Robin sits up straighter with her pencil poised to answer. She's an interesting girl.

"How do you know so much about Aerlings?"

Robin looks over at me with an expression that clearly says I'm completely nuts. She starts scratching out a hurried answer. *I had one of my own, of course! My family has been Caretakers for generations. Hasn't Olivia's family?*

Part of me wants to explain how Olivia found me, tell her about my other family. Maybe she could help me make sense of everything. But if she knows how this is all supposed to work, she'll realize that somehow my life got screwed up. What if she tries to change things, or take me away from Olivia? I make a snap decision, not willing to risk losing Olivia, not even for answers that have plagued me my entire life.

"Yeah, of course they have," I lie. "It's just that we've never met anyone else who is, uh, a Caretaker. I didn't want to assume."

Robin nods as if that makes perfect sense. *Okay, my turn again. When did you realize you were an Aerling? Or did your parents tell you right away?*

This question brings back another round of painful memories as well. One of the few clear memories I have before meeting Olivia is of wandering around the city crying and begging for help, confused why no one would look at me, let alone help me.

"No," I say, "they didn't tell me. I figured it out when I was five."

Robin shakes her head. *I don't understand why Caretakers don't tell Aerlings who they are. It only hurts them later to realize they've been lied to. I mean, I get that they don't want to make them feel like they're different, but it's the truth.*

"Yeah, I'm with you on that one." Maybe if they had told me, I would have known what to do. Instead, I was alone and terrified.

Chapter 3

Sentinel

I don't know where Mason has been, but when he pops up near the cafeteria I latch onto his arm and refuse to let go. "Where have you been all morning?"

"Getting to know our new friend," Mason says.

"What?"

Mason shrugs, as if my question barely fazes him, but I can see the tension in his shoulders.

"I decided to go to class with Robin."

"Why?"

"Why?" Mason asks. "Because she can see me and talk to me. That's reason enough."

I can certainly understand the appeal, but I'm still miffed. "You could have at least told me where you were going. I turned around and you were gone."

Mason rolls his eyes. "And interrupt your fascinating conversation with Hayden Benton?"

"Fascinating?" What on earth is he talking about? Hayden returned my pencil and asked me if I knew when our next test was.

I shake off Mason's weirdness and say, "Look, I know you're excited that someone other than me can see and hear you, but we know nothing about this Robin chick. What if she uses something you tell her against you?"

"What's she going to do? Tell people you have an invisible guy living at your house? I'm sure that will go over well."

"Would you please be serious about this for five seconds?" I snap.

Mason's body bristles. He takes a step away from me and turns the corner. Knowing the drill, I follow him to the abandoned drinking fountains and pull out my phone. I hold it to my ear, so if anyone walks by they'll assume I'm arguing with whoever is on the other end of the call and not that I'm totally insane, yelling at a wall.

Usually we can manage to talk without anyone else noticing, thanks to the crowds and noise. Pulling a stunt like this means if we continue this conversation, people will notice. I don't like these kinds of conversations.

Locking eyes with Mason, I ask, "What is going on?"

For a moment, Mason doesn't respond. He seems to be considering his words very carefully. That's never a good sign, either.

"Robin knows stuff," Mason says slowly.

"Like what kind of stuff?"

● ● ●

After a minute of shuffling, Mason responds. "Stuff like naming ceremonies, Caretakers, how good my memory is."

"What do you mean? How much does she know?" Everything he's saying is only making me more anxious.

"Well, she knew enough to ask me questions about my name, for starters. She knew what a big deal it was to my family, and she acted like that was totally normal."

I can feel my nose crinkle. Evie tells me every time she sees me doing it that I'm wrecking my skin with all the scrunching and I'll end up with winkles like cat whiskers. I'm not vain, or at least I don't think I am, but that does concern me a little. I try to unwrinkled my nose and think.

"Okay, so what does that mean?" This time my forehead wrinkles. "When she called you an Aerling and acted like it was no big deal, I guess I figured that meant there are more people like you out there somewhere. How does she know this stuff?"

Mason fidgets again, folding his arms across his chest. "She said something about Caretakers, people who watch over Aerlings. She said her and her ancestors have been Caretakers for a long time, and get this … she used to have an Aerling."

"She used to *have* one? That sounds like she's talking about a toy car. What is a Caretaker, anyway? Like some kind of foster family?"

"I guess," Mason says with a shrug. Now he really starts getting antsy. His feet shuffle and eyes go to his shoes. I know that look as well.

Sighing, I ask, "What did you tell her?"

"I may have told her that you and your family are Caretakers, too," he admits. Mason looks up, searching my expression for a reaction. He seems shocked when he gets one.

"What?" I demand. "Why would you do that? What if she asks me some kind of Caretaker question, or wants to compare notes, or has some kind of secret handshake?"

Mason snorts, only maddening me even more. "Really? A secret handshake?" His laugh is incredibly annoying.

"Well, it isn't any weirder than living with an invisible person!" I defend.

His head shakes back and forth. "What else did you expect me to tell her? Was I supposed to admit that my real family …"

Suddenly, Mason looks away. When I realize his hands are balled into fists and his jaw is quivering, I reach out to him. I can hardly stand here hugging a bunch of thin air, but I slide my hand around one of his fists. I know thinking about his family is never easy. His reaction right now is more intense than usual, though. Worry that Robin dredged up memories he'd rather forget makes me edge away from concern about her and toward dislike.

It takes another minute before Mason continues. "I couldn't explain all of that to her."

"I know." My hand tightens around his. "I'm sorry I snapped at you."

Mason shakes off my apology. "It's more than that, too. She obviously knows what's supposed to happen with Aerlings. If I tell her what really happened, what would she do? Maybe there's some kind of Aerling Child Services, or something. What if she told someone and they tried to take me away from you?"

"Mason, Mom and Dad would never let anyone take you from us. *I* wouldn't let that happen."

"Who knows what *people* might be involved, or what they're capable of?" Mason says.

The worry that has been niggling at my mind worsens. Mason has never shared the exact details of what happened to his real family, but I know enough to understand it was bad. It had to be for a five year old to end up wandering the streets alone. If that wasn't proof enough, Mason's nightmares are more than enough to convince me.

The first night he stayed with me, we were huddled together on my bed, sleeping after a full afternoon of playing in the backyard. It was the shaking that woke me first. I tried to ask him what was happening, but he wouldn't wake up. Then he started screaming. I was so freaked out that I ran into my parents' room crying, begging them to help me. They thought I was the one having bad dreams, because, of course, they thought Mason was imaginary, but it did the trick. Mom took me back to my room and sang songs to me while I held Mason's hand. I wouldn't let her leave until he stopped crying.

"Mason, what if what happened to your family ..." I pause as his hand cinches around mine. "What if Robin has something to do with them?"

"I don't know, Olivia. I know we just met her, but she seems so genuine. She's pretty stoked about finding me. Whatever she knows, I don't think she, herself, is dangerous," he says, "but if she tells people about me, and word gets back to the wrong people, it could be bad."

No kidding, I think, as I turn and lean against the wall. I can admit that I have always been curious about Mason's past. If it means risking his safety or not having him in my life, I will happily leave those questions unanswered forever. I push away from the wall and meet his eyes. My seriousness is hard for him to dodge. He straightens up as well.

"So, how do we handle this?" I ask.

Mason shrugs. "We go to lunch, I guess."

● ● ●

16

Okay, so maybe he isn't going to be serious. My narrowing eyes have no effect on him. "Mason," I growl. "We need a plan."

"I already told you my plan. You pretend you're my Caretaker and we find out as much as we can from Robin at lunch."

"Your plan sucks," I grouch. Even still, my shoulders slouch because I don't have a better one. "Fine. Let's go to lunch."

I don't realize Mason is still holding my hand until he starts toward the cafeteria and my arm is yanked after him. Apparently he didn't realize either, because he stops and looks down at our hands. He smiles sheepishly, no doubt embarrassed that his earlier anxiety affected him so much.

His hand slides out of mine as he says, "Sorry."

I bump against Mason's shoulder with a smile before continuing on to the cafeteria. As soon as we walk through the double doors, I spot her. It's hard to miss her sitting all by herself at a table meant for eight. Her bright red glasses stick out just as much as her big, goofy grin. I can't help cringing when she sees us and starts waving enthusiastically. People already think I'm kind of weird. Robin certainly isn't going to improve my reputation.

Mason is already five steps ahead of me before I commit myself to sitting down next to Robin. By the time I actually sit down I am convinced she is about to explode. The mental image of her head bursting like a party balloon does nothing to improve my mood. Normally, I don't mind perky people. Perky and question hungry, possibly a threat…that, I'm not so keen on.

"How was your morning, Olivia? I had so much fun with Mason! He hung out in my classes with me and we talked about all kinds of stuff. I love the name your family picked out for him! He only told me about his first name, though. I can't wait to hear about the other names. I was too little when my parents chose the name for our Aerling, but I loved hearing the meanings. I am so excited to get to talk about this stuff again! It's been forever since I've had Caretaker friends to chat with. Aren't you excited?" Robin says, the words bulleting out of her mouth.

A quick glance over at Mason almost makes me laugh. With one eyebrow cocked and his mouth hanging half open, he looks a little surprised by Robin's free flowing enthusiasm. He hasn't had to spend nearly as many hours listening to Evie prattle on about everything under the sun as I have. Needless to say, I recover first.

"Excited might be a little strong," I say simply.

Now Robin looks shocked. "What? How can you not be excited? I always hated keeping secrets. It feels so awesome to be able to talk about this stuff with someone who understands."

Regardless of the fact that Robin is acting completely clueless, I'm not buying it just yet. I lean back in my chair and eye her carefully. "We prefer keeping to ourselves, actually. Having other Caretakers around, well, it feels a little claustrophobic."

"Hmm," Robin says, tilting her head to one side. "I guess I might be a little out of the loop since it's been a while since we've had much contact with the others, but I didn't think the conflict was still going on. Grandma said it had been bad when she was younger, but she made it sound like most of it had resolved. Mom and Dad never really talked about it. Has it gotten worse? Was there an actual split? Oh wow, if there was … maybe I should call my grandma when I get home and ask her about it."

Sure that Robin will continue to ramble without stopping, I step in and shut her up before she totally loses me. "Look, I have no idea what you're talking about …"

Mason's eyes widened, thinking I am about to bail on his not-so-carefully laid plan. I roll my eyes and refocus on Robin.

"I never said anything about a conflict or splitting. All I said was that my family prefers to keep things private. We don't have much contact with the other Caretakers or anyone else involved in all this, for that matter."

"Why not?" Robin all but demands.

"Why should we?" I counter. Not my best comeback, but I am grasping at straws here.

Robin's shoulders drop in defeat. "Because…because other Caretakers are the only ones who understand. We help each other and give each other support when we need it. It's not easy walking around with secrets all the time."

For some reason, Robin's chin dips down. I can't say for sure, but I think I see a hint of tears in her eyes. Is she hiding something? Guilt would be my guess, but guilt for what? I'm suddenly so fixated on what mistakes she might have made, or secrets she might have let her runaway mouth spit out, that when she speaks again I jump.

"What about Mason? Staying in contact with the other Caretakers gives all the Aerlings a chance to socialize and help each other," Robin says, just a touch indignant.

Her tone gets under my skin. Is she judging my family for our choices? In the back of my mind I know she has the whole situation screwed up because we're lying to her, but all the same, what right does she have to judge?

"Mason has me," I snap, "and Evie and Mom and Dad. Why would he need anyone else?"

Again, I look over at Mason, expecting him to back me up. The expression on his face makes me falter. There is longing and guilt reflected in his eyes. I don't understand. He would never want to leave us, right? There's no way he would ever want other Aerlings more than us. It hurts to think he would even consider it. I am stunned...until Robin starts talking again.

"Why would he want to be around other Aerlings?" Robin asks in disbelief. She shakes her head at me, like *I'm* the crazy one. "Olivia, you seriously can't imagine what it's like to be like Mason? His world consists of his family, *only* his family. Even though I'm sure you all love him a lot, that's a totally tiny world!

"Sure, he can go anywhere, do anything, and no one will ever see him. Nobody else sees the talents he has or gets to experience his personality and sense of humor. The only people who hear and see him are obligated to love him because they're his family. It makes it pretty hard to ever feel truly accepted!

"And they're so different. They experience life here in a way we can never understand. They have to be hidden, kept secret, lied about. It hurts to always be viewed as a potential problem, don't you get that? Being around other Aerlings is the only time they're *actually* free to be themselves! Why would you want to take that away from him?"

Her accusing stare pins me. I am too shocked to say anything. My eyes dart to Mason, hoping he will stand up for me, for my family. I am stunned all over again when I see his defeated posture, his glassy eyes downcast. Suddenly, it doesn't matter that everything Robin is judging my family for is all ridiculous because we never actually made choices to keep Mason away from people like him. We didn't even know they existed. We did the best we could, but it doesn't make any difference.

I realize as I watch Robin's hand slide comfortingly over Mason's that it's all true regardless of reality. Mason has felt isolated. He hates being our secret...our problem. Practical jokes aside, it kills him to be locked inside the little box that is my family. I know he loves us, but Robin is right, he will never have the opportunity to experience life in a way that truly gives it meaning.

Mason's funk this morning seemed so strange to me at the time. Now, I am astounded that I have been so blind not to see how much he has been struggling lately. I sniff against the inevitability of tears, tilting my head up just enough to keep them from falling.

"Olivia," Robin says, sounding rather far away.

When I don't respond right away, she says my name again. Eventually, I turn in her direction, but don't actually look up at her. Only Mason's hand closing over mine gives me enough strength to meet her gaze. When I do, Robin looks embarrassed.

"Olivia, I'm so sorry. I didn't mean to be so awful to you. I wasn't thinking, something my mom says happens all the time when I start talking." She rolls her eyes. "It's just that the other Caretakers we knew were so supportive through everything and it made such a difference to know them. I didn't think that maybe your family had experienced something different until Mason explained." Robin shakes her head, chastising herself. "I know, that's not an excuse. I shouldn't have judged, either way. Sometimes my mouth just gets the better of me. Friends?"

I stare at her, completely dumbfounded. I turn and stare at Mason. "You told her?" I squeak.

Mason meets my eyes directly, speaking slowly when he begins. "I told her about the other Caretakers your parents knew. I told them how they betrayed some of the families in our area and told their secrets, and the harm they caused. Robin understands now that your mom and dad were just trying to protect me by distancing us from the others."

His gaze doesn't waver until I nod slowly.

Where did he come up with that? I am amazed that he was able to fabricate a convincing lie so easily, and deliver it so calmly. More importantly, I am so relieved that he stuck up for our family, no matter how much Robin's words rang true with him.

Both of Mason's hands are on the table, but I pat his leg gently in thanks. Mason's eyes dart over to mine at the feel of my hand on his thigh. I feel badly for startling him and pull my hand back, but suddenly his hand is gripping mine, holding it tightly in place.

Knowing that he is probably still hurting from what Robin said earlier, I don't try to pull away again. Instead, I turn back to Robin. I am no longer in the mood for a question and answer session, but I do have one thought scampering around in my mind that won't be put off for later.

"Robin, you mentioned the Aerling your family used to take care of, but obviously he or she isn't with you anymore. What happened?"

Robin's already pale face turns ghostly. "Her name was Eliana, and she isn't with us anymore because the Sentinels killed her."

Chapter 4
Nightmares

Screaming wakes me from an already troubled sleep. The sound of Mason's voice calling out in fear and pain jolts me out of bed and sends me running down the hall. Pushing through his door, the yelling doubles in volume. Mason lays on the bed thrashing. I hurry over to him, unfortunately all too familiar with this routine.

"Mason," I call out as loudly as I dare. I don't want to wake the rest of the house. "Mason!"

With his eyes squeezed shut, he continues to thrash and mumble words I can't pick out of the chaos. I try calling his name several more times, but he won't respond. Worry begins building in my heart. It's never been this hard to wake him before. With all the new revelations and stress he's had to deal with today, I am concerned this is more than just nightmares.

Dodging his flailing arms, I reach in and grip his shoulder hard. My plan was to give him a quick shake, but before I have the chance, Mason's eyes snap open wide and terrified. His whole body freezes, his eyes not seeing anything but the horrible memories I know are replaying in his mind.

"Mason," I whisper. My fingers tighten on his shoulder, but I am afraid to move him. "Mason," I try again.

When his whole body starts shaking, I panic.

"Mason. Mason! Wake up. Please, you're scaring me!" I grab his other shoulder and hold on tight as he continues to shake. I am half a second away from calling out for my dad when Mason suddenly wakes up.

For a moment he seems confused, then his eyes find mine and his arms practically strangle me as he yanks me into his lap. His face is buried in my hair, hiding from everything before I can even react.

"Ollie," he whispers. "Ollie, you're here. Don't leave, Ollie. Don't leave."

The torture in his voice breaks my heart. My arms tighten around him. "I'm not going anywhere, Mason."

We hold each other until Mason's body stops trembling, until my heartbeat climbs the ladder back down from rabbit-speed to normal. Even once the night no longer feels like it is collapsing in on us, we stay in each other's arms. I am afraid to let go. The irrational fear that the nightmares will start again if we slip apart keeps me from doing anything. I don't know if Mason feels the same fear, but he makes no move to push me aside either.

Time is indeterminable in this moment. It doesn't matter. All that matters is Mason.

"Thank you," Mason whispers in the darkness. "Thank you for staying with me."

Gently, I push back just enough so we can see each other. "Are you okay now?"

There is indecision in his eyes before finally saying, "Yeah, I guess."

"Liar," I say. I start to stand up, but Mason latches onto my arm before I can get more than a few inches away, proving my point. Instead of saying so, I press my hand against his cheek. "Hey, I'm not going anywhere. I'm just moving so I can rub your shoulders. It always helps you calm down after a nightmare, so scoot up."

Mason does as he is told and I settle on the bed behind him. I have to stack a couple of pillows beneath me so I can comfortably reach his shoulders, but as soon as my fingers start kneading away at his knotted up muscles I hear him sigh in relief. As I work at his stress, my mind works at puzzling out tonight's odd events.

Most nights, Mason has nightmares about what happened to his family. They are always scary and leave him feeling the loss all over again, but tonight was different. I have never heard him screaming like he did tonight. It scared me half to death when he woke me. Not being able to wake him for so long was even worse. Something about his nightmare tonight was different. I want to ask him about it, but usually all asking questions gets me is silence and a sour mood. Still, I am worried enough to risk it.

"Mason, what happened tonight?"

His shoulders shrug under my fingers. "Nightmares," he mumbles.

"The same as usual?" I question. "Because you haven't called me Ollie since we were little. And even then, you only called me that when you were really upset."

When Mason hesitates, I know I am right. Maybe pushing him to talk is selfish, but this feels important and I am not willing to let it go. My silence is enough of a push after several minutes.

"It started out the same," he says slowly.

"It was about your family at first?"

Mason nods. "Every night it's the same. Screaming, crying. Watching them come, watching them hurt my family...my sister."

Sister? My hands slow as I falter. Mason has never said anything about a sister before. I knew he wasn't an only child, but he's never shared any specifics with me. Just talking about them is too much. It is a struggle to continue massaging his shoulders with my shaking hands as I realize Mason may have witnessed his sister's death.

"Everything was the same until I got away," Mason says quietly.

When Mason doesn't continue right away, my mind is taken back to the day I saw Mason standing in our front yard. He was filthy, but I barely noticed. His tears were what captured my attention. I had never seen him in the neighborhood before, but I quietly went out the front door even though I knew I wasn't supposed to go in the front yard without my mom. When I sat down on the front steps beside him, he nearly jumped right out of his shoes.

For a moment, I thought he was going to run away. Then, suddenly, he stopped crying. He looked at me as if he was confused about something. When he reached out and touched my cheek, I didn't flinch away. Wanting to make him feel better, I asked him if he wanted to play with me.

I was too young to question where his parents were. Later that night when he asked if he could stay the night at my house, I was more than happy to say yes. I had no idea at the time that his entire family had been murdered and he had nowhere else to go. I was just happy to have made a new friend and I wanted to do everything I could to make sure he was happy and didn't cry anymore.

"Mason, how did the nightmare change?" I ask.

"I found you," he says slowly, "which I usually don't. It always ends with me running away, scared and alone. This time, I made it to your house, and then all of the sudden we were older, the same age we are now. I thought everything was fine until they came back. Then it started happening all over again."

"What started?"

Mason shudders. "The killing."

"The…what?"

"They found me. They wanted to hurt me again, but they couldn't get to me. They hurt your mom and dad instead. I tried to protect Evie, but no matter what I did it wasn't enough. And then …" Mason's voice breaks. His head drops and his hands come up to press against his head. "…then they came after you. I couldn't stop them. They hurt you. They took you away from me."

It isn't just his nightmare that shocks me. I haven't seen Mason cry since the day we met, but I can feel his body shuddering now as he tries to hold back sobs. When I slide one of my hands to his face, he presses against it and the tears tumble over my fingers. Words come slowly, yet my breathing is rapid as fear sets in.

"Mason, it was just a dream. No one is going to hurt us," I say, more of a prayer than a statement.

"What if it's not?" Mason asks when his body begins to calm.

More frightened by that statement than I let on, I say, "What do you mean?"

Mason reaches up and stops my hands from rubbing his back. Gentle pressure pulls my arms over his shoulders. I quickly fold them around him in a hug, resting my chin on his shoulder. His own arms follow suit.

When Mason doesn't answer my question, I say, "Mason, as scary as it was, it's just a dream. All that stuff with Robin today has you freaked out. No one is going to hurt us or take you away."

"Why did it happen the first time?" Mason demands.

"You mean to your family?"

I can feel all my hard work getting reversed as Mason's body begins to tense back up. His voice is rough when he says, "Why did they die? Who killed them?"

He knows I have no clue what even happened, let alone who was responsible. But after talking to Robin today, I know what he is really asking. "Do you think those Sentinels Robin mentioned had something to do with what happened to your family?"

As if having someone other them him voice his thoughts makes them easier to deal with, Mason's shoulders relax slightly. "I don't know. Maybe." Leaning his head against mine, Mason sighs. "If they killed Eliana, maybe that's what they were trying to do to me."

"But, why would they hurt your family? Robin's family wasn't harmed."

"My family would never let anyone hurt me," Mason says almost angrily.

"And Robin's would?" I ask. I don't question his family's commitment, but I wonder why he doubts Robin's.

Mason doesn't answer right away. His jaw works back and forth as he chooses his words. "She feels guilty about something."

His words remind me of the way she teared up when she talked about secrets. I doubted her then, and I found myself siding with Mason now, as well. Robin is hiding something.

"Besides," Mason interrupts, "they couldn't find me when they showed up. My mom was making pancakes that morning. When she went to the pantry to look for syrup, I hid under the sink. I loved to surprise her. It made her laugh, and I loved the sound of her laugh."

I sit absolutely still and perfectly quiet as Mason talks about his mother, afraid that the slightest sound or movement will end his sharing. I wait as Mason swipes at a stray tear. He sniffs before continuing.

"I was under the sink when I heard a loud bang. My mom screamed. I tried to get out of the cupboard, but she pushed the door back shut. They didn't know I was there, but I remember an unfamiliar voice calling out for me. Whoever they were, they wanted me."

● ● ●

24

Without warning, catching my breath seems impossible. I don't know if I can handle the thought that someone might actively be trying to hurt Mason. Before I can stop myself, I feel tears begin sliding down my cheeks. I'm not the only one who feels them. Mason reaches up and touches my face, seeming startled when he realizes I am crying. Not that I can blame him. I'm about as much of a crier as he is.

"Oh, Ollie," he says softly. His strong, but gentle arms easily pull me out from behind him and nestle me against his body. I curl against him as I try to shut out the fear that is quickly swallowing me up.

"Mason, I can't bear the thought of losing you," I whisper against his chest.

His arms press me against him so tightly there is no space left between us. "I've already lost one family. I won't lose you, too."

The night quiets as we lay in each other's arms. Slowly, Mason's breathing calms. As he relaxes, my own fears begin to calm as well. They don't disappear, but they come down to a manageable enough level that I can think and ask the question lingering in both of our minds.

"Mason, what do we do now?"

He sighs. His fingers stroke my hair softly. "I don't know. I'm not sure how to get more information out of Robin without telling her the truth."

"We can't tell her the truth. We have no idea who she's really involved with. It's too big of a risk."

"I know, but we have to stay close to her, too. If she is a threat, we can't be blind to it."

I know he's right, but I don't like to think about Mason being so close to someone who could potentially hurt him. But what choice do we have? I look up at Mason and find him already staring down at me with a look of concern. Something about the moment makes my heart lurch. It takes me a few seconds to gather my thoughts.

"Mason, we'll figure this out," I promise.

As his fingers brush against my cheek, that strange sensation flashes again, but I am too anxious to pay it much attention.

"Out of everything Robin told us today, do you know what hurt the most?" Mason asks, surprising me by his change in topic. He doesn't wait for me to answer. "Robin said something like sometimes it's hard to remember 'I wasn't human,' that I was sent here to be raised by Caretakers. Do you realize what that means? Not only am I not human, my family isn't even my real family. All of the sudden, I've lost another family, one I never knew, maybe one that didn't even want me to begin with."

"We'll find answers, Mason."

I know it's not much as far as comfort goes, but I don't know what else to say. I have no idea why anyone would give up someone as wonderful as Mason. If his biological parents didn't want him, their stupidity was our gain. I can't imagine my life without Mason.

I have no idea what time it is, but weariness begins to creep over me. My eyes are starting to close when Mason asks one last question.

"Do you think Robin is right about me not being human?"

A yawn stretches my jaw before I can answer. "I don't know. Maybe. You *are* invisible."

"Does that bother you?" he asks quietly.

My shrug is more of a twitch as sleeps tries to steal me away. "Why would it? I love you no matter where you came from."

Chapter 5

Separation

I am exhausted, but having Olivia's body tangled up with mine makes it impossible for sleep to claim me. Both my body and mind are begging me to give in and rest, but I know this is a rare opportunity I would be a fool to squander. So I hold her quietly, breathing in her scent as I contemplate her last words.

Denying that what she said sent a rush through my body would be a lie. I know she didn't mean it like I want her to, but hearing her say that she will love me even if I am some kind of freak…alien…whatever I am, means more to me than she will ever understand.

I freeze as Olivia shifts, crossing her leg over mine and snuggling even closer. It takes a moment for my heart to stop racing. The desire to turn my head enough to press my lips against her forehead is very nearly too much. Lying in my bed with her is pure torture, anything more and I wouldn't be able to stop myself from waking her and admitting how much I want her.

But I know how that would go over. Seeing an expression of disbelief or disgust on Olivia's face as she tries to comprehend her "brother" telling her he's in love with her is not something I want to experience.

That thought alone is depressing enough to make me reconsider sleep. My eyes close, but a sound in the hallway snaps them back open. Memories spring up uncontrollably, flashing back to that day. My arms tighten around Olivia's body. I am ready to scoop her up and run if my fears prove true.

The sight of Olivia's dad shuffling down the hallway sends a shot of relief through me. I laugh at myself for being so paranoid and relax my grip on Olivia. A second later, panic sets in that he will realize Olivia isn't in her room and is in fact sleeping with me. Olivia may only see me as a brother, but her dad saw the potential for something more from the first day. Before I can wake Olivia and warn her, her dad appears in the doorway calling Olivia's name softly.

It takes me a moment to remember that he can't see me. All he can see is Olivia sprawled awkwardly across my bed. In a moment of desperation, I opt for rolling away from her and pretending I am still asleep. I quickly decide to let Olivia figure a way out of this.

"Olivia," Olivia's dad calls again as he crosses the room, more awake now. "Olivia."

She doesn't stir until he reaches down and gently shakes her. Slowly, her eyes blink open. "Dad?"

●●●

27

She pulls away from me as her dad sits down on the edge of the bed. I am working hard at pretending to be asleep, yet I can't help but notice that Olivia doesn't even seem embarrassed at being found in my bed. Grimacing, I realize that the thought probably never crossed her mind that something more than her comforting me was going on.

"Olivia, what are you doing in here? Is everything okay?" her dad asks.

Rubbing her eyes, Olivia mumbles, "Yeah, Mason was having nightmares again. They were pretty bad. He woke me out of a deep sleep."

Olivia's dad puts an arm around his daughter, ruffling her already mussed hair. "Sorry, kiddo. I wish I could hear him. I feel bad that you're always the one who has to get up in the middle of the night to help Mason. That should be mine and your mom's job, not yours."

"I don't mind," Olivia says, and I know she means it. Not smiling in response to her kindness is a challenge.

"Is Mason okay?"

Olivia shrugs. "I don't know, Dad. I'm worried about him. Tonight's nightmares were really bad. I'm scared that Mason thinks something terrible is going to happen."

Rather than brushing off her fears as nothing, her dad considers what she said. His nose scrunches just like Olivia's always does. "Mason has nightmares all the time. What made these different?"

One of the things I love about Olivia most is her honesty. She knows how to keep a secret when it's absolutely necessary, but she prefers to be open and up front about what is going on in her life. She tried to tell her whole family about me the day we met. No one believed her, but she kept trying. She knew she needed help, and she doesn't believe in prolonging a difficult situation by being stubborn or keeping secrets. Olivia handles my nightmares in the same way.

The concern in her voice is clear as she tells her dad not only about my nightmare tonight, but about Robin and everything we learned from her today. Her dad listens thoughtfully, carefully considering everything. As I quietly eavesdrop on their conversation, I marvel at their closeness. They are so alike it's no wonder they have always turned to each other when they needed support or someone to laugh with.

I listen raptly, waiting for one of them to come up with a solution. When Olivia speaks next, I am not prepared for her question.

"Dad, do you think Mason's nightmares could be more than dreams? Premonitions?"

When Olivia's dad doesn't immediately discount the idea, my breathing stops.

"What makes you think they aren't just dreams?"

Olivia shrugs. "I don't know. Nothing, I guess. It's just that, well, Mason is special. He's amazing and unique. He's invisible. Obviously there's something we don't understand about him. What if he has abilities we don't know about?"

Silently, I hope that he'll just brush off her theory. I can't stand the thought of anything I saw tonight being even mildly close to reality. Sweat begins to bead on my forehead. Please, I beg, tell her it's a ridiculous idea.

"I can't say whether his dreams are more than that or not, but I think you're smart to be wary. Mason is very special, and it wouldn't surprise me at all to find out he has abilities beyond the average person."

Clearly, that wasn't the answer Olivia wanted to hear, either. The way her shoulders bunch up and her arms tighten around her slender body prove the idea terrifies her.

"Dad, I don't want Mason's dreams to come true. I don't want to lose him." A quick sniff and brush at her eyes makes my chest constrict. She leans her head against her dad's shoulder and he pulls her in tightly.

"Olivia, I'm not saying that his dreams are real. Most likely, they're just dreams brought on by meeting Robin. But even if they are real, don't you think that if Mason has one special talent, he may very well have others, too? I don't think you need to start worrying yet."

Turning just enough that I can see her profile, Olivia smiles weakly up at her dad. "I'll try not to."

He kisses her forehead. Having reassured her, he moves as if to leave, but stops and settles back onto the bed. The turning of his head toward me forces me to shut my eyes feign sleep just in case Olivia's gaze follows. My ears, however, stay open and ready. Olivia senses something has changed. The feel of her shifting to a more wary posture on the bed makes me even more nervous. Maybe she wasn't as unconcerned about being found in here as I thought.

"Olivia, since we're talking about the future, I need to ask you a question. I've been meaning to talk to you for a while, but we've both been so busy I can't ever seem to find the time," her dad says.

"A question about what?"

Olivia's dad shifts for a moment, not speaking right away. Eventually, he says, "Olivia, this is your last year of high school. I know we've talked about colleges and majors, but ..."

"Dad, do we really need to talk about this right now? I'm still thinking about what I want to do. I won't even apply anywhere until next semester, and even once I start college I can take all my Gen Ed classes if I'm still not sure about a major."

● ● ●

Patting her leg, her dad waves off anymore arguments. "That's not what I was going to ask you. Take a breath. You have plenty of time to decide all that."

Confused, Olivia asks, "Then what?"

"What about Mason? Has he talked to you at all about what he wants to do after high school?"

It is an innocent enough question, but it makes me go cold. Not only does Olivia seem stumped by the question, I am floored. I have to admit that I haven't thought about it for even a second. It never occurred to me that Olivia graduating might change things. Being separated simply isn't an option.

The sound of Olivia's voice startles me. Suddenly, I am hanging on every syllable.

"I guess I really haven't thought about it, and I don't think Mason has either. He hasn't said anything to me, anyway," Olivia says. She fiddles nervously with the bedspread. "I just figured he would come with me. He could study whatever he wanted, but we would still be together. That's what's important, right?"

Her dad doesn't answer right away. He glances back at me again before turning back and speaking. "I know you and Mason are very close, but this is something you both need to talk about, something we all need to talk about. It won't be as simple as you and Mason just going off to college."

No, it won't be that simple, I suddenly realize. Where would we live? If Olivia decides on a college away from home she'll be housed either in a dorm or an apartment. Either option would require a roommate. Roommates will be a problem. How would Olivia explain her live-in invisible friend? I don't think either of us could stand having to pretend I didn't exist that often.

The other obvious problem is that even though I am invisible to the majority of the world, I still need a bed, food, and the occasional shower. Explaining an empty room that definitely looks lived in, but never has an actual tenant would definitely be a problem.

The only real option would be sharing Olivia's room. That thought is staggering as I consider the unlikely possibility of having Olivia in my arms every night. Olivia's dad's voice seems distant as he spells out all the same problems that just ran through my mind. Paying attention seems too difficult. I can feel my skin flushing as fantasy takes over. There is no way that Olivia would remain oblivious to how deep our connection could go if we spent that much time together being that physically close. I have no delusions of my limits. It wouldn't take many nights for me to breakdown and admit everything. It is a thought that both terrifies and excites me.

● ● ●

30

I think I might have spent the rest of the night entertaining such thoughts, but Olivia's voice pulls me back to reality.

"Dad, none of that stuff matters. All that matters is that me and Mason stay together."

The thrill her words send through me is hard to describe. Her dad doesn't seem to appreciate the sentiment.

"Olivia," he says wearily, "you're not being realistic. It's one thing to have you both living here, but the two of you going out and living together is completely different."

"Why is it so different?" she argues. "We manage well enough now."

"Because we have rules here. You have separate rooms, boundaries. Plus, we all know about Mason. He can come home and he doesn't have to hide. You won't have that at college in the dorms."

Folding her arms stubbornly, Olivia stares her dad down. "Then I won't live in the dorms. I'll get an apartment off campus."

Olivia's dad raises a finger to interrupt, but Olivia powers over him.

"I know the budget. I'll get a job to pay the difference not having a roommate leaves me with." She refuses to back down. "I'm not leaving Mason behind, and I'm not letting money stop me. Mason deserves to have as normal of a life as he can possibly have."

If anyone had inexplicably asked me for my thoughts in that moment there is no way I would have been able to express how much Olivia standing up for me meant. After Robin's comments today about not having other Aerlings around and the companionship I was missing out on, my frustration at being the family "problem" has been weighing on my mind even more. Clearly it has been bothering Olivia as well.

Her dad has other problems on his mind. "Olivia, I appreciate your willingness to make sure Mason has a place to feel at home. I'm glad you're thinking about his feelings, but that isn't really the main problem."

When Olivia's nose crinkles in confusion, it manages to deflate my mood quite a bit.

"Olivia ..." Her dad rubs his forehead, obviously not sure how to proceed. "Honey, I know you and Mason have been together for a long time. You're closer that a lot of siblings are, but the fact is...well, Mason isn't your brother. It wouldn't be appropriate for the two of you to live together."

"It's not like anyone would know," Olivia says quietly.

Her dad sighs. For once I don't want to join him. The slightly guilty quality of Olivia's voice gives me hope that she at least thought of where living together might lead.

"Honey, your mom and I would know. We're not comfortable with you and Mason living together on your own."

"Why not? We've never done anything to warrant you not trusting us," Olivia argues. "I'm trying to make sure Mason has an opportunity to get on with his life. You can't possibly expect him to stay here at home forever."

Olivia's dad pats her shoulder in an effort to calm her down. He shushes her quietly, glancing in my direction. Once he's sure his daughter won't start yelling at him again, he continues. "I am not saying that I don't trust you and Mason. You are two of the best kids I know. It's just that…well, things could change when you're off on your own."

"Dad," Olivia whines, embarrassment creeping into her voice. "Mason is my best friend. Can't we just leave it at that?"

"I'm afraid not." Her dad's hint of a smile lingers for a moment. "Look, I'm not saying we have to figure this out tonight. But I do want you to think about it. Ask Mason what he wants to do. He may have a completely different idea of what he wants out of life after high school. I just want the two of you to think about it."

Olivia flops back against the headboard. I am once again forced to pretend total unawareness. That isn't easy considering that Olivia's knee is pressed against my shoulder.

Sighing, Olivia gives in. "Ugh, fine. I'll ask him later, okay?"

"Thank you," her dad says.

Ready to head back to bed, Olivia's dad stands and holds his hand out to Olivia. "Come on, let's get some sleep."

Olivia's dad and I are both surprised when Olivia hesitates. I can't stop myself from flinching when her hand brushes over my shoulder. My breathing is stalled as I wait for her answer.

"Dad," she asks, her breathing quicker than it was a second ago, "would it be okay if I stayed in here tonight?"

I don't have to open my eyes to know the look on her dad's face. After the conversation he just had with Olivia, concern and just a bit of disapproval are a foregone conclusion. The agitated sigh only confirms it. I am sure he's about to order Olivia back to her bed, but she speaks up before he can speak the command.

"This isn't about relationships or whatever," she argues. Her hand strokes back and forth across my shoulder. "Dad, Mason really scared me earlier, and he was pretty freaked out, too. I'm afraid that if I leave he'll have another nightmare. You said you trust us. Let me prove I can live up to that. I just want to make sure he's okay."

As much as I hate to believe that is Olivia's only reason for wanting to stay with me, I know her dad can hear the sincerity in her voice as much as I can. When I hear him sigh, I know she has won.

● ● ●

"Fine, but …" He doesn't finish the thought. Instead, he kisses Olivia's forehead. A second later I can hear his slippers shuffling out of the room.

I start to relax knowing he has left the room, but right after his departure I feel Olivia lie back down next to me. I don't expect much other than having the comfort of knowing she is so close by. When her hand slides across my body and closes around my hand, I am too stunned to react. I don't know how long I lay there frozen. Olivia's breathing slows to the regular pattern of sleep before I regain control and tighten my fingers around hers.

"Mason," Olivia whispers, startling me into gripping her even tighter.

"Yeah?" I say, knowing it is a risk to admit I am still awake.

Olivia's quiet chuckle surprises me. "I knew you were awake."

Embarrassed, I mumble a quick apology.

"You heard everything Dad said?"

"Uh, yeah."

There is a moment of quiet as Olivia gathers her thoughts. "Don't worry about what he said," Olivia says softly. "I'm not saying you have to go to college with me…I mean, I want you to, but whatever you want to do after high school, I'll make sure Mom and Dad go along with it."

"Thanks." It's a simple answer despite the complex mixture of emotions swirling around inside of me.

"Um, so, do you know what you want to do?" Olivia asks.

There is so much that begs to spill out of my mouth. I have to bite the inside of my cheek to keep myself in check. It takes me a minute to give her an answer. "I want to go to college with you."

Again, Olivia is quiet for a while. After several long minutes, she says, "We could make it work, right?"

Whether Olivia has any inclination of ever looking at me as more than her brother or not, I have no intention of discouraging her. "Yeah, we can make it work."

This time Olivia is the one to pull closer to me. Her head rests against my back, and suddenly everything else takes a backseat to the simple pleasure of having Olivia pressed against me. I want to take the peace she inspires into my dreams, but as sleep begins to claim me, fear of returning nightmares threatens to overpower. Even more, fear that my dreams are more than what they seem, that Robin's arrival has set off a series of events I have no control over tightens every muscle in my body. Olivia backed me up with her dad, but I can't shake the feeling that sometime soon I will be the one protecting her from a separation more permanent than college.

Chapter 6

Anything but Horror

I slide into the chair next to Mason and fix my stare on Robin. She remains as perky as usual and chomps on a carrot stick. I have a zillion questions firing around in my mind, but the annoying sound of her crunching scrambles my thoughts. I already have my doubts about Robin. Getting very little sleep last night is not helping me play nice. Not that I blame Mason, of course, but I'm still pretty beat.

I take a long swig of Coke and hope the caffeine will help clear out the ache behind my eyes as well as my short temper. I'm halfway through my meal before I can focus, be nice, and form a question all at the same time. Having to wait for Mason and Robin to stop chitchatting almost pushes me back toward grumpy, but I hold onto my pleasantness by sheer force of will.

Finally, there is a lull in the conversation and I break in.

"So, Robin, that split you mentioned, I tried asking my parents about it, but they didn't really want to tell me anything. I've never really been in contact with any other Caretakers to hear about it, but I was curious about what you said," I say casually. "If there's something going on that might put Mason in danger …"

Robin shakes her head quickly. "Oh no, nothing's going on that's dangerous. Not anymore anyway. At least, not that I know of. We're not really involved in Caretaker business so much anymore, but we still get news of anything major happening. I'm sure my parents would have heard about anything dangerous."

I take a deep breath. Her rambling may be more than I can take today. "So the split," I say, bringing her back to the point, "what exactly happened?"

"Well," Robin says, putting her fork down and getting serious, "a long time ago, like when my parents were kids, the network of Caretakers used to be really connected, like downright glued together at the hip kind of connected. There were organized groups, a database, geographical boundaries that separated everyone into units, leaders who controlled each unit. Crazy! Everyone knew where everyone else was and who had Aerlings, you know like Big Brother almost."

"Sounds a little spooky," Mason says.

Robin's eyes get big. "I know, right?" She shakes her head at the idea. "I guess some other people started thinking the same thing. The leaders were getting really controlling and it was making Caretakers nervous. Then it got even worse when rumors started going around that there were spies or traitors or something. I'm not really sure about all the details, but they thought someone was getting information about where Aerlings were and using it to track them down and kill them."

"What made them think that?" I ask.

Robin gives me a "wow, you really are a blonde" look, and turns to look at Mason. "They thought that because Aerlings were disappearing."

"Disappearing like …"

"Like gone, dead, most likely. Sentinels aren't known for their mercy. They have no use for Aerlings anyway. They just want to kill them."

"Why?" I demand.

Again, Robin gives me a look that says I am asking really obvious questions. "Because, they're like Nazi's. Aerlings aren't human. They think they don't belong here. They think they're bad news and they want to get rid of them. That's what my parents told me, anyway. Sentinels are certified psychos, though, no doubt about that."

Robin shudders, and I wonder if she has personal experience with Sentinels. I know she said they killed Eliana, but I hope that doesn't mean she saw it happen. I turn to look at Mason, thinking about what he said about his sister. The sad expression on his face makes me think the same thoughts are running through his mind. I pat his knee gently and he smiles a bit.

"So, what happened once people realized their information wasn't safe?" I ask.

Shrugging, Robin says, "Exactly what you'd expect to happen. A bunch of people wanted out. Not from being Caretakers, just out of the Caretaker network of death. Aerlings might not be their biological children, but they love them fiercely. No one was going to stand by and watch their kids die if they could stop it. People went into hiding. The leaders tried to stop them, even tried to force people to stay by threatening them, but it didn't work."

"How do you all stay in contact now?" Mason asks.

After pushing her tray and away and parking her elbows on the table, Robin continues. "Now, everyone is organized in groups of three. The three families in the group help each other and take care of each other. We have the contact info for one person outside of our group that can contact another group if we need reinforcements. There's still a possibility of someone betraying us, but it's a lot smaller."

"Then how did Eliana die?" Mason asks, his voice sharper than usual. When I look over at him, his eyes are fixed on Robin. I remember his concern that Robin felt guilty about something and is hiding the truth about Eliana. My eyes turn to spear her as well.

● ● ●

"Nobody betrayed us, if that's what you're asking," Robin says. Her hands start fidgeting and she stands abruptly. "Sometimes the Sentinels find us all on their own."

Robin picks up her tray and makes a hasty exit. Mason and I watch her go without saying a word. I think we both need a few minutes to process everything. It's not just about Sentinels infiltrating the Caretakers, or possibly one of their own betraying everyone. We both realize that Mason was right. Whatever happened to Eliana, Robin carries a lot of guilt for her death.

"I wish I could remember," Mason says suddenly.

"Remember what?"

He rubs his head with his hand. "My real…I mean, my first family. My Caretakers." He looks up, but his expression is pained. "There's so much I can't remember about them. Did they ever take me to play with other Aerlings? Did they keep me secluded? I don't know. I can barely remember anything good about them anymore. Only the bad memories stay at the top."

"I'm sorry, Mason."

Smiling at my words, Mason still seems bothered. "I'm going to go find Robin. I didn't mean to upset her. I'll catch up with you later, okay?"

I nod and he hurries off in the same direction Robin just went. Maybe he can get her to tell him a little more about the Sentinels and Eliana. They definitely have a few things they could bond over. A shiver runs down my spine thinking about the things Mason most likely witnessed. Even if he didn't see the actual deaths, whatever he did experience was enough to scar him. The nightmares are proof of that.

No longer in the mood to eat, I dump my tray and head for my next class. My feet tread the familiar halls easily. We're only a month into the school year, but I've been wandering these halls for over three years now. It's weird to think this is my last year in high school. Thoughts about graduating inevitably lead to college, and from there, to my conversation with Dad last night.

My cheeks flush slightly thinking about it. I was shocked when Dad said he thought it was inappropriate for me and Mason to live together. I've never thought about Mason like that before. He's my best friend and I've never done anything that would give Dad the impression that living with Mason would lead to us sharing a bed.

The whole argument seems ridiculous, but as I stop off at my locker, thoughts of lying next to Mason last night creep into my mind. How did it feel? I struggle to define it. There is no question that I feel safe and happy with Mason. I love being with him. Nothing will keep me from always being with him. But as I move books around, I remember that moment when he squeezed my hand and my heart jumped. I don't know why I pulled him closer after that. It just felt right. I wanted him near me. What does that mean?

"I have never seen anyone think so hard about what books to take to class before," Hayden says, making me jump.

The book I was holding tumbles out of my hands and I pull my foot back just in time to keep it from getting smashed. I can feel my face turning red as I stoop to pick up my book. Standing back up, I shove it in my locker and swing the door closed.

"Lost in thought, I guess." It's the only response I can think to say.

Hayden laughs and smiles at me. "Sorry, didn't mean to scare you."

"It's okay," I say, smiling back.

I turn away from my locker and toward class. I don't know why Hayden stopped in the first place, and I don't know why he starts walking with me, either. I look over at him with a curious expression and find him watching me. He smiles again and laughs at being caught staring. I know Mason thinks Hayden is an idiot, but he's always been nice to me, and he has a nice smile.

I don't really know what to say to him, though.

"So, I noticed you sitting with that new girl, Robin, at lunch. I have her in a few of my classes. She seems nice," Hayden says finally.

Glad he spoke first, I nod. "Yeah, she's a little odd, but she's nice."

Hayden laughs. "She's kinda quirky, and man can she talk. We have AP chemistry together and I happened to ask her about ionic bonds and she went off for ten straight minutes. Nice girl, though, and really smart."

I don't know about the smart part since we've never talked about classes, but I can definitely sympathize on the talking. She makes it even worse by speeding through what she has to say without breathing. It's hard to focus on her words when she does that.

"She says pretty much whatever she's thinking," I agree.

Hayden shakes his head, but he's still smiling. I try to figure out why we're talking about Robin. We've never really had a conversation that didn't revolve around assignment due dates or what chapter we're supposed to read. Mason's fascination with Robin from day one was partly due to her being able to see him, but I do have to admit that Robin is a cute girl. Maybe that's it?

"Are you interested in Robin?" I ask, realizing how blunt that sounds after it leaves my mouth. I try to follow it up with something a little more smooth. "Because if you are, I'm sure she'd want to go out with you."

"Really?" Hayden asks, a smile creeping onto his lips as he steps in front of me and forces me to stop. "What makes you think that?"

I shrug. "You're a nice guy. Good looking. Sweet." I shrug again. I'm sure any girl would be happy to have Hayden ask them out.

Hayden's smile turns into a grin. "You think I'm good looking?"

"Sure, but you're nice too." That's more important. I may not know Robin very well, and I'm not totally convinced she's safe for Mason to be around, but that doesn't mean I'd want her get involved with some dirtbag either.

I'm startled when Hayden suddenly moves closer to me. He's taller than me, forcing me to look up to meet his eyes. He's still smiling, but it's different than before, more sultry. I feel my heartbeat pick up involuntarily.

"I appreciate your blessing to ask Robin out," he says, "but she's not really the reason I wanted to talk to you."

"She's not?" I ask. The scent of his aftershave seems to be filling the space between us. My hands suddenly feel clammy.

Hayden picks up a strand of my hair and gently pushes it back over my shoulder. "No, I wanted to ask you what kind of movies you like to watch."

"Why?" I gulp.

"Because I was hoping you'd like to see one with me sometime."

"Oh." My brain seems to be having trouble working right now. He's standing too close and his aftershave is making me dizzy. "Um, anything but horror," I manage to mumble.

Hayden must think I'm a total idiot. The corner of his smile is twitching, like he wants to laugh. "Is that a yes then?"

"I don't know. Maybe?"

He seems to find that funny. I'm not sure why.

The touch of his thumb gliding across my cheekbone startles me, but not in a bad way. He smiles again. "Well, when you decide, let me know. I'd love to take you to a movie, one that's not horror."

"Okay."

Before I can manage to embarrass myself any further, Hayden steps back and continues on his way to class. I have a hard time doing anything. I've known Hayden for years and I have never reacted to him like that before. As I remember how to breathe and walk, I try to figure out whether what just happened was a good thing or a bad thing.

Chapter 7

Up to Something

Walking up to Mason after my last class, I scan the crowd for Robin. Mason didn't say much after lunch about how his conversation with her went. I'm curious to know if he got any more details out of her.

"So, you never really told me what Robin said," I start. "You were pretty quiet this afternoon. Was everything okay?"

Mason looks over at me with a strange expression. "Things are fine with Robin. I just apologized for making her feel bad. She said it was okay. We went our separate ways."

"So what's wrong?"

His shrug doesn't say much, but he is clearly upset about something. I try not to be obnoxious and pry it out of him. It's not easy. With everything he's been going through lately, I worry that it will become too much at some point.

When we get to the Jeep, I try again. "Are you worried that Robin will cause problems for you?"

Like she apparently did for Eliana.

"Why were you talking to Hayden?" Mason asks, dodging my question.

The strange sense of embarrassment that spreads through my chest catches me off guard. "I don't know," I say with a shrug.

"What did he want?"

"He asked me if I wanted to see a movie sometime."

I look over at Mason and am surprised by his sour expression. I didn't even realize he had seen me with Hayden. I know he doesn't like him much, but the way his fingers curl into fists seems a little intense. What is going on with him?

"What did you tell him?" Mason demands.

Shaking my head, I say, "I said maybe."

Mason's shoulders drop. I don't know what I expect him to do, but I'm startled when he jumps out of the Jeep and announces he's going to walk home. The door slams shut before I can say anything. That doesn't stop me from jumping back out of the Jeep and trying to get his attention without looking like a total wacko in front of the whole school. Mason knows I'm limited on what I can do without drawing too much attention and keeps walking.

I intend to get back in the Jeep and follow him home, but Robin catches me when I turn around.

"Where's Mason going?" she asks.

All I can do is shrug. "I don't know. He's in a weird mood."

I start to brush past Robin, but a thought occurs to me. I'm still not convinced Robin isn't bad news, but I'm leaning toward her not being a direct threat to Mason's safety. She's got such a big mouth and no social filter to stop her from saying whatever's on her mind, so I doubt she could really carry out a complicated, underhanded mission without giving herself away. I'm hoping, though, that her big mouth can be put to use in a more helpful way.

"Hey, do you want to come over and hang out?" I ask Robin.

Surprised by my offer, it doesn't stop her from accepting. "Sure! I can't wait to meet the rest of your family."

Her enthusiasm gives me a moment's hesitation, but I figure Mom and Dad will both be at work for a while still, so it shouldn't be a problem. "Hop in," I say with a smile I'm not sure is completely honest.

The ride to my house is short and filled with Robin talking nonstop about her day. I'm glad when we finally pull into the driveway and I have an excuse to jump out. Robin goes right back to her story about the guy who sits behind her in French when she comes around the Jeep and I have to stop myself from groaning.

"Hey," Robin says, grabbing my arm as I reach for the front door, "what's with the creepy car over there?"

My eyebrows scrunch together in confusion. "What creepy …?"

My words trail off as I turn toward the street and spot a black sedan. The guy sitting in the front seat looks to be intently checking email on his phone, or maybe playing Angry Birds. He's got a t-shirt and sunglasses on, which seems normal enough. But I think that's what he was trying for.

I live on a street where it's fairly rare to see a For Sale sign. Most of my neighbors have been here my whole life. The newest family moved in five years ago. This guy, I've never seen him before. His car doesn't look familiar, either. Even more suspicious is the fact that the house he's parked in front of belongs to a widow whose only family is her middle-aged daughter.

"Uh, let's go inside." I grab Robin's arm and shove her into the house.

Both of our backpacks get ditched next to the door and we move in concert over to the window where we push back the curtains just enough to peek through. Mr. Casual's phone has disappeared. His eyes are now focused on the house, watching, clearly waiting for something to happen. Or someone to show up. Immediately, I think of Mason, but that doesn't make sense, does it?

"Can Sentinels see Aerlings?" I blurt out before thinking.

"What?" Robin asks. "No, of course not. Only Caretakers can see Aerlings."

I notice that she doesn't brush off my concern about who might be in the sedan. In fact, her lip is tucked firmly between her teeth to keep it from trembling and her hands are clenched into fists. She's thinking the same thing I am.

"Is it one of them?" I ask quietly.

"I...I don't know. It's not like they look any different than normal people."

My eyes narrow at her. "Normal people don't sit around in parked cars watching people's houses."

Before Robin can respond, Evie plops onto the couch next to us. "What're we looking at?"

"The creeper watching our house," I say without looking away from the window.

Evie crowds in next to me. "What?"

I don't relish the idea of taking my eyes off this weirdo, but Evie shoves me out of the way. With her eyes peeking just over the window sill, she glares at the guy in the car. "What's he waiting for? He's giving me the creeps."

My thoughts exactly.

"Maybe his car broke down," Robin says weakly. She cringes when Evie and I both pierce her with a fierce glare.

"Is this guy looking for Mason?" Evie demands. "One of those Sentinel nutjobs you told Olivia about? Did you bring them here?"

Robin's eyes fly wide in a panic. "What? No! Of course not! Why would you even think that?"

"We never had fishy looking guys staring at our house before you showed up," Evie counters with her usual sassy flare. "We really don't know that much about you. How are we supposed to know what you're really after?"

"After?" Robin asks. "Who says I'm after anything?"

As Evie stands, hands on hips, Robin hops up and stumbles back. Evie matches her step for step. Usually, my little sister's knack for speaking her mind and getting in people's faces makes me want to disown her, but I'm perfectly happy to let her back Robin into a corner.

"Is that guy a Sentinel?" Evie demands.

"I don't know!" Robin counters, finding her footing and stopping her retreat.

I step forward, eyeing Robin. "Take your best guess."

"Probably," she mutters. "He looks the type."

"Why would he be here? How did he find Mason?" Evie demands.

● ● ●

Robin shakes her head. "He may not be here for Mason. Did either of you think he might be watching me? The Sentinels know my family. They tend to pop up every once in a while to make sure we're not up to something."

"So it is your fault he's here," Evie says with narrowed eyes.

The beginnings of panic start showing in Robin's eyes and I decide to step in and give her a break. After all, she might be right about why the Sentinels are here. If it even is a Sentinel. It's not too farfetched to think we may not have noticed it following us and parking before we got to the front door.

"Robin may be right," I say, mainly to Evie so she'll back down, "but even if she is, Sentinels poking around still puts Mason in danger."

"Where is Mason?" Evie asks.

For the first time, I wonder the same thing. With him walking and me driving, it wouldn't be surprising for us to get home first, but I never saw Mason walking on the way. Earlier, I assumed he had wanted to go hole himself up in his room and ran home like he usually did when he was upset. Clearly, that didn't happen.

"He isn't here?"

Evie shakes her head. "He usually rides home with you. You didn't see him after school?"

"Well, yeah, but he said he was walking home. He was in a bad mood."

Robin takes a hesitant step forward. "You didn't see him come home?" she asks Evie.

"*See* him?" Evie asks. She gives Robin one of those "you're so stupid" looks that Robin is always giving me. "No. I didn't hear the door either. He isn't here."

Anxiety blossoms on Robin's pale face. My thoughts are heading down the same path. Where could Mason be? Surely the Sentinels don't have a clue about him. Robin has to be right that they're only here for her, checking up. They wouldn't be sitting around watching the house if they already had him, right?

"Where's Mason?" Evie demands.

"Is there somewhere he might have gone?" Robin asks.

The concern in her expression seems genuine, but part of me still fears that she isn't the innocent girl she appears to be. Regardless, I try to focus on her question. Where else would Mason have gone? We live in the middle of a big subdivision. Escaping would mean driving somewhere a good distance away. Mason has no way of getting that far on his own.

"Robin, please," I beg, "you have to be honest. Could the Sentinels possibly know about Mason?"

Dropping back down to the couch, Robin presses her hands to her face. "Of course it's possible, but you guys have been cut off for so long, who would want to betray Mason?"

Robin's words actually calm me down a tiny bit. What did the other Caretakers think had happened to Mason? Did they think he was dead with the rest of his foster family? Did anyone even know he still existed? There was no way to know for sure, but surely it was a slim chance anyone would know enough to tell anyone anything about Mason.

Evie opens her mouth to say something, and judging by the scowl on her face it won't be pretty. I slip my hand over her arm and pull her out of Robin's face. After reigning Evie in, I turn back to Robin.

"Look, whether this guy is here for you or Mason, he's bad news. We need to find Mason and tell him what's going on."

"Tell me what?" Mason demands as he walks into the room.

Immediately, I spin around and sigh in relief to see him whole and unharmed. I can't seem to say or do anything for a moment. The huge dose of fear I had been holding at bay slithers off of me and I want nothing more than to wrap my arms around him and not let go. Robin seems to be having a similar reaction, which kind of irritates me. Evie seems to be the only one still at a loss.

"What's going on?" she asks worriedly.

Robin glances over at Evie with another one of those looks. She seems dumbfounded that Evie would ask such a stupid question when Mason was standing right in front of her. Her expression and her earlier question about whether or not Evie had "seen" Mason makes my mind whirl.

I stand back as Mason touches Evie's shoulder and tells her that he's home and everything is okay. Knowing where he is now, Evie throws herself around him in a hug. I don't miss how Robin's curious eyes follow the both of them. Something isn't right here. She can sense that. Realization that Robin wasn't the only one in her family that could see her Aerling hits me square in the face.

Of course her parents had to be able to see Eliana! Robin was a baby when Eliana arrived. She couldn't have taken care of an infant when she was one herself. Mason's Caretakers could see him as well. All of them.

If Robin realizes that I'm the only one who can see Mason, the jig will be up. I don't know what that will mean. Will she tell someone? Will they try to take Mason away from me and give him to a real Caretaker family? I can't let that happen. I *refuse* to let that happen.

●●●

Chapter 8

In This Together

A little unsure why Evie is hugging me like she didn't talk to me in the halls just an hour ago, I look over her head at Robin and Olivia. My curious expression does nothing to inspire an answer.

"What is going on?"

Robin's head dips for some reason. Olivia folds her arm across her chest. Their reactions tell me I'm not going to like whatever they're about to tell me.

"There's some guy out front watching the house," Olivia says calmly.

The tremble in her hands makes a liar out of her, though. She's clearly pretty worried. Given the way she's been freaking out about every little thing lately, that shouldn't surprise me, but this feels different. She's scared and doesn't want to show it. That makes me worried.

"What do you mean 'watching the house?'"

Robin's voice makes a reappearance as she tells me about seeing the car when they got home and how he's still sitting there watching the house. At some point during the explanation Evie stops trying to strangle me, but keeps a hand on my arm to make sure she can hear anything I say. She stumbles when I dart away from her and head for the window. She stays close, though, and discretely touches my arm so she can hear me.

I don't worry about anyone seeing me standing in front of the window where the curtains are pulled apart. My eyes zero in on the man sitting in his car with his eyes glued to the front of the house. Medium brown hair, average build, youngish but not too young, he's completely nondescript. The perfect guy to act as a one-man surveillance team.

Spinning around, I spear Robin with a glare. "This guy is a Sentinel?"

"I don't know. Maybe," she says. "He might be here to watch me, though. Sometimes they check up on known Caretakers to see if they contact anyone else."

"Isn't that what you're doing," Evie snaps.

Robin's eyes water. "I…It's not…You were never part of our group. There's no reason to think I would even know any Caretakers in this area. They can't suspect …"

The usual life and vibrancy that follows Robin around breaks down. Her whole body deflates. Afraid she'll collapse, I grab her arm and pull her against me. Her weight leans on me heavily as she turns her face into my chest. Caught off guard, I look to Olivia for help. The prickly nature of her stance doesn't offer much and I figure it's better to handle this myself.

● ● ●

Walking Robin over to the couch, I gently sit her down with me. "Robin," I say quietly, "what is going on?"

"I'm so sorry," she wails. "I should have known better. That's why we move around so often, to protect the other Caretakers. I never should have talked to you guys at school. What was I thinking?"

Olivia and Evie look like they have a million questions buzzing around in their heads. I can tell that they're both itching to lay into Robin after that admission. Neither one of them has been terribly keen on her from the start, though. Waving them off before they attack and run Robin off, I gently push Robin to look at me.

"Robin, I'm not following what you're saying. Why weren't you supposed to talk to us at school?"

"Because my family is marked!"

We all stare at her, not sure what she means. Our confused expressions make her eyes widen and I get the impression that if Olivia's family were real Caretakers they would know exactly what she is talking about.

"Eliana died," Robin says, as if that should clue us in.

Trying to preserve our lie, I take a guess at what she's telling us. "So, after Eliana died, it meant the Sentinels knew you and your family were Caretakers, right? And you aren't supposed to talk to other Caretakers in case the Sentinels are keeping an eye on you?"

Robin nods. "I just got so excited to see another Aerling that I couldn't resist."

My eyes glance up to Olivia, and I am surprised to see the glint of anger in her expression. I grimace at the sight. I know Robin didn't mean any harm, but Olivia is clearly seeing the implications. Robin may have just outed me to the Sentinels.

"You guys weren't supposed to be here," Robin says in her defense.

"What do you mean?" Olivia asks.

Shaking her head in confusion, Robin looks at Olivia. "We move every few years to keep the Sentinels from bothering us too much. We go where there are no other Caretakers, so even if the Sentinels follow us, there's no chance of us leading them to anyone. There weren't supposed to be any active Caretakers in the area. I don't know how they got it wrong."

I do. As far as whoever does the Caretaker organizing and assigning knows, my family, *and me*, died twelve years ago. There's no way Robin's family could have known I was still alive and living with Olivia's family. When I glance back at Olivia to confirm that she has come to the same conclusion, I'm glad to see that her hostile stance has softened a bit.

"Olivia's mom and dad may not have reported where they were," I say in an effort to comfort Robin.

● ● ●

"But still, I should have known to walk away so I didn't put you at risk." Robin sniffs, her face splotchy and red from crying. "It's just that it's been so lonely on our own. I was so excited to meet you both. I didn't think."

As tears start welling in her eyes again, I slip my arm around her shoulders. It's a strange sensation to have Robin turn into my shoulder as she cries. I've never had to comfort a crying girl before. Olivia almost never cries, and she's usually so together that I rarely have to comfort her. It feels oddly natural to hold Robin, not romantic, but nice.

When Robin stops crying, I ask, "What's going to happen if the Sentinels figure out I'm here?"

"You know what will happen," Robin whispers. "They'll take you. They'll…kill you."

Evie and Olivia both tense at her words and start forward as if attacking Robin is going to change anything. I wave them off, glaring at them until they back off.

"When the Sentinels came after Eliana," I begin slowly, "did they try to hurt your family?"

Confused by the question, Robin sits up and cocks her head to one side. "No. Why would they? It's just the Aerlings they're after."

"Did your family try to stop them?"

I know mine did. Maybe that wasn't how it usually happens, though.

"We never got the chance," Robin admits. "They came for Eliana at night. Everyone was asleep. We only woke up when she screamed, but by then it was too late."

"What if …" I scrub my hand through my hair in frustration. I'm not sure how much I can say without rousing Robin's suspicions. "What would the Sentinels do if they couldn't find the Aerling they were looking for? Would they hurt the Caretakers?"

Robin shakes her head as if my question makes no sense. "I've never heard of that happening before. They would just wait and try to find the Aerling later."

I don't understand. What made my family so different? If I was the only thing the Sentinels wanted, why kill my entire family? Something isn't fitting, but I have no idea what it is. Fear and confusion fill my mind. What if it happens again? Is there something about me that makes things different? I can feel my body rising toward panic, but I can't stop it.

The feel of Olivia's fingers slipping onto my shoulder and squeezing it lightly feel more like a warm embrace. Everything I am feeling takes a back seat to her touch. I want to reach up and take her hand, press it to my lips and pull her to me. Her voice breaking the silence scatters such thoughts.

"How do the Sentinels find Aerlings?"

Robin shrugs. "Short of someone betraying a family, they stalk families like mine, haunt places Aerlings have been known to be housed, watch for suspicious occurrences."

"Like what?" Evie asks looking more than a little nervous. No doubt she's thinking of the myriad of pranks we have pulled over the years that could definitely be categorized as suspicious.

"I've heard that they pay a lot of attention to claims of hauntings, rescues no one can explain, things that just don't make sense. I'm sure that has gotten easier with everything people post on the internet these days." Robin looks down at the ground. "They've been doing this for centuries. If you give them even a small chance to find you, they will."

"How do they usually come after Aerlings?" I ask.

I want to believe that it will never happen, but I have to be realistic. We may have given them dozens of chances to figure out who I am. Robin showing up with a troop of Sentinels watching her probably hasn't helped, either. I have to know what to expect.

Robin doesn't seem overly fond of talking about this subject, but we all wait, refusing to let her get out of answering. Sighing, Robin starts talking.

"They operate like any other sicko trying to take a kid, wait until the right opportunity presents itself." Robin swipes at another tear before continuing. "Getting them at night is fairly common. Or public places when one of the parents looks away for a second. Crowded areas, walking home from school, all the usual techniques."

So it could be anywhere at any time. Great. That doesn't help me know where to focus.

"It's easier when the Aerlings are young," Robin says quietly. "They can't resist or put up much of a fight."

"How old was Eliana?" Olivia asks.

Sniffing and batting at tears again, Robin says, "Seven."

"So you've been moving around the country for ten years with these freaks following you?" Evie asks.

Robin nods. "I thought they had given up. No one in my family has seen anyone that looked like a Sentinel in years. I guess I just got too complacent. I wasn't careful enough."

"Robin, it's not your fault," I say. Olivia and Evie seem to disagree with me on that count, but I ignore them.

Somehow, I think this has more to do with my first family than it does with Robin. I want to ask Robin, see if she could find out more about the Caretakers I first lived with, but that would require telling her the reason behind the request, the truth. I may not think she's in league with the Sentinels, but that doesn't mean I trust her with my secrets.

● ● ●

Olivia fires out a few more questions about the Sentinels, but Robin doesn't know enough to lend any more insight. She offers to ask her parents, but that only causes a round of silence. I can see the fear shining in Olivia's eyes. I feel the fear as well, but the burning desire to know the truth tries to overwhelm it. Unable to determine the best course, I stay silent.

"My parents are going to be expecting me home soon," Robin says.

"I'll drive you home," Olivia offers unexpectedly. When no one says anything, Olivia shrugs. "If they think we're hiding something, we just have to prove them wrong. We're just two friends hanging out. Nothing weird about that."

Robin nods, a small smile tentatively turning her lips up. I feel bad knowing she wishes that were true, that Olivia was her friend. She may not want to hold her breath on that one. Olivia clearly blames her for the Sentinels' presence. Someone putting her family in danger isn't something Olivia will forgive easily.

When Robin stands and waits for Olivia to get her keys, her hands twist together, knuckles white. Knowing that Olivia will think I'm not taking this threat seriously keeps me from offering Robin any more comfort. I do, however, catch Olivia's arm before she makes it past me. She looks up at me expectantly, almost daring me to say something to defend Robin.

"Be careful," I say instead.

A flash of surprise lights on her face before mellowing into a warm smile. "I will. Keep an eye on Evie."

"I won't let anything happen to her."

My promise brings Olivia's arms around me in a quick hug. "I'll be right back."

She hustles Robin out the door and I watch them pretend to be natural and carefree as they walk to the Jeep. It's not very convincing. Hopefully the guy in the car buys it. From here, it's difficult to catch any facial expressions. Watching his head turn to follow the girls is easy enough. I expect him to take off after them, or maybe approach the house. He surprises me by driving away in the opposite direction.

I stay at the window with Evie parked on the couch watching for more strange vehicles until the familiar rumble of the Jeep rolls back into the driveway and shuts off. Olivia hustles up to the house and bursts through the door a few seconds later.

"Where'd the car go?" she demands.

I shrug. "Drove off in the opposite direction after you left. Maybe he really is just watching Robin."

"We can't assume that," Olivia argues.

"Yeah, I don't trust Robin," Evie pipes in.

* * *

48

I know arguing with them won't help. "Evie, don't you have homework to do?" I ask after placing two fingers on her forearm.

Groaning and rolling her eyes, she starts for the stairs.

"Wait a minute," Olivia says. Evie is all too happy to obey. She immediately puts a hand on my shoulder so as not to miss a single word.

Curious, I ask, "What's wrong?"

"I think Robin's whole family could see her Aerling. I think that's how it's supposed to work, not just one person like it is with me." She turns and looks at me with a searching expression. "Can you remember? Did everyone in your first family see and hear you?"

Olivia knows how hard it is for me to think about my family. She wouldn't ask me to dredge up those kinds of memories without a good reason. That is the only reason I try. Did they all see me? Hear me? I know my mom did. Flashes of my dad trying to teach me how to say the alphabet flicker through my mind, as do memories of my sister drawing on my face with a marker as I laughed at how it tickled me. I remember my older brother getting mad at me for taking his drumsticks without asking. He looked right at me as he lectured me.

It's all just bits and fragments, but it's enough. "Yeah, I think they could."

Olivia sighs. "That's what I thought. We have to be more careful around her. She'll realize we're lying if she figures out I'm the only one who can see you."

Evie cringes. "I didn't even think."

"It's alright," Olivia says. "I'll mention it to Mom and Dad too, just in case she's over again."

The expression on her face as she says that makes it clear Olivia hopes that won't happen again. Evie shares her opinion.

A few minutes later after Evie has disappeared upstairs to do her homework, I flop onto the couch feeling suddenly worn out. Olivia follows me, leaning her head against my shoulder. Neither one of us speaks for a while. I'm too lost in my own thoughts to attempt conversation.

What Robin said about how the Sentinels hunt keeps scratching at my mind, making me obsess over why my family had to die when hers didn't.

"I would have gone with the Sentinels willingly if it meant my family wouldn't be hurt," I say quietly.

Olivia sits up and faces me solemnly. "I know you would have."

"If it comes to that again …"

She doesn't let me finish. Olivia's hands grasp my face firmly. "I'm not letting anyone take you away from me."

"I won't let them hurt you just to save myself."

● ● ●

49

My heart rate jumps up a few notches as Olivia's hands slide down my neck to rest on my shoulders. My own hands come up to grip her arms. I barely stop myself from pulling her in, from kissing her until she understands how much I love her and that I would give up anything to make sure she is safe. The fierce seriousness in her eyes is the only thing that makes me hold back.

"Mason," she says almost angrily, "whatever happens, we're in this together. Do you understand me? If I ever hear you talk about leaving again, I'll duct tape you to a chair. You aren't going anywhere. I won't let you."

Olivia's forehead rests gently against mine. The temptation is almost too much to bear. My fingers tighten around her shoulders. I want to tell her that she's right, that I'll never leave and we'll always be together. She wants me to say it. Her expression, her eyes beg me to speak the words. I almost give in to the delusion.

I don't want to lie to her. Leaving Olivia is a crippling thought. Imagining my life without her breaks down my restraint and I pull her into my arms, squeezing her almost to the point of hurting her. Only one thought causes me more pain that leaving Olivia, and that is seeing her hurt. I want to tell her I'll never leave, but if that's what it takes to keep her safe, I'll have no other choice.

Chapter 9

Golden Waterfalls

"I'm starting to regret telling Dad about the creepy guy in the car," Evie moans as she folds a pair of jeans. "It's like being in prison, only worse."

Rolling my eyes, I toss a pair of balled up socks at her. "And you would know what prison is like how?"

"I watch TV."

The socks come flying back at my head. It's not too hard to bat down her weak throw. "You're not even supposed to be dating Aaron, and you still get to see him at school all day. What exactly are you missing out on?"

"Hello…" Evie says, "getting a ride home from Aaron. It's like the only time we actually get to be alone. Now I have to ride home with you every day. This sucks."

"Being kidnapped or dead sucks even more."

Evie sticks her tongue out at me and sloppily folds another pair of jeans.

It's only been three days since the weird guy in the car parked his suspicious self in front of our house. Nobody has seen him since, but I'm still on edge. Evie acts like it's been years since she's seen Aaron. It's not like he's that amazing of a catch anyway. He has a super annoying laugh and the only thing he seems capable of having a conversation about is video games. Personally, I think Dad did Evie a favor.

Myself, I'm feeling rather grateful for the lack of freedom. It gave me a good reason to get out of going to the movies with Hayden when he asked yesterday. I was a little offended that he laughed when I told him I was grounded—which is basically true. He didn't believe it for a second and I was forced to explain that some creepy guy had been hanging around the neighborhood and my dad was being overly cautious for the foreseeable future.

That he believed.

He also promised to check back with me next week and see if the ban on outings had been lifted.

I don't know why his invitation to see a movie with him causes me so much turmoil. He's a nice guy, pretty hot, and seems genuinely interested in me. So why not go out with him?

Why not?

Because every time I think of going out with Hayden, my conversation with Dad that night creeps back into my head and starts taking me down strange paths. It's really starting to get on my nerves. Eyeing Evie, I wonder if her talent for chatter can talk me out of my funk.

● ● ●

"Dad asked me about college a while ago…about what Mason plans to do after graduation, too," I say.

Evie glances over at me with a crooked eyebrow. My tone has definitely alerted her that I don't want to talk about majors. "Mason? What does he want to do?"

"Come to college with me," I mumble as I straighten the collar of the shirt I just hung up.

Going from bent over the dryer to standing hipshot with her eyebrow climbing even higher, Evie watches me. "What do you mean *with you*? Like go to the same college, or live with you? 'Cause that's not gonna be the easiest thing to explain to a roommate."

"That's what Dad said…among other things."

The clothes are abandoned as Evie jumps up to sit on the dryer. He eyes are fastened on me. "So he does want to live with you?"

"Well, where else is he supposed to live?" I snap, suddenly defensive. I ditch the waiting clothes as well and lean against the washer.

Evie laughs, one of those high, quick laughs that is clearly meant to mock. "And you thought Dad was going to go for that?"

"I hadn't really thought about it before then. I just assumed Mason would come with me. I wasn't thinking about roommates and all that," I say. "Besides, what's so weird about living with Mason. Siblings share apartments."

The glare Evie sends my way is scathing. "Are you really that oblivious, or are you just trying to be dense?"

"What?"

"Mason is not your brother," Evie says, emphasizing each word. "Of course Dad is going to freak if you tell him you and Mason want to move in together. It's not too hard to figure out where that might lead, and Dad is not ready to think about that. Geez, Olivia, he just about died when Mom was out of town last month and my period started! You expect him to think about you and Mason shacking up and not have a problem with that?"

My whole body flames red with embarrassment. "Shacking up? Who said anything about that? I'm talking about living with Mason, like we do now!"

Evie snorts. Prissy, prim Evie actually snorts at me! "You are delusional. Are you actually trying to make me believe that the thought of you and Mason tangled up in the sheets has never crossed your mind?"

"No!" I snap. "Not until Dad brought it up, anyway."

The silence that fills the basement minute after minute is unnerving. Evie is never this quiet. She's never stopped talking for this long. Ever. Each excruciatingly long moment peels away a layer of confidence. I start to wonder if she's right, if I've really been deluding myself this whole time. But, it honestly hadn't even occurred to me that living with Mason would be a problem before that night. Why would I?

"How could you not have thought about Mason like that?" Evie asks finally. The disbelief in her voice makes me feel foolish without really knowing why.

"I don't know. I've always thought of him as my brother."

"What is wrong with you?" Evie demands.

Shocked by the strength behind her words, I struggle to form a coherent response. "Are you saying that you've thought of him like that?" My nose wrinkles. "What's wrong with *you*?"

Evie's Sketcher-clad feet slap on the concrete floor as she jumps down from the dryer and glares at me. "For one, Mason is not and has never been our brother. Do I love him? Absolutely. But is he my brother? No."

"How can you say that?" I demand.

"It's not some personal attack on him! It's just the truth. He's not our brother." Evie shakes her head at me. "I care about Mason just as much as anyone else in the family. It has nothing to do with that. I'm just being honest here."

I don't understand her, but I know I have no right to criticize her for not thinking about Mason the same as a blood brother. Am I the one that's seeing this situation abnormally? I thought everyone in the family viewed Mason like I did.

"Secondly," Evie continues, "Mason is just about the most awesome person I've ever met. He's completely hot! How could I not think about him like that? Not that I fantasize about him or anything, but the possibility of you two being together has certainly crossed *my* mind."

"How would you know whether or not Mason is hot?" I snap, regretting very much ever starting this conversation. Evie has thought about Mason like that? Eew!

Evie starts chucking mismatched socks at me, startling me into tripping over a basket and landing hard on my hip. When she runs out of socks, she stares me down. "You have got to be the most hypocritical person I have ever met if you think I was talking about Mason's looks."

I scrunch up my face in confusion, wondering if she has lost it.

"You of all people," Evie snaps, "Miss I'm Gorgeous But It Doesn't Matter. Miss Every Guy Practically Drools Over Me As I Walk Down The Hall! Who cares what Mason looks like? He is the most caring, loving, sweet, doting, selfless guy I know. He's practically perfect and you act like he's just some run of the mill average Joe. Is he unattractive? Is he? Because if that's your problem with him, you don't deserve him!"

Completely stunned, I have no idea how to respond to any of that.

"Well?" Evie demands.

"Well what?" I ask. Was there actually a question somewhere in her tirade she expected me to answer?

"Is Mason ugly? Is that why you don't like him?"

Is she serious? This whole conversation has turned into a nightmare!

"I never said I didn't like Mason," I snap. "I just said I hadn't considered our relationship going in that direction until Dad brought it up because I've always thought of Mason as a brother—which I'm apparently alone in! And no, he isn't ugly. That has nothing to do with it. Why would you even say something like that?"

Folding her arms across her chest smugly, Evie says, "Well, I honestly can't figure out why you wouldn't be jumping at the chance to be with Mason. The only thing I can come up with was that you're way shallower than I expected."

"Thanks. Thanks very much! This is the last time I ever try to talk to you about something like this."

Throwing the loose socks off my body and pushing myself up off the floor, I wince when a sharp pain shoots through my thigh. Yeah, this is definitely the last time I ever go to Evie for advice! She can finish the laundry by herself. I'm done!

Pushing past Evie, I try to shake her off when she grabs my arm. Getting away from Evie has never been easy, though.

"Olivia, wait. I'm sorry. Don't storm off all mad, please?"

"When have I ever judged someone based on how they look?" I demand angrily.

Her head falls, ashamed. "Never. I shouldn't have said that. I know you wouldn't turn Mason down just because he was unattractive. I just don't get it."

"I don't get why you don't think of him as your brother. He's been here since you were three!"

Evie shrugs. "I don't know. I just don't think of him that way. He's always been more like this amazing friend who gets to stay over every night. It doesn't mean I love him any less."

Sighing, I sit down on the bottom stair, grimacing again when my hip aches. "I know. It just surprised me. I didn't realize everyone saw him differently than I do. It's confusing."

"No kidding!" Evie laughs and nudges me with her elbow when she sits down.

For a while, we just sit there. The thought crosses my mind that we better clean up the clothes now scattered on the floor before Mom sees them, but I don't get up to do anything about the mess. I feel really drained all of the sudden.

Evie elbows me again. "So, is Mason hot? I've always wondered what he looks like."

I can't help but smile when I picture Mason's face. Until Robin showed up, I had never thought about whether or not Mason was *hot* in the sense of whether or not I was personally attracted to him. I always knew he was gorgeous, though.

"You already know Mason is tall," I say, "but he has this athletic build that seems so effortless. He's not all muscle-y, bursting out of his t-shirt or anything, but you know he's strong just by looking at him. His strength is quiet, like it's waiting for just the right moment to jump into action and do something amazing.

"The color of his hair depends on whether he's inside or outside," I say. "When he's inside, it's almost red. When he's outside, though, it turns the color of those really neat fireworks on the Fourth of July that look like golden waterfalls. His hair usually looks a bit like those fireworks too, especially lately because it's a little too long."

I laugh thinking about the first time I tried to help him cut his hair. It was a good thing no one else could see him. Now he does it on his own, but it still makes him nervous.

"The way Mason smiles…it's something that would catch every girl's attention if they could see him. He always seems like he's about to laugh when he smiles, but not in a mean or hurtful way. It's more like he's excited about something. It's infectious, and he could always cheer me up with his smiles when we were little."

My hand bumps against Evie's and I smile. "His eyes are the best, though. They're so unique, it's hard not to stare."

"What do they look like?"

"I've never seen blue eyes as dark as his. When he gets mad, they almost turn black, all but the silver ring around his pupil. It's the coolest thing I've ever seen, well, aside from when Mason is really happy."

"What happens when he's happy?" Evie asks quietly.

Grinning is inevitable when I think of Mason being that happy. "The silver almost seems to take over his eyes. You've heard people say someone's eyes sparkle? Well, Mason's really do. It's amazing."

It's something I realize I haven't seen very often lately. The thought saddens me until Evie leans her head against my shoulder and asks, "Are you sure you aren't in love with Mason, because it sure sounds like you are."

Chapter 10

Every Bloody Memory

Leaning against Olivia's locker, I watch her for a moment. It's kind of weird how obsessive she is about trading books between every class. A lot of the other students only stop by their lockers once a day. Maybe she doesn't like carrying very much weight in her backpack. Or...my mouth turns down...maybe she thinks Hayden will stop by.

"Hey," Olivia says. "Sorry, I couldn't find my math notebook. What's up?"

Shaking off thoughts of Hayden, I say, "Don't wait for me after school today. I think I'm going to hang with Robin for a while."

"Why?"

The way she nearly snaps at me makes me pause. Is it just because she thinks Robin is a danger, or is it something else? Jealousy? I can only hope.

"Why?" I repeat. "Because you tend to be a little intense and judgmental when Robin says anything about Aerlings and Caretakers. I think she'll open up a bit more if it's just the two of us."

Olivia's nose wrinkles. I don't care what Evie says, I love it when she does that.

"Just the two of you?" She bites the corner of her lip nervously. "Mason, I don't know if that's a good idea."

"It'll be fine. I want to know more about the Sentinels and Eliana. If that guy in the car really was a Sentinel, we need to be prepared. Robin knows more than she's told us." It's hard to decide whether Robin is lying, scared, or something else, but I know she's hiding something.

Olivia sighs. "You're going to go whether I say it's okay or not, aren't you?" My expression is answer enough. She sighs again, her lips frowning anxiously. "Please be careful. Don't go too far away, okay?"

"Just the park down the street from the house."

She frowns again, then does something unexpected. Her fingers curl around mine for just a moment before sliding away. "Fine, but...just watch yourself around her, okay?"

It takes me a moment to respond. "I will."

As she turns and heads for her next class, I follow wondering about Olivia taking my hand.

***

● ● ●

56

When I slip up next to Robin, I startle her so badly she drops the books she's carrying and stumbles over the mess. I can't help laughing as she kneels down to pick them all back up. I'd help her if I could, but that would only make more people stare than are already watching and shaking their heads. Robin doesn't seem to notice and stands up with a smile.

"So, did you come by just to scare me half to death, or was there some other reason?" Robin asks as we walk toward her car.

"What are you doing right now?" I ask.

She shrugs. "Homework. Why?"

"Just wanted to see if you'd wanna hang out for a while." I'm sure that didn't sound nearly as casual as I meant it to, but Robin doesn't notice. She grins at me in response.

"Sure!" Her eyes dart around the parking lot. "Just us, or should we wait for Olivia?"

"Just us," I say. "I thought we could head over to the park near my house. Olivia's dad still doesn't want us wandering around too much since that guy in the car showed up, but I thought it'd be nice to get out for a while."

Robin skips the last few steps to her car and unceremoniously dumps everything she's carrying into the backseat. "I'd love to! Let's go!"

Pretending to look at something on her phone, Robin lets me slide in through the driver's door, so no one asks questions about the passenger's door opening on its own. Once I'm across, she climbs in and throws the car into reverse. A few seconds and one near collision with a group of teens trying to get past Robin later, we pull onto the street and make the short trip to the park.

We repeat the same process getting out of the car just in case anyone is watching, and I start to walk away. Robin doesn't follow, instead grabbing her backpack out of the backseat.

When I give her a questioning look, she says, "I can pretend I'm doing homework if anyone walks by."

Knowing her, she really will be doing homework. I shake my head, smiling all the same, and head toward the back of the park where a stand of trees provides a little more privacy. I flop down and stretch out on the grass. Robin pulls out a couple of books and organizes her notebooks and pencils next to them.

"You are a nerd," I tease.

Robin grins. "Yeah, and what of it?"

"Nothing," I laugh. "Just thought it needed to be said."

"Anything else you need to get off your chest?"

I can see the teasing glint in her eyes, but I can also see that she is honestly curious about why I asked to hang out with her today. "I've never had a friend that wasn't family before. I'm not sure family even counts as friends, since they're family. If they don't, I guess you're the only friend I've ever had," I admit. "Which is kinda weird."

"Weird?" Robin leans back against the tree. "How so?"

Shrugging, I look up at the sky. "It feels strange not to have Olivia or Evie with me. Like I'm exposed without them here as a barrier to protect me."

"You don't think I'll keep you safe?" Robin asks quietly.

"It's not that." To be honest, I don't know if Robin will keep me safe, or not. I don't really need anyone to keep me safe. I'm invisible, after all. It's more … "Protect isn't the right word. It feels good to have them close by, familiar, comfortable. I don't like being away from them."

Robin moves away from the tree and lies down on the grass next to me. Her nearness makes my body tense. As she props herself up on her elbow, she smiles. "They're all you've ever had…up 'til now."

Part of me wants to pull away from Robin. The anxiety her smile and closeness inspires is intimidating. I'm not sure what to do with it. She's probably waiting for a response, but I'm not sure what she expects me to say.

"I know I'm kind of a spaz," Robin says, lowering her eyes, "and I blurt out things I shouldn't, so I can understand if hanging out with me feels weird …"

"Robin, it's not any of that. I mean, you are a spaz and you talk a lot," I say, pausing and smiling so she knows I don't hold any of that against her. "You don't make me feel weird about being here. It's just strange to think that you can see me."

"Why?"

"Because I don't know you that well. Seeing me has always felt like such an intimate thing, something personal and private. No offense, but you're still kind of a stranger, and even though I love that you can see me, it takes some getting used to."

I look over at her, hoping I haven't hurt her feelings and wondering if what I just told her makes sense. She grins back at me and pokes me lightly.

"There's a simple solution to this."

Raising one eyebrow at her, I wait for an explanation.

Laughing, she says, "You just have to get to know me better. Starting now. Ask me whatever you want."

Not nearly distracted enough by the unique situation to miss an opportunity for answers, I know jumping into the big questions right away will only scare her off. So I start small.

"Where did you grow up?"

"Pennsylvania."

"Did you like it there?"

Robin nods. "It was so pretty and we had all this land to explore. I loved it there."

"Why did you move?"

The cheeriness drops out of Robin's expression immediately. "We had no choice," she whispers.

For a moment, I hesitate asking a new question. Robin turns to look up at the clouds, but I know what she's really doing is trying to keep the tears brimming in her eyes from falling down her cheeks. I don't doubt that Robin's guilt has something to do with Eliana's death. Suspecting her of being the deliberate cause...I seriously doubt it.

Scooting closer to Robin, I set my hand on her forearm. "What happened?"

"After …" Robin sniffs, but turns to look at me. "After Eliana died we couldn't stay where we were anymore. The Sentinels knew where we lived. We had to cut off all contact with other Caretakers for over a year."

"Why?" I ask. "Aside from hoping you'd lead them to other Caretakers, I mean. Did they think you might take in another Aerling?"

The expression on Robin's face is quizzical for a moment. Then, for some reason it turns into frustration. She doesn't let me wonder why. "Mason, I know I don't know your Caretakers, but I don't understand why they've kept you in the dark about so much. They've kept you from making friends, from exploring your abilities, from knowing who you are. Why would they want to limit you so much?"

"What do you mean *exploring my abilities*? Olivia's parents have never held me back from learning and developing skills."

I watch as Robin's eyes go from mild frustration to full on anger. "They never told you?"

"Uh, told me what?"

"About your talents!"

"What talents?"

Robin sits up on the grass with her feet crossed and yanks me up next to her. "Haven't you ever been able to do something unusual, out of the ordinary?"

"You mean aside from being invisible?" I drawl.

Rolling her eyes, Robin slaps my knee. "I mean something more than that. It could be knowing what someone is about to say before they say it, guessing the weather, sensing someone's emotions, strange dreams …"

"Dreams?" I practically demand.

Robin stares at me. "Do you have dreams that don't seem like dreams?"

"I…maybe, I'm not sure."

"What are they like?"

A shiver runs through my body. "Terrifying. I have nightmares all the time. They feel so real. I wake up screaming sometimes."

"What are the dreams about?" Robin asks.

I freeze, suddenly wanting to kick myself for bringing it up. "I, uh, they're just…nightmares. Bad things happening to me or my family."

"Have any of your dreams ever come true before?"

"What?" I snap. "No, and I hope they never do."

Robin holds up her hands. "It was just a question, Mason. I didn't mean anything bad by it. I'm just surprised you haven't had any other talents manifest that you're aware of."

"Why? Do all Aerlings have talents?"

"Well, yeah, and they usually show up pretty early, like by three or four years old."

Feeling more than just uncomfortable, I try to shrug off the conversation. "Maybe I'm just not all that talented."

Or maybe watching my family die killed that part of me.

Pouting, Robin folds her arms. "This doesn't make sense. You have to have a talent."

"What was Eliana's talent?" Anything to get the focus of the conversation off of me.

"She could talk to me without speaking," Robin says, a bit of her smile reappearing. "She couldn't talk to anyone who wasn't a Caretaker, but it was a fun talent."

Why couldn't I have had that talent? Maybe I could have figured out how to talk to Olivia's mom and dad and Evie without having to touch them every time I needed to say something. No, I get nightmares instead. That's not even a talent. It just sucks.

"Robin," I ask slowly, "how did Eliana die? How did the Sentinels find her?"

Her smile drops away immediately. "That's not something I want to talk about, Mason."

And to really make her point, she starts tossing her books and papers back into her backpack. I panic, knowing I should have been more subtle, but just not having the patience for it. I grab Robin's arm and pull her away from her bag. For a moment, fear flashes through her eyes. Guilt for being so rough with her loosens my grip, but not enough for her to get away.

"Robin, please. I need to know if I'm putting Olivia and everyone else in danger."

"You aren't," she says as she tries to pull away from me.

"How do you know?" I demand.

Her struggle to get away from me falters. Whatever the source of the pain Robin is holding onto, she recognizes the same in me and stops fighting me. Her frantic expression softens into one of understanding. I don't realize I'm still gripping her arm until she brings her hand up to rest on my face.

"Mason, I can't promise you that the Sentinels will never find you. I wish I could," she says, "but you're doing everything you can to keep your family safe. You don't make scenes that cause suspicion or draw attention. Olivia and Evie are just as careful, protecting you every second. I can see how much you love each other. You would never do anything to put them in danger, and neither would they. It's the best anyone can do."

A tear slips past Robin's control. I don't know why, but I release my grip on her arm and brush away her tears. When Robin's head drops, I push her chin back up. As if she thinks I can see something more than her pain-filled expression, her body convulses in a sob. Instinct pulls her into my lap and I hold her as she cries.

"You and Olivia are so blessed to have each other," Robin says through her tears. "I wish…I wish Eliana had been so lucky. Instead, she ended up with me."

"Robin, what happened?" I ask.

Pushing away from me, Robin swipes at her tears. "I have to go, Mason."

She reaches for her backpack and stumbles to her feet. I am right behind her. I don't want to scare her or hurt her, but I need to know everything. I need to be sure that Olivia will be safe. My hand reaches for her arm again. She's too quick, and I end up hooking her waist instead. She gasps when I pull her back to me.

"Please," I beg.

Robin's palms press against my chest, as if she's trying to get away again, but there is no force behind it. Finally, her head falls against my shoulder. She doesn't look at me when she begins to speak.

"Everyone was telling secrets. It was my first sleepover. I was seven and I wanted everyone to like me. I waited my turn, listening to the other girls tell about watching a movie they weren't supposed to or getting into their sister's makeup. It all sounded so silly when I was keeping a secret like Eliana. I knew I had the best secret, but the others got bored of the game before it was my turn. They all started to turn away and I was forgotten. It was the first time I had been invited to someone's party. No one ever paid attention to me or even liked me. I just wanted them to think I was interesting…so I told them about Eliana."

"What did they say?" I ask.

"Everyone laughed at me," Robin whispers, "except for one girl I didn't know very well. She just stared at me. She stared at me all night. I should have realized."

Robin sobs again and I hold her more tightly.

"The Sentinels came for Eliana the next night while we were in bed. Nobody knew they were in our house until Eliana screamed, but by then it was already over." Robin's body starts shaking. "There was so much blood. She was right next to me in bed and I didn't protect her. I told her secret and I slept while they murdered her."

I can't speak, or move. I can't respond at all. I want to tell Robin that I understand what she's feeling, that I carry similar guilt and horrible memories. I want to tell her that my mom and sister were murdered right in front of me as I cried in the corner because I didn't know what to do. I want to tell her everything and cry until every bloody memory is washed away. I want to share my pain with her and share hers, but I can't. I don't say anything. I keep the agony I hold close deep inside my heart and stroke her hair as I struggle to keep my own secrets.

"I'm sorry," Robin mumbles against my shirt when her tears finally calm.

"Sorry for what? You were only seven, Robin."

She shakes her head. "No, I can never be forgiven for that. I meant that I'm sorry for ever coming into your life. If that guy was a Sentinel, it has to be my fault that he's here."

"You don't know that."

"Nobody else even knows you're here."

"There's nothing to say that anything has changed," I argue, praying I'm right. "More likely than not, with your family having just moved, the Sentinels are just checking up on you."

Robin is quiet for a moment. She wants to believe that as much as I do. Bringing her gaze up to meet mine, Robin says, "I won't make the same mistake twice, but if you don't want me to hang around you and Olivia anymore, I understand."

Olivia and I might have different opinions on this, but I smile down at Robin. "I don't want to lose my only non-family friend just yet."

"Are you sure?" The expression on her face makes it apparent she thinks I might be making a mistake. Despite Olivia's misgivings, I trust Robin.

"I'm sure."

Robin has a knack for catching people off guard, but I'm shocked when she lifts onto her toes, kisses my cheek, and spins out of my arms. She has her backpack and is halfway to her car before I snap out of it. I watch her drive away wondering what just happened.

Chapter 11

Breaking Glass

I know I'm dreaming. I know this is another nightmare, but the panic and fear racing through my body feels too real to ignore. Images flash through my mind. Dark hallways, glass breaking, footsteps. The roar of blood rushing through my body makes it hard to hear the intruder. My head whips back and forth as I search for him, as I search for Olivia. I don't know where she is!

Not running is painful. I want to barrel through the house screaming her name until I find her.

All of the sudden, I'm outside, standing in the street, staring at a nondescript sedan filled with shadows. My feet carry me closer, against my will. The shadows start writhing. I fear they are going to come after me. Sweaty hands reach for the car and it takes me a moment to realize they are mine. I try to pull them back. Get away from the car. Run.

Olivia's face breaks through the haze of shadows.

My fingers are tearing at the handle, beating against the glass. I scream her name, no longer caring if I am quiet. She reaches for me. I can't get through the door! I scream her name again as her face begins to disappear. I can't stop screaming. I can't stop her from disappearing!

"Mason!" someone shouts at me. Their hands claw at me, trying to keep me from saving Olivia.

"Mason!" the voice hisses again. I can't see them, but I strike out, desperate to get away and reach Olivia.

"Mason, please," a gentle voice whispers in my ear. The ache in the voice breaks through my panic, making me listen, recognize.

The dream's power dissolves. My eyes snap open to find Olivia hovering over me...no sitting on top of me. Confusion sets in as I realize she has my arms pinned to the bed and is sitting on my chest with her knees on either side of me. I'm too disoriented to really enjoy the moment.

"Olivia?"

"Are you awake?" she asks.

My eyebrows knit together. Am I? Would I be in this position with Olivia in real life? It takes me a moment to answer. "I think so?"

Olivia collapses on top of me. "Thank goodness!"

"I'm sorry I woke you again."

"It's okay," she says. "It just scared me. What were you dreaming about?"

"Someone had broken into the house. They took you, I think. It was confusing and frightening."

Olivia blows out a shaky breath. "You're telling me. I thought you were never going to wake up. You were scaring the living daylights out of me, Mason!"

That last part comes out a little angry and she follows it up with a punch to my shoulder. She rolls off of me and sinks into the bed looking exhausted. I'm about to ask her what exactly happened, but when I turn to face her my mind goes completely blank at the site of a bruise forming on her cheek.

"Olivia, what happened?" I demand.

She sighs. "You were having another nightmare. Don't you remember? It was awful. You were screaming for me and thrashing around like a crazy person. I couldn't get through to you at all."

"No," I say angrily, "what happened to your face?"

Olivia turns to scowl at me. "You whacked me when I tried to wake you up and knocked me off the bed. Thanks for that."

The blood drains from my fingers, leaving them cold as I gently touch Olivia's face. She winces, but doesn't pull away. "Ollie, I'm so sorry."

She smiles up at me. "I know. It's okay. I'm just sorry you were having such a rough night."

"Does it hurt?"

"Stings a little, but I'll be fine. Really, Mason. It was just an accident."

Before I can think about it rationally, I press my lips to her cheek just above the bruise. I hear the sharp intake of her breath and freeze. I should pull back, pretend it didn't happen, spontaneously fall asleep. I don't do any of that. I can't.

Olivia turns to face me, her eyes wide. The expression on her face is unreadable. I can feel my heart rate speeding up as panic sets in. What have I done?

Olivia's lips part to say something, but she never gets the chance. The sound of breaking glass yanks us both up to sitting as everything but fear leaves our minds completely.

"Mason!" Olivia squeaks. "There's someone in the house!"

"I know," I whisper back.

I start to swing my feet over the side of the bed, but Olivia clamps down on my arm with strength born of terror. "Don't go."

"Stay here."

"No!"

Prying her hands off of me proves nearly impossible. "Olivia, let go, I'm just going to scare him off. He won't see me."

"What if it's a Sentinel?"

"It's not a Sentinel," I say, though I hardly believe it myself.

"Who else would it be?" she demands.

"A criminal," I hiss at her. She's wasting time! He could be halfway up the stairs and on his way to Olivia! "Olivia let go!"

Her hands clamp down tighter and she screams.

As the shrill, piercing noise of Olivia's scream dies, everything happens at once. I finally break out of her grip, Olivia's dad's bedroom door crashes open, and the noises from downstairs intensify as the intruder makes a run for it.

Olivia's dad and I crash into each other as I come barreling out of my room. Confusion and panic grips him because he doesn't immediately understand what just happened. Grabbing his shoulder, I steady him and say, "It's just me, sorry."

Relief droops his shoulders, but it's short-lived. "What is going on?"

"Someone is downstairs," I say, "or was. I think Olivia's screaming scared him off."

The downstairs area seems abnormally quiet now.

"Still," he says, "get me your bat."

It only takes me a few seconds to dash back to my room and grab the bat. Olivia's dad takes it and brings it over his shoulder, ready to swing. I've seen him hit a ball, and I know he can do damage, but I still step in front of him and start down the stairs. Olivia hisses at me from the top of the stairs, telling me to get back, but I don't listen. I do spare a moment to hope her dad doesn't realize she just came out of my room again.

My heart speeds up with every step, but I make it to the bottom of the staircase without having a heart attack, so I figure things are going pretty well so far. Part of me wants to stop and take a few deep breaths. Olivia's dad won't know I stopped, though, and will probably end up running into me, so I keep going.

From playing hide and seek outside on summer nights, I know my night vision is quite a bit better than anyone else's. I can see the living room and dining area as I slip quietly into the foyer. Nothing. The dining room has some vicious rose bushes beneath each window, so I take a logical guess and move toward the living room. Still nothing.

When we reach the kitchen, I can hear Olivia's dad stop behind me at the same time my feet come to a halt. Glass from the open back door sparkles in the moonlight. He curses and the bat falls from his shoulder. He brings it back up right away.

"We should check the rest of the house just to be sure," he says.

Feeling more secure, we split up and make sure the rest of the rooms are empty and undisturbed. Ten minutes later, we're back in the foyer empty handed.

"Is he gone?" Olivia asks from where she's huddled on the stairs.

Her dad nods. "Go call the police and tell your Mom everything's okay."

Olivia darts back up the stairs.

"Is this the work of those Sentinels you told me about?" he asks.

"I don't know, but it's possible," I admit. I wanted what I said to Robin earlier today to be true. I wanted it so badly.

"The police are on their way," Olivia says as she comes back down the stairs. Her dad pulls her into a hug, but she wiggles out of his embrace after a moment and wraps herself around me.

Olivia's dad doesn't say anything about the way Olivia holds me, but he watches her carefully, no doubt picturing my arms locked around her body as well. I'm beginning to think he saw Olivia come out of my room.

"Mason, was this the dream you were having?" Olivia asks. "Did it come true?"

"What?" Olivia's dad demands.

I shake my head, trying to reject the idea.

"You said you dreamed about someone breaking into the house and taking me," Olivia pushes.

"Nobody took you," I say fiercely. "I would never let that happen."

Olivia pulls against me more tightly. "I know, but you dreamed about this…and it came true."

"It was just a coincidence," I say desperately.

My nightmares can't come true. They can't. Olivia has to stay safe. No one can hurt her. Nothing bad can ever happen to her. My hands press Olivia against me. My fingers tangle in her hair and cradle her against my heart. Breathing…it's not working right. I can't get enough air suddenly. My chest starts heaving.

"Mason?" Olivia asks as she tries to pull back. "Mason, calm down!"

"Mason?" It's her dad's voice now. His hand grips my shoulder. "Son, what's wrong?"

Olivia stops trying to pull away from me and starts whispering. "It's okay, Mason. Nobody took me. Everything is okay. Please calm down. It's okay."

I struggle to control my breathing as red and blue lights start flashing through the living room windows. Olivia's dad walks to the front door, leaving Olivia to calm me down. She pulls me out of the foyer and into the living room. We're huddled on the couch before I finally begin to relax.

"You called me Ollie again," Olivia says quietly as her dad talks to the officers.

"Did I?" I can't remember. Everything seemed too chaotic when I first woke up.

She rests her had against my shoulder. "Yeah, you did."

"Does it bother you when I call you that?" I ask.

Her hand slips into mine. "No."

The conversation between Olivia's dad and the officers quiets as he leads them to the broken windows in the back door. Olivia's mom makes it down the stairs with a wide-eyed Evie in tow. Neither of them notices us on the couch and they walk toward the noise, leaving us in the quiet of an interrupted night.

"Would it bother you if I called you Ollie more often?" I ask, not really sure why I'm making the request.

Olivia is quiet for a moment before saying, "I would like that."

I pull her against me even more and we hold each other until the police and the fear leaves.

Chapter 12
Selfish Choices

"Someone broke into our house last night," I snap at Robin when I finally corner her.

"What?" she squeaks.

My eyes bore into her. "Someone. Broke. Into. Our. House. Last. Night."

Robin fumbles with her backpack and almost drops it. "Olivia, that's terrible! Is everyone okay?"

"We're fine, but I want some answers."

I watch as Robin's eyes dart around for help or reassurance that I'm not crazy. She doesn't find any. "Answers about what?" she asks.

"I think it was a Sentinel that broke into our house last night."

"And you think I had something to do with it?" Robin asks, clearly confused.

"No," I snap, although the thought had crossed my mind many times. Mason talked me out of the idea, but I'm still not completely convinced. "But I want to know how Sentinels find Aerlings. The truth this time."

"What do you mean? I told you how they find them."

Robin tries to back away, but I won't let her get away from me. "After the police finally left, all I could think about was how there had to be some other way for the Sentinels to find Aerlings. It couldn't just be luck and tabloid stories. There has to be something else that draws them to Aerlings. I simply can't believe there isn't something more."

"Don't…don't you, um, have to get to class?" Robin asks.

"Mason will let me know what I miss. You, on the other hand, have a free period right now, so don't think you're going to escape answering," I say.

Robin's mouth opens. It closes right after. Something seems to go out of her as her head drops. "Can we go somewhere else to talk?"

The practice gym is empty this hour, so I turn on my heel and head in that direction knowing Robin will follow. I don't look back to make sure. The shuffle and squeak of her sneakers dragging her after me is confirmation. I don't really need it, though, because I know she understands that if she doesn't tell me, her friendship with Mason will be over. It's obvious that she cares about him and doesn't want that to happen. So she follows.

My nose wrinkles as the smell of old sweat that always seems to permeate the practice gym hits my nose. I toss my backpack down. Robin slumps to the first bleacher, her own backpack landing at her feet with a thud.

On the way over here, a dozen questions about Sentinels were running through my mind. When I open my mouth, none of those questions come out.

"Mason told me about Eliana," I say quietly.

Robin's head pops up. The surprise on her face doesn't make sense to me. "He did?"

I nod. "We don't keep secrets from each other."

"He told you everything?" Robin asks, her hands trembling.

"He told me how you told your friends about Eliana and the Sentinels killed her the next night. It was clear how much it affected you. He was pretty upset himself just telling me about it. I know he believes you." I take a deep breath, trying to keep my opinions from overruling everything else. "Mason told me that you offered to step back and stay away from him in order to protect him and he told you no."

Robin shudders and wraps her arms around her body. "You disagree with him."

It's not a question. The temptation is there to agree, to tell her to back off and get out of our lives. I'm not sure that sparing Mason's feelings is worth the risk, but he asked me to try. Being wrapped up in his arms last night as we waited for the police to leave made it impossible to deny him anything.

"I don't trust you like he does," I admit. Robin holds her breath. "But I don't think you'll hurt him either."

Robin's breath stutters out haltingly.

"That may change, though, if you don't tell me how Sentinels really track Aerlings."

Her posture makes it obvious that she isn't any more keen on telling me now than she was in the beginning, but she squares her shoulders and opens her mouth. "They can feel them," she says simply.

Goosebumps pop up all over body. "What do you mean they can *feel* them?"

"It's not something I really understand," Robin says with a shake of her head. "Sentinels look like anyone else, but there's something about them that lets them sense when an Aerling is near them. I don't know if it's something they're born with or a talent they develop, but it's their biggest tool in finding Aerlings."

"Why didn't you tell us this when we first asked?" I demand.

"All it was going to do was scare you both. It doesn't help you keep him safer," Robin argues. "Unless you plan on locking him up in your house so

● ● ●

70

no one can ever come in contact with him. But given how you've practically done that already, maybe you will."

I tried to give her some latitude because Mason wants her around, but she just hit my last nerve. My palm knocks into her shoulder angrily. There's no guilt when she falls back between the two bleachers, scraping her back on the one above her.

"How dare you judge us!"

Robin winces as she pushes herself back up to sitting. "Do you know what Mason told me yesterday?"

I don't answer.

"He told me that I was his only friend," Robin says, shocking me.

"What? Why would he say that?" I ask. "Mason is my best friend."

Robin folds her arms across her chest. "He said he wasn't sure if you could count family as friends, and since the only friends he's ever had were his family, I was his first friend."

I don't count?

Grabbing her backpack up off the ground, Robin stands stiffly. "You claim you're trying to protect Mason, but I wonder if it isn't just selfishness fueling your choices. Seems to me like you're afraid that if he actually has the chance to live his life, it won't be with you."

"That's not true," I whisper, but in the deepest, most honest part of my heart, I like Mason being my secret. I don't want him to be friends with Robin because that may mean he won't have room for me.

Robin shoulders her backpack and starts walking toward the door. A small amount of guilt plagues me as she rubs her back. Some of what she said might have a kernel of truth to it, but she doesn't understand as much as she thinks she does. It kills me that I can't fix that. Maybe I can at least try to make her see more.

"Robin," I say before she reaches the door, "I love Mason."

She stops and sighs. "I know you do."

"It does scare me to think of Mason being away from me and finding something better. He's my best friend, the person I can't imagine living without." My breath catches at the thought of not seeing him every day. "But if Mason did want to leave, I wouldn't stop him. I would miss him like you could never understand, but I want him to be happy more than anything else."

Slowly, Robin turns back around and faces me. She looks tired, sad.

"I do understand what it's like to miss someone so much it physically hurts." She pushes her glasses up on her nose, brushes her hair back, anything to keep her mind off what she's saying. "Eliana was *my* Mason. My best friend. My only friend. It was my fault she died. I'll never forgive myself, and I'll never stop missing her. My selfish choices cost her everything. I worry that you're going to fall into the same trap."

Shaking my head, I say, "I would never tell anyone about Mason."

The pain that flashes through her eyes makes me cringe. I didn't mean it as a judgment of her. I try to apologize, but Robin waves me off.

"That's not what I meant. I know you won't tell anyone about Mason, but there are other ways you might betray him to the Sentinels."

"What?"

"Why hasn't your family helped Mason develop his abilities?"

Abilities?

"The dreams he has, you can't tell me no one in your family recognized them as an ability he needed to develop. Most Aerlings are fully trained by now. Mason acted like he'd never heard of such a thing. His abilities are meant to keep him safe from the Sentinels and your family has done nothing to help him develop them." Robin glares at me, watching my expression carefully.

I'm not sure how to respond to her. Of course, no one in my family had any idea we were supposed to be looking for something. It was only when Mason brought it up himself that I began to wonder if his dreams were something more than simple nightmares. I don't want to give away that we are clueless about this, but I struggle to find an answer for Robin.

"We...Mason's dreams, they, uh, until just recently they were nothing but nightmares. The same thing every night. We didn't realize they meant anything."

Robin's eyes narrow. "Until recently?"

My head bobs slowly. "He had a nightmare about someone breaking into our house last night, before it actually happened."

A strange sense of excitement builds around Robin. "He's never dreamt something that came true before? He said his dreams are always very real. What about those?"

"He doesn't tell me much about his nightmares usually. They've never come true before, thankfully. They're bad, really bad. And most of them are about stuff that already happened."

"What kind of stuff?" Robin demands.

Now I'm the one folding my arms. "The kind that's very personal and Mason wouldn't want me talking about."

"Does Mason have any other abilities?" Robin asks. Well, it's more of a demand, but I can tell she's trying to be patient.

I shrug. "I don't know. There are things Mason is better at than other people, but maybe he's just stronger or whatever."

"Like what?"

"He seems stronger than a normal guy of his height and build. His endurance is really good. He outlasts everyone else when we go running, including my dad who was All American in cross country when he was in college. He sees better than us, especially at night. His hearing is better." I shrug again, not sure whether his edge over us is enough to qualify as special abilities.

Robin doesn't seem impressed. "No, that's all just regular Aerling stuff. He's got to have something more," Robin says. Her fingers curls around her backpack strap as if suddenly nervous. "He should have had an ability that manifested much earlier."

"What if he doesn't?"

She shakes her head worriedly. "I don't know. It's not supposed to be like that. He should have shown signs of some kind of ability as a toddler. I don't know what that means if he didn't."

"You don't think the dreams are enough?"

Robin chews on her lip. "I don't think so. Many Aerlings start developing secondary abilities in their late teen years. They usually aren't as strong as the primary ability, though."

Neither of us says anything for a moment. Fear builds in my mind that I missed something in Mason that could make the difference between staying hidden from the Sentinels and being killed. What escaped our notice? Could he possibly have hidden some ability out of fear that we wouldn't understand?

I push that thought away quickly. Mason wouldn't keep secrets from me. He knows I would never turn away from him just because he was different. No, Mason must not have seen anything unusual in himself either. He would have told me, wouldn't he have?

"Maybe…maybe you should come over this afternoon and we can talk about it with Mason," I say dejectedly.

Spending more time with Robin isn't my idea of a nice time, but despite her baseless accusations, she has me scared.

"Sure," Robin says. "I know you don't trust me, Olivia, and I know I haven't known either of you that long, but I care about Mason and I don't want to see him hurt. You don't have to like me, but I hope you can at least believe me."

"I do believe you," I say, surprising us both.

Robin nods. "See you after school then."

I watch her walk away and slump down to the bleachers. My head drops into my hands. I feel like every time I turn around lately, Robin is dropping some kind of bomb on me. Mason is an Aerling. Mason isn't human. There

● ● ●

73

are Sentinels trying to kill him. You and your family screwed up his chances of surviving. Mason only loves you because he has no one else.

Okay, maybe she didn't say that last one quite like that, but it's what she meant.

I don't want to doubt how Mason feels about me, about my family, but he's been different since Robin showed up. To be honest, it started before she showed up. Everything Mason was already feeling, everything I had been blind to, is now being validated by Robin. I want to believe that he'll always stay with me, but I'm not so sure anymore, and it breaks my heart to admit that.

Chapter 13

Meltdown

The weird vibe between Robin and Olivia when I find them standing together at Olivia's locker after school doesn't make sense with the polite way they're treating each other. I suspect something happened between them earlier. Neither one seems interested in explaining, though, so I leave it alone for now.

Olivia announces that Robin is coming over to hang out and we head for the Jeep. Evie is already waiting for us there, with Aaron making a hasty retreat. He's well aware that Olivia thinks he's an idiot and tries to make himself scarce when she's around. Since I don't like him either, I'm glad to see him go.

Evie stops staring after Aaron in time to turn and hear Robin say she'll meet us at the house. Evie's hands snap to her hips as she fixes a glare on Olivia. "Am I the only one who remembers what happened last time she came over?"

"We need her help," Olivia admits.

Now, I am more curious than ever to know what she and Robin talked about.

The drive home is quiet and sullen. For some reason, Olivia keeps looking over at me with a sad expression I don't understand. As we approach the house, everyone's eyes are scanning the streets for suspicious cars, but everything seems perfectly average. Evie is hardly appeased.

As soon as Olivia puts the Jeep in park, Evie jumps out, slamming the door behind her. I'm shocked Evie is being so dramatic about this. When I turn to Olivia, she puts a hand on my arm and says, "This has more to do with her not being able to see Aaron than with you or Robin. I'll go talk to her."

Olivia gets out and holds the door open long enough for me to slide out after her. I want to ask her what's going on between her and Robin, but she walks away before I get the chance. Sighing, I head for the house, hoping Robin will have some answers.

As my body flops onto the couch next to Robin, she looks over at me and smiles. It's the first pleasant expression I've seen all afternoon. There is something infectious about Robin's grin. I can't help smiling back.

"Hey."

"Hey," she says. Robin sets the notebook she was flipping through down on the coffee table and turns sideways to look at me. She tries to

● ● ●

maintain her smile, but it falters and slips away. "Olivia said you told her about Eliana."

I nod, hoping she doesn't expect me to apologize. Olivia was struggling to trust Robin. She needed to know that what happened to Eliana was the mistake of a naïve little girl and not a vicious betrayal.

"She said you don't keep secrets from each other."

"No, we don't."

Robin fidgets with one of her dangly earrings. "You didn't tell her everything."

She doesn't have to explain for me to know what she's talking about. I look away, not sure whether I'm embarrassed when I think about Robin kissing me, or glad she did it. "No," I admit, "I didn't tell her."

"Why not?"

I shrug. I don't want to admit that I didn't know how to tell Olivia, because I couldn't figure out how she would react. Would she be glad I had found someone that I might have a real chance at a relationship with? Would she be angry? Jealous? Would it affect her at all? Without knowing the consequences, I couldn't tell her.

A thought suddenly occurs to me. I turn to Robin, hoping I didn't just figure out why Olivia seemed so down on the way home. "Did you tell her?"

Robin laughs. "Olivia dislikes me enough without me adding fuel to the fire. No, I didn't tell her."

I start to ask what she did tell Olivia that upset her so much when I hear the front door open. Assuming it's Olivia's mom, but not wanting to be caught off guard, I check the driveway for her car and relax when I hear her voice calling out that she's home. Her head peeks around the corner a few seconds later.

"Robin, how nice to see you," Olivia's mom says. "Where are the kids? Did they all abandon you?"

Realizing my mistake right away, I jump up from the couch and try to reach her before Robin makes the connection. I'm not fast enough.

Robin cocks her head to one side. "Evie and Olivia are upstairs, but Mason's right in front of you."

My hand lands on Olivia's mom's shoulder. Her eyes widen, knowing we're both in trouble. "I...I meant to ask where the girls were. Of course Mason is right here."

She reaches out and gives me a quick hug before dashing off to the kitchen. I want to follow her, but Robin grabs my shoulder. My head drops to my chest. She's way too smart of a girl not to have connected all the dots.

"What just happened?" Robin demands. "Olivia's mom acted like she didn't even see you."

"Sure she saw me," I answer lamely.

Folding her arms across her chest like she so often does, Robin glares at me. "You're lying."

That's right about when Olivia bounds down the stairs. She slows to a stop at the sight of Robin facing me down. "What happened now?"

"Your mom walked into the room and asked why I was sitting there all alone when Mason was right there! Add that to the way Evie was acting the other day, and something is clearly not right here!" Robin yells. "What is going on?"

Olivia tries to brush off the outburst. She'd have to be invisible for Robin not to notice her shifting feet and darting eyes. Still, she tries. "What are you going on about, Robin. Mom just didn't see him. I don't know why you're having a meltdown about it."

"He was standing right in front of her!" Robin eyes are darting back and forth.

Olivia's mom walks back into the room slowly, her eyes on Robin. I remember her approaching an injured cat the same way once, when it wandered into our yard. In the weeks we have known Robin, Olivia's mom has never expressed an opinion one way or the other about whether she believes Robin is a threat. Now, there is fear in her eyes.

"Robin," she says calmly, "I'm sorry if I upset you earlier."

The cautious approach doesn't fool Robin. She backs away slowly.

The clomp-clomp of Evie clambering down the stairs momentarily distracts everyone. Her hand appears first, gripping the hand rail and swinging herself around the landing to start down the last half flight. She skids to stop when she realizes everyone is staring at her.

"What is all the yelling about down here? And where's Mason? I need him to help me with my math homework," Evie says. Her eyes dart around expectantly. Olivia and her mom groan.

Robin's eyes double in size. One hand covers her mouth while the other starts pointing at Evie. "See? See?"

Evie's hand drops from the rail. Her face falls as she realizes her mistake. "He's standing right here, isn't he?"

I reach over and touch Evie's shoulder. "Sorry, right here."

"Mason, I'm so sorry," she says.

"You mom blew our cover first," I say with a laugh.

Olivia's mom can't hear me because she's not touching me, but Evie looks over at her and grimaces. They both feel terrible. Really, I'm not sure how long we were going to be able to keep this up anyway. I'm not even sure why we're keeping the truth from Robin anymore. I trust her, so I take the lead.

● ● ●

Taking Robin's hand like I might a frightened child, I wait until she looks at me. From the corner of my eye I can see Olivia clenching her fists. I still don't know what happened earlier today, but Robin deserves an explanation. She doesn't resist when I pull her over to the couch and make her sit down. Evie and her mom crowd around us, each making an effort to touch my shoulder or arm so they can hear me.

"Mason, what is going on? You guys are really freaking me out!"

I don't quite know where to begin, so I start with the first thing that comes to mind. "Olivia is the only one who can see me."

"What? Why?"

The only response I can give is to shrug.

"That's not an answer!"

"I'm sorry, Robin, but we don't know."

"This doesn't make any sense. If you're all Caretakers, why is Olivia the only one that can see you?"

Everyone starts squirming except me. "Um, it's probably because they aren't Caretakers. Not even Olivia."

For a moment, I think Robin might faint. Just in case she pitches forward and smacks her head on the table, I put my arm around her shoulder and keep her upright. The hand Robin never let go of when I led her to the couch clamps down on mine, but she stays conscious.

"How…did you…this doesn't make sense!" Robin cries. "How did you get an Aerling if you aren't Caretakers?"

Her hand slaps over her mouth as her eyes grow larger than I would have thought possible. The way her breathing spikes to near hyperventilation puts everyone on edge, including me. "Robin? Calm down. It's okay. *You're* freaking *me* out now!"

Robin isn't paying attention to me. Her eyes snap over to Olivia's mom. "Did you steal Mason from his Caretakers?" she demands.

"Whoa!" Olivia jumps in. "Is that what you're having a conniption fit about? Good grief, Robin! We're not kidnappers!"

"How…how?" Robin stutters.

Before this turns into a fight, which it looks like it's about to, given Olivia's and Evie's outrage, I force Robin to look at me. "Robin, no one stole me. Olivia saved me, and she's been protecting me ever since."

I'm not sure my words have made any impact. Robin seems intent on going into freak out mode. I've stayed pretty calm up to this point, but panic starts to creep in. If Robin starts telling people someone kidnapped me, who knows what the real Caretakers will do. I'm ready to start shaking Robin when she finally takes a deep breath. Everyone holds very, very still.

Robin breathes out slowly and says, "Someone needs to tell me what on earth is going on. Right. Now."

"Do you remember how I told you that I figured out I was an Aerling when I was five?" I ask.

Robin nods slowly.

"Well, that wasn't completely true. I hadn't heard the word Aerling until the day you ran into us in the parking lot. The only thing I figured out when I was five was that no one could see me. I was alone, wandering the city trying to find someone to help me, but no one heard or saw me."

"Why...were you alone?"

Talking about this has never been easy, but for some reason a tenuous calm settles over me as I begin telling Robin my story.

"I don't remember very much about my life before I found Olivia. I know you said something about how Aerlings remember everything, but watching my family die took most of those memories away."

Robin gasps. "What?"

"I can't tell you what happened for sure. I was hiding in a kitchen cabinet when it started," I say. "I tried to come out when my mom screamed, but she held the cabinet door shut so they couldn't find me. When the screaming stopped, I thought it was over, but it wasn't. She fell in front of the cabinets. I didn't see the blood at first. Not until I pushed the door open a little further. Then I saw it spreading across the tile."

Evie reaches over and takes her mom's hand. She curls her fingers around her daughter's hand with tears in her eyes. Olivia sits down next to me on the couch. She just sits, letting her nearness give me strength. Facing the returning memories of my family's deaths, I need more. My fingers slip around hers and she squeezes my hand tightly.

"I could hear whoever had hurt my mom moving through the house. My dad started yelling. There was noise everywhere. I had no idea what was going on and I panicked. All I wanted was to get to my dad. I didn't want to hurt my mom, but I had to push the cabinet door against her to get it open far enough so I could get out. She wouldn't answer when I tried to talk to her. When I got out, I slipped in the blood and fell beside her. I think I might have just stayed there next to her if Dad and Cami hadn't come running down the hall."

My eyes close as images start flooding back in. I'm back on the floor, kneeling in my mother's blood, crying, when my dad comes sprinting down the hallway with little Cami in his arms.

"I had never seen such a wild look in his eyes. Cami was bawling, terrified out of her mind. The knife flashed through the air so fast I only saw it once it stopped moving. My dad fell to his knees, dropping Cami to the floor."

I can't tell Robin about what happened next. Just thinking about it hurts my heart, squeezes it until it seems ready to split in two. The ache spreads through my body, pulling me inward as I try to fight off the memories and pain. I don't want to remember my dad looking over at me, his lips mouthing the word "run" on his dying breath. I don't want to remember the new puddle of blood forming and creeping toward me as I screamed.

More than anything, I beg myself not to remember the man snatching Cami up of the floor and adding her to the dead. I couldn't stop myself from disobeying my dad and crawling over to her. I picked up her hand and held it. That's when they realized I was in the room.

"I watched them die," I whisper. "I tried to hold my little sister. They must have seen her arm move. One of them grabbed me. I thought I was next."

"Oh, Mason," Olivia whispers.

"I'm not even sure how I got away," I continue. "One second they had me, and then suddenly I was free, running to find my older brother and sister."

The room is silent as I struggle to find my will to continue. Olivia leans her head against my shoulder. Her hand rubs back and forth across my back slowly. Every stroke lends me some of her strength.

"They were already gone by the time I found them. I didn't know what to do, so I hid under my brother's bed when I heard the men coming again." The images keep coming, but I push them away. "I don't know how long I stayed under there. It felt like days as the men searched the house for me. Even after the noises stopped and I was sure they were gone, I stayed under the bed, too terrified to come out."

"How did you end up on our front porch?" Olivia asks quietly.

I shake my head. "Someone must have called the police. A neighbor, maybe."

How long did I lay curled up under Brian's bed? I remember the knocking, the door swinging open slowly, the gasps as the officers saw the blood and bodies. I had no idea who they were. Already terrified, I didn't even have a word to describe how I felt in that moment.

I think it was the walkie-talkies that finally started to calm me down. Even at the time I knew it was a strange thing to focus on, but Brian and I had played with our own set just the day before. Every time one of the officers spoke into his walkie-talkie, I felt another bit of terror drop away. It was a long time later that I forced myself to crawl out from under the bed.

My eyes were closed as I stepped carefully around Brian's body, only opening once I got to the hall. All I saw were my dad's shoes before snapping them closed again. The tears streaming down my face didn't garner any more attention than my crying. Officers walked up and down the hall, but nobody saw me.

"None of the officers knew I was there, but I had no idea why. Out of desperation, I ran out of the house to the neighbor's houses. I banged on doors. Most stayed closed, but even when someone answered the door no one helped me. They just stared into the empty space looking confused."

"So you just kept going?" Robin asks.

"I kept thinking someone would finally see me. Maybe it was all just a nightmare." I shake my head. "I just kept walking until something made me stop."

"What made you stop?" Robin asks.

Finally, a good memory. "It was Olivia."

I turn to face her and all the bad clawing at me slips away. "I saw her sitting in the living room window. She was breathing on the glass and drawing pictures in the fog. For a moment, I thought she saw me. It was the first glint of recognition in two days, but I wasn't sure so I sat down on the porch. I was so tired and hungry."

"I did see you," Olivia whispers. "You looked so sad. All I wanted to do was make you feel better."

My arms tighten around Olivia. I am so overwhelmed in this moment that I can't even begin to find the words to tell her how much I love and appreciate her. One thought keeps repeating in my mind and it slips past my lips as a whisper. "I love you, Ollie."

Chapter 14

On Our Own

When I finally start to pull out of Mason's arm, he pulls me back in tight against his chest. No one says anything as he holds me a few more minutes. Slowly, his arms begin to loosen from around me. Now I am the one trying to hold onto him. We pause, halfway between pulling closer and letting go. A sound from somewhere in the room tips the balance and we lean back. Our hands stay fastened together.

"Mason," Robin says quietly, "I'm so sorry about what happened to your family, but I don't understand any of this."

"What's to understand," Evie snaps. "Those Sentinel freaks found his family, probably because some other supposedly trustworthy Caretaker betrayed them, and they killed Mason's family. Seems pretty straightforward to me."

Mom puts a hand on Evie's shoulder and pats her gently. It's obvious Evie wants to continue harassing Robin, but Mom's soothing presence is hard to ignore. Evie eventually sits down on the coffee table with an annoyed thud. She lets her gaze slip from Evie to Robin.

"Not that I want to start an argument, but it would appear that Evie is right. What happened to Mason sounds like it happens fairly often." Mom glances over at Mason with a sad expression, so deep you can almost feel the weight of it on your skin.

Robin shakes her head vehemently. "That's just the thing, though. What happened to Mason does *not* happen regularly. Or ever. Like *never* ever. Sentinels don't kill Caretakers. It's never happened before. It just isn't done."

"You said yourself that they're complete psychos," I remind her.

"Complete psychos when it comes to killing Aerlings. I have never once heard of Sentinels killing Caretakers." She shakes her head and rubs at her temples. "I mean, why would they? Caretakers are potentially very useful. They can lead them to other Caretakers, but even if that doesn't happen, they know that family will get another Aerling eventually."

"Really?" Seems like leading a lamb to the slaughter. If the Sentinels already know that family is a Caretaker, all they have to do is wait for the next one to show up.

Everyone else seems to be thinking the same thing. Robin waves us off, explaining quickly. "Not right away, of course. That would be stupid. It usually takes generations before that family is allowed to have a new Aerling, along with name changes, relocation, the works. Because of what happened to Eliana ..." Robin pauses for a moment, taking a deep breath.

"Because of her death, I'll never raise my own Aerling. Not unless they're really desperate and have no one else. Even if that happened, I'd have to leave my life, start over somewhere new, as someone new, in order to protect the Aerling."

"You would do that?" Mason asks.

Robin doesn't even hesitate. "Of course I would. I know I screwed up with Eliana, but this is my family's heritage. It's what I've been raised to do, to believe in. It's my purpose."

"So, why did the Sentinels kill Mason's Caretakers?" I ask.

Shaking her head, Robin says, "I have no idea."

Evie's hackles start twitching again, so I beat her to the next question. "There has to be a reason. How can we find out what they wanted with Mason's family? Surely there must be some kind of records we can look at that might give us a clue."

"Records?" Robin shakes her head. "Maybe at some point there were. You know, before the whole split thing happened. Nobody keeps records like that now because it would be too easy to get into."

"What about his real family, where he came from?" I demand, exasperation thick in my voice.

Robin stares at me with the infuriating look that says I have once again asked the world's stupidest question. "We have no idea where Aerlings come from or who their real families are."

"What?" Mason asks. "But you have to know something."

"So, what? Aerlings just pop up out thin air and drop on Caretakers' doorsteps?" Evie asks. The sarcasm is hard to miss.

"They must come from somewhere," Mom adds softly. "Someone must deliver them to the Caretakers, Robin. Surely someone will know something that might help Mason."

Confusion is plastered across Robin's face. For all her snotty looks, it's pretty plain that this is the first time she's actually tried to answer these questions. Apparently, she's coming up blank. Her eyes dart back and forth to each of us. "I...I don't know."

"Is there someone who could help us find out?" Mason asks.

Before Robin can answer, I start shaking my head. "No way. We're not telling anyone else about this. Robin knowing the truth is bad enough."

Looking wounded, Robin doesn't jump to her immediate defense. She takes a few moments to gather herself before speaking. "Olivia, I'm not going to hurt Mason. I feel like I have been given a second chance to prove myself and there's no way I'm going to squander it. Even more, I care about Mason a great deal. I would never do anything to hurt him. Please, you can trust me."

A great deal? My mind seems stuck on those few words. What right does she have to say that? She's known him for a couple of weeks. I've known Mason for twelve years. I've been the one protecting him! Shouldn't I know how best to keep him safe?

"You can't tell anyone about Mason," I say through gritted teeth. "We've already got Sentinels sniffing around and breaking into our house. It's too much of a risk."

"What if you can't protect him from this on your own?" Robin asks.

What if? What if Robin had never stumbled into us? What if we continued living our lives just as they were? What if she hadn't led Sentinels to us, on purpose or not? What if Mason could have just stayed with us forever, safe and lost to this other world Robin claims he belongs in?

The rant continues in my head. It might have continued forever if Mason squeezing my hand didn't draw my eyes up to his. The blue of his iris are so dark they're almost black. The pain filling them makes my heart ache, but what really stops my runaway thoughts is the glint of hope sparkling in the silver ring, turning my thoughts in a new direction.

What if Mason had been forced to continue his life in the background? What if his unhappiness at being *the guy no one can see* burdened him to the point of misery? What if his true identity had never been revealed and he spent his life feeling like a mistake? What if Robin hadn't shown up and warned us about Sentinels? What if there is a way to give Mason the life he deserves?

I look over at Mom for help. I don't know what to do. What if Robin isn't being honest? If she trusts the wrong person or speaks too candidly and Mason is taken or harmed, I'll never forgive her. I think Mom sees every thought running through my mind. Her expression is thoughtful as she says, "The choice is yours, Olivia."

"What? Why?" I need help. I want to cry. I want someone to tell me what to do!

Mom smiles, small and thin. "I love Mason like my own flesh and blood, but he belongs to you more than anyone else. You took him in, took care of him when no one else believed you, protected him. The two of you share a bond more powerful than I can understand. I trust whatever decision you make because I know you would never do anything to put Mason in danger."

A shaky breath pours out of me as I fall back against the couch. I feel like the weight of the world has just been laid on my shoulders. Or maybe just the weight of Mason's life. It presses down on me, making me unsure, afraid. Everyone seems to be looking to me for answers, but I don't have them. I just don't know.

"What would the other Caretakers do if they found out Mason was living with us?" I ask quietly.

Robin's mouth pops open, at first eager to fill the silence, but it snaps shut immediately after. Her eyes drop to her lap. "They would insist on taking him to a new Caretaker family."

The tension in the room triples.

"Not because you guys haven't done a great job," Robin hurriedly says, "but just because we have rules, laws. Caretakers make very serious covenants to protect Aerlings with their lives."

Evie's face screws up in disgust. "Some people must take those promises more seriously than others." She sneers at Robin. "We've done well enough on our own, no promises needed. For us, it's enough that we love Mason."

"Evie!" Mom snaps. The harsh tone surprises everyone. It's such a rare thing to hear coming out of her mouth. She seems a little surprised herself. After taking a deep breath, Mom continues. "It is not your place to doubt Robin's love for her Aerling or her devotion to protecting her."

"But …" Evie begins. Another sharp look from Mom cuts her off.

Mom looks over at Robin. "I apologize for Evie's attitude. We're grateful that you're willing to help us, but I think we all agree that we have no intention of handing Mason over to anyone, Caretaker or Sentinel."

"Absolutely not," I agree. My hand tightens around Mason's. He smiles at me appreciatively and echoes my words.

"I…I wasn't suggesting that," Robin says. "I don't want Mason taken away either."

"Then what?" I ask.

Robin looks up nervously. "I could ask a few questions without mentioning Mason. Find out what I can about where Aerlings come from…if anyone even knows."

"Someone knows," Mason says, his voice low and very nearly menacing.

"Who would you ask?" I demand. From what she said earlier, they're cut off from most of the other Caretakers.

The way her shoulders square up gives me hope. "I could ask my parents."

The hope fades. "No."

Everyone looks at me with a questioning glance. Really? Am I the only one that sees what a terrible idea that would be? I shake my head, refusing to relent.

"Robin, your parents move you around every few years to protect you from the Sentinels. What do you think they'd do if you started asking questions about Aerlings when you just admitted that you'll never have one of your own? There's no way they wouldn't be suspicious."

"I would be careful," Robin says. The defensiveness in her voice in no way changes my mind.

I'm not trying to hurt her feelings, but the snort escapes my lips before I can stop it. "Robin, you're not subtle. At all. I know you would try, but more likely than not, your first question will tell them something is up. What do you think they would do if you told them you found an orphaned Aerling hanging out with some random family?"

She doesn't answer.

"They'd freak out, haul you off to who knows where, and send someone to collect Mason."

I want information, but I will only risk so much to get it. Making sure that Mason is safe is my top priority. Going to the Caretakers is too dangerous. No matter how good of a job we've done hiding and caring for Mason, they'll want him back. As far as I can figure, they must assume he was killed by the Sentinels that murdered his family. I think it should stay that way.

"I'm sorry, Robin, but we're going to have to figure this out on our own."

Surprisingly enough, no one argues with me.

Mom pats my arm gently and nods while Evie continues to glare at Robin. I wasn't really expecting Evie to side with Robin on anything, so that's not surprising. I look over at Mason to make sure he's okay with this plan. He isn't looking at me, though. A look passes between him and Robin. When they both turn to face me, they nod in agreement, but that wasn't what their look said a minute ago.

Chapter 15
But Not Everything

I question the wisdom of this plan the farther I get from the house. The light breeze causes a piece of hair to fall in my eyes. I brush it away distractedly as I walk past the green grass and sand of the park Robin and I met at a few days ago. Every step makes me doubt myself and I almost turn back. The sight of Robin waiting for me at the corner spurs me on. I need answers.

I don't blame Olivia for not wanting to take the risk. I know her main concern is keeping me safe. Once, that would have been enough. Not anymore. It started before Robin ever showed up this feeling of need, need to know why my family had to die. Why I am different? Would it ever be different for me? Would I ever live a normal life?

When Olivia's dad started the conversation about college and living arrangements, it was the first time I had thought of those kinds of details. It wasn't the first time I thought about my future with Olivia.

Robin waits, leaning against the car, pretending to be busy on her phone as she watches my approach. She smiles when I reach her and opens her car door for me. I slip in without a word. Once we're both settled, Robin turns to me with a concerned expression.

"Are you sure about this?"

I nod wordlessly.

"We can tell Olivia if you want." She chews on her bottom lip. We both know how that conversation will go. She breathes a sigh of relief when I shake my head no.

"Okay. To grandma's house we go." Robin smiles in an attempt to lighten the mood. As usual, it's hard to resist smiling back.

"Thanks, Robin, for bringing me with you."

"Thanks for trusting me," she says.

The next few minutes are quiet. I watch the houses go by, feeling a sense of loss as we leave the neighborhood I have spent the last twelve years in and venture into a new part of town. This is a chance for answers that have plagued me since the night my family died. I almost expect the air to change as we get farther from Olivia. It seems like the world should be different so far from her side, but block after block appears to be perfectly average, mundane.

Robin signals for a left turn. The sound startles me and I look over at the building unable to breathe. Plain in its appearance, with cream colored walls and light pink trim, the nursing home seems to emanate a sense of foreboding. It isn't about trust. It's fear.

"Mason?" Robin says softly.

I don't answer. I can't.

The touch of Robin's fingers sliding into mine startles me into looking at her. Her breathing catches at the sight of my panic. "Do you want to go home? We don't have to do this."

"We do," I croak. "I need to know. I have to find out why my family was murdered."

"Why?" Robin asks.

Her hand tightens on mine as if she fears the answer. She should. "Because I think it's going to happen again."

Robin's head dips down. "The dreams?"

I nod. "They're too real. After the break in, it's hard to deny they're more than just nightmares." I shake my head. "Not that they're prophetic or anything—the dreams didn't play out exactly how I saw them—but it's clear they're a warning. There's something more behind this than me being an Aerling."

"I think you're right," Robin says quietly.

"You do?" I ask, not surprised she agrees with me, but curious about her reasoning.

Leaning back against her seat, Robin sighs. "Aside from what happened to your Caretakers, which seems like proof enough, there's Olivia. She shouldn't be able to see you. Nobody can see Aerlings but Caretakers."

"Why? What makes you guys so special?"

Robin tucks her bottom lip between her teeth as she considers her words. "It's an ability we're born with. There are stories about the origins. They sound ridiculous, things like eating an apple from wherever Aerlings come from, some kind of god-given blessing, intermixing of species, stuff like that. I have no idea whether any of them are true. I don't know if anyone does. I just know that this is how we were meant to be.

"And as much as the Sentinels don't want to admit it, they're in the same boat. It wasn't just luck that they were born with the ability to *feel* Aerlings. Someone or something wanted it that way. They hate Aerlings because they aren't human and they don't think they belong here, but it's not like they're pure either."

Shaking her head and sinking down in her seat, she stares at the doors of the nursing home. "If you're right about the Sentinels coming after Olivia and the others, we need to find out why."

"I know," I say, "but I'm afraid of what she's going to tell us."

● ● ●

88

Robin snorts. "Well, there's no guarantee she's going to tell us anything, but if she knows something that could help ..."

"That's not why I'm scared," I blurt out, regretting it almost instantly.

As Robin turns in her seat to face me, my head dips in shame. Her fingers press lightly against my cheek. She tries to make me look at her, but I can't. "Why then?" she asks.

"What if it's my fault?" I demand. "What if there is something about me that isn't good, that has to be killed? Who knows who my real family is or why they sent me here. What if I'm dangerous or...or I'll hurt people...Olivia. What if your grandma tells me that I'm the problem? What if Olivia finds out who and what I really am and it changes the way she looks at me?"

This time, when Robin pushes me to look at her, I don't resist. Her smile is warm and kind, confident. "Nothing my grandma might tell us will change the way anyone feels about you. I think you're getting a little ahead of yourself. Why don't we just go see what she has to say and then figure out how to deal with it?"

My head starts shaking, but Robin releases me and steps out of the car. She waits, holding it open for me. I get the impression she will wait as long as it takes and I sigh. When I slide out of the car, her pleased expression is more kind than gloating.

I trail behind her through the parking lot, focusing on the patches and lines of tar as we walk. Looking up at the building is too daunting. Coming here seemed like a good idea when Robin first mentioned it. I try to remind myself of that now. Robin is right. Nothing will change the way Olivia feels about me. I came here as a baby. What could I have possibly done in my first home that would be so terrible?

Robin reaches for the door, but it swings outward at the same moment and slams into her forearm. The guy that comes barreling out barely pauses when he sees Robin stumble and rub her elbow. His muttered "sorry" draws an annoyed huff from Robin. She isn't one to hold a grudge, though, so a few seconds later she's back to smiling when we approach the surprisingly classy looking reception desk. I feel like I'm about to check into an expensive hotel.

"Good morning, Robin," a middle aged woman says with a friendly smile.

"Hi, Lola. Would you happen to know where my grandma might be right now?"

Lola gestures down the stately hall. "Resting in her room. She just finished a game of checkers with Arnold. You know that always tires them both out."

For some reason, Robin cracks up. She thanks Lola, still laughing, and heads down the hall. Hurrying up next to her, I ask, "What's with the checkers?"

"Grandma is very competitive, and she's also not all there half the time, so it usually gets pretty interesting. Last time I watched her play, halfway through the game she thought she was shelling peas with her mom, and every time Arnold tried to pick up a checker she'd slap his hand and tell him to keep his mitts off the peas. He didn't appreciate that and started swearing her."

And Robin really thinks her grandma will be able to help us? I groan inwardly thinking this may turn out to be a huge waste of time, but what other option do we have?

Robin slows next to a half open door and calls out rather loudly, "Knock, knock!"

The sound of shuffling echoes around the room. "Robin, dear? Is that you?"

Grinning, Robin pushes into the room. Her grandma is half up from her plush arm chair and sits back down heavily when she sees her granddaughter. Her face lights up with joy. "Robin! I'm so glad you came today! How are you, dear?"

"I'm just fine. How are you?"

Her grandma shrugs and makes a few noncommittal gestures. She looks to be on the verge of speaking when her eyes land on me. The recognition in them startles me even though I knew she would be able to see me. Even more than that, I'm shocked when her face screws up in fear.

"Close the door!" she demands. Robin seems startled as well, but jumps to do as her grandma asked.

Closing the door, but finding no lock, Robin turns anxiously back to her grandma. She doesn't even get a second to explain anything. Her grandma points a trembling hand at her. "What are you doing with *him*?"

The way she says "him" sets me on edge. Does she know me? Is everything I feared about to be revealed? The sudden weakness in my knees begs me to sit down. Aside from the floor, the only option is the bed. I grip the lip of the pale pink wainscoting surrounding the room instead.

"Grandma, do you know him?" Robin asks with wide eyes made even bigger by her glasses.

"Of course not!" her grandma snaps, "but I know *what* he is. Where did he come from? And why would you bring him here? You know better than to contact Aerlings after having been marked, child. You are putting him at risk!"

Robin stumbles to explain. "But, it's not like you're thinking! I bumped into him, literally, and I…he needs help. Answers. He needs someone to tell him. Explain. And I don't know enough. Please, Grandma. Just let me explain before you freak out or tell Mom and Dad."

That may not have been the best thing to say. Her grandma's eyes become big and fearful. "Your parents don't know about this Aerling?"

"I couldn't tell them. Please, Grandma, just listen. Please, I'm begging you."

"Please," I beg, startling them both.

Robin's grandma stares at me, piercing everything and scouring me from the inside out. I don't know what she sees. Desperation, maybe? Hope? Whatever it is, her menacing glare softens just a bit. Her eyes slide away from me and fasten onto Robin. She waggles a finger at her with a frown.

"This story had better be worth the heart attack you nearly gave me."

"It will be," Robin says, "I promise."

Her grandma still seems rather unconvinced, but Robin's smile is slowly creeping back onto her face. At least *she's* confident. I'm beginning to think Olivia was right about this. Robin walks across the tile and pulls me toward the bed, which appears to be a regular bed until I see the controls hidden away on the side. We both sit on the edge of the mattress and face the old woman glaring at us.

Not sure how to approach her grandma, I'm happy to let Robin take the lead. As she speaks, I'm not the only one drawn in by her words. I knew Robin was smart, incredibly intelligent even, but I had no idea she had an artistic side as well. My story flows from her lips as if she lived it herself, capturing fear in the beginning, hope at the sight of Olivia, and the turmoil the past few weeks have inspired. No one utters a word as she spins the story of my life into a tapestry that seems to envelope the whole room.

"His dreams seem to be warning him that the Sentinels will try again and will hurt his family in the process," Robin says as she begins to wrap up her tale. "We need to know why so we can stop it from happening."

Robin's grandma unfolds her arms from across her chest, and I notice for the first time that she is quivering. Given her strength when we first arrived, I worry that it is fear and not age causing the tremors. Seeing her tremble sends a sharp stab of fear straight to my center.

"They aren't his family," her grandma says.

Robin and I look at each other, confused. "Huh?" Robin asks.

"The people you live with, they aren't your family," she repeats.

"They've loved and protected me for twelve years," I say, trying very hard to keep my tone polite. "I don't care whether they're Caretakers or not. They're family."

"Caretakers weren't you family either."

A rigid anger spreads through my body. "Then where is my real family? Why am I not with them? Why am I here?"

"You real family is where they are supposed to be, in their own world. You are here because they had no choice. They sent you here to be protected," she says calmly.

"Didn't work out so well, now did it?" I snap.

She shakes her head slowly, the trembling increasing. "Too often, no, it does not work out as we would want. There are too few Caretakers left, too many Aerlings to protect."

"How would the Sentinels have found Mason?" Robin asks. "It sounds like his Caretakers kept him pretty secluded."

"There is no way to know," her grandma answers sadly.

"Why would they kill my fam...my Caretakers?"

This is something that Robin is absolutely certain is out of character for the Sentinels. I'm not sure if I want to hear her grandma tell me that it happens all the time and my story is not nearly as unique as I might think, or if confirmation that there is indeed something about me that inspires such violence is the real truth.

Robin's grandma clasps her hands together. "I don't know why they would do such a thing. As vicious as the Sentinels are, they do not harm Caretakers. The Sentinels rarely do something without a good reason, though. If they attacked your Caretakers, there would have been justification for the decision."

"Justification?" I snap. "What could possibly justify them killing a loving mother and father and three children?"

"They justify killing innocent Aerling children every day," she says with equal heat behind her voice. "I'm sure it wasn't as hard as you think for them."

Smoothing her hands along the material of her housecoat, Robin's grandma breathes in and out slowly. "On occasion," she says, "an Aerling will come to this world that is considered unique. Special. He or she may possess abilities that would be considered very important to their kind. I have no way of knowing, but I could imagine that if the Sentinels found one of these Aerlings they might push the limits of their usual laws in order to see that Aerling dead."

"But, I barely have any abilities at all," I argue.

She shrugs. I expect her to continue...but a strange glassiness fills her eyes. Her lips turn up in a sweet smile that hardly seems to fit the tenor of our current conversation. I hear Robin sigh next to me. About to ask her what is going on, I jump when a set of cold fingers land on my wrist.

"Rodney," she croons, "I'm so glad you stopped by today. It's been weeks since we've seen each other and I was beginning to think you had forgotten me here."

Not sure what to do and thoroughly creeped out, I turn to Robin for help. She looks severely deflated, but offers no help other than to mouth, *play along.* I don't know what else to do.

"Uh, no...Um, of course I didn't forget you ..." What's her name? I have no idea. I glance back at Robin again, but my eyes aren't a good enough communicator to tell her what I need. She stares at me with a crooked eyebrow, her shoulders shrugging helplessly.

"Rodney, you missed the social last week. Where were you? I looked everywhere for you, but I couldn't find you."

"I, uh, was out of town? For work?"

Thankfully she doesn't seem to hear the uncertainty in my voice. Her grip tugs gently on my hands. Feeling extremely uncomfortable, I step closer. She tugs again and again until I am standing at her side. When her head leans against me, I'm begging Robin for help.

Without any explanation or warning, Robin's grandma straightens up, her hands falling back into her lap. She stares at Robin curiously. Me, she pulls away from as if I might be contagious. I need no further encouragement to go back to my seat.

"What were you saying?" she asks Robin.

"We were talking about Mason and why the Sentinels killed his Caretakers."

Her grandma's head bobs seriously. "Yes, that's right, but that's not really the most important question, now is it?"

"It's not?" I ask.

She shakes her head. Her expression is firm, but I swear I can almost make out the hint of a smile. "No, what you should be asking me is why Olivia can see Mason."

When silence falls over the room, Robin rolls her eyes. "So why can she see him?"

Her grandma startles, taking a moment to come back to herself. "She can see him because she is his Escort."

Robin laughs, covering her mouth immediately after. "His what?"

Yeah. My what? I stare at Robin's grandma impatiently. The smile I thought I saw earlier widens.

"It is rare to find an Escort so young. The two of you must be quiet special indeed to have been led to each other as children."

I turn to Robin. "Do you know what she's talking about?"

Robin shakes her head. "I've never heard of an Escort before, but my training pretty much stopped after Eliana died. I know there's a ton I didn't learn."

She turns back to her grandma. "What is an Escort? What do they do?"

"Do?" Robin's grandma stares at her like she has just asked a very foolish question. I almost laugh, realizing that's where Robin got that look from. She shakes her head at Robin. "Escorts take Aerlings home."

"Home like ..." Robin leaves the question unfinished, hoping her grandma will continue.

"Home to their own world, of course."

The wave of nauseating fear that sweeps through me nearly doubles me over. Digging my fingers into the edge of the bed is the only thing that keeps me upright. "What? I have to go home? Will Olivia come with me? Will I ever come back?"

The questions shoot out of my mouth rapid-fire, but the glassy expression is back in her eyes. Her serious mood melts back into an innocent smile. "Can you please pass me the syrup, Clarence?"

Too unbalanced to move, Robin steps in and hands her a bottle of lotion. I stare blankly at her as she dribbles lotion onto a piece of paper Robin stuck in her lap at the last second. The minutes tick by as Robin's grandma remains lost in some memory of breakfast with her family. Fear and desperation sink in as she continues to live in her memories with no sign of coming back to reality.

"Robin," a voice calls from behind us, making Robin and I both jump. Robin lets go of the throw pillow her grandma is convinced is her infant son, Albert, and lets her rock it back and forth. She stands and turns to the nurse watching the scene with sad eyes.

"Do you need her?" Robin asks.

The nurse nods. "It's time for her physical therapy session. I'm sorry, but I need to take her."

Robin nods, looking half relieved. Part of me feels the same. I have never had to deal with this before, but I'm desperate for answers as well. Robin must sense my turmoil. Her hand clasps mine briefly as she nods toward the door. Her goodbyes to her grandma are short, and then we are hurrying about of the room and back to Robin's car.

She handled her grandma so well, I didn't realize how much she was struggling until she falls against the car and breathes out shakily. "She wasn't going to come out of it any time soon, anyway," she says.

Her arms wrap around her body protectively. Approaching Robin slowly, I'm not sure what to do until she looks up at me with tears in her eyes. A moment later my arms are around her, holding her.

● ● ●

"I'm so sorry, Robin. I had no idea how hard that would be for you."

I was so worried about myself, my answers. She stayed so calm in the room when her grandma slipped back into her memories, but it was clearly just an act. My arms tighten around her protectively. Robin's arms unfold from around her body and cinch around mine. She doesn't cry, but she doesn't let go either.

The sun travels slowly across the sky, dipping toward evening. Blue becomes orange as day gives way to night. I don't pressure Robin. Thoughts of Olivia push me to untangle myself from her grip, but Robin's body pressed against mine feels oddly natural. It's a strange feeling, not exactly one that urges me to turn it into something more, but one that makes me reluctant to let go.

Robin is the one to finally pull back. "I'm sorry," she whispers.

"You don't have to be sorry. You handled it better than I did."

"I've had practice," she says. Her bottom lip quivers and she tucks it between her teeth. "I keep thinking it will get easier to see her like that, but it doesn't."

"You two were close?" I ask, stroking her back slowly, though I don't know why.

Robin nods. Her eyes close, but this time not out of fear. "She was the only one who didn't treat me like a criminal after Eliana died. Everyone knew it was my fault. I felt so horrible, I confessed right away. No one in my family has ever looked at me the same since that night. Only Grandma held me when I cried for Eliana. She loved me even after what I did. Maybe she shouldn't have, but I'm glad she did."

Disbelief pauses my hands. She was seven! A child who, yes, had been taught to keep Eliana a secret, but a child who craved acceptance and made a mistake. I can't believe her family would turn on her like that. "Robin, I'm sorry."

Shaking her head, Robin turns away from me but remains in my arms. I get the hint that we are done talking about her family when she changes the subject. "Are you going to tell Olivia about coming here?"

"Yes." The plan was never to hide what I found out, only to take a risk she wouldn't blame herself for if it turned out badly.

Robin nods slowly. "But not everything."

I look down, not sure what she means by that, and find her staring up at me. One hand curls behind my neck gently. The slight pressure of her hand bends me as she lifts onto her toes and presses her lips against my cheek. My eyes close as the feeling of her lips on my skin sends a strange sensation through me.

* * *

She pulls away slowly. Our eyes meet and I am startled to see tears in her eyes. "Thank you," she whispers.

"For what?" I reach up and brush away a tear that has fallen.

Robin smiles shakily. "For being my friend. I haven't had one in a very long time."

She doesn't need to tell me that the last friend she had was Eliana, that every day without her is torture, and that the guilt she feels over her death will never leave her. She doesn't need to tell me because I understand already. Pulling her back against my chest, I don't say anything. I don't need to.

Chapter 16

Last Conscious Thought

The door knob twists slowly. My shoulders tense, waiting for him to see me. He's halfway across the room before his eyes are drawn to me sitting cross-legged in the center of his bed. Jumping back, Mason bumps into his dresser.

"What are you doing in my room?" Mason gasps.

"What are you doing *not* in your room?" I ask. My mouth turns down in a frown. "You told me you were coming up here to read, that you needed some time alone."

His mouth opens. I can see the excuses running through his mind. None of them make it past his lips. His shoulders fall.

The corner of my mouth twitches. "You were out with Robin, weren't you?"

"Yes," Mason says quietly.

"Getting answers, or just hanging out?" I ask, though I have to force the words out of my mouth.

I don't know which one is worse. Would I feel better about him spending time with Robin if it were only to find more information, even though that meant going behind my back? Does the lie hurt less if he just needed a break and turned to Robin instead of me? Tricking me, cutting me out should be the worse option, but it's the one I can bear more than the other.

"We went to ask her grandma some questions," Mason admits. He sits lightly on the edge of the bed.

Despite the relief that washes through me, I hold onto my stern expression. "Why didn't you tell me?"

"You know why."

Frustration tears at me. I look over at him with a scowl. "So you went behind my back instead? If you didn't agree with me, you could have just said so. We could have talked about it."

"You were done talking," Mason argues.

"I'm just trying to keep you safe!" How could he risk himself like that? Robin said the Caretakers would try to take him back. Doesn't that matter to him?

Mason looks down at his hands. The passive posture doesn't match the clench of his jaw and I am more confused than ever. "Safe, or to yourself?"

"What?"

"Which one are you more angry about, that I lied to you, or that I was with Robin?" When his eyes come up to meet mine, the mixture of pain and anger behind them hits me like a physical blow.

Stunned, confused, I slide off the bed and take a step back. What is going on with him? Why is he treating me like this? We've always been careful. He's my main concern no matter what, yet now he's acting like all the times I've looked out for him were out of some selfish desire to keep him from experiencing some bigger, magical life. My head starts shaking, hurt and angry myself now.

I turn away. I have no intention of standing here and being treated like some cruel captor, but before I can take a step Mason is towering over me. "You're not going to answer?" he demands.

Shaking my head angrily, I try to push past him. He moves again, blocking me. Never, in the twelve years I have known him have I been so angry with him! My hands push against his chest. "Get out of my way, Mason!"

"Answer the question," he growls back.

Knowing I have no chance of escaping him, my frustration boils over. "Fine! You want to know?" I shove him once more, bouncing back rather than moving him, which only makes me angrier. "I can't believe you would lie to me! You want to hang out with Robin, fine. Go ahead. I was actually kinda glad you and her were becoming friends because I know being around her made you feel more normal, happy.

"Is it hard for me to share you? Of course it is, Mason. You've been everything to me since I found you on my porch. You're the first thought on my mind when I wake up. I can't imagine my life without you, but I would never want to force you stay with me if you didn't want to."

Throwing a pillow from the bed at Mason, I stare straight at him. "I thought we didn't keep secrets from each other? I thought we could trust each other no matter what. Did all of that disappear because you have someone else to talk to now?"

"Olivia, please," Mason begs.

"Please what? You're the one accusing me of being selfish and jealous!"

"I'm sorry!" Mason exclaims. He flops down on the bed and presses his palms against his eyes. "I'm sorry, okay? Sorry I lied, sorry I said those things, sorry I didn't just tell you in the first place."

Sitting down on the bed next to him, I keep my distance. "You're just saying that so I'll stop yelling at you."

"Partly," Mason mumbles from under his hands.

Sighing, I flop down next to him. There's still a good bit of distance between our bodies, but much of my anger has disappeared. I look up at the ceiling as I ask, "Why did you lie?"

Mason drags his hands down his face slowly. "I knew you would think it was too risky."

"Mason, it was. What if her grandma tells her parents, and they tell someone else? I can't stand the idea of someone taking you away from me."

"She won't tell," Mason says quietly. "She probably doesn't even remember we visited her."

When I look over at him, he is watching me already. "Her grandma has Alzheimer's. It was touch and go while we were there. Most of her new memories don't stick around very long."

Shaking my head and looking back up at the ceiling, I say, "You could have told me that. I would have understood. I want answers too, you know. I just care about having you more."

"I know you do," Mason says, "but it's different for me."

I look over at him feeling suddenly afraid. Different how? I wonder, but don't ask. Different because answers mean more to him than I do? Different because the lure of finding out who he really is beats out a surrogate family? I see the weight of his thoughts reflected in his eyes, but I am too scared to ask.

Mason stares back at me, the silence eating away at him. "Why are you looking at me like that?" he asks with fear in his voice.

"Like what?" The ache in my voice makes it thin.

"Like you're getting ready to say goodbye."

My breath catches in my chest. Pain I cannot begin to describe floods through my heart. "Maybe because I'm terrified that's what you're going to ask me to do."

Suddenly, I am being swallowed up by Mason's arms, cradled in his embrace. "Ollie, oh Ollie," he says softly. "I don't want you to say goodbye. I never want to leave you, Ollie."

"But?" I whisper. He can't tell me that's it because I can hear it in his voice. He wants to promise we'll always be together, but something is stopping him. "But what?" I beg.

Slowly, achingly, Mason tells me about his conversation with Robin's grandmother. I listen, nestled in his arms, as he talks about special Aerlings that might attract more Sentinels than usual. He seems doubtful, but I have no problem believing Mason could be one of these unique children.

It kills me to hear the guilt speaking these words inspires in his voice. He doesn't seem to understand that even if he was sought after more than other Aerlings, it wasn't his fault. Nothing he could have done would have preserved his family. Thoughts of his family send him to a new topic, to his *real* family, his Aerling family. He can say little, only that Robin's grandmother claimed they had no choice but to send him here. It is a bright moment in his retelling as he takes a second to believe, to hope that his birth family stills loves him.

"I know why you can see me," Mason says.

That pulls me out of my thoughts quickly. I lift my head from his shoulder with an expectant expression. "Why?"

"Apparently, you're my Escort."

My nose crinkles. "Your what?"

"Escort."

"What is that?"

Mason widens his eyes mockingly. "How do you not know what an escort is? Surely you know how guys can call an agency when the need *companionship*."

Slapping at Mason's shoulder, I scowl at him. "Somehow I doubt I'm meant to be your *call girl*! Stop being an idiot and tell me what she really said."

I turn my nose up at him like he's being utterly ridiculous, but the word "escort" keeps bouncing around in my head. Could it be something similar? Am I really meant to be with Mason that way? Suddenly my head on his shoulder, my hand on his chest, our feet crisscrossed, every point of contact seems to grow warm. My fingers curl up, afraid of touching him too much.

"It means you're supposed to take me home," Mason says, startling me back to the conversation.

"What? Home?" I ask. Reeling my brain back in seems harder than usual.

"My...real home. Wherever Aerlings come from, I guess."

My hand digs into Mason's chest as I push myself back up to sitting. "What?" I shriek.

Mason sits up slowly. "That's what she said. Nothing more. She was completely out of it by then, so I have no idea when or how, just that you're supposed to take me home."

"I don't know how to take you home! I'm not sure I would even want to," I blurt out. The way Mason cringes scales back my panic. Swallowing my own desires takes a great deal of effort, but I force myself to think of him first. "I mean, of course I would take you if that's what you wanted."

"I don't know what I want," Mason says. The agony in his voice kills me.

Tears threaten to betray me, but I hold them back as best I can. "Could I go with you?" I ask quietly.

"Would you want to?" Mason stares at me so intently it's impossible to look away. "Would you leave your mom and dad and Evie?"

The quivering starts in my chin and quickly spreads to my fingertips. "I don't know," I admit, "but I would want the option. I couldn't just leave you somewhere not knowing if you were safe or happy. I couldn't...I couldn't leave you at all, I don't think."

Mason grabs me and pulls me against his chest. "I don't think I can leave you either."

I don't know if it is Mason that moves first, or me, but somehow we end up lying on the bed, foreheads pressed together and arms around each other. Neither of us speaks. We just lie there blinking at each other until our eye lids start opening more and more slowly. Mason's stop moving first, but mine aren't far behind. My last conscious thought is that I never want to move from this place.

Chapter 17
Pinchy

A sharp pain that stabs at me yanks me out of sleep. Disoriented, I reach for my lamp only to have my hand fall through empty air. Another crack makes me wince, but forces my senses to wake up. That's when I realize the thrashing body next to me is Mason. Responding takes a moment as I try to figure out how I ended up in bed with him. Memory flashes back quickly and a second later I am trying desperately to wake him up.

Getting my hands past his flailing arms is a challenge. I get whacked a few more times before getting a hold on his shoulders. His arms, though, are still trying to fend off the nightmare. Letting go of his shoulders for a moment, I grab one arm and pin it to his side. It takes a feat of near-acrobatic talent to keep one arm pinned with my knee while I throw my other leg across his chest to catch the other arm before he hurts one of us.

Straddling his chest as I keep his arms in check, I grip his shoulders again and try to shake him awake as gently as I can. "Mason!" I whisper harshly.

The last thing I want to do is wake up Mom. She'll realize I'm still wearing my clothes from earlier and it will be a quick leap from that to figuring out I've been in here all night. I have enough to deal with right now without getting another lecture.

"Mason, wake up!"

A particularly violent bout of thrashing nearly knocks me off of him. I have to practically throw myself on top of his body to keep myself from being tossed onto the floor. Either the weight of me landing on him heavily, or my voice calling out right next to his ear, snaps him out of his nightmare.

His eyes fly wide in a panic. "Ollie!" he calls out.

His chest is heaving as he tries to clamber out of bed. I realize he hasn't even noticed me sprawled on top of him and try to slip off before he dumps me on the ground. I get one knee back on the bed before he realizes it's me squashing him and stops moving. Neither of us says or does anything for a full minute. I'm not totally sure he's awake. I'm not sure what he's waiting for.

The feel of his hands suddenly gripping my waist makes me jump, especially when his fingers slide up my body as he attempts to lift me up. I feel like a ragdoll as he pushes me gently back to sitting. He stops when I am back to my original position from when I first tried to restrain him, one knee on either side of his chest. Only this time, instead of my hands trying to shake him awake, they are held in his. All he can do for a moment is stare at me.

"You're safe," he whispers in relief.

"Is that what your nightmare was about?"

Mason's shoulders roll forward, dropping his head. "They took you, snuck up behind you at night and just took you. I couldn't stop them."

"No one took me," I reassure him. "I'm not stupid enough to walk around at night alone, anyway. Not with Sentinels hanging around."

I smile when Mason chuckles. He falls back against his pillow, still holding onto my hands. "Are you okay?" I ask.

He shakes his head all around, neither a yes nor a no. "I wish I could make these nightmares stop," he groans.

"I wish I could make them stop too, especially since I seem to take the brunt of the failing and thrashing."

Mason uncovers his eyes looking pained. "Did I hit you?"

Shaking my head, I pat his cheek playfully. "I was just kidding. I'm fine. Just a few nudges here and there."

He doesn't seem convinced, but I smile and refuse to let him worry about it. Getting knocked around a bit won't keep me from rescuing him from those horrible images. I slide my foot off the bed to the floor and shift my weight so I can get off of Mason's chest. I'm not all that eager to leave, but he grabs my wrist with a look of panic in his eyes.

"Where are you going?"

I can't deny the shot of warmth that shoots through me. Placing my free hand on his chest gently, I smile. "I'm not going anywhere. I just realized I'm sleeping in my jeans."

"So?" He gestures at his legs, now uncovered since the blankets are dangling off the end of the bed in a tangled mess. "I am too."

"Yeah," I argue, "but guys' jeans are all loose and comfy. Mine are tight and pinchy."

"Pinchy?"

Laughing, I push off of him. "Yes, pinchy. They're really uncomfortable to sleep in."

I turn and start toward my room. I only get a few steps away before Mason crowds in front of me. I don't realize he's holding anything until he presses it toward me. I stare down at the plaid, drawstring pajama bottoms, not sure what to say. When I look up, Mason's expression is tortured.

"Don't go, please." His eyes close against the possibility of me denying him.

"I was going to come back," I whisper.

Mason breathes in slowly, then out just as carefully before speaking. "You were?"

"Yes." I hold my breath, silently begging him not to ask me why. I don't know if I can answer that question coherently.

My fingers tighten around the pajama bottoms just as Mason releases his hold on them. His hands fall away, but he hesitates a moment before turning back. I watch him walk to his dresser. When he is intent on finding another pair of pajamas, I quickly wriggle out of my jeans and tug on the pj bottoms.

I want to turn around, for just a minute, but fear keeps me rooted to the floor. Blocking out the sound of him undressing is impossible. I could describe every movement. My breathing stops entirely when I hear him pull on the pajama bottoms and take a step toward me. Even knowing he is coming, I still jump when his hand touches my shoulder.

"Why are you just standing here?" he whispers.

My whole body floods scarlet. I cannot even express how grateful I am that this room is dark. Any answer I could give would sound completely idiotic. So I don't say anything. I turn away and head to the bed, dropping onto it graceless and awkward. I just want to pull the blankets over my head, but when I reach for them and find nothing I remember the tangled heap on the floor.

A second later, Mason settles a light blanket around my shoulders. His hand lingers. The recollection of how to breathe escapes me entirely. The way his fingers slide down my arm sends a shiver through my body. The ability to breath returns, but now I can't seem to stop breathing! My chest pumps in and out at a manic pace.

The mattress shifts as Mason's weight distorts the surface. I feel absolutely paralyzed as he lies down next to me. His hand still rests tentatively on my shoulder, his body keeping its distance. The air in the room freezes. Sound melts away. All either of us can hear is my breathing, rapid and frantic.

"Are you okay?" Mason asks worriedly.

Am I okay? I wonder. Am I losing it completely? How many times have I ended up in bed with Mason over the years? Dozens, but this is different. This isn't just two friends talking or comforting each other. I can't lie next to him without wanting more. When did this happen? Does it matter? Do I want it to be any different?

"Ollie, are you okay?"

No, I don't want it to be any different. That admission slows everything back down.

"Yes," I say, finally gaining control of my breathing. "I'm fine."

● ● ●

Reaching up for Mason's hand on my shoulder, I pull it around me. Never one to waste an opportunity, Mason scoots in closer. For the second time tonight, I fall asleep in Mason's arms.

Chapter 18

Traitorous Jeans

Waking up feels like trying to peel wallpaper off the wall. My eyes simply refuse to open when the morning sunlight attacks me from the window. Why are the curtains open, anyway? I always close them at night ever since I caught our neighbor, Timothy Dugger, staring at me one day. Intent on getting up, closing the curtains, and falling back into bed, I finally force my eyes open. The sight of navy blue curtains instead of the deep purple ones in my room that block out light so well freezes thought and movement alike.

The reason for why I'm so tired comes back to me when I realize my arm is draped across Mason's chest. Even better, my head is on his shoulder with his arm around me and my leg is crossed over his, putting my knee in a very delicate place.

My first thought is to close my eyes and pretend I'm still asleep. My second, more realistic thought, is that if someone finds me in here, we are both going to be grounded for the rest of our lives. Self-preservation beats out self-indulgence. It kills me to do it, but I wriggle out of Mason's arms and make a break for the hallway.

I feel like I just ran a marathon as I pull the door closed behind me. My eyes dart up and down the hallway. It's a miracle that it's empty at this time of day. Usually everyone is scurrying around getting ready for work and school. I'm halfway down the stairs before I remember Dad is out of town until late tonight. That takes care of one person.

One look at the old pendulum clock hanging in the hallway tells me it's barely six in the morning. That takes care of Evie, who never crawls out of bed a minute before she has to. Mom is always up at the crack of dawn, so it's not surprising when I stumble into the kitchen and am welcomed by eggs and pancakes.

"You're up early," she says with a smile.

"Long night," I grumble.

Mom puts an arm around my shoulder. "Mason's nightmares again?" When I nod, she frowns. "I really wish you'd come and get one of us. You shouldn't have to deal with that every time."

I nearly choke on my orange juice at her suggestion. She looks over at me curiously. "It's fine," I say after a coughing fit. "I don't mind handling it."

If she has the same doubts Dad does about Mason and I—which apparently are well grounded—she doesn't express them. She only smiles

● ● ●

106

and goes back to flipping pancakes. Fifteen blessedly quiet minutes later, Evie ruins the moment when she plops into the chair next to me looking like she rolled down the stairs.

I doubt I look much better, though, so I save any snappy comments for later. If only my dear sister would be so kind.

"Are those Mason's pants?" she asks through sleepy eyes.

The spatula Mom was just holding clatters to the pan. She picks it back up quickly, but I can tell from the tension in her shoulders that she's listening very closely.

"I borrowed them. So what?" I ask, glaring at Evie.

"Why? They're way too big."

"I couldn't find mine."

Evie looks over at me, no longer half asleep. "Not a single pair?"

As a smile creeps onto her face, I have no doubt her big mouth is about to get me in serious trouble. So I run. I push away from the table and my half-eaten breakfast, all but running for the stairs. I am cursing Evie as I grab for the bathroom door knob. One quick twist and the hope of a few minutes alone evaporates at the sight of Mason.

Standing in the middle of the bathroom with nothing but a towel around his waist, one hand on the door knob as if he were in the middle of opening it, he stares at me looking as caught off guard as I feel.

"Mason, I…I'm sorry, I…"

Red as a cherry tomato, I turn for the door. Mason is faster, pushing it closed before I can escape. I spin around as if caught in a trap. My heart rate spikes at the sight of him only inches away from me. I stumble back against the counter.

"You were gone when I woke up," Mason says softly.

I try to say something, I do. I can't stop hyperventilating long enough to form an actual word. My fingers begin strangling the lip of the counter out of fear that I might faint. I don't know what to do when Mason's hands slide over my cheeks. His fingertips brush my eyelids, closing them with a feather touch. His breath washes over my skin softly. Slowly, my own breathing calms to match his.

"Why did you leave?" he asks.

"Someone might have seen me." Do I really have to explain that? Dad would freak out!

Mason's fingers slide up over my cheeks to nestle in my hair, opening my eyes as they go. The smile on his face is like nothing I have ever seen on him before. Mischievous, eager…my breathing stutters…sexy and full of desire.

"So what if they saw you. Blame it on my nightmares. No one would doubt you, and it wouldn't be a lie," Mason says as he closes a little more of the distance between us.

"They would doubt if they saw the how we were laying," I mutter.

Mason's hearing is too good to miss it. His lips curve up a little more and I add devilish to the list. "You're the only one that can see me. To anyone else it would just look like you were sprawled out awkwardly."

I try not to admit he's right, but I can't lie to myself. No one would have realized. I panicked and ran. That's why I really left.

"Mason, I don't know what's happening," I say in a moment of complete honesty.

His grin turns suddenly serious. "What do you think is happening?"

My mouth opens. It closes. My eyes close, just to pretend for a moment this isn't happening. I open them again and truly see Mason. Not only is he absolutely gorgeous, he is the best friend I have always treasured, the companion I want to share my life with, the one person I would trust with every secret, my first and last thought, the man I am undeniably in love with.

"You're not my brother," I whisper.

Mason's entire being lights up. "I'm so glad you finally realized that."

He leans in before I can think to do anything at all, crushing his lips against mine, spilling out love and passion like I have never experienced. My hands reach up to his neck, pulling him to me hungrily. Mason groans and yanks me away from the counter to press against his chest. His lips drink mine in as if he needs me to live. My body sinks against his in complete surrender.

Thought completely disappears from my mind until the bathroom door cracks into the back of my head. "Olivia," Evie snaps, "why are you standing right in front of the door?"

Her eyes widen as she stares at us…well, at me. I must look completely crazy with my arms seemingly sticking out strangely, pressed up against an invisible wall. I hastily yank myself away from Mason, but the damage is already done. Evie's hand slaps over her mouth.

"Are you freaking kidding me?" She laughs and reaches out a hand to locate Mason. She isn't disappointed. "This is so awesome! Dad's totally going to kill you both, though."

"Shut up, Evie," I snap. Spinning away from her, I shove the door against her.

Mason grabs my arm before I can escape. "Your jeans are still in my room. I didn't think to grab them before."

I'm thankful for the warning, knowing that if Mom tries to straighten up and finds them in there, we'll have to face a whole slew of inquisition-like questions.

"No!" Evie says with bulging eyes.

It's only then that both Mason and I realize Evie was still touching his arm and heard what he just said. Mason shakes her off and runs his hands through his hair in frustration. Furious at Evie, I snap, "That's not what happened."

"Sure," Evie drawls.

"It's not," Mason says evenly.

"Don't say a word about this," I say to them both. Red with embarrassment, I slam the door behind me and go off in search of my traitorous jeans.

Chapter 19
Quietly, Painfully

It's a good thing we only live half a mile from the school, because after Olivia took off without either of us, I dreaded the idea of asking for a ride. After Olivia's blow up, I have no doubt her mom has a pretty good idea about what happened. Olivia's dad is not going to be happy when he gets home tonight.

As Evie stalks along behind me, it's hard not to be pissed at her. I know it wasn't her fault. I should have locked the door, for one, but I can't help tossing away my anger when I think of how excited she was at the idea of Olivia and I being together. It was the reaction I wanted from Olivia, but now I'm afraid it's been jeopardized.

Evie and I part ways without a word when we reach the school grounds. She heads for Aaron while I go in search of Olivia. Her obsessive nature leads me to her locker. My palms immediately turn sweaty as I spot her. She pushes the locker closed and leans her head against it.

My body responds immediately, carrying me toward her. I only get within five feet before she senses my presence and looks up. The deer-in-the-headlights look she sports stops me cold. I don't know what to do when she turns and bolts for her first class.

I want to run after her, talk to her, something! Falling back against the locker, I force myself to take a deep breath and think.

Of course Olivia is freaking out! Before Dad brought up living arrangements after high school Olivia had never looked at me as more than her brother. Romance, kissing, sex, those had never before crossed her mind. It kills me to admit it, but kissing her may not have been the best plan. What was I thinking?

Banging my head against the locker, the sound draws a few strange looks, but I ignore them. I need someone to tell me what to do. Should I back off, let her process the fact that I'm in love with her? Will she freak out again if I hold her hand or try to get close? I don't know what to do!

A scuffle in the middle of the hall draws my attention, even more so when Robin pops back up to her feet after probably tripping on something. Her bright red glasses draw my gaze and I freeze. She's the only other one who can see and hear me, but how do I talk to her about this? I'm not as blind as Olivia. Robin clearly has feelings for me. I have no idea what to do about that either. I like her, a lot, but I'm in love with Olivia.

I am on the verge of ditching school entirely and taking a mental health day, but Robin catches sight of me first and ping pongs off the other students

● ● ●

milling in the hallway to reach me. This is the first time her grin doesn't rub off on me.

"I kissed Olivia!" I blurt out, independent of thought.

Robin blinks. Her eyes widen. The delicate arch of her eyebrows flies up. Her lips part as she stares at me. "Uh, what?"

"I kissed her." My breathing takes a vacation, leaving me staring at Robin like a fish.

Robin closes her mouth and fiddles with her glasses. "Okay." She breathes out slowly. "How did Olivia react?"

"Uh, great, at first." I drag my hands down my face wanting to shake myself violently. "Until Evie walked in on us and figured out what was going on. That's when Olivia freaked out, took off without us, and now she practically ran away from me."

Covering her mouth with her hand as she thinks, Robin looks like she trying not to laugh. "So, it could have gone better, then?"

The final bell blares through the hall saving me from having to say anything in response. This was a mistake. I turn toward the outer doors. Robin snatches at my hand and refuses to let me go.

"Uh-uh," she says. "You're coming to class with me."

I could break free if I want to, but I let Robin drag me down the hall to her first class. As soon as she drops into her seat and releases my hand, I slide down the wall to the floor and hang my head. I want to stay here for the rest of the day. Robin nudges me with her shoe. I ignore her. So, she kicks me, hard enough to make me yelp.

Glaring up at her, she glares right back and points to one of the two notebooks on her desk. I groan. Talking about this was a really, really stupid plan. Still, Robin won't give up. She gets me in the shin with the next kick and I pull myself up off the ground so I can see whatever she wrote.

Look, I know you're in love with Olivia. That was pretty obvious the second we met, but it's also been pretty obvious that she thinks of you as her brother. What were you thinking kissing her?

"It wasn't like that," I argue. "She's been different the last few weeks. I knew the way she thought about me was starting to change. Then last night, we got in this fight after she found out I went with you to your grandma's. She was mad at me for lying, but I thought she was more jealous than anything."

Was she?

"That was definitely part of it, but she was pretty mad about the lying, too." I sit on the top of an empty desk in front of Robin feeling exhausted. "Anyway, we worked it out and we ended up falling asleep on my bed."

Robin peers up at me with a quizzical expression. I roll my eyes at her. "Nothing happened. If it had, I probably would have blurted out that I had sex with Olivia rather than that I kissed her if it had."

Nodding, Robin looks back down at her notebook and writes, *Okay, no sex, but something obviously happened.*

"I had another nightmare. Olivia was kidnapped. It was pretty bad and Olivia had to wake me up. I thought she'd leave after that, but ..."

She didn't?

I shake my head. She didn't even want to. She wanted to stay with me.

You spent the night together? Robin asks.

Nodding, I continue. "When I woke up, though, she was gone. I took a shower, but when I went to leave, Olivia walked in on me and it just happened." I scrub my hands through my hair and look at the ceiling.

For a long time, Robin doesn't write anything else. I look down, thinking perhaps she is taking real notes, but her pencil sits between her fingers unmoving. When my eyes travel up to her face, her expression makes me want to kick myself. The quiver in her chin is faint, but it's only accentuated by the way her bottom lip is being held between her teeth. She blinks her eyes rapidly. I am such a jerk.

"Robin," I say, reaching down and covering her hand with mine. The touch seems to startle her and she looks up with a tortured expression. What was I thinking?

Standing, I let my hand slide away from hers. "Robin, I'm so sorry. I know you don't want to hear any of this."

I turn to leave but Robin sticks her leg out in front of me. I could just step over her, but I look back. Her notebook is tilted up so I can see it.

SIT! DOWN!

My face screws up in confusion. She taps the same message and glares at the seat in front of her. Not sure what I'm doing, I sit back down on the edge of the desk. Her pencil starts flying over the paper.

I can't do this through notes. I have a free period next. Do. Not. Go. Anywhere!

For some reason, I listen to her. The last thing I want to do is hurt Robin. It was an idiot thing to do going to her with this problem in the first place. I can't figure out why she's so intent on making me stick close by, but her intensity pushes me to do as she says. I slink down in the empty seat and try to focus on the lecture, on anything other than Robin and Olivia.

The ring of the bell startles me nearly right out of my chair half an hour later. I stumble to my feet. Before I can take a step, I feel Robin's grip latch onto my hand. She's not letting me get away. Once again, I am drug through the halls to the parking lot. Robin yanks me over to an empty bench and unloads her stuff on ground next to the bench.

"Sit," she demands.

I sit.

She looks over at me with an expression I can't puzzle out. Guilt spreads through me like a sickness. "Robin, I'm so sorry for coming to you with this. I wasn't going to. It just kind of slipped out. I shouldn't have said anything."

"Why?" Robin asks. "We're friends. You can talk to me about anything."

"Yeah, but …"

I seem to have developed a talent for getting myself into stupid situations. She's acting like this has nothing to do with her, but it does, doesn't it? I can't have possibly misread the way she acts when we're alone. Feeling incredibly lost, I figure I can't make this any worse by telling the truth.

"Robin, I shouldn't have said anything, because I know you like me." I look over at her with a pained expression. "Don't you?"

Robin's infectious grin returns. "Of course I do. As you well know, you usually don't kiss people if you hate them, and I've kissed you twice."

"But …?"

My head shakes back and forth. Did I lose part of my brain at some point during the night? What is going on?

"Mason," Robin says, sliding her hand into mine, "I like you a lot, but like I said, I know you're in love with Olivia."

"Then why did you kiss me? Twice?"

She grins again. "I knew how Olivia saw you, and I just thought that if you ever got tired of waiting around for her, you'd know I was here."

I can only stare, still feeling rather off center. Robin smiles sadly and leans her head against my shoulder. "You kissing Olivia, yeah, that threw me for a minute, but I knew my chances from the start. I'm still your friend first and this was obviously tearing you up."

"You looked pretty upset in class," I say quietly, afraid she's just being nice now.

Robin's body goes unnaturally still. When she speaks, her voice is strained. "Yeah, but not about what you think."

Her words send a chill down my spine. Gently, I push her up to look at me. "Robin, what's wrong?"

"It's not about Olivia," she says, her chin beginning to quiver again. "It's about you."

"What do you mean?"

The tears I thought she was trying to hold back in class spring to her eyes in a glassy sheet. "After I dropped you off, I went home and asked my mom about the Escort thing."

I suck in a breath as fear stabs straight into my chest.

Robin hurriedly tries to reassure me. "I didn't say anything about you. I told her Grandma had been rambling on about Escorts and I wasn't sure what they were."

Scaling back my panic is a slow process. "Did she know?" I ask shakily.

"Some," Robin admits. "She didn't know how Escorts are able to take Aerlings home. She said it's not something Escorts really talk about. She did know when it's supposed to happen, though."

Robin's voice catches on that last point and I know whatever she says next is not going to be good. Her fingers cinch around mine more tightly. I don't want her to say it, but I need to know. "When?"

"Your...on your eighteenth birthday. I tried to ask her if there was any way to avoid it, stay here, but she said there wasn't. Aerlings have to go home when they turn eighteen." She tucks her lip between her teeth, biting down almost to point of drawing blood as she attempts to stop trembling. "I'm so sorry. You only have a few more months here before you'll have to go back, Mason."

"Five," I whisper mournfully.

Robin looks up at me. "What?"

"Five months. My birthday is February 16th. That's only five months away."

A tear slips down Robin's cheek. "I'm so sorry, Mason."

Leaning back against the bench, I breathe out slowly. "This changes everything."

"I know."

I shake my head back and forth in frustration. Anger sets in so strongly I can't contain it. My fist slams down against the bench, leaving a sizable dent. Robin jumps next to me, but isn't scared away. Her hand tightens around mine. Both our knuckles are pale from the strength of our grips.

In five months, the only life I've ever known will be over. Somehow I'll be sent back to a world that is completely alien to me. Olivia's parents, Evie, Olivia, I'll never see them again. No more playing catch in the backyard. No more cooking next to Mom, listening to her laugh as ingredients and utensils float through the kitchen. Evie will never laugh at my antics again. And Olivia...my heart convulses in on itself.

I never could have imagined a time when kissing Olivia would be something I considered a mistake, but now that is the only thought running through my head. I would never have been so cruel had I known.

● ● ●

"I can't be with Olivia," I say in amazement.

"You still have five months," Robin says.

Shaking my head, I know where that would lead. Five months to be together, love each other, only to be torn apart. It could never be casual between us. I felt the passion behind her kiss this morning. She's scared right now because this is new an unexpected, but I know Olivia.

Giving someone her love isn't something she would take lightly. Olivia's love is fierce. It's what has kept me safe all these years. Loving me as a brother kept her focused, made me her first concern. Giving herself to me with a deeper love isn't something that could ever be broken. When I am forced to leave…that isn't something I could ever put her through.

"Robin," I say quietly, painfully, "I need you to do something for me."

Chapter 20

What. Just. Happened?

After I ran away like a scared little girl this morning, I wasn't surprised when Mason didn't show up in class that first hour. When he didn't reappear for second hour, or lunch, or any class at all, I started to panic. It was stupid to take off like that, I chide myself as I race for the Jeep. I have to explain that I was just overwhelmed, confused. Between last night and this morning, I needed some time to think and sort out the jumble of emotions I was feeling.

Mason will understand that, right?

I stumble to a stop when I get to the Jeep and find it empty. Evie comes up behind me with a scowl.

"Thanks for making me walk to school this morning."

Her prissy, snotty schoolgirl attitude doesn't have the effect on me she was hoping for. "Where's Mason?" I demand.

Evie stares at me like I'm crazy. "How would I know? You two usually head out here together. What, you haven't seen him?"

"No! He's been gone all day. He didn't come to any classes."

"Serves you right," Evie snaps. "Next time the guy of your dreams kisses you, you might want to try for excited rather than running off like a lunatic."

Scowling back at her, I say, "It was kind of a lot to take in at once, and you barging in and sticking your nose in our business certainly didn't help."

Evie cocks one eyebrow at me and puts her hands on her hips. "Look, it's your own fault that you're way too dense to figure out that Mason was in love with you all these years. I think everyone else realized it! It's your own fault, too, that instead of falling into his arms when you finally woke up you ran away like a rabbit from an angry farmer."

Spinning on her heel, Evie waves at Aaron and tells him to wait for her even though she knows Dad would be pissed. Before bailing, she turns back around and says, "You know, I was really happy for you this morning, but now maybe I'm thinking that Mason could do better if this is how you're going to act about it."

Evie flips her hair over her shoulder and stomps over to the waiting Aaron. I am left staring at her backside in shock. She acts like I just doomed myself to being alone for the rest of my life! I just needed some time to think, for crying out loud! Is that so shocking? I certainly wasn't expecting to find myself making out with Mason in the bathroom this morning. My whole world feels like it's been stood on its head. It's felt like that since the day Robin showed up, but this morning was the real kicker.

She's wrong, I tell myself as I climb into the Jeep. What does she know about something like this? Panic sets in as I realize my little sister knows way more about relationships than I do. I think just about everyone knows more about relationships than I do. The Jeep barrels down the street to the house.

I can't even begin to describe the strange feeling that settles over me when I pull into the driveway and spot Robin's sedan next to the curb. What is she doing here? I tear my seatbelt off and scurry into the house. As I round the corner, I almost collide with Mom on her way out of the kitchen.

"Olivia!" she gasps. "Slow down! What on earth are you in such a hurry about?"

"Have you seen Mason?"

Mom chuckles, "Technically, no, but he just let me know he was home."

I start to run off, up the stairs to his room. My mom's voice stops me.

"He's only going to be here for a few minutes, though. He said he and Robin were going out."

"Where?"

Mom shrugs. "He just said they wanted to hang out for a while."

I try to take off again, but Mom grabs my arm. "Olivia, I hope you don't think I was completely blind to whatever was going on this morning between the three of you."

"Mom," I groan.

"I'm serious, Olivia. I know your Dad talked to you about life after high school with Mason, but don't think those same issues don't exist right now." She looks at me sharply. "Don't think that because your father isn't here right now you can get away with things. We will all be having a serious discussion about this when he gets home."

"Fine," I say, more intent on finding Mason right now than worrying about a lecture from Dad.

This time when I stalk away from her, she doesn't stop me. I hurry up the stairs to Mason's room. I try not to burst in like a lunatic, but the door still swings open rather abruptly. I'm caught off guard when I find myself in an empty room. Where is he?

I head back down the stairs, wondering if they went out back for some reason. Before I make it to the bottom, Mason and Robin emerge from the basement. "Mason," I call out.

* * *

He looks up at me, but instead of excitement in his eyes, I am startled by the pain etched into his features. I reach the bottom of the stairs and slow down. Did something happen? Why wouldn't Mom tell me?

"Mason, what's wrong?"

His jaw clenches. "Sorry, Olivia. Robin and I were just on our way out."

"But, wait! We need to talk."

"I can't. Not right now. I'll be back later," he says as if the words are hurting him.

"If something's wrong ..." I say, reaching for him.

Mason pulls away from me slowly. "Everything's fine," he lies and turns away.

I start to say something more, but I choke on my words when Mason reaches for Robin's hand. She slips her hand into his without looking at me, but I can see the corner of her mouth twitch. Robin's eyes travel up to Mason's. Something seems to pass between them, but I can only see half of Robin's face and it makes no sense.

As the door closes behind them, I sink down to the stairs. My head thunks against the railing painfully, but I barely notice it. What. Just. Happened?

Mom walks out of the kitchen, but slows when she sees me. "Olivia, is everything okay?"

All I can do is shake my head back and forth slowly. Mom's mouth turns down in concern. "What happened?"

"I don't know." Tears begin welling at the back of my eyes. I don't want to cry in front of my mom, but I don't know if I can help it.

"Olivia, honey, you're making me worry. Why are you so upset?"

She tries to take my hand, but it makes me think of Mason holding Robin's and I snatch it away from her and stand up. "I don't think we'll be needing that talk with Dad anymore," I say slowly.

"Why not?" Mom asks.

"Because Mason just walked out the door holding Robin's hand."

Mom stares at me, confused. Well, she can join the club. Pushing past her, I mumble something about needing to leave and bolt for the Jeep. I don't know if she follows me. I don't look back. If I look back I'll want to curl up in her arms like I used to when I was little and tell her everything, tell how I finally admitted to myself how much I love Mason, how I ran because I was scared, how I may have lost him for good.

I can't tell her all of that, so I drive.

And drive.

I'm not even sure when I stop driving. At some point I just realize that the Jeep is no longer running and take my hands off the wheel. The last time

I cried was after Mason told me he thought the Sentinels were going to come back for him and kill him. The last time before that, I can't even remember.

The thought of Mason dying was terrifying. The thought of losing him because I was too scared to love him cuts deep into my heart. Tears start running down my cheeks in sheets. My shoulders shake uncontrollably as I feel my heart breaking.

A sharp rapping on my window yanks my face out of my hands in fear. I look up, tearstained, broken, right into the startled gaze of Hayden Benton.

Chapter 21

Dark Shadow

My door flies open as Hayden suddenly crowds in on me. "Olivia? Are you okay?"

"Hayden?"

Embarrassed, and more than a little confused, I start wiping away tears frantically. It's no use, though, because they just keep falling. Hayden doesn't say anything when I flop back against the seat and cover my face with my hands. I try to breathe, to get control of myself, but it seems impossible. Every passing second I expect to hear the door shut as Hayden walks away.

It would be the absolute cap on today if he bailed on the obviously crazy girl he had previously been nice to. He's probably better off making a quick exit. I wait for the sound, but it never comes.

When my tears finally wear themselves out, Hayden's hand slips over mine and gently uncovers my face. The concern written on his face seems so genuine, but I know he must be thinking that I'm a total nutcase at this point. I try to turn away from him, but he won't let me.

"Olivia, what's going on?"

Sniffing and wiping away tears, I say, "I'm just having a really horrible day."

"That was pretty much a given." Hayden smiles. "Do you want to talk about it?"

I shake my head violently. Not only can I *not* talk about it, I don't want to. Not with Hayden. Not with anyone.

Hayden nods. "You wanna take your mind off whatever's bothering you?"

Surprised that he moved on from me crying so quickly, I just stare at him for a moment. "What?"

He gestures past me to a basketball court. I look at the court in confusion. "Where am I?"

Laughing, Hayden looks at me curiously. "Really? You don't know where you are?"

I rub my hand across my forehead wishing this day would just end. "Sorry, I just needed to get away from my house and started driving. I don't even remember pulling over."

"No worries," Hayden says. He nudges me softly. "And here I thought you came to watch me play ball."

"I didn't even know you played basketball," I admit sheepishly.

● ● ●

Hayden laughs out loud. "Wow. You really know how to keep a guy's pride in check, don't you? I've been on the basketball team at school for four years."

"I've never been to a game."

"Never?"

I shake my head. Hayden shakes his head right back. I've just admitted to him that even though I've known him since junior high I know almost nothing about him. Why he doesn't say goodbye and look for a girl who hasn't gone through her life completely oblivious to…well, apparently to just about everything, I have no idea.

Instead of running for the hills, he asks, "Have you ever played?"

"Basketball?"

"Yeah," he laughs. "Unless there's some other sport you're *actually* interested in."

I shake my head. The closest I've ever been to a sport is watching Dad and Mason play catch in the backyard. Instantly, my lips turn down and tears threaten. I try to shake thoughts of Mason away, but that has never been easy.

"Come on," Hayden says softly.

He tries to take my hand and get me to leave the Jeep, but I pull away and cross my arms over my chest protectively. "I should probably just go home. Go to bed or something. You don't want to hang out with me right now. Nobody does."

"I absolutely do want to hang out with you. I've been trying to talk you into hanging out with me for weeks, remember?" He tugs on me again.

"But, I'm a mess. I just want to go home."

He shakes his head. "You're fine for a little one on one, and home is where you were trying to get away from, remember?"

But Mason left. He was the one I was running away from. The idea of curling up in my bed and never coming out again seems awfully appealing. He'll come home eventually, though. Maybe he's already home. I have no idea how long I've been gone. My chest constricts thinking that Mason might already be home and I would have to face him.

"Okay," I say weakly.

Hayden grins and pulls me from the Jeep before I can change my mind. I'm glad he has the presence of mind to lock it up, because I didn't even think of it. I also notice that he thought to take my keys out of the ignition first. I sigh, embarrassed to be such a train wreck. Dad would have killed me if I had walked away from the Jeep with it unlocked and the keys still in the ignition. No doubt it would have been stolen.

"Thanks," I say, gesturing at the Jeep.

Hayden smiles and pockets my keys.

* * *

"Are you going to give those back?" I ask.

"Eventually." He smiles again and heads around the Jeep toward the courts.

I really have no other choice than to follow him. Shaking my head, I trudge through the grass a few steps behind him. It seems like an incredibly long walk. I'm exhausted by the time we finally reach the court. When I look back at the Jeep sitting lonely by the curb, I sigh. Resigned to spending the foreseeable future watching Hayden shoot baskets, I collapse on the grass like an egg dropped on cement.

Hayden walks over with a basketball in his hands and shakes his head at me. "Nope. Not gonna happen. Get up."

"What?"

"How do you expect to play sitting on the grass?"

"Play?"

"Yes, play."

My face scrunches at him. "But, I don't know how to play."

"Lucky for you, I do. Get up here," he demands.

When I show no intention of moving, he drops the ball and comes to get me. My frown stays firmly in place as he hauls me up from the ground. He practically has to drag me out to the center of the court. I feel like crying again, but he just laughs.

"Stubborn, huh?"

"Depressed," I counter.

Hayden picks the ball back up and approaches me slowly. "I know exactly how to cure that."

"I highly doubt it."

Pulling off a perfect imitation of me wrinkling up my nose at him, Hayden laughs and starts dribbling the ball. "You clearly don't watch basketball," he says, "but you must know at least some of the basics."

"You'd probably be surprised."

Hayden catches the ball and holds it up like Vanna White. "Ball," he says sarcastically. Then he points at the hoop. "Hoop. Are you following so far?"

My scowl is ruined a bit by me laughing.

"The ball …" He points again. "…goes in the hoop." Again, he points.

"Thanks," I say in a snotty voice. I wait for him to continue mocking me, but he offers nothing more. "And?"

"And what? Those are the basics. I wouldn't want to overwhelm you on your first try."

"First try? That implies there will be a second attempt."

Hayden stalks up to me. "There will definitely be a second go at this."

● ● ●

I shake my head and take a step back. I have zero interest in basketball, and my interest in spending time with Hayden isn't much better at this point. I can tell by the grin that springs onto his lips that getting him to back off isn't going to be easy. I sigh, feeling awkward.

As Hayden tries to fill the empty court with real instructions on how to play basketball, I only half-listen. After a few minutes, he warns me that he's going to pass me the ball. That should probably mean I am ready for it, but I flinch away from the ball and it goes sailing past me. Hayden stares, looking somewhat amused and just a little surprised.

"Wow, you really aren't athletic, are you?"

"I tried to warn you."

He grins back at me. "You're not getting out of this that easily. Go get the ball."

I look over my shoulder distastefully. Turning back, I say, "You get it."

Hayden marches toward me, in what I'm sure is meant to be an intimidating way. His laughing at me ruins it. He grabs my hand as he marches by and tows me along with him. When we reach the ball, he scoops it up and presses it against my middle until I relent and take it. The ball slips, and that's when I realize Hayden still has a hold of my other hand. Flushing pink, I yank my hand away from his and head for the court.

I start doing what Hayden says, mainly out of desperation to keep him from getting too close to me or having an opportunity to touch me again. Half my attention stays on what he's telling me to do. The other half struggles to figure Hayden out. I don't do very well on either count.

Hayden stands to the side when I try to shoot the ball for the first time. We both watch as it goes about half the distance to the basket and sinks like a rock. Hayden busts up laughing, and I can't help but join him. That was pretty sad.

"I can honestly say," Hayden says through his laughter, "that I have never met anyone as terrible at this sport as you are."

"I tried to warn you."

He laughs again and scoops up the ball on his way to me. "Yes, yes you did. I didn't believe you, but you have done a magnificent job of proving me wrong."

I can't help it. The corner of my mouth turns up. Hayden doesn't miss it. He shoves the ball back into my hands and slides around behind me. I jump when his hands touch my shoulders. He presses down lightly, and when I resist starts wiggling me around until I begin to loosen up.

"There," he says finally, "you're like a stick figure, all stiff and awkward."

"Your chances of their being a second basketball session are sinking fast," I say.

Hayden peeks around my shoulder looking thoroughly shocked. "Signs of a sense of humor? Wow, we are making progress."

I roll my eyes and shove him away from me. He goes back to showing what *form* is supposed to look like. I feel like a manikin as he scoots my feet into position and shows me how to hold the ball properly.

After an interminable amount of prodding and shifting, Haden says, "Try it again."

My hands feel awkward as I push the ball up and away from me. My confidence is pretty low, but I watch hopeful it will go somewhere this time. It goes maybe two feet further that my first try and sails back to the court with a smack-smack-smack as it bounces into the grass. Hayden puts his hands on top of his head and tries really, really hard not to laugh at me.

"I suck at this."

Hayden reaches his limit and busts up. "You do. You suck at this pretty bad."

He runs off after ball and tosses it back to me. I flinch again, but somehow still manage to catch it. "What?" I whine, "I have to do it again?"

"Uh, yeah. Again and again and again."

Groaning dramatically, I raise the ball and look at the rim. Hayden groans as well, mumbling about how he *just* showed me how to hold the ball correctly! He hardly seems put out about having to come back and reposition me again. Every touch seems to linger a little longer. I try not to squirm, for the sake of not messing up my position again, but having Hayden touch me brings up more miserable emotions than pleasure right now.

When Hayden finally stands back, I shoot again. He groans as it falls way short of the hoop. He's still smiling, though. He tries over and over again to turn me into an only halfway terrible basketball player, but he's going to have to get used to failure because not a single shot makes it anywhere near the rim.

We try one on one next, and it's no surprise that Hayden beats me soundly. The really sad thing is, I don't think he was even trying. At some point, I actually start having fun. Not the kind of laugh out loud, never want to leave fun. Just less miserable.

As the sun fades, even Hayden starts missing shots. After one bounces off the backboard and nearly hits me in the head, I grab the ball off the ground and refuse to give it back. "We're done!"

"Ah, come on. There's still enough light!"

"No!"

Holding the ball behind my back, I sneak away from him and make a run for the grass. It's not very hard for Hayden to catch up to me. He snatches the ball out of my hands. The force spins me just enough that I stumble over Hayden's gym back. My foot tangles in the strap and I topple over and land on my backside.

"Olivia," Hayden laughs, "I'm sorry. I didn't mean to knock you down."

"It's okay," I say.

Hayden extends his hand in an offer to help me up. I take it, but right away my hand goes clammy. I can't seem to hold onto Hayden. My hand slips, but he drops the ball and grabs my forearm with his other hand. There's no chance of me getting away from him now. He pulls me up with hardly any effort, but doesn't let go.

I start to pull away, afraid he wants to do something other than basketball. Hayden's gentle voice stops me.

"Olivia, thank you for staying."

"Why are you thanking me?" I ask shakily. "I'm terrible at basketball. I'm sure you had better things to do with your afternoon, uh, and evening."

Hayden smiles. "Not at all. I had a lot of fun. I'm just sorry it took you having the worst day possible to get you to spend time with me." Hayden reaches down and untangles my foot from the strap of his gym bag. When he stands back up, he says, "I know you didn't really want to stay. If you don't want to talk about what made you run away from your house, that's okay, but if you do ever want to talk, about today or anything else, you can call me any time."

"I don't even have your number," I remind him. The thought slips out before I can think better of it. When Hayden starts smiling mischievously, I know I just painted myself into a corner.

"I can fix that pretty easily."

He snatches up my phone from where I left it on a bench near the court and as he walks back to me I see his fingers flying over the keyboard. He hands me my phone, open to the contacts screen, his number right there to wipe away any excuses.

"Thank you," I say, not entirely sure whether I am grateful or not.

Hayden holds his phone out to me, but I just stare at him in confusion. He uncurls my fingers and sets the phone on my palm. "Now, I want your number."

"Why?"

"So I can call you the next time I need a self-esteem boost when it comes to basketball." He grins when I laugh.

The thin piece of metal and plastic feels heavy in my hands. I don't move right away to enter my number. Hayden doesn't push me, but he waits. In some ways, it feels like a betrayal to give him my number. Just as that thought pops into my head, the image of Mason's hand slipping into Robin's slaps me right across the face.

My fingers start typing furiously, tapping out my anger. If Mason wants to kiss me like he did and then run off with Robin, fine! Screw him. He may not think I'm worth waiting a few hours for, but Hayden just spent his entire afternoon and evening trying to cheer me up. At the least, he deserves my phone number.

I hand the phone back with shaking hands. Satisfaction and regret mingle in my heart, but I refuse to turn back. I manage a small smile when Hayden takes the phone. "Thank you," I say, "for putting up with me today. I know I was lousy company."

"You were great," he says softly.

The sun has fully set now, and the park has taken on a decidedly creepy vibe. I dread actually going home. Avoiding Mason forever is hardly a plan, though. Sighing, I shove my phone in my pocket and ask for my keys. Hayden hands them over reluctantly.

"I better get home. My parents are probably freaking out about now."

The way Haden's hand touches my arm, hesitant, almost afraid, keeps me from moving away. He stares at his hand on my arm for a moment before looking up at me with an equally concerned look in his eyes.

"Olivia, when you first got here, you said you had to get away from your house. I know you don't want to talk about it …" He pauses and takes a step closer. "If you're scared …"

"Hayden," I interrupt, "it's nothing like that."

I don't think he believes me totally, but he doesn't pressure me for more. "I hope you know I was serious when I said you could call me if you needed me. Any time. For any reason."

It's impossible for me to doubt him. The honest worry in his eyes melts away my lingering fear. "Thank you," I whisper, my voice raw.

Unable to stand there any longer without breaking down again, I turn and start for the Jeep. Hayden calls for me to wait up and offers to walk me to my car, but I feel guilty for having already taken up his night and tell him I'll be fine. I can hear him hurriedly shoving things back in his gym bag so he can catch up, but I don't stop.

I've covered half the distance when a dark shadow jumps out at me, stopping my heart and tearing a scream from my throat.

Chapter 22

Indescribable

I am falling to the ground as my scream dies in my throat. My breath blasts out of me as my attacker's body falls against mine. Terror races through my veins as I try to kick out at him, hit him, knee him, anything! My elbow connects with something hard. The attacker groans, but his grip only tightens.

Suddenly his weight shifts on top of me. He rolls to the side and yanks me up to my knees. I try to scream again, but he shoves a hand over my mouth and yanks me upright. Desperate, my foot crashes down on his instep.

The pain loosens his grip just enough that I can turn myself in his grip and wedge my hands between us. The fierce fury in his green eyes stabs at me viciously. A lock of blonde hair falls out from his hood, across his forehead and scarred cheek.

Even that seems terrifying, sending my panic into overdrive. I shove against him, trying to break his grip. A surge of relief shoots through me when I gain a little separation. I bring my knee up hard into his groin, hoping it will be enough. He doubles over, groaning in pain, and I spin out of his arms.

The two steps I take are fueled by panic before his hand snaps down on my ankle and my feet jerk out from beneath me. Screaming and kicking out with my free foot, I connect with his shoulder. He growls as he launches himself forward, crashing down on top of me. His fist follows, right into the side of my head.

Spots of light wink in and out as my head falls back to the ground. Pain throbs through my skull as a dark shape flies in from the side and crashes into my attacker. The sudden loss of crushing weight on top of me makes me roll onto my side. Trying to get up only sends me sprawling.

Shaking my head, I try to clear the spots away. The pain of moving sends a wave of nausea coursing through me and I collapse back to the grass. Breathe. Breathe. It's all I can manage. The seconds that pass feel like hours, but when I finally manage to look up and see Hayden grappling with the attacker my head suddenly clears.

"Hayden!" I call out in panic.

I scream when the attacker's fist pummels Hayden. He fights back, landing a punch to the guy's chin, but takes one to his side right after. A million thoughts race through my mind as I try to reach Hayden. I don't know how to fight. My phone is nowhere to be seen. I have no idea what to do, but I have to help Hayden!

● ● ●

Blue and red lights flash through the neighborhood, pulling the attacker up off Hayden in an instant and sending him running for the opposite street. Hayden scrambles back up to his feet and tries to take off after him, but I grab his arm and hold him back.

"Don't!" I cry. "Please!"

"Olivia," Hayden calls out as he folds me into his arms, "are you okay?"

I don't have time to respond. An officer rushes up to us, but Hayden hurriedly points him in the direction of the fleeing attacker. Just as he takes off after him, another officer comes running up.

"Are you two alright?" he demands.

Hayden pushes me back and takes a look at me. "Are you?"

I don't know, but as I stare at him my heart breaks to see the blood running down his lip, the bruises springing up on his arm and face, and I know the hits to his side have got to be agonizing. "I'm fine," I say, "but you …"

"I'm okay," he says as he pulls me against his chest. "It's okay. Everything's alright now."

The officer puts a hand gently on my shoulder. I flinch at his touch, but his calm and reassuring voice keeps me from freaking out. "My name is Officer Kimball. You both look like you're going to need some medical attention. Stay put for a minute while I call this in, then we'll figure out what happened."

We both nod, but I don't think either of us was planning on going anywhere anyway. I lay my head against Hayden's chest and close my eyes. I start to curse my luck, wondering why some idiot would try to attack me like that when Hayden was still nearby. My body goes completely numb when I remember Mason's nightmare from last night.

That lunatic wasn't trying to rob me, he was trying to abduct me! This wasn't some random mugging in a park! I know without a doubt that this was a Sentinel attack. They've probably been watching me since the day we saw the car. This is just the first time I've been away from the house without Mason or Evie for a significant length of time since then. They saw their chance and took it. Dread fills me as I realize this won't be the only attempt to find out where Mason is.

"Paramedics are on their way to check you both out," Officer Kimball says. "Now, can you two tell me what happened?"

Hayden takes the lead, thankfully. He starts off by giving the officer our names and explains me heading for my car after we finished playing basketball.

"I should have just waited for you," I whisper, feeling like an idiot. Mason had even tried to warn me about walking around at night alone. I told him I wasn't that stupid, but here I was being *exactly* that stupid.

"It's okay," Hayden says as he strokes my hair. He finishes telling the officer about seeing the guy jump out and attack me, calling the police as he ran over to me, and launching himself at the attacker.

The Officer Kimball doesn't say anything for a moment while he finishes his notes. When his pen goes still, he turns to me. "Is there anything else you want to add, Olivia?"

I shake my head.

"What about a description?" he prods.

"He was blonde, with green eyes."

"Taller than me by a few inches," Hayden adds, "and pretty well built. The guy was strong."

I close my eyes and force myself to picture him again. It makes me cringe to think of his horrible eyes and twisted sneer, but as I picture his mouth screwing into disgust I say, "He had a scar that ran from his cheek to his lip."

I draw my finger across my own face to show him what I mean, starting at the height of my cheekbone and moving down to the section of my lip just below the corner of my nose. The officer notes it down in his notebook and thanks us for our help. About that time, the first officer comes back, panting and empty handed. I'm not surprised.

"I couldn't catch up to him," he says apologetically. "He jumped into a waiting car a few blocks away and they took off. No license plates on the vehicle, but I got the make and model."

Not that that will help us, I think. Unless it just happens to be an exotic, rare vintage, we'll never find it. And let's face it, that only happens in shows like CSI. In real life, the getaway car is something plain and common, impossible to track.

As the two officers confer with each other and talk into the walkie-talkies on their shoulders, the paramedics arrive, sans flashing lights and sirens. The officer must have told them it wasn't life threatening, because they walk over to us with just a portable medical kit.

After giving us both an initial once over, the two paramedics lead us over to a picnic table and start cleaning up our cuts and bruises. It doesn't take too long, and the paramedic working on me announces that I'll live.

"Just keep a bottle of pain reliever on hand for the next few days, okay?" one of the paramedics tells me. I nod, but my attention is on Hayden as the second paramedic lifts his shirt to examine his abdomen. I cringe at the red and purple blotches dotting his side.

Hayden winces a few times as the paramedic presses on his abdomen, but he toughs it out for the most part. The paramedic finally lowers his shirt and says, "I don't think there are any internal injuries, but if the pain worsens or you have any unusual bruising you need to go to the hospital for further examination, okay?"

When the paramedics step back, the officer who took our statements, Officer Kimball, moves back in and asks for our contact information. That leads to questions about parents. I don't think he realized we were both seventeen at first.

"I'll need phone numbers for you parents as well. We need to call them and let them know you're both okay and let them know we'll be bringing you home."

"I can drive home. I'm fine," I argue.

The officer shakes his head. "Someone can come pick up your car later. Now both of you follow Officer Carl over to the cruiser, please."

"Can you ask my parents to meet me at Olivia's house?" Hayden asks. "It'll be more convenient that way."

Officer Kimball nods that he can do that and clears us to go gather up our belongings strewn all over the grass.

It takes a few minutes for Hayden to gather up everything he abandoned when he saw me getting attacked and for me to figure out where I dropped my keys and phone. Once we finally have everything, Officer Carl ushers us over to the cruiser and shuts the door behind us once we're seated. Hayden automatically wraps his arm around my shoulders and leans his head against mine.

"Boy, when you say you're having a really bad day, you meant it."

"It's enough to make a person want to steer clear of me, right?" I ask, not sure whether I want him to agree or not.

Hayden smiles and pulls me closer. "Not a chance."

It seems to take a really long time for the paramedics to shove off and the officers to join us in the car. I can feel the weariness settling into my bones by the time we finally get moving. The officers mainly just talk to each other as we drive. They find my house without any problem and pull into the driveway. Seconds later, my parents come barreling out of the house. Evie is close on their heels. It doesn't escape me that Mason is nowhere to be seen, but I refuse to dwell on that.

I want to throw myself into my dad's arms, but I can't open the stupid car door on my own. Locked in like a criminal, I have to wait for Officer Carl to let me out. When he does, my dad snatches me up before I have the chance to say or do anything else.

● ● ●

"Olivia, sweetheart, are you okay? We were so worried when the police called!"

"I'm fine, Dad, I promise. Just a few bruises and a black eye."

Hayden comes around the side of the cruiser and Dad surprises me by releasing me and wrapping Hayden up in an almost violent hug. "Thank you!" he says to Hayden.

Right away I am smothered my Mom and Evie, but I watch Hayden as my dad nearly strangles him with his hug.

Dad holds Hayden out at arm's length and thanks him again. Hayden looks a bit embarrassed and mumbles a quick *your welcome*. He seems relieved when his parents' car screeches to a stop in front of my house. They come hurrying up the driveway and wrap him up in fierce hugs as well.

After that, the questions start flying. The officers fill in both our parents on everything we told them, give them their cards, and let them know that they'll be in touch to follow up and possibly have Hayden and I sit down with a sketch artist. I nod willingly, but I know they'll never catch the guy. Not with him being a Sentinel, which I am positive he is now.

It's kind of a relief to watch the officer's drive away. In the back of my mind I know this is far from over, but I want it to be over for tonight at least. I want to crawl into bed, carefully, and sleep for the next two days. Instead of granting my wish, Dad invites everyone inside for a few minutes to calm down and decompress.

Mom refuses to let go of me as we head into the house. Someone's hand slips into mine on the way, and I half expect to see Evie clinging to me when I look over. I see Hayden instead, and look away immediately. But I don't pull my hand from his.

As soon as we reach the living room, Mom finally lets go of me. She introduces herself to Hayden's parents and leaves me to escape to the couch. Since Hayden is determined to keep a hold of me, I tow him along behind me and collapse. Neither of us says anything. I don't want to lean on Hayden, but exhaustion drops my head against his shoulder eventually. As my eyes start to close, I think I hear a noise from the back of the house, but I'm too tired to care.

Only a few minutes later, Mason steps into the chaos. My whole body goes rigid as I watch his eyes fill with confusion as he surveys the crowd. I shrink in on myself as his eyes find mine and sees me sitting with Hayden, sporting a bloody lip and black eye. The expression on his face is indescribable.

Chapter 23

Make it Right

Panic. It screams through my veins as I stare at Olivia. Anger and disbelief chase it down as my body goes white hot with rage. What happened to her? My first instinct is to throw my arms around her and never let go. I only get one step into that plan before the crowd of random bodies in front of me ruins it.

I want to scream at them to get out of my way! It infuriates me that none of them can hear me. All I want is to get to Olivia! I stare at the faces of the people standing in my way in confusion. Who are they? What are they doing in our house?

Blonde, middle-aged, I nearly push them out of my way until I hear the name Hayden slip tearfully past the woman's lips. Hayden? What does he have to do with anything? I look toward Olivia for answers, for help, and am stunned when I realize she's not sitting there alone. What in the hell is Hayden doing with his arm around her!

Absolutely desperate, I start to push my way through. Evie is the first to get knocked into. Her eyes spring open in recognition even though she can't see me and her hands grope for my arm. She isn't strong enough to stop me, but her nails dig into my skin painfully enough that I stop and look down at her.

She shakes her head violently and starts pushing me away, out of the living room and into the hallway. She doesn't let go of my arm, though, and listens carefully.

"What is going on?" I demand angrily.

"I don't know," Evie snaps. "All I know is that Olivia got attacked at some park across town."

"What? By who?"

Evie glares at me. "How am I supposed to know? They didn't catch the guy!"

"Why is Hayden Benton here? And why does he have his arm around Olivia?" I shriek.

Throwing up the hand that isn't latched onto me, Evie growls in frustration. "She was with him, I guess. I. Don't. Know! And as for why he's getting all cozy with her, I suspect you know more about that than I do." The glare she fixes on me is deadly.

"What? Why would I know?"

"All I can tell you is that when Aaron dropped me off, I saw Olivia come tearing out of the house looking like someone just stomped all over her

● ● ●

heart and drive off nearly in tears. You were already gone. Mom was calling Dad with her voice sounding all weird and worried and she spent the next hour on the phone with him talking about you and Olivia."

Evie puts her free hand on her hip and stares me down. "Care to explain?"

"This is none of your business, Evie," I snap.

The look on her face turns absolutely murderous. "My sister just got attacked! She could have been killed or kidnapped. It is my business! And it's your fault she was out there!"

Evie whirls around on her heel and stomps away from me. I try to call after her, but she can't hear me, of course. I don't think she would have stopped even if she could.

My feet feel like lead as I trudge back to the living room. Everyone is sitting down now. Evie is parked right next to Olivia, holding her hand and leaning on her shoulder. Hayden no longer has his arm around Olivia's shoulders, but nausea sweeps over at me as I see his hand curled around hers protectively.

My whole body feels numb as I listen to the pair of them explain what happened. When Olivia describes "running into" Hayden at the basketball park, a look passes between them that says there was much more to it than that. Right then I realize that Evie is right and it buckles my knees.

Olivia glances over at me as I slump to the ground, but she tears her eyes away right after. I look away, ashamed and furious at myself for putting her in this situation. If I hadn't ditched her to hang out with Robin...if I hadn't been so stupid to think backing off would protect her from pain, I would have been with her this afternoon like always. She wouldn't have run from the house, scared and broken. She never would have set foot in that park.

I am sure I can't feel any more agony than I do already, but when Olivia talks about walking back to her Jeep in the dark and having a man jump out at her my head falls into my hands. Images from my nightmare flash into my mind like gunshots, each one piercing and wounding me.

I knew this was going to happen. I was warned that I needed to protect Olivia, to keep her by me so she was never alone to be attacked. I could have kept her from this pain, yet I wasn't there. I walked away and let her be attacked and hurt.

The sudden, seemingly orchestrated movement of everyone in the room startles me. I cringe back against the wall as everyone stands before I realize they're just ready to call it a night. Hayden's parents shake hands with Olivia's parents as they are thanked again for their son's help. He deserves every word of their praise, but my stomach sours listening to it.

My ears tune them out as I focus on Hayden standing up stiffly and gently pulling Olivia up after him. She hesitates a moment before wrapping her arms around him and leaning her head against his chest. My heart shatters as he strokes her hair softly. He whispers something in her ear and kisses her cheek so lightly I don't know if she even feels it.

They walk past me to the front door, Olivia's hand still in his. They hug again. It's feels like someone is stabbing me repeatedly as I watch them. I expect relief when the door finally closes on Hayden and his parents, but the misery only deepens when Olivia walks past me without a word.

She probably would have continued up the stairs if her dad's voice hadn't stopped her. "Olivia, is Mason here?"

"I thought he'd be home by now," Mom says worriedly.

Olivia's feet drag tiredly as she walks back toward the living room. She stops in the doorway and points at me sitting on the floor. "He's right there."

That's it. She doesn't even look at me. Her mom and dad look at each other worriedly when Olivia simply turns and heads for the stairs again. Olivia's mom is the first to approach me. Her hand reaches out, questioning. I touch her fingers so she knows where I'm at, but don't say anything.

"Mason," she says as she kneels down next to me, "are you okay?"

No. And I don't know if I ever will be again, but I know that's not what she's asking. I can see the fear in her eyes that what happened to Olivia wasn't an isolated incident.

"I'm fine," I choke out.

"Are you sure? You sound like you're hurt. Did anyone try to come after you?"

I shake my head slowly. "No. Robin and I were fine."

Olivia's dad crouches down next to me and lays a hand on my shoulder. "Mason, what's going on?"

"I had a nightmare about Olivia getting attacked last night."

"What?" they both ask.

"I should have protected her. It wasn't a mugger. It was a Sentinel. I should have been there."

Olivia's parents look at each other. I can tell they aren't sure whether to believe me or not. They're fools if they don't.

"Mason," Olivia's mom asks gently, "what happened between you and Olivia?"

Standing up suddenly and knocking them back a step, but not so far that they let go of me, I say, "I ruined everything, that's what happened."

Neither one of them tries to stop me as I march out of the room and up the stairs. I intend to head straight for my bedroom, but stumble when Olivia steps out of the bathroom and right into my path. Her hands grip the bathroom door frame. For a moment I think she is scared of me for some reason. When I see her knees shaking and the pain in her eyes, I realize she's trying to keep herself from falling. It kills me to see her in so much pain. I can't stop myself from crossing the distance between us and reaching for her.

"Don't touch me!" she snaps.

Shocked, hurt, I stumble to a stop inches away from her.

"Get away from me," she says with tears in her eyes.

I take a step back. My breathing escalates as I look into her angry eyes. I have never seen her so hurt and afraid before. Every cell in my body screams at me to make it right, hold her, fix this between us. Thinking I could step back after what happened this morning and not hurt her was the stupidest thing I could have done. I want to tell her I'm sorry, beg for her forgiveness.

Olivia pushes away from the door frame and marches to her room. The door slams and I sink to my knees in agony.

Chapter 24
Confess

Driving to school with Mason and Evie is torture. Mason at least had the decency to sit in the back today. Evie tried to come talk to me last night about everything that happened, but I couldn't stand the idea of reliving it one more time and refused to let her in. She sits beside me quietly as we pull into the parking lot.

As I kill the engine, Evie looks over at me as says, "Come find me if you need me today, okay?"

All I can do is nod. She slips out of the car, and I follow quickly, desperate to get away from Mason. He keeps his distance as I make my way to my locker. Mom offered to let me skip school today and rest up, but I have a research paper to turn in. In all honesty, though, I didn't want to stay because I knew Mason would stay as well and the idea of being trapped in the house with him all day is a million times worse than showing up at school looking like I got in a bar fight.

As I step into the building, it's acutely obvious that my makeup isn't doing nearly enough to hide the black eye or split lip. Furtive glances dart at me as I walk down the hallway. I'm sure they're all wondering, but I don't care to fill them in. I spot my locker and make a beeline for it. I'm yanking open the door when Hayden slides up next to me.

"Hey," I say.

He smiles. "That's all I get? A *hey*?"

"Sorry," I say with a half-smile—the half that doesn't hurt to move. "Not feeling like my usual peppy self today."

"You have a usual peppy self?" Hayden asks. "Why have I never seen it?"

I roll my eyes, amazed at his ability to cheer me up. "Okay, I may not have a peppy side, but I'm certainly feeling worse than my usual quiet, loner self. How's that?"

"Much more accurate," he laughs.

Hayden's fingers brush along my cheek carefully. I try not to wince, but even breathing on that side of my face hurts. His fingers slide down to my chin. Thankfully he doesn't get too close to my lip. His mouth turns down. "You look even worse than last night."

"Thanks, that makes me feel better," I grouch. "You do too, by the way."

He grins. "I know."

"How's your side?" I ask. I remember the attacker punching him repeatedly in that area.

Hayden lifts the edge of his shirt and I gasp at the mottled bruises covering nearly half his stomach. Several of the students around us stop and stare. "Oh my gosh, Hayden! That looks terrible!"

"Yeah, I won't be playing basketball for a few weeks, which I'm sure you're devastated about, but I'll be fine." He drops his shirt back down and leans against the lockers. I can see him wince at the movement.

"I feel so terrible about last night. It was my fault you were there so late. If you hadn't been there trying to make me feel better …"

"If I hadn't been there you may have gotten hurt a lot worse, or taken, or…or other things I'd rather not think about," Hayden finishes. He grabs my hand and pulls me over to him. "But if you're feeling guilty, you can always make it up to me by having lunch with me today, and every day."

"Lunch?" I stare at him. How is he being so calm about all of this? "Uh, sure. Okay."

Hayden grins and pushes away from the lockers carefully. "See you at lunch then."

The final bell rings a moment later and the hallways begin to clear. I shuffle off to my first class in a daze. I hold the door open for Mason out of habit when I reach class, and nearly jump out of my shoes when I feel him slip in past me. I don't look at him, though.

I keep my eyes squarely in front of me as I walk to my desk. I can still see Mason parking himself on the window sill like he usually does from the corner of my eye, but I refuse to acknowledge him. I'm relieved when he doesn't try to talk to me.

All morning he follows me around like a ghost. We don't speak to each other. I pretend I can't see him anymore than anyone else, but his eyes never leave me. It's honestly the first time I can say having Mason near me makes me uncomfortable. And that's underneath the anger and hostility I'm still carrying around against him, too. Needless to say, I am completely drained by the time lunch finally arrives.

I dump everything in my locker and practically run for the cafeteria in an effort to escape Mason. I know he's not far behind, but halfway there he backs off a bit and gives me some space. As I round the corner to the cafeteria, I spot Robin approaching the door as well. She freezes, eyes wide before walking over to me.

The last thing I want to do right now is talk to *Robin*. I do my best to make that obvious by turning away from her, but she isn't deterred. "Olivia, are you okay?" she asks. "I heard about what happened."

Spinning around to face her, I say, "I have nothing to say to you after what you've done."

"What I've done?" Robin asks. "Look, Olivia, it wasn't my idea. I told Mason …"

"I don't care what you told him or who's idea it was. I don't want to see either of you. Keep him away from me. That's what you're good at."

Stalking away from her, I'm so angry I am tempted to pick up a chair and throw it at a wall. Luckily, I spot Hayden sitting at a table on the opposite side of the cafeteria from where I usually sit with Mason and head in that direction. I collapse into a chair next to him with no food and a scowl that seems to be on its way to becoming permanent.

"Everything okay?" Hayden asks.

I want to snap at him for asking such a stupid question, but I don't. I watch as Mason and Robin sit down at our usual table. My eyes narrow. I want to scream when Robin puts her hand in Mason's. They start talking a few minutes later and I look away.

"I'm sorry, Hayden," I say, "I'm not very good company again today."

"Well, it would be hard to have a worse day than yesterday, so you can at least feel good about that." He pops a fry into his mouth and looks at me with a knowing expression.

Tired of feeling like crap, I decide to ignore Robin and Mason completely and focus on Hayden, who has been nothing but nice to me—pretty heroic actually—and force myself to be in a better mood.

"Not all of yesterday was horrible," I say. "I was having fun before that psycho tried to grab me."

"So was I," Hayden says. "I think we should do it again."

Cocking an eyebrow at him, I say, "I thought you were grounded from basketball for the time being."

"True. I guess we should go see a movie then."

Hayden is so sweet, but the idea of going out on a date with him makes me feel…weird. I don't know what to think. Being furious at Mason doesn't change the fact that he has been my best friend for twelve years or that I am in love with him. I want him more than anything in this world or his.

But no one has ever hurt me as badly as he did.

"Sure," I say quietly. "When?"

"Friday night?"

"Um, okay." Given my glaring lack of extracurricular activities—sports especially—I'm pretty sure I'm free. "Do you have a movie in mind?"

Hayden shakes his head. He leans closer to me, his hand coming up to brush against my uninjured cheek. My heart stutters a moment, but whether in fear or something else I don't know. He smiles as he says, "Why don't you choose?"

I really couldn't even tell him a single movie at the theaters right now. Needing some space and a moment to think, I turn to grab my phone so I can check the movie listings. Without meaning to, I elbow Hayden in the side. I don't get him very hard, but it's on his injured side and he groans. I gasp and spin back around more carefully.

"Hayden, I'm so sorry!"

"It's okay," he says after taking a deep breath. He looks anything but fine.

Gently, my hand presses to his abdomen where I elbowed him, as if it does any good to protect that area now. His heart is beating so rapidly, I can feel it echoing through his whole body. Did I hurt him that bad?

I look up and find him staring down at me with a look that is not filled with pain, but with something else entirely. His hand covers mine gently and slowly pulls it north to his chest where he curls his fingers around mine and simply holds onto me.

"Can I confess something?" he asks.

"You lied about how bad I hurt you?" I guess.

He shakes his head with a chuckle.

"Then what?"

"I've wanted to ask you out since sixth grade."

Honestly surprised, I ask, "Really?"

He nods.

"Then why didn't you?" I ask not so much because I would have jumped at the chance anymore more back then than I did today, but more out of curiosity.

"I wasn't sure you even knew who I was. I didn't think you were interested. You always seemed to be, I don't know…like you were happy just being on your own. You never talked to me unless I asked you a question about one of our classes."

I always knew people thought I was a little strange, but it's embarrassing to hear how out of it I have been. "It wasn't anything personal," I say. "I did know who you were. I was like that with everyone, though."

"Well, I hope that won't be the case anymore, because I actually enjoy talking to you."

Smiling, I say, "I like talking to you, too."

And surprisingly enough, it's true.

Hayden finally releases my hand and pulls out his phone so he can bring up the movie listings for the nearest theater. I steal a French fry from his tray while he scans the movies. I don't really care what we watch. I'm not even totally sure if I want to go to a movie with Hayden. I do know that he makes me feel better about my life and the lousy turns it has taken recently, and for now that is enough.

"Comedy?" Hayden asks.

"Sure."

"Seven o'clock?"

I nod.

"Is it okay if I pick you up, or would you rather drive separately?"

I don't answer right away. Driving separately would give me a getaway car if I got desperate and wanted to bail. Letting him pick me up will force me to sit through the entire movie, ride to and from the theater with him, rely on him. The idea of that scares me at first, but then I think it might be nice to rely on someone else…for a little while.

"You can pick me up, if you don't mind."

Hayden attempts to put his arm around my shoulders, but only moves his arm a few inches before thinking better of it and takes my hand instead. "I don't mind at all," he says.

Chapter 25

Nothing in Between

My hands are pressed flat against the table as I watch Hayden and Olivia. Why is he so close to her? Why does he have to touch her so often? What is with his stupid smile? My fingers curl under into fists. Why is she letting him act like this?

"Mason."

"Mason."

"Mason!" Robin snaps.

I can't bring myself to look away from Olivia, but I snap right back at her. "What?"

"Stop staring at them. It's not going to do you any good."

"It might," I argue.

She shakes her head. "It won't. Now stop it." She gives me a moment to comply on my own, but when I don't she kicks my shin from under the table.

"Ow!" I rub my leg angrily.

Robin just shrugs. "I told you to knock it off."

"I bet he was involved," I grumble.

Looking over at me with a confused expression, Robin asks, "Involved in what?"

"The attack last night. I bet Hayden lured her out into the open …"

"Give it a rest!" Robin snaps. She'd probably yell if she could, but that would draw a lot of attention. "Hayden had nothing to do with Olivia getting attacked last night and you know it."

"He could have. He could be a Sentinel."

Robin rolls her eyes. "If he is, he's a pretty lousy one. You said you've known him since sixth grade. If he were really a Sentinel he'd have figured you out by now. They may not be able to see you, but they can feel it when you're nearby, remember?"

"He could still …"

"Mason," Robin says firmly, "he's not a Sentinel. Drop it."

Sinking into my chair, I fold my arms over my chest and continue to glare at Hayden. I knew he was interested in Olivia. He has been for a long time. It's a miracle Olivia remained completely oblivious to his advances as long as she did. How can my luck be so lousy that the second I try to step back from Olivia, Hayden is right there to sweep her off her feet like some kind of freaking fairytale hero?

"Hey, Angry Boy," Robin calls out to me.

I sneer at the nickname, but still look over at her.

● ● ●

"So, what are we going to do about these Sentinels running amuck through your neighborhood?"

"What can we do?" I ask. If I get too close to one of them, they'll recognize me for what I am.

Robin shrugs. "I don't know, but moping certainly isn't useful."

"Shut up," I growl.

Tossing down her fork, Robin glares at me. "Look, for the record, I told you the whole pretending to date me thing was a stupid idea. I told you Olivia would be hurt. I *told* you to just tell her the truth about leaving."

"I couldn't tell her."

"Haven't you ever heard that whole 'tis better to have loved and lost than never to have loved at all' saying?"

Rolling my eyes at her, I say, "It's not that simple. As far as you know, once I leave, I'll never come back. I'd be holding Olivia back when she could be finding someone she has an actual future with."

"Isn't that what she's doing with Hayden?"

Hunching my shoulders, I refuse to answer that question. Why did it have to be Hayden? I can't stand him!

"So you thought pissing her off and making her think you're a total dirtbag would be a better way to spend the next five months?" Robin shakes her head at me when I don't answer.

Of course it isn't better. I hate it. I am furious with myself that Olivia got hurt because I wasn't there to protect her. Then again, if I had been there, the Sentinel would have found me and then I'd be dead.

"I didn't think she'd hate me," I mumble.

"Well, you're an idiot."

My eyes snap up to Robin angrily.

She shrugs. "You spent the night with her, kissed her that morning, all but outright told her you are so head over in heels in love with her that you can barely stand it...and then you hooked up with another girl. You really thought she'd still want to be friends after that?"

My chin drops to my chest. Yes, I did, and Robin is right that I'm an idiot. I just didn't think Olivia could ever look at me like she did last night. Then again, I'm sure she never thought I would do something so horrible to her, either.

"Mason, maybe if you explained to Olivia …"

"No," I say automatically.

She tries to say something else, but I cut her off. "What are you complaining about, anyway? You got what you wanted out of this deal."

Robin stares at me, wounded. "I went along with this because you begged me to. I didn't do this because I wanted to date you at the expense of Olivia."

She starts gathering her trash and slamming it back onto her tray. I sit up quickly and grab at her wrist. I catch her before she can bolt. Forcing her to look at me, I say, "Robin, I'm sorry. I never should have said that. I didn't mean it, and I know you didn't want to hurt Olivia. It was a terrible thing to say."

Robin stops trying to escape my grip and calms back down. She doesn't push me away when I turn my restraining grip into a gentler one. She pulls her hand back slowly until my palm falls into her hand.

"What are we going to do about the Sentinels?" she asks again.

This time I have an answer. "We're going to find them."

"And do what?"

"I don't know. I just know I won't let them hurt Olivia again."

Robin looks down at the table. "They'll never give up, Mason. There's no way to stop them from feeling your presence. The only way to make sure they don't kill you is to kill them."

"Then that's what I'll have to do."

"How?"

I shake my head. I have no idea. I've never killed anyone before, let alone some kind of super hunter. I'll figure it out as I go along.

"Even if you kill them," Robin says, "the other Sentinels will realize they're missing. They'll send more to figure out what happened and look for you."

"I don't have to keep this up forever," I remind her, "only until February. Then they should be safe."

My hopeful words linger between us. I want to believe they are true, but I have no way of knowing. I won't even be here to find out. How can they expect me to leave not knowing whether or not my family is safe? *They.* I don't even know who they are. My biological parents? Someone else? I have no idea.

"What if …" Robin begins. She takes a deep breath and starts over. "What if the same thing that happened to your Caretakers happens again?"

"It won't. I won't let it."

Robin's other hand comes up and presses over our already joined hands. "Mason, you can't promise that. We need to find the Sentinels. What if we could capture one and figure out why they're so keen on you?"

"If we capture one, he could never be let go. He would know I'm an Aerling and where to find me."

Fighting back fear, Robin says, "I know."

It brings me a sick sense of relief to hear her say that. "Okay. This afternoon, then, we need to find out where they're watching us from."

"Then what?"

"Then we find out how many of them there are, what their weakness are, and how to get rid of them. What happened to Olivia last night won't be their last attempt."

"No," Robin agrees, "it won't."

I want to ask Robin to do one more thing, but fear keeps me quiet for a moment. I know Olivia was right when she said talking to other Caretakers was too dangerous, but I can feel the clock ticking now and I don't think we can afford to be in the dark for too much longer.

"Robin, without telling your parents about me, do you think you could try to find out more about all of this?"

Robin nods carefully. "I can talk to my grandma more, and I'm sure I can ask my parents about a few things without raising their suspicions. I'll find out as much as I can."

"Thank you, Robin."

The bell rings, but Robin doesn't move right away. Instead, she looks up at me with a sad expression. "Can you do something for me?"

"What?" I ask warily.

"Quiet hounding Olivia and Hayden." I start to react right away, but she cuts off. "Look, I still think you should tell her the truth, but if you're really set on this stupid plan, you have to back off and actually let her move on. It's either one way or the other, nothing in between, do you understand me?"

I hate knowing that she's right. Being with Robin so Olivia can move on won't work if I'm constantly hovering over her shoulder reminding her of what might have been. I would only be hurting her more. Despair crashes over me as I say, "Fine, I'll back off."

Chapter 26

Jealous Much?

The drive home from school is just as miserable as the drive to school was this morning. No one speaks. Even Evie is quiet, which is a small miracle. It's a not so pleasant reminder that she is still pissed at me, though. As soon as we pile out of the Jeep and into the house, everyone goes their separate ways. For Olivia and Evie, that means up to their bedrooms. Me, I crash on the couch waiting for Robin to text me.

I wanted to get started on our Sentinel hunt right after school, but Robin had an eye appointment. She promised to text me as soon as she was done. Realizing now how incredibly horrible it was for me to show Olivia that we couldn't be together by moving onto Robin right in front of her, I told Robin I'd meet her at the park instead of having her pick me up.

Flipping through channels on TV quickly gets boring. I settle on a favorite, but even that has trouble keeping me occupied. The minutes tick by slowly as I watch reruns of Uncle Si and Willie getting into one crazy situation after another.

The house is so quiet with Mom at work for the afternoon. The mental and emotional exhaustion of the past few days starts to catch up with me and my eyes slowly drift closed.

Images start flickering through my mind, all of Olivia. Her on the phone, opening the front door. She takes a plate out of the dishwasher. Suddenly she's on the kitchen floor, the broken plate lying next to her.

Buzzz! Buzzz!

My phone vibrating against my hand jerks me awake. The images fall away as I blink and try to open my text messages. Robin's number pops up with a new message.

Finished. Meet U @ the park in 10.

It's only takes a few minutes to walk to the park, but I don't wait. Eager to get out of the house, I shove my phone in my pocket and head for the front door. Evie's hand on my arm stops me before I can escape. I'm not sure how she knew I was there, but I suspect she's been watching me.

"Where are you going?" she demands.

"I just need to get out for a while, okay?"

"With who? Robin?"

The way my body goes still must give me away because Evie's face screws up in disgust. I sigh, wishing I could explain. "Evie, I know you're mad, and you have every right to be, but please believe me when I say that this is the only way I know how to protect Olivia."

● ● ●

Confusion spreads across her features, but I don't wait for her to respond. I slip away from her and out the front door, trying not to look back. I only last until I reach the front sidewalk before my eyes dart back at the house. It isn't the front door or Evie that trips me up. I only see Olivia's curtain swish closed, but it's enough to know that she saw me leave, and just like Evie, she can probably guess who I'm going to see.

There's nothing I can do about it now, so I keep walking. The park is empty when I arrive. To the rest of the world, it still looks empty even after I sit down. Five minutes later, Robin pulls up to the curb and gets out of her car. She looks completely casual as she sits down next to me, keeping her phone in her hands.

"Do we have a plan?" she asks.

Not much of one. But to her I say, "They've got to be watching the house from somewhere nearby. It wasn't by chance they found Olivia in a basketball park across town. Someone followed her and waited for the right opportunity."

"So if we find their lookout spot, we can watch them."

"Exactly."

"Great," Robin says, "then let's get started."

She pulls a pair of earbuds out of a black case strapped to her arm and pops them into the top of her phone. I watch her turn on the music, wondering what she's doing. Robin sticks one earbud into her ear and slides her phone into the case on her arm. She stands up, and I realize she isn't wearing the same clothes she had on at school.

It catches me off guard to look up and see her tight running shorts and a green tank top. I think it's the first time I've ever noticed how slender and athletic Robin is. I feel like a creep staring at her, but I can't seem to look away. She starts jogging in place, which only distracts me more.

"Okay, so you'll have to lead me because I'm not very familiar with this neighborhood yet and I'm bound to get us lost," Robin says.

I try to come up with a response to that. "Um, yeah, sure."

Robin looks over at me with a curious expression. I shake myself and try to focus. "Ready?" she asks.

"Yeah, sorry."

Glad that I had been feeling like crap this morning and didn't feel like dressing up beyond gym shorts and a t-shirt, I start leading Robin around the neighborhood slowly. She does her best to keep an eye out without looking like a peeping Tom or tripping herself. Scanning the area is much easier for me.

While Robin stays on the sidewalks, I look over plants and bushes to peek in windows looking for anything suspicious. We make it to the corner and past my house before anything catches my eye. Across the street sits a dark blue sedan with medium tinted windows. That's not so odd in and of itself, but the guy sitting in the driver's seat with his eyes glued to our house is definitely suspicious.

"Robin, blue car across the street."

She peers over at it with a critical eye. "It's not the same car we saw last time, but it definitely looks creepy. Let's check it out on our way back around."

I lead Robin on a circuitous route that gets us over on the opposite side of the road. We're two blocks behind the car in question when we cut across. I'm about to ask Robin if she has a plan when she suddenly slows and tugs her phone out of its arm band holder.

"What are you doing?" I ask when she shuts the phone off and messes with the back of it.

She smiles slyly and says, "Don't worry. When he's distracted, crawl under the car and mess it up. He shouldn't be able to sense you from under the car. You normally have to be within a few feet of them for them to feel you."

"I know nothing about cars."

"Me neither, but I suppose all those hoses and things are supposed to be hooked up for it to run. So just pull something apart. Anything that'll make him have to call for help."

I'm not sure about this, but I don't have anything better. "Fine."

Robin keeps her phone in her hand as she walks up to the car. I almost yank her back when her hand comes up to knock in the window. Trust I'm not totally sure is warranted holds me back. Her knuckles wrap on the tinted window and I wait anxiously for something to happen. A few seconds later, the window rolls down halfway.

"Can I help you?" a male voice asks.

Robin beams at him. "Do you know what time it is? I was supposed to meet a friend in a little while. I had an alarm on my phone, but it died a few blocks back."

She wiggles the phone at him as proof.

"It's a quarter to five," the voice says.

Robin cringes convincingly. "Oh shoot. I'm supposed to meet him in five minutes, but I'll never make it time. He's going to be so mad at me." Robin sniffs and makes her bottom lip tremble. "I don't know what's wrong with this stupid phone. It keeps turning off on me for no reason."

"Did you try holding the power button down?" the voice asks.

The confused expression on Robin's face makes me chuckle. "Huh?"

I hear the seal of the driver's door pop and I drop down to the ground. He steps out a moment later and beckons Robin over so he can look at her phone. My heart is racing as Robin motions for me to get busy before walking around the car. The asphalt digs into my back as I squirm under the car and start looking for something to tamper with.

"You are so sweet," Robin croons. "Thank you for looking at it."

"It's no problem," the guy says.

I can hear a few clicks and "hmms" as he attempts to fix Robin's phone. Eventually he realizes Robin loosened the back and made sure the battery wasn't making full contact before putting it back in the case.

I have no idea what I'm looking at as I stare up at the underside of the car. Most of the parts don't look like I'll be able to do anything to without some serious tools. There are a few hoses here and there, but I have no idea whether unhooking them will keep the car from starting.

A few years ago Olivia's dad had to fix something on her mom's car. I sat out there and watched him, but there wasn't a lot that stuck. I know the problem was something electrical, a wire coming off a round metal piece. I think it was the starter. I look for something similar on this car. It takes some shifting and digging around, but I think I find what I'm looking for. It's round and has wires coming off of it, anyway.

Fearing that Robin may be running out of ideas to keep that guy busy, I grab a fistful of wires and yank them away from the starter. The force of my pull is a bit much and my hand bangs into something sharp. Pain slices through my hand as I jerk it away. I grunt in frustration as blood drips down my arm.

Getting out from under the car takes some maneuvering, thanks to my throbbing and bleeding hand, but I make it out without any other incidences. I stay down and keep my distance, just in case. I drop to the pavement across the street from the car and wave at Robin so she knows I'm done.

A quick nod in my direction lets me know she saw me, but she continues to listen to the phone genius as he shows her something on her now-working phone.

"Oh, wow! I didn't know there was an app to track my running." She touches his arm and smiles like the app is the most amazing thing in the world.

The guy grins back like an idiot. He turns and leans against the car. I roll my eyes as he hands the phone back to Robin. His fingers trail down her hand. Mr. Smooth doesn't stop there. The elbow he has propped on the roof of his car drops down and his hand brushes against Robin's face.

●●●

148

My hand tightens into a fist at his touch. Robin giggles and slaps a hand lightly against his chest, effectively pushing him back enough that his hand falls from her face.

"I think you missed your date," the guy says, stepping closer.

Robin shrugs, but somehow makes it incredibly sexy. "I guess I did."

"Maybe I could make it up to you sometime."

I have the sudden urge to punch him.

Robin shakes a finger at him. "I don't accept dates from strangers." She sidesteps gracefully out of his reach. "Maybe I'll see you around, though. I run here fairly often."

"I'll definitely keep an eye out." He grins at her.

When he tries to step closer and touch her again, Robin spins out of his grip and takes off jogging down across the street. The guy calls after her that he'll see her around. Robin answers with a flirty wave. When she jogs past me, she makes a gagging noise and motions for me to get up and follow her. I'm more than happy to oblige.

We run to the end of the block, me trailing blood along the way and Robin trying to shake off that creep's touch. Robin makes a graceful turn at the corner. I follow, grimacing as my hand throbs incessantly. We collapse on the lawn of a house halfway down the block and recoup.

"Ugh," Robin says with a shiver, "that guy was such a creep. I mean really? Picking up on some random runner while he's supposed to be doing surveillance?"

In his defense, Robin looks *really* good in her running clothes. I don't say that, though. "My thoughts exactly. What was with all the touching?"

Robin turns her chin up. "Well, I had to keep him distracted, and it worked pretty well."

"You're actually pretty good at that."

"Yes I am," she says with a grin. "Thanks for sounding so surprised." She rolls her eyes at me.

"That's not what I meant, though, about the touching."

"No?" she asks.

"I meant, why was he touching you so much?" I grumble.

Robin looks over at me with a curious smile. "Jealous much?"

I try to turn away, but Robin stops me with a light touch to my shoulder. She waits until I turn back to look at her. When I meet her gaze, her smile is warm and soft.

I want to look away, but I can't. "It bothered me...to see him touching you like that."

"It bothered me to *have* him touch me like that," Robin says. Her fingers spread out over my chest. "I would have preferred it was someone else."

My hand comes up, but before I can do anything with it I groan in pain as the throbbing intensifies. Robin gasps.

"Mason, what on earth happened to your hand?" she squeaks.

"Scraped it on something under the car. It's fine," I insist. "Already stopped bleeding. It just won't stop throbbing."

Robin hops up and slips her hands under my biceps to help me stand. "We need to get you home," she says as she helps me up.

"No, we need to keep an eye on that car and see who comes to help him."

"But, Mason …"

"No, Robin. I'm fine."

She huffs at me and lets go of my arm. "Fine, lead on."

I do. Robin can't risk that guy seeing her again, so she stays back behind a scarlet bush while I watch from the front yard. I'm disappointed to see that nothing has happened. He's back behind the wheel staring at my house.

"Anything happening?" Robin whispers.

"Not a thing."

She grumbles, annoyed that she can't watch as well. After that she lapses into silence, only telling me what time it is occasionally. It isn't until five o'clock that Mr. Handsy tries to start his car. He seems perplexed when the engine doesn't turn over. I can see him looking around the dashboard and panel. Eventually he gets out of the car.

I hear Robin sneak up behind me. She pulls out her phone and snaps a few pictures of the guy as he kicks the tire—like that's going to help. It only takes the genius ten more minutes to figure out he can't fix the car. Fear and excitement are stirred up as he pulls out his phone and calls for help.

The car driving up behind him twenty minutes later is expected, but the guy walking out of the house across the street from mine is a shock. At first, I think maybe it's just a coincidence. I've never seen him before, though, and I know Mr. and Mrs. Dewalt's only child is a woman, and she lives in New Jersey. Worry fills my mind as he approaches the car we're watching and starts poking around. Where are the Dewalts?

Robin keeps taking pictures as we watch the Sentinels mess around for half an hour before finally giving in and calling a tow truck. Neither of us moves until the street is empty. Even then, we fall back on the grass in silence. My mind is swimming with a million questions.

● ● ●

"I think it's safe to say," Robin eventually says, "that the Sentinels weren't watching me like I thought in the beginning."

"Apparently not."

"They're watching your house every second." Robin shivers.

Rubbing my hand against my forehead, I say, "Olivia's mom and dad are going to freak out when I tell them."

"I'll send all these pics to you so you can show them who to look out for. I'd come with you, but …"

"Yeah, I know. Sorry, Robin."

She shrugs and stands up. Robin slips her hands under my arm to help me up again. My hand stopped throbbing so bad a while ago, but it still hurts. Once we're both up, Robin puts her ear buds back in, but doesn't turn on any music. We start back toward my house. Robin only mumbles a quick goodbye when we reach my house so as not to draw attention, but promises to call me later and check on me. I skirt around to the back of the house and go in through the back door where no one will see a door open seemingly by itself.

On my way to the stairs, Olivia comes out of the kitchen. She stops cold when she sees me, and I can tell by the expression on her face that she wants nothing to do with me. An ache settles into my chest. I turn away, not wanting to force my presence on her. I try to hide my hand from her, but she catches sight of the blood and gasps.

Chapter 27

Sick Satisfaction

I stare at the blood caked all over Mason's hand, angry and concerned at the same time. I'm not sure what the black gunk is smeared in patches across his arms, but it's pretty apparent Mason was out doing something he wasn't supposed to be doing. I want to walk away, make him deal with his cut up hand on his own, but I just can't do it.

"What happened?" I demand.

"Uh …" He looks down at his hand. I can tell he is choosing his words carefully, which only makes me madder.

"Where were you?" I snap.

Mason finally looks up at me. "Spying on the Sentinels."

"What?"

How did he figure out where the Sentinels were in order to spy on them? Why didn't he tell me? Why would he do something so stupid and risky? A dozen other questions start flying through my mind. They jumble and stick, keeping me from uttering a single one of them.

My hand rubs across my forehead slowly. The desire to walk away is compelling. I know he'd never be able to bandage up his hand on his own, and as angry as I am with him right now, I still can't bear to leave him in pain.

Shoving him toward the stairs, I say, "You talk, I'll bandage. And you better tell me everything."

"I will," Mason says quietly.

At the top of the stairs, we both freeze. Suddenly, I can't stand the thought of being in the bathroom with him again. I could barely handle coming in here this morning on my own. I reach for the door handle, but I can't do it, not with him standing next to me.

"Go down to the kitchen," I command. "I'll get the first aid kit."

Mason nods wordlessly and makes a beeline for the stairs. My breath shudders out of me shakily, painfully. Determined to not be a wimp, I reach for the door knob. That's as far as I get for a few minutes. I feel like an idiot. Tears sting the backs of my eyes, but I refuse to cry over Mason again. Fighting back every emotion, I shove the door open and dig through the cabinet desperately. I'm not even sure I got everything I need when I dart back down the stairs, but I don't care.

When I round the corner to the kitchen Mason is standing at the sink trying to rinse off his injured hand. He winces as he gently rubs away the clotted blood around the cut. Not running over to him kills me. At the same

● ● ●

time, seeing him in pain gives me a kind of sick satisfaction. I don't help him.

As he finishes washing his hand, I open the kit and sort through the bottles and ointments I grabbed for some hydrogen peroxide and antibacterial cream. I'm so focused on not thinking about Mason, I jump when he sits down next to me. He doesn't say a word as he lays his hand palm-down on a towel. I grimace at the cut running from his middle knuckle across his hand to just below where his thumb connects with his wrist. The flesh around the cut is red and swollen.

"How long ago did you cut this?" If it had just happened it wouldn't look so agitated yet.

"About an hour ago," Mason mumbles.

Staring at him angrily, I say, "Then why didn't you come clean it up?"

"I couldn't. I had to wait for the other Sentinels to show up."

"What?" I demand. Then shaking my head, I hold up a hand. "Start from the beginning."

The clippity-clop of Evie bounding down the stairs momentarily distracts us both. She skids to a stop just inside the kitchen door. Her eyes pop open wide at the scene before her. "What's with all the bandages? Is Mason hurt?"

"Cut his hand," I say curtly.

Evie plops down on the stool behind Mason. "How?"

"That's what he was just about to tell me," I snap.

Evie shuts her mouth and places a hand on Mason's shoulder—once she finds it. She jabs him in the ear first, which almost makes me laugh.

I dump hydrogen peroxide over Mason's cut, making him groan, and say, "Start talking."

"After you were attacked in the park, I suspected the Sentinels were watching you more closely than we realized. They must have followed you to the park that night. I didn't remember seeing any cars lurking around, so I wondered if they were using something else, a house maybe, or a camera somewhere."

"So you decided to go hunt them down?" I ask.

Evie frowns. "Mason, that wasn't safe. What if they spotted you, or felt or you or whatever?"

"I kept my distance," Mason argues. He glances down at his hand. The guilt in his expression warns me that he's hiding something.

"Well, did you find them?" Evie asks.

Mason nods. "There was a car parked down the street. He was far enough away not to be noticeable right away, but he was definitely watching the house." Mason pauses and takes a deep breath. "He wasn't the only one, though."

As I smear antibiotic ointment over Mason's cut, my whole body tenses up. Whatever he's about to say is not going to be good. I want to slap Mason every time I see him, but that still doesn't mean I want to lose him.

"I messed around under the lookout car and pulled out some wires so it wouldn't start. That's how I cut up my hand," Mason says gesturing at his now goo-covered hand. "I figured when he tried to start it he'd have to call someone when it didn't work. Who better to call than another Sentinel."

"Did it work?" Evie asks anxiously.

Mason nods slowly. "Yeah. Some other guy drove up and tried to help him. I have pictures, but that wasn't what really freaked me out." Mason flinches as I set a large piece of gauze over his cut. "Have either of you seen the Dewalts in a while?" Mason asks.

Evie and I both stare at him, confused by this sudden change in topics. We both shake our heads. I haven't seen them in a few weeks. They're fairly homebound because of their poor health, so it's not like anyone would really notice if they weren't seen for a few days at a time.

"I haven't either," Mason says looking pained. "When the first guy couldn't fix the car, they called someone else...and he came out of the Dewalt's house."

"What?" I demand.

Mason nods. "I think they're keeping tabs on us from the Dewalt's house."

"What happened to the Dewalts?" Evie asks. He pale skin looks a bit green.

"I don't know," Mason says, "but I'm afraid it might not be good."

"We have to tell Mom and Dad."

Evie nods. "Maybe Mom can call their daughter and ask her if they're alright. Say we hadn't seen them in a little while and were worried.

"That's a good idea," I say. Walking over and knocking on their door is out of the question, even for Mom or Dad. A phone call could at least give us an idea whether or not they're alive still. I don't know them very well, but it makes me sick to think they might have been hurt by these disgusting Sentinels.

Looking up at Mason, I ask, "You said you had pictures. Where are they?"

Now Mason is the one who looks green. "I, uh...check my phone, but I'm not sure if they're on their yet."

"Yet?" Evie asks. Her forehead wrinkles, because that makes no sense at all. If he took pictures, why wouldn't they be on there already?

● ● ●

Evie holds out her hand for Mason's phone. He won't look at her as he hands it over. I watch, suspicious, as she taps through several screens in search of pictures. "There's nothing here," she complains.

The sudden buzzing of the phone nearly makes her drop it. The bizarre thing is, it keeps buzzing, and buzzing, and buzzing. Mason's head drops to his chest. "Check the text messages," he mumbles.

Still confused, Evie taps again. I don't understand why her face screws up in disgust. She looks ready to either throw the phone or hit Mason. She does neither, although depending on what she says, I may not have stopped her from doing the latter.

"Texts from Robin," Evie says with a sour expression. "They're pictures of the Sentinels you were watching, I'm guessing."

"Yeah," Mason says.

From Robin? The tape I was holding snaps down on Mason's hand painfully. He hisses, but doesn't say anything. I yank my hands away from him and hold my hand out for the phone. Evie hands it over dutifully. I don't look at Mason as I flip through the pictures.

The blue sedan isn't the same one we saw watching the house that first time. The guy sitting in it means nothing to me. His average brown hair and eyes match his rather average physique and looks. He wouldn't stand out in a crowd, which I suppose is the point. I keep jabbing at the pictures, moving on to the next one.

The next guy who shows up in another car is only slightly more memorable. His dark hair is cut stylishly and his blue eyes are something that would catch a girl's eye. Other than that, I don't think I'd remember him five minutes after I saw him. His car doesn't look familiar either. That makes me a little sick, because it means there are more of these creeps somewhere.

When I scroll down to the next picture, I gasp and drop the phone on the counter. The blond hair and green eyes staring up at me knock the breath right out of my body. Flashbacks of the night I was attacked skitter through my mind. I wouldn't have even needed to see the scar to know it was him. I don't realize Evie and Mason are crowding around me until Evie reaches in and snatches the phone up off the counter.

"No way!" she shrieks. "I know this guy!"

"You do?" Mason and I both demand.

Evie nods frantically. "He was here last week. He fixed dishwasher. Remember it wasn't draining and Mom called the repair place? This is the guy that showed up to fix it!"

"Are you sure?" Mason asks.

"Positive," Evie says, still shaking her head. "He gave me the willies, and that scar isn't something you forget."

● ● ●

She drops the phone like it's contagious when I hold out my hand for it. I set the phone down in front of Mason. "That's the guy that attacked me in the park."

Mason looks up at me, his face ashen. He doesn't question me. His head falls into his hands. "That's the guy that came out of the Dewalt's house," he says. The agony dripping off each word makes my hands shake. "He's over there right now."

Chapter 28

Forming Plans

Walking back up to my room after a tense conversation with Mom and Dad, I find it impossible to think of anything but the repair guy turned stalker and attacker. I wholeheartedly agree with Dad instituting the buddy system for the foreseeable future. Knowing those guys are across the street spying on us twenty-four-seven makes me feel sick to my stomach.

I hate walking around scared. I want them gone, but I have no idea how to make that happen. Knowing how close they are to catching Mason might be helpful. Figuring out why they want him so bad would be even more of a bonus. Admitting I agree with Robin that they seem to have a special interest in Mason makes me want to throw something, but I fear it's true.

Mason's presence crowds behind me and my whole body tenses. He doesn't say anything. There was a moment when I was bandaging his hand that my anger at him started to calm, but then Robin's texts came through and stirred it back up.

"Why did you have to go with her?" I ask quietly. No doubt he can hear the hurt in my voice.

Mason sighs. "Who else was I supposed to ask? No one was talking to me."

Clenching my jaw, I fight with myself on how to answer that. It doesn't matter that he's right, that I would have sooner poked my eyes out than listen to him. He still should have asked. I deserved the chance to know what he was planning, didn't I?

"We could call him," I say, changing the subject.

"Call who?"

I twist my hands together anxiously. "The repair guy. I'm sure he left his card. We could tell him the dishwasher is broken again …"

"No!" Mason snaps, yanking me around to face him. "Absolutely not. It's too dangerous, Olivia."

"And what you did today wasn't?"

"Robin kept me safe. She kept the Sentinel distracted while I worked."

Shoving away from him, I say, "Robin! I don't care what Robin can do. I want those freaks gone! How long are we supposed to live with them next door?"

Mason blanches and turns away. He shakes his head slowly. "It's too dangerous. We'll find another way."

"What way?" I demand.

He doesn't have an answer. I storm away from him and slam my door behind me. Sleep seems like a distant possibility when I fall onto my bed, but exhaustion sneaks up on me quickly. I wake the next morning face down on my pillow still wearing my clothes from yesterday. Stiff and grouchy, and I drag myself through getting ready for school and skip breakfast entirely.

I'm up so late and take such a long time getting ready, the kitchen is empty when I wander by. I almost walk right past, but a thought stops me and pulls me over to the drawer where Mom keeps important papers. I pull it open quietly and fish through a container filled with various business cards. I find the plumber, the electrician, the guy that replaced a window a few years back, even Mom's hairdresser.

Frustration threatens to boil over when I reach the last business card. Tossing them back down, the force knocks the container to the side. The corner of a green business card peers up at me from under the container. I move it aside carefully, scared and hopeful at the same time, and pick the card up.

Reliable Appliance Repair

I palm the card right away and push the drawer shut. Seconds later, sounds of Evie coming down the stairs send me scurrying for the hall. I step out a few seconds before she hits the last step. Mason trails behind her morosely. I grab my keys off the side table and head for the car, forming plans as I go.

***

As I wait for Hayden to show up for lunch, I pull the card out of my pocket and start dialing before I can talk myself out of it. A man picks up on the third ring.

"Reliable Appliance Repair, how can I help you?"

"Hi, this is Karen Mallory. One of your repairman fixed my dishwasher last week. I can't remember his name, but the dishwasher isn't draining again."

"I'm sorry to hear that, Mrs. Mallory. I can send a technician out this afternoon at no charge to rectify the problem. What time will you be available?"

I gulp, terrified of going through with this. "Any time after three o'clock would be fine, but the closer to three, the better."

Sounds of computer keys being tapped echo over the line. "I could have someone there at three-thirty."

"That would be great," I say, "but could you make sure you send someone different. The last guy obviously didn't solve the problem. I'd rather not have him come again."

"No problem, Mrs. Mallory. Alex will meet you at your house at three-thirty this afternoon."

"Thank you," I say quickly and hang up.

Breathing hard, I struggle to calm myself back down. I wasn't exactly sure what I was going to do with the card when I first stuck in my pocket this morning, but when I overheard Robin asking Mason if they were going to get together to watch the Sentinels again this afternoon, all I had to do was hint at Evie that she should go over to her friend Allison's house after school in order to have the house to myself.

Mason's angry refusal to help me only served to make me more determined to follow through. He did make me reconsider how wise it was to invite my attacker back into the house, though. Requesting someone different still gets me a Sentinel, but one that won't know I recognize him for what he is. Now I just have to figure out what to say to him in order to get some answers.

Before I can think on it too much, Hayden slips into the seat next to me.

"I love that I didn't have to beg you to sit with me today," he says with a grin.

"I'm a girl who keeps her promises." My smile is small and timid, but Hayden grins even wider.

Hayden bites into his burger, but his attention is still mainly on me. He eyes my salad suspiciously. "Please don't tell me you're a vegetarian."

"Huh? No, I just wasn't very hungry today."

He looks unconvinced and pushes his tray closer to me, French fries first. I laugh and take a fry off his plate. He really is a sweet guy.

"How's your side feeling?" I ask.

"Better." He shrugs the question off. "How's your face?"

"Sore, but less puffy at least. These bruises are so gross looking and I keep biting my lip," I say grumpily.

Hayden looks over at me...at my lips specifically. His lips turn up slowly. "You look beautiful, even with a split lip and bruises."

He's lying, but I appreciate the compliment. When I smile at him he sets his burger down and looks over at me. His fingers twitch, as if they want something, but instead he says, "You should see my side. It looks like my little sister spilled watercolors all over me."

"You have siblings?" I ask. I assumed he was an only child after his parents showed up at our house the other night on their own.

Hayden nods. "Two brothers and one sister. I'm the oldest."

"I didn't know that. I only have one sister, Evie."

"I know. I've met her. My brother, Matt, is friends with Aaron."

"I'm sorry," I say without thinking.

Hayden laughs. "Aaron's actually not that bad. A little immature, but a nice kid."

I crinkle my nose in response.

"My brothers thought the bruises and stuff were pretty cool. Lydia, who's five, told me I looked like a zombie," Hayden says.

"You don't look that bad." I chuckle, though, imagining his little sister.

We go back to eating our lunches then. As I munch on lettuce and French fries, I'm surprised to realize that being around Hayden isn't nearly as confusing and awkward as it was only a few days ago. It's actually kind of...nice.

When the bell rings, Hayden grabs both of our trays and carries them to the trash. I wait for him to return before heading out. It's strange to not have Mason by my side as we stalk through the hallways. I know he's never far away, but it's weird to feel so alone. I realize that since I was five I have spent almost every waking minute of my life with Mason. It's a sobering thought I'm not really sure what to do with.

As we approach my class, a goodbye forms on my lips, but Hayden isn't ready to let me go just yet. His hand slips into mine and he pulls me to a stop. Something pushes me to take a step closer to him.

His fingers come up and brush my hair back. Worry creases his forehead. "Are you doing okay?" he asks. "You seemed kind of distracted or upset."

"Just some stuff at home," I say quietly. "I'll be fine."

"Can I call you later?" he asks.

"Um, sure."

Hayden chuckles. "Don't sound so excited."

"No, it's not that," I laugh, "but you don't have to ask permission. You can just call if you want."

He seems surprised by this, but nods his head in acceptance. "Good to know. I'll talk to you later then."

"Okay."

With that, we go our separate ways. I turn toward my next class, but catch sight of Mason watching me from across the hall. He looks positively sick, but I can't let myself be drawn in by him. Not only do I hope he *is* sick, I have no intention of talking to him before I follow through on my plan for this afternoon. Knowing him, he'd somehow guess, and wring all the details out of me.

● ● ●

I yank the door to the classroom open and step inside. The door swings closed behind me, but that hardly means it shuts Mason or the Sentinels out of my mind. I spend the rest of the afternoon distracted by them both.

After the final bell, I take my time at my locker. I want to avoid watching Mason and Robin head off together, but they pass by me in the hall on their way out. I turn away as soon as I see them, but not fast enough for Robin not to catch my eye. I hate the sad look in her eyes, like I'm the one hurting them.

I shove my locker door closed and stalk out to the Jeep. Intent on getting a step closer to ridding ourselves of Sentinels, I drive the short trip back to the house. The house seems unnaturally quiet when I walk in. I'm sure that's just my imagination, but it creeps me out all the same. I busy myself trying to figure out how to make it look like the dishwasher isn't draining.

Given how little I know about the workings of dishwashers, in the end I settle for dumping a pitcher full of water into the bottom of the dishwasher and hope it doesn't disappear before the guy gets here.

The buzz of a text message distracts me for a moment. I check Evie's message saying she made it to her friend's house safely and set my phone down on the counter. A moment later, my heart jumps out of my chest when the sound of harsh knocking shatters the silence.

Walking toward the door, I try to calm my racing heart, but that proves impossible. The pounding only gets worse the nearer I get. I feel like I am about to faint by the time my hand touches the door knob. I stand there quaking for probably a full minute before finally turning the handle and opening the door.

"Hi, can I help you?" I ask. I recognize the guy from the pictures of the Sentinel in the second car. His blue eyes are even more striking in person. They kind of freak me out, to be honest.

"I'm Alex, from Reliable Appliance Repair. We got a call saying your dishwasher was having trouble again."

"Uh, yeah. My mom is running a few minutes late, but she told me to let you in when you got here. The kitchen is right through there," I say, pointing.

I'm not about to turn my back to this guy. I wait for him to step inside and start toward the kitchen before closing the door and following him. He doesn't say much as he walks, but his eyes take in absolutely everything. It's more than a little disturbing.

Heart still racing, I sit down on one of the kitchen chairs and watch him get his tools ready. A few minutes later, I have no idea whether he's fixing the dishwasher or making things worse, but I've had enough of waiting.

"You look familiar," I say. "I feel like I've seen you recently."

Alex—or whoever he really is—shrugs casually. "Can't think of any time we've met before."

"Are you sure?" I decide to push a little harder. "I think it's your eyes. They're so blue. I'm sure I've seen them somewhere before."

Alex turns to look at me. Something seems to be going on inside his head. I have no idea what, but it makes me want to cringe. He sets his tools down and dusts off his hands. When he sits back on his heels, I begin to wonder if this was a really bad idea.

"I think I would have remembered meeting you," he says. "You're a very pretty girl."

"Uh, thanks."

He stands slowly and I begin to *know* this was a really bad idea. I try not to show any signs of fear, even though I want to bolt. Alex steps around the open dishwasher and approaches me slowly. The smile on his face is playing at being seductive. I'm pretty repelled by it, knowing this guy is a killer, but I do my best to pretend I find him appealing.

"When did you say your mom was going to be home?" Alex asks as he leans against the table right in front of me.

"Soon," I say shakily. "She got held up at work."

His hand slides over my cheek, making me want to hurl. I don't move a muscle. This was a *really, really* bad idea. I try to think of something to say that will help me, but before I can, Alex's hand snaps away from my face and around my throat. I lash out immediately, scared out of my mind.

"Next time, don't try to flirt information out of someone, Olivia. You're really quite terrible at it," he laughs.

Choking, terrified, desperate, I still have enough presence of mind to take offense. I slap at his hands even more fiercely. He yanks me off the chair and throws me to the ground. My head rebounds off the tile painfully. Before I can react, Alex has one knee on my chest. Nothing I do budges him. Tears start rolling down my cheeks.

"Why did you call me here?" Alex demands.

"I wanted to know why you're watching my house," I say.

Alex leans down, his face hovering above mine. "You know why we're watching your house."

I shake my head in a panic.

"Yes, you do," he counters. "You know we're looking for your invisible friend, your Aerling."

"I have no idea what you're talking about. Get off of me!"

Alex jerks his knee up and smacks it down on top of me. Every spec of air in my body blasts out and I gasp frantically for a breath I can't catch. Panic grabs hold of me, pouring terror over me like a waterfall.

● ● ●

"Where is the Aerling?" he demands. "We know you have one."

"We don't!"

Alex presses down on me, his lips practically touching my skin. "I want the Aerling, Olivia. Tell me where he is and we'll never bother you again."

"You're a liar," I croak. "You'll kill us after you have what you want."

"No," he snaps, "we'll kill you if we don't find what we want!"

My fingers tear at his hands, desperate to get him off of me. I scratch and claw, throw my knees at him, but nothing works. I hear a noise from the other room and panic, thinking more of his friends have come to find Mason. I nearly lose it when I see Mason scrambling into the kitchen doorway instead.

Fear stronger that I have ever felt in my life grips my heart. My mind races to know what to do. If I warn him, the Sentinel will know he's here and go after him. I would rather let this psycho strangle me than give up Mason.

Mason seems paralyzed as well. He knows what will happen if he tries to help me. Suddenly, his eyes narrow and he takes a step forward.

"No!" I scream. Mason freezes. The Sentinel's hand tightens around my neck, thinking I am talking to him. I try to keep it up. "Leave us alone, please! We don't know anything about an Aerling."

The Sentinel intensifies his control over me. His knee slips off my chest, and for a moment I think I have a chance to escape, but it falls to the side of me so he is straddling me, pinning me helplessly under his grip. I gasp as his weight threatens to crush me. Mason tries to take another step, but I shake my head violently. I can see the panic in his eyes, though. I won't be able to stop him for long.

"Tell me where the Aerling is!" the Sentinel screams.

"I don't know." I gasp again, trying to gain enough breath to mount some kind of attack or escape. I try to buck him off of me, but it barely moves him. The only advantage I gain is that I see my phone on the table. My eyes jerk from Mason to the phone, praying he gets the point.

"How long do you think you'll be able to hide him, Olivia?" Alex says. "You're not a Caretaker. I know what you are. You're the only one that can hear him, talk to him, see him. You won't last. We'll find him, and then we'll kill you both."

Shaking my head, I claw at his face, kick, and try to force him away from me. He fights back. My head slams into the ground as I see Mason skirting around the far side of the kitchen. He'll get me the phone. He'll get me the phone. I repeat that over and over in my mind as Alex and I struggle.

Desperation claws at me as I catch sight of Mason reaching over the table for my phone. I get one hand wedged between me and the Sentinel. My nails dig into the exposed flesh of his chest. My other hand reaches out, praying Mason can get me the phone. Twisting, yanking, I do everything I can to distract him. He grabs a chunk of my hair and yanks my head back until I cry out in pain.

Another shot of agony darts through my right hand as something hits it. The sting of nearly having my hair ripped out almost keeps me from realizing what just happened. My hand slaps frantically across the tile looking for my phone. Alex yanks my head back again, drawing a strangled yelp from me.

The cool, trembling feel of Mason's fingers dropping the phone into my hand almost makes me snatch my hand away. Fear snaps my fingers around the case instead. I don't think. I can't spare a second. The phone slams against my ear desperately.

"Help!" I screech into the phone. "There's a man in my house trying to kill me!"

The Sentinel's eyes whip up to my face. Panic drenches him. His body lurches toward the phone. His fingers tear at me, scratching my face and hands. My free hand slaps at his face. I wedge the phone between my ear and floor so he can't get it.

"I'm at 367 Sycamore!" I yell. "Hurry! Please! He's going to kill me!"

My words freeze the Sentinel. He jumps back as if I just burned him. Scrambling to his feet, he stumbles away from me. "The police can't stop us," he says, but the fear in his eyes calls him a liar.

He backs toward the hall when I lurch up to my feet. I hold the phone against my ear as I stare him down. "They'll be here in two minutes," I say calmly.

His eyes widen. I expect him to attack me again, but he runs, throwing the door against the wall as he bolts into the street. I don't move a single muscle until the sound of his truck has disappeared completely. I am so baffled I can barely even think. Mason throwing his arms around me is barely enough to break through the shock.

"Are you okay?" he demands. His hands start wandering over me, checking for serious injuries. When his hands come back up to my shoulders, he shakes me roughly. "Olivia, are you alright?"

"Yeah," I say slowly.

Mason stares at me, his concern deepening. "Olivia, the police are going to be here any second. We need to figure out..."

"No they aren't," I say numbly.

"What?" Mason asks.

Shaking myself, I hold the phone out to him. Its blank screen confuses him. "Why didn't you call the police?"

"There was no way I could see the phone to dial or even get it to turn on. I couldn't do anything. Pretending was all I had. I didn't even think it would work, but he bought it...and ran away." My face screws up in confusion again. "Why did he run?"

Mason stares at the phone. He looks as confused as I feel. An uneasy feeling settles over the room. "I have no idea," Mason says, "but I doubt it means anything good."

Chapter 29

The Reason

Sitting on Olivia's bedroom floor instead of lying next to her is torture. Torture I deserve for being such an idiot, but torture nonetheless. After the attack, we spent an hour cleaning up the kitchen in silence. I watched her every move, my stomach twisting as new bruises joined the ones already there from the last attack. The urge to storm across the street and tear every Sentinel hiding in there apart was nearly impossible to resist.

Realizing that I would have to leave Olivia to accomplish that—along with the fact that I have no idea how to fight—kept me at bay. When the kitchen was clean, Olivia finally spoke to me, but it was only about what happened. Anything personal got ignored. She tried to pretend my refusal to be more than a few feet away from her annoyed her, but the way her body relaxed when I got closer gave her away.

Thinking about her makes it impossible to resist being next to her. I scoot closer to her bed and curl my hand around hers. She sighs in her exhausted sleep, but doesn't wake up. We spent the rest of the afternoon arguing about the attack. I still thought she should have called the police. Olivia argued that they would start to think something was wrong with us after the break in, her being attacked, and now being attacked again. It would attract attention, something we can't really afford. Plus, neither of us really thought they could do any good against the Sentinels.

Olivia didn't even want to tell her mom and dad, which surprised me, but I agreed. All it will do is make them worry even more. Neither of them has any idea about how to get rid of the Sentinels, either. This whole situation is beginning to feel hopeless.

Every day I hold out hope that I won't get Olivia and her family hurt or killed. I hope that I'll figure out how to stay here past my eighteenth birthday, how to fix what I broke with Olivia. I cling to my hope, but reality edges in closer and closer. Tonight, I feel as if it is about to win. There's only one person left to turn to for answers and hope.

I pull out my phone and open a message to Robin. *Any new info from your parents or grandma?*

It's one in the morning, so I don't hold my breath for a text. I just need something to distract myself with and answers seem like a good distraction. My foot starts tapping after five seconds.

Not much, comes Robin's reply ten minutes later. Followed by, *Sorry*.

My fingers start tapping madly. *Nothing about how I can stay here or why I have 2 go back?*

● ● ●

It's not easy 2 get answers without them figuring it out. It's hard to tell through texts, but I swear she just snapped at me.

I'm not feeling all that polite either. *I need answers, Robin.*

Her response seems to take an eternity. I start to think she must have fallen asleep before I finally get another text.

Something happened, didn't it?

I don't respond right away. It's not about trust. Not exactly. Robin wants answers. She knows she can get them if she pushes hard enough. Pushing could reveal me, though. We both know that's a risk. Olivia would never take a risk like that, but I know I could push Robin far enough if I really wanted to. I just wish I knew what would happen if I did.

Olivia lured a Sentinel 2 the house & he almost killed her.

What!? Robin replies instantly.

Trying to explain that I wasn't in on the plan and Olivia's motivations will take too long through texting. I can tell her more tomorrow. For now, back to the answers.

Can I leave before my eighteenth birthday? I ask.

The pause between my text and her response makes me think my question has rattled her. I can picture her thumbs poised over her phone as her thoughts race.

Why? she finally asks.

Because it may be the only way to protect Olivia.

She has to take you there, remember? Robin responds. I think I detect a bit a bite hidden in her words.

Answer the ? Robin!

I half expect a huffy response, but instead her words feel weighted. *No, U can't leave early, but Olivia may be able to go with you when it's time.*

I nearly drop my phone when I finish reading her text. The breath I just inhaled feels impossibly heavy and incredibly light at the same time. What does that mean? Has Olivia changed her mind about coming with me? That's an all too real possibility. Would I want to take her away from her family like that? She may never be able to come back.

Another question hits me.

I thought U said U hadn't learned anything. I hope the accusing tone travels across the signal.

I didn't want 2 get UR hopes up B4 I knew 4 sure.

I think I believe her. Maybe. Well, I don't disbelieve her enough comment on it. She's the only one still talking to me on a regular basis, so I have to be careful. Tomorrow we'll have plenty of time to talk.

After Olivia pretended 2 call the police, the Sentinel ran off. Any idea why?

Another slow response makes me hope she's taping out a long explanation that makes sense. Nope. All I get is a suspicious, *No clue. Let's talk tomorrow. Going 2 bed now. Really tired. Sorry.*

That, I definitely don't believe. I try texting her again, but after twenty minutes I give in and become very annoyed. She's obviously hiding something from me. Tomorrow is not going to be fun for her if she doesn't start talking as soon as I see her.

I stew over my annoyance for hours, until my mind is eventually drawn back to the attack. I think maybe there are some answers there, something he said perhaps. I replay everything I witnessed over and over again, begging for some kind of clue. My eyes are drifting closed before I latch onto something he said to Olivia.

He tried to convince Olivia that keeping me a secret was too hard because she's the only one who could see or hear me. He'd said earlier that he knew exactly what Olivia was…that she wasn't a Caretaker. He must have been referring to her being my Escort, but that doesn't make sense because Olivia isn't the only one that can hear me.

Exhaustion is begging me to climb up in bed next to Olivia and fall asleep. There's no way that's happening now. This one thought keeps nagging at me. Why would he say that no one else could hear me? As much as I hate the guy for hurting Olivia, he should know about this stuff, right? But he's wrong.

I don't know how long I sit staring at the wall before my wondering changes directions. Myself, Robin, her grandma, we all agreed that Olivia can see and hear me because she's my Escort. I think Robin's grandma was right about that. That hardly explains what I can do with Olivia's parents and Evie. Why can they hear me? It isn't about Olivia being the reason. I think…I think I might be the reason.

Maybe it's like my clothes, how they disappear when I put them on, or my phone when I put it in my pocket. It's not about me touching them. Evie used to love it when I would carry the cat around because it looked like it was flying. The cat didn't disappear like my clothes. I've wondered about this for years, but without Caretakers to explain everything to me, I always just assumed it would never make sense. That's just how it was.

Now, I wonder if my clothes and the things I put in my pockets disappear because I want them to…because I make them disappear. I never wanted the cat to disappear because it made Evie laugh. What if I'm the one controlling this? What if I'm responsible for more than I ever thought I was capable of?

The theory forms slowly, but as it takes hold there is a certain weight that seems to follow it. Yes, Olivia is my Escort. I've never had to *try* to make her see or hear me. She didn't have to accept me in order to see me. Even though I might enjoy having to touch her every time we talk, she hears me from clear across the room.

This thing that makes Olivia special, it didn't transfer to the rest of the house. I think I did something to make them hear me. Something that isn't supposed to happen. My conversation with Robin about abilities I should have already developed comes charging to the front of my mind. Could this possibly be what she was talking about?

If I made Olivia's parents and Evie hear me…can I make them see me too?

Chapter 30

A Wonderful Gift

Riding to school with Olivia and Evie this morning, I consider my next words and actions very carefully. I can now freely admit that lying to Olivia was the absolute stupidest thing I could ever have done. Doesn't do me a lot of good at this point since she pretty much ignores everything I say. I tried a dozen times yesterday to explain, but she refuses to give me even a second to speak. I have no intention of giving up, but I have to be very careful.

Olivia pulls into a parking space and reaches for her door handle. I grab her arm gently, but firmly. Her body stiffens at the contact. The sick feeling in my stomach has to be ignored for now. She won't look at me, and doesn't say a word.

"I won't be in class this morning," I say slowly.

Olivia tries to jerk away from me, but I hold on tightly. She continues to struggle for a few seconds with Evie staring silently. I feel her fingers land on my shoulder so she can listen in. I don't shake her off.

"I need to get some answers …"

"From Robin?" Olivia snaps, still refusing to look at me.

I wish I had any other answer for her, but I don't. "Yes."

Olivia tries to yank her arm away from me, but I won't let go.

"This isn't about Robin," I say, "or me and Robin. There isn't even a *me and Robin*. I just need answers from her."

I watch as Olivia's eyes turn molten. "It sure as hell looked like there's a *you and Robin*," she seethes.

"I was just …"

With strength I'm not prepared for, Olivia wrenches her arm away from me and nearly throws herself out of the car. Her eyes drill into me. "I don't care what you do with Robin, or what answers she has. I'll never trust a word that comes out of her mouth. Not after …" Olivia swipes at her eyes angrily. "She proven more than once that she'll betray her friends if it gets her what she wants."

She slams the door and storms toward the school. Evie gets out of the backseat slowly. She opens my door and pretends to rummage around, giving me time to get out without rousing suspicion. I start to turn away, expecting Evie to ignore me as well. Her gentle touch on my arm stops me.

"What did you mean about you and Robin?" she whispers.

I want to tell Evie everything, hope she'll tell Olivia for me. Not only do I doubt Olivia would believe her, but it's the coward's way to do this. I need to tell Olivia what an idiot I am and beg for her forgiveness myself.

● ● ●

"I made a very bad decision, but I never meant to hurt Olivia. I was trying to protect her. I just went about it in the most idiotic way possible," I admit.

Evie zips up her backpack slowly. "Why would dating Robin protect Olivia? You had to know it would kill her."

Running my hands through my hair, I sigh heavily as my shoulders slump. "I guess I didn't realize how much it would hurt her. I've spent so much time knowing she doesn't love me like I love her that I thought it would be easy for her to forget one kiss and move on, be safe. I never expected…this."

Evie squeezes my hand softly. "I don't think she realized how much she loved you until she saw you with Robin, either." Her voice is sad. It adds to the weight in my heart. She looks up at where she estimates my head to be. "You need to explain to Olivia. This is killing her, thinking she's lost you."

"I've tried, but the second I start talking to her she runs or yells at me. I don't want to drag you into the middle of this, Evie, but…could you try…I mean, just try to convince her that I still love her, and if she ever stops hating me long enough to listen, I'll explain everything?"

"I'll try," Evie says, "but it may take a while."

I cringe inwardly. Time isn't something I have a lot of. If nothing else, I'll sit on Olivia. I'll force her to listen to me. I have to try.

But first, I need to deal with Robin. She is the worst liar I've ever met, and last night is not something I'm going to forget. I march toward her first hour class. By the time I get there, class has already started and there's no way for me to get inside without causing a stir, so I stand in front of the window staring at her.

There's no way she doesn't see me, but she keeps her eyes trained neatly on the whiteboard. Her fingers move precisely as she takes notes. I watch every stroke, waiting for her to run out of words. She's so focused, she jumps when the bell rings and knocks her water bottle off her desk. Some kid I don't know sets it back on her desk and moves on without speaking. Robin fumbles through getting her things back in her bag, moving slowly toward the door.

She tries to pretend me latching onto her arm and dragging her through the halls doesn't affect her. Nobody finds it odd that she's tripping over her own feet and bumping into people. It's Robin, after all. I yank her out to the empty football field and gesture harshly for her to take a seat on the bleachers. She does.

Sitting down next to her, I try to limit my frustration to only the portion she deserves and not everything simmering inside of me. I'm not terribly successful.

"You lied to me last night." The heat in my voice makes her shrink in on herself.

Robin squirms a minute before answering. "I know."

"Why?" I demand.

Her bottom lip quivers. "Because…I couldn't tell you how I knew about Olivia going with you, maybe, or why mentioning the police scared away the Sentinel." She drops her head into her hands.

I don't give her an easy way out. The weight of my body sitting down next to her makes the old bleachers creak. My presence seems to have a similar effect on Robin. She groans as she squeezes her head.

"I told my parents…about you."

Every cell in my body becomes electric. Energy sizzles across my skin as panic begins flooding through my veins. I am almost too freaked out to speak. Somehow, my voice erupts of its own free will. "You what?" I scream.

"I had to, Mason. It was the only way to find out what you needed to know, and it's okay. They promised not to tell anyone. None of the other Caretakers know. Only my mom and dad, I promise."

Robin sits trembling at my feet, her eyes wide and fearful as she waits for me to respond. Her words jumble in my head. I can't seem to figure out what they mean. The pounding need to act, to run, is overpowering everything else. I have to force myself to breathe and think in order to respond.

"What?"

Okay, not much of a response, but it's all I can manage at the moment. I feel like I am on the verge of losing it completely.

"I tried asking my grandma more, but she hasn't been well the past few days. I tried asking my parents, but they got suspicious right away. I had to tell them or they were going to pack up and make me move again. I couldn't leave not knowing if you were okay." Robin's voice is pleading, begging me to understand.

I don't know if I understand. I don't know if I can forgive her for breaking her promise, shattering my trust. Right now, I don't even want to speak with her, but I have to know.

"Why didn't they tell anyone? How do you know they didn't? What if they've sent someone to come get me already?"

More questions roll through my mind, but Robin speaks before I can ask them. "I told them about what happened to your Caretakers, about you being special, about Olivia being your Escort. I told them that you would never leave Olivia." She looks down at her hands. "I told them I'd leave if they told anyone else."

● ● ●

Her shoulders shrug. "I don't think me threatening to leave made half as much impact as your story. They got really scared, but they agreed that being with Olivia is probably the safest place you can be right now. Being with her protects you somehow. My mom wasn't sure on the specifics, but she said she'd find out more. So long as the Sentinels only have suspicions, and don't actually try to take you, they'll leave you alone."

"But if something changes, they'll swoop in and abduct me?" I growl.

"It was the best deal I could make," she says quietly.

I am furious with her. The anger pouring off of me feels hot enough to scorch. Stuffing it away in favor of answers…I can't find a word to describe how impossible that seems. Somehow, I do it, enough to unclench my jaw and speak, anyway.

"What does this have to do with the police scaring away the Sentinels?"

Robin's pale skin turns green. "Well, when I said my parents agreed not to tell anyone, that wasn't exactly, technically true." She holds up her hands when I take an angry step toward her. "There are specially trained policemen all over the country, all over the world. They're Caretakers by birth, but they are chosen to protect all Aerlings rather than one in particular."

"Chosen?" I demand.

She nods slowly. "They're Caretakers who are more sensitive to differences in people. They can identify Sentinels, and when it comes to Sentinels, Caretaker law supersedes everything else. They'll kill them without a second thought, and once they ID them, they never forget. They'll hunt them down relentlessly. My parents told them about the guys watching your house."

I sit back down silently, struggling to process everything.

"Was the Sentinel that came to your house young?" Robin asks.

I nod mutely.

"They're usually more scared of the police than the older Sentinels. The older ones are better at getting away."

Shaking my head, I try to get my scrambled thoughts in order. It doesn't work. I'm going to have to sort all of this out later. Right now, I need another answer.

"What about Olivia going with me?" I demand.

Robin all but sulks at this question. "It was my dad who found out about it. He said Escorts have the ability to cross the barrier between our world and yours. There wasn't a lot of information, but he knew stories of Escorts disappearing along with their Aerling. It may be that they can stay there if they want, or it could mean …"

"It could mean they died trying to get some poor, confused Aerling like me through the barrier."

Robin nods grimly.

"You have no idea which one it is?" I ask, feeling the panic creeping back in.

"Not yet," Robin responds.

With nothing else to offer me by way of answers, and me too angry and confused to think, we part ways. I go through the rest of the day in a haze. Olivia still isn't interested in talking to me, but a concerned expression graces her face every time she looks at me.

The ride home from school is only slightly less pleasant as I tell Olivia everything Robin told me. The news about Escorts being able to cross the barrier between worlds brings a spark of hope to her eyes no matter how hard she tries to hide it.

Finding out that Robin told her parents…I have to say I have never seen Olivia turn that shade of purplish red before. I don't say a word as she storms through the house, marches up to her room and shuts the door quietly. I wait by her door, listening to her vent her frustration. I had no idea Olivia knew that many swear words. I'd laugh if I weren't afraid she was going to kill me for trusting Robin.

Eventually, Olivia's bedroom door reopens. I step back, not eager to be in her path. She looks up at me and says, "We will discuss this after dinner with Mom and Dad. Until then, if I hear her name, I think I might punch you in the face."

The other thing that has been consuming my mind today—what little was left idle after talking to Robin—has been latched firmly onto the theory I came up with last night. I need to test it. I *have* to test it. Not alone, though.

"I have something I want to try," I say slowly, "and I want you to see it if it works."

Olivia looks at me, confused with the sudden change in direction. One eyebrow crooks up at me, but she nods her head sharply. She may hate me right now, but she's never been able to turn down witnessing me do something interesting.

Olivia follows me down toward the kitchen in silence. I heard Olivia's mom come in a few moments ago. The sound of bags rustling is a sure sign that she's in there putting away groceries. When I stop at the entrance to the kitchen, Olivia stops as well.

I really have no idea how to go about this. I try to understand how I make my clothes disappear, but not the cat. It's my choice what becomes invisible and what doesn't. Even the rest of the family being able to hear me—I don't think there was some preset rule saying that they had to accept my existence as fact before they could hear me. I think *I* made that rule, because I was scared.

● ● ●

174

There is no guidebook for this. All I can think to do is focus. My thoughts zero in on Olivia's mom, on her being able to hear me. She's already accepted me. I have no fear of being revealed to her because I know she loves me. I *want* her to hear me, to break the need to have a physical link that protects me from her. I don't need to be protected from her.

"Karen."

Her movements stop. Her head quirks to one side as if she's not sure what just happened.

"Karen, can you hear me?" I ask.

She jumps. Her eyes dart to her shoulders. Her hands brush along her arms, up to her shoulders, but she feels nothing. Spinning around, she spots Olivia. She looks vaguely alarmed as she tries to guess where I might be.

"Mason?" she asks quietly. "Where are you?"

"I'm standing next to Olivia," I say.

Her eyes widen, but they begin to fill with excitement. "You are? But how can I hear you?"

"I think I could have let you hear me this whole time, I just didn't realize it."

Slowly, her feet carry her across the kitchen to stand right in front of me. There are tears gathering in her eyes. "Can I...?"

My eyes close. I know what she wants to ask. Can she see me too? It's the same question on my mind. I want to know the answer as badly as she does. Closing my eyes, I try again to focus. It seems harder to do this time until Olivia slips her hand into mine. For a moment, I don't feel her hostility. I feel her love and encouragement, and it gives me the strength to allow myself to be vulnerable in a way I never thought I could be.

I watched the first family I knew be murdered in front of my eyes. Being invisible was the only thing that saved me. It protected me. I've used it as a shield all these years, not knowing I could let it down, not trusting anyone but Olivia enough to even want to. Knowing that my time here is so limited pushes me even further. I want the woman who has raised me, protected me, loved me, to finally see me and know me.

Peace settles over me as I let go of the fear of being hurt, of losing those I love. My fingers tighten around Olivia's. She responds in kind and I hear her mom gasp. My eyes snap open to see her crying. A second later, her arms reach out and wrap me in a massive hug.

"Mason!" she cries out joyfully. She pulls back enough to look at me. "Look at you! You look just how I imagined you would!"

Surprised, I ask, "I do?"

She smiles and presses her hands against my cheeks. "Of course you do. Look at your kind eyes. This is the smile I pictured every time you pulled a

● ● ●

prank. The way you hold yourself, so strong and ready to protect. This is such a wonderful gift," she says tearfully.

Her arms wrap around me again. I smile as she laughs and cries at the same time. My eyes drift over to Olivia in wonder. The smile she wears sinks through me to my core. It's the first time she's looked at me with something other than anger in days. I am desperate to hold onto the moment, but Evie comes bounding down the stairs, drawing everyone's eyes.

"What's going on?" she asks. "And who on earth is Mom hugging?"

Chapter 31
Any Hint

I am completely drained. The emotional ups and downs of today have sapped my strength. Sitting on the back porch watching Dad throw baseballs to Mason, actually knowing where to throw them for once since he can see him now, makes me smile tiredly. It's a small smile, though, as I try to sort through everything that has happened today.

By far, the biggest hurdle today has been not driving over to Robin's house and beating the living daylight out her. My fingers clench over the armrests of the deck chair. I breathe in slowly as Dad throws the ball back to Mason with a laugh. It hits smack in the middle of the glove. I smile again and relax my hands.

This...watching Mason interact with my family like he's no different than us...it's the only thing that has stopped me from killing Robin. I never knew playing catch could be so beautiful.

"Pretty awesome, right?" Evie asks as she plops down next to me.

"Amazing," I say.

Evie grins as Dad throws a wild pitch and teases Mason for not catching it. Yesterday, he would have had no idea whether or not Mason was near enough to attempt catching the ball. They both laugh and Dad throws an arm around Mason before they step back and resume their game of catch.

"You were right about Mason," Evie says. "He's gorgeous."

A few days ago, I would have been happy to gush over Mason. Today, my body tenses up. Hurt, confusion, and uncertainty swim through my mind. He said there was nothing going on between him and Robin, but he held her hand! He walked away from me. Why would he do that?

Noticing my reaction, Evie's body stills. She sits quietly for a moment. I watch her bite the corner of her lip. Her fingers wind together. "Have you talked to Mason about it?" she asks.

I stare at her incredulously. "Why would I?"

"He might...he might have a reason for what he did." Her heads dips, as if she's not convinced of what she's saying. Well, neither am I!

"Nothing Mason can say will erase what he did."

I expect anger to fill my voice, but I'm surprised to hear the words come out sounding defeated. An ache builds in my chest. I don't want to be angry with Mason. I want him to take me in his arms and hold me, tell me all the insane events of the last few weeks will disappear if I just wish it hard enough. I don't want to feel such intense pain every time I look at him, but I can't let go of the hurt.

◦ ◦ ◦

Evie shifts in her chair. Her eyes dart up to me before dropping again. "I think you should talk to him."

"You were as pissed at him as I am yesterday. Why the change of heart? Just because you can see him now, it doesn't change anything," I argue. Maybe this is too overwhelming for her to hold onto her anger, but it isn't for me.

"It's not about seeing him," Evie says sadly. "It's about the truth."

Part of me argues that I should just brush her off. I want to walk away and not let myself feel any sympathy for Mason. A much smaller, infinitely more fragile part of me is begging for any shred of hope I can find.

"The truth?" My voice is weak and trembling.

Nodding, Evie looks up at me. "He said...he said he was trying to protect you the only way he knew how. I don't know what he meant by that. He seemed to think it would be better if he told you himself."

Evie touches my arm gently. "He told me it was the worst mistake he's ever made and when you're ready, he'll explain everything."

"Protect me?" I choke out. My lungs constrict, refusing to take in air. "But he...he kissed me, and not just a peck on the cheek. He *kissed* me. The kind of kiss I will never, ever forget. The kind that spawns an addiction with one touch. It was a kiss that I can't get out of my mind no matter how hard I try!"

My hands press against my face, holding hostage emotions and tears alike. I refuse to cry over Mason again. I refuse!

"And then he walked away like it never happened, like it meant nothing," I whisper. "Does he not understand how much that hurt?"

"He does now," Evie says, "but I don't think he did at the time."

The fire I felt in that instant reignites as I think about Mason's lips pressing hungrily to mine. Terrible heat spreads through my body. I know he felt it too. It wasn't just me.

"How could he not know?" I ask quietly.

Evie's eyes slip past me to Dad and Mason. I don't know what she's thinking, but her expression flashes between a smile and a frown. Her face echoes the turmoil she must be feeling. When she looks up at me, her eyes are filled with careful determination.

"You know Mason is in love with you, right?" she asks.

My face scrunches. "He was, maybe."

Evie shakes her head. "There's no maybe, no was. He *is* in love with you. Desperately."

I don't say anything. I don't want to contradict her, because I want it to be true so badly, but I just don't know if it is anymore.

"Are you in love with Mason?" Evie asks.

Maybe saying no out loud will make this less painful. Maybe it will make it true. It's a foolish hope. "Yes," I say, almost a whisper.

"Does Mason know that?" Evie asks.

I wrinkle my nose at her, not because I think she's being a snot, but because I realize I don't know the answer to that question. Evie shakes her head slowly.

"Mason said something to me today. He said he's spent so much time knowing you don't love him the way he loves you that he thought it would be easy for you to forget one kiss and move on so you could be safe." She holds up her hands apologetically. "I don't know what he meant about being safe, but you're lying to yourself if you think the rest of it isn't true."

"But ..." My voice trails off.

"Maybe things between you two have been inching closer to something more physical, but you've never given him reason to think he'd break your heart if he backed off. Sure you guys kissed, and even if it was as amazing as you make it sound, you ran away from him, Olivia."

My throat tightens painfully. I look over at Mason feeling like I suddenly can't breathe. My eyes dart back to Evie.

"I don't know what Mason found out, but whatever it was it convinced him that you'd be better off without him. The way you've acted toward him made him believe you'd be able to brush it off and get on with life. With Hayden, apparently," Evie says, grumbling that last part.

"I just…things just started to change and I…he didn't give me time, I mean …" A million thoughts jumble in my head and only gibberish comes out.

Sitting back in her chair, Evie reaches out a hand and takes mine in hers. "I know you're hurt, but you know Mason better than anyone else. Does all but confessing his love for you and then skipping off into the sunset with Robin really sound like something he would do?"

"But he did," I argue.

Evie gives me a stern look.

"No," I say, "it doesn't sound like Mason."

Squeezing my hand, Evie says, "Then I think you should talk to Mason and find out what's really been going on."

The anger and pain I have been keeping close company with the last few days begins to fade. Slowly, it is replaced by concern. "Did he give you any hint about why he did this?"

Evie shakes her head. "All he said was that he was trying to protect you."

A terrible thought occurs to me and my fingers strangle Evie's. "What if he knows something bad is going to happen to him? What if he's trying to distance himself from me?" Dread sinks into the very deepest parts of my soul. "Evie, what if he dreamed something?"

"Has he had any nightmares the past few nights? I know you're the only one that can hear him, and I know you usually end up in his room when they come. Has he mentioned anything?"

Guilt like I have never known assaults me. I nearly break down right there on the porch. "Yes," I whisper, "he's had nightmares the past few nights, but I don't know what they were about. Oh, Evie, I heard him yelling, but I refused to go to him. I made him suffer because I was so angry with him. How could I be so cruel?"

Evie grimaces, but pats my arm. "Well, under the circumstances, I think you'd have to be a saint to be willing to get up in the middle of the night and go comfort the guy who stomped on your heart." She shrugs apologetically.

Mason would have done it for me if the situation were reversed. I know he would have, but I was too stubborn and vindictive. As I laid awake the past few nights listening to him cry out, part of me was glad he was scared and alone. Don't get me wrong, I had to nearly tie myself to the bed to stop myself from going to him, but a small part of me felt like he deserved it.

I close my eyes and focus for just a moment on what a horrible person I have been the last few days. The ache I feel when I think of Mason settles in deep, chastising me for ever taking any enjoyment from his pain. I should have seen that something was wrong, that the Mason I knew would never do something so horrible to a person just because he could. I was too wound up in my own pain to realize something had him so scared he was willing to lie to me and hurt me.

Taking a deep breath in, I resolve to set things right.

"Hey, everyone," Mom says cheerfully as she steps out onto the porch. "Dinner is ready."

I watch with a small smile as her eyes find Mason and watch him all the way to the door. The grin on her face is infectious. She's so happy just to watch him walk! She and Dad clasp hands briefly as he walks by, but Mom slides an arm around Mason's shoulders and ushers him into the house. I look over at Evie and notice she too can't seem to stop staring at Mason.

"I'll talk to him after dinner," I say to her.

Her expression brightens. "Thank goodness." She turns to me and grins. "I already thought he was pretty darn near perfect when he was invisible. Add in actually being able to his gorgeous self...you better snatch him up before somebody else does."

That's exactly what I intend to do. Smiling, I don't say that to Evie. Instead, I say, "Come on, let's get some dinner."

We both head back into the house and make our way to the kitchen. Everyone else is already seated and Mom is dishing out chicken cordon bleu. There is a seat next to Mason, and one on the opposite side. Lately, I have taken to sitting as far away from Mason as I can get. Evie doesn't even ask me where I want to sit. She just heads around the table, leaving the seat next to Mason open.

When I sit down next to him, he freezes. His chest stops moving, no air going in or out. It takes a few seconds before he looks over at me with a strained expression. It takes a little effort for me to smile at him, but I manage it half-convincingly. He stares at me for a moment before the corner of his mouth twitches up.

That's about as much as I can handle at the moment, so I turn to grab a plate from Mom and stick a piece of chicken in my mouth. We're halfway through dinner—a meal filled with chatter mainly directed at Mason—when the sound of a car nearing the house steals all the life out of the room. With everything that's happened lately, and the fact that Mom hasn't been able to get a hold of the DeWalt's daughter to find out if they're alright, anyone approaching the house unexpectedly makes us very wary.

All eyes go to the window above the kitchen sink. Fears of Sentinels coming to kill Mason stiffen my body. The blue four door truck doesn't look familiar, but I choke on my food when I see Hayden step out on the sidewalk.

Chapter 32

Everything Winks Out

"What day is it?" I demand of everyone at the table once the hunk of chicken stuck in my throat gets washed down with water.

"Friday," Evie says with a confused expression. "Why?"

How could I forget? My heart rate skyrockets as I realize Hayden is here to pick me up for our date! My eyes dart over to Mason. His tight expression kills me!

I watch Hayden start walking up the driveway. My stomach twists painfully.

Dad looks over at me and says, "Were you expecting Hayden tonight?"

"Uh, yeah ..."

"For?" Mom prompts.

"For our date," I say quietly.

Everyone freezes. Dad looks rather shocked. Mom scrunches her nose. Evie's eyes bug. None of their reactions draw my attention as much as Mason's. I cringe as his head drops. Hayden's knock sounds on the door, bringing Mason's eyes up to mine. The agony holding his body tight kills me.

I turn to Mom and ask, "Can you get the door?"

Then grab Mason's hand and yank him up from his chair. "I need to talk to you."

Mason doesn't object as I tow him through the hall to the kitchen. When we're safely away from the front door, I drop his hand. It's not that I don't want to touch him right now. I just can't think being so close to him. I take a step back and look up at Mason.

Clearly confused, Mason doesn't say anything. He just waits.

"Mason, I'm sorry. I forgot Hayden was coming tonight."

He shakes his head. "You don't have to be sorry. I'm the one that screwed up. I have no right to hold you back."

"No, Mason, I think I screwed up too. Evie told me you wanted to talk, and I want to hear everything, but I think I need to go with Hayden right now."

"Olivia?" Mom calls from the hall, her voice questioning.

I glance at the hall, but my eyes are pulled back to Mason. "Just a minute," I yell to Mom.

Turning back to Mason, I sigh in frustration. "I don't want to go, but...I feel bad being mean to Hayden when he's been so nice to me, and I'm pretty sure he still thinks I'm being abused, and ditching out at the last minute might make him more suspicious."

"What? Why would Hayden think you're being abused?" he demands.

"Uh…it's a long story." I shake my head and grab Mason's hand. "Just, um, wait for me, okay?"

"Of course," Mason says.

I throw my arms around him quickly. "Thanks, and sorry."

As I pull away, it's hard to make my eyes leave him. It feels good to let go of my anger at him, but there's still something he's hiding from me. Anxiety prickles around me as I finally exit the kitchen. What made Mason lie to me in the first place? I approach the hallway afraid to find out.

The smile that spreads across Hayden's lips makes me stumble. Mom looks over at me curiously, not sure what's going on.

"There you are," she says with one eyebrow raised. Her head tilts to one side as if she's waiting for an explanation.

"Thanks for keeping Hayden company, Mom. Sorry I took so long." That last part is directed toward both of them.

Hayden is the first to answer. "It's no problem, but we better get going if we're going to make it to the movie on time."

"Oh, of course."

"What time will you be back?" Dad asks as he comes up behind Mom. I see Evie leaning against the kitchen doorframe, her face pinched as she stares at me.

Hayden puts his arm around my shoulder casually. "I'll have her back before ten, if that's okay."

Mom glances up at Dad, the corner of her mouth twitching a bit. "We're supposed to be over at the Harpers by 9, but that should be okay, don't you think?"

"Uh, yes, that should be fine."

Hayden seems to catch onto the fact that something is a little off. "If you're worried about Evie being here alone, she can always come with us," he offers.

"Oh no," Mom says quickly, "Evie can come with us. The Harpers have a daughter her age. You two have fun."

Her smile seems a little tight, but it's convincing enough for Hayden. He smiles. "Well, you guys enjoy your evening. I promise I'll look after Olivia."

With that, he takes my hand and leads me out the front door before I can say anything. He's opening the passenger door for me before I shake myself and wake up. I don't know what else to do but climb up into the truck and buckle myself in. Half a dozen thoughts run through my mind as I watch him walk around to the driver's side.

Hayden has been the one bright spot in my life the last few days. He is a decent, sweet guy. And I have to admit that he is very handsome. My interest in Hayden was more survival instinct that actual romance, but I know it's real for him.

As he climbs in with a smile, I'm not sure if I've used him the last few days, or just leaned on him. To be honest, I have so little experience with relationships or even friends that I have no idea what I'm doing. Hayden is a great guy, and I don't want to hurt him, but I know I would never choose him over Mason. Whatever Mason is lying about …

Nothing could be bad enough that it would break us apart. I can't let Hayden think there is a future between us when I know there isn't. I may be nearly clueless about relationship etiquette, but I know that one at least. I have to tell him.

"Hayden," I start.

He looks over at me with a smile so sweet and kind that I can't go on. My chest hurts as I look at him. He waits expectantly. My willpower caves to his warmth. I'll tell him after the movie.

Forcing a smile, I say, "Thanks for picking me up."

Hayden grins. "No problem." His hand squeezes mine, but doesn't linger. "I'm glad you came. I was almost sure you were going to back out."

If he only knew.

"It's, uh, nice to get out of the house," I say.

"Yeah," Hayden says, "it sounded like you're parents are still pretty worried about you and Evie being on your own. I'm sure the mugging really rattled them."

"Uh huh."

Sure, let's go with that. It's better than him thinking my parents are abusive and controlling. By the sideways look he gives me, I get the impression that concerns about them hurting me are still swimming around in his head.

I breathe a sigh of relief when we pull into the parking lot of the theater a moment later. It feels like I am suffocating in the truck. I jump out and breathe in a steadying breath. The tips of my fingers twitch as I walk slowly to the back of the truck to meet Hayden. He, on the other hand, is grinning.

Quickly, I fold my arms across my chest. I don't want to hurt his feelings and pull away if he tries to hold my hand. Better to take away the option. Or so I think. His arm settles easily around my shoulders. He keeps it casual, like he might sling an arm around a buddy. I'm not that easily fooled, though. I'm pretty sure that if I give him any signs that I could handle more,

● ● ●
184

he'd pull me against him like I have seen so many other couples do. Like Mason has done with me, but I was too blind to realize what it meant.

Hayden doesn't seem to feel the awkwardness I do as we walk up to the ticket window. I shiver when his arm falls away to pay for our tickets. Thinking quick, I step away from him and pretend to look at the "Coming Soon" posters lining the wall. When he turns away from the counter with tickets in hand, I pull the door open and wave him through.

All the way to through the concession line and to our seats, I manage to keep a small buffer between us. The previews are already rolling by the time we sit down, and I hope that rules out conversation. Just like the rest of this night, luck is just not in my favor.

"Are things any better at home?" he asks quietly.

"What?" I try to sound casual, but the anxiety in my voice is hard to miss.

"Since we ran into each other at the basketball park, I mean. I know you didn't want to talk about it, but I…I've been worried about you, Olivia." He looks over at me seriously. If I was a normal girl, I'm sure the look would melt me to the core. "Things seemed really tense at your house when I picked you up."

My mouth opens, but what am I supposed to tell him? My invisible friend, who has been living with us for twelve years, is being hunted by a group of wackos who may have killed our neighbors and want to kill Mason as well? I want to bang my head against something. When did everything get so screwed up?

Hayden's brow furrows at my lack of reassurance. He looks away for a moment, then surprises me by reaching up and pushing down the high collar of the shirt I'm wearing. Blood drains from my body, turning my fingers icy.

"I noticed these yesterday," he says. The pain in his eyes tears at me. "They aren't from the mugging. I know because I memorized every bruise that creep gave you. These…Olivia, it looks like someone had their hands around your neck."

I push his hand away from my throat. I tried to cover them up. When did he see them? Panic whirls through my mind as I try to come up with some kind of believable excuse for the strangulation marks on my neck. Nothing comes to mind and my stomach plummets to my shoes.

The movie starts. I stare straight ahead. Can this night get any worse? Now if I tell Hayden that I can't see him anymore, he'll think it's because of this. He'll become even more suspicious, and even though he hasn't moved on his suspicions yet doesn't mean he won't. He's a good guy, an honest guy. The type of guy who would tell someone what he thinks is happening to me in order to protect me.

I can't let him tell anyone that my parents are abusing me. Not only is it not true, it would draw attention, it would mean letting people into our house to investigate. How would we know if they were real social workers or Sentinels in disguise? The Caretakers have people working in law enforcement. Social services would be a perfect place to hide a bunch of Sentinels.

My head falls back against the seat as all my energy abandons me. Everything is such a huge mess right now and I have no idea how to fix things! My gut tells me it's only going to get worse, too. Mason is still hiding secrets. More than the threat of Hayden making false claims against my parents, I am terrified of what he is going to tell me.

Hayden stays silent through the entire movie. What feels like forever later, the credits begin to roll. I have no idea what we just watched. I just want to get out of here. I jump up from my seat and power past Hayden. The doors loom in front of me like an escape hatch, but as soon as I push through them, Hayden grabs my arm and yanks me to a stop.

"Olivia, what is going on?" he demands.

I shake my head, scared and frustrated.

When I try to pull away from him, he grabs my other arm and pins me against the wall. He isn't rough, just firm. There is no anger in his eyes. The depths of his concern for me would be bliss if the situation were as simple as he thought it was. Part of me wants to blurt everything out, the real truth, and dump my problems on him, but I know I could never do that.

"Olivia," Hayden says more softly, "please tell me what's going on. It's been killing me not say anything, not confronting you about this. I want to respect the fact that you don't want to talk about it, but I'm scared that someone is hurting you and I can't stand by and let it keep happening. Please just tell me the truth. Are your parents hurting you?"

I slump against the wall. "No, Hayden, my parents are not abusing me. This has nothing to do with them."

His face wrinkles. I can tell he wants to believe me, but he just can bring himself to do it. "Someone gave you those bruises. I want to know who."

"The same guy who gave me these bruises," I say, pointing at the lingering yellow-brown stain on my cheek."

"What?" Hayden asks. He shakes his head, confused or maybe angry because he thinks I'm lying to him.

I am, but I can't help it. The only idea I can come up with rolls off my tongue with abandon.

"The guy from the park, he attacked me again, at my house this time. He must have followed me home, or maybe he was following me from the beginning, I don't know. He knocked on the door and I was stupid and didn't look to see who it was first. I thought maybe it was Robin because she said she might come by. He pushed the door into me and grabbed me. I couldn't get away. I don't know what he was planning to do, but my mom pulled into the driveway and he ran out the back."

"Did you call the police? Are they watching your house? No wonder your parents were so freaked about you going out tonight and leaving Evie at home." Hayden's grip on my arms becomes less restraining and more of a caress. He steps closer to me and looks down at me worriedly. "What did the police say? Do they have any idea who this guy is?"

"I…didn't call the police."

I'm not sure why I admit that to him. When his eyes fly wide, I wish I could take it back.

"What? Why not?"

"Because, he said he'd hurt my family if I did," I say quietly. While not exactly what happened, the threat is there all the same. I reach up and touch Hayden's shoulder softly. "I don't know who this guy is, or what he wants, but he knows my name, knows where I live, and I don't know what to do about it. I don't know how to get him to leave me alone, but I'm scared he'll come back."

Hayden draws me against his chest. His heavy breaths pulse against my cheek. "Olivia, I'm so sorry. I know you're scared, but you have to tell the police. They can have someone watch your house. You won't be able to watch for him every second."

"He meant it when he said he'd hurt them, Hayden. I can't tell anyone."

Pain etches his features. I can tell he wants to argue with me until I give in, but I won't. To be honest, I don't know if we can trust the police now that we know Caretakers are hiding out in their ranks, loyal to Caretaker law over anything else. What if they find out about the second attack and decide Mason is in too much danger? They'll take him away from me.

My shoulders start to shake. I can't let them take him away. I can't lose Mason. I just can't. Hayden's arms tighten around me painfully. He isn't the one I want to have his arms around me right now, but I just want this all to be over. I want my life back, my friend back. I want to stop living under a cloud of fear. I want to be with Mason always.

"Olivia," Hayden croons as he sweeps tears from my cheeks, "everything is going to be okay. I won't let anyone hurt you, okay? We'll figure this out."

I pull out of thoughts of Mason and feel the weight of guilt settle on my shoulders. I shouldn't be dumping this on him. It will only put him in danger if the Sentinels think he has some idea of who they are. I try to shake my head at him, but he won't have anything to do with it. His hands press against my cheeks to stop my head from shaking away his promise.

"I won't let anything happen to you, Olivia."

Before I can change his mind, his mouth presses against mine. Without warning, every thought drains from my head. The gentle pressure of his lips eases away my fear. I start to respond, moving my mouth with his, but reality slaps me in the face a moment later and I pull away from him wide eyed.

Hayden stands back, startled and breathing heavy. The question in his eyes haunts me.

"I'm sorry," I blurt out.

His hands fall to his side. "I didn't...I mean." Seemingly at a loss, he scrubs his hands through his hair and groans. "Olivia, I'm so sorry. I thought...I didn't mean to upset you."

"You didn't," I start. No. I start over. "It's not that, Hayden. I'm not mad or anything. You're an amazing guy ..."

"But?"

"But," I say, feeling sick to my stomach, "I should tell you why I ended up at the basketball park that day."

Hayden leans against the wall. The way his body sags against the bricks makes it obvious he knows this won't be good news. I feel horrible for making him feel like this, but I know what I want, who I want. I won't string him along and hurt him like that.

"I have this friend," I begin. Hayden grimaces. I struggle to continue. "We've been friends almost all our lives, and things had started to change between us lately. Well, I guess things changed for him a while ago, but I didn't realize it at first. I waited too long, and when he told me how he felt, I freaked out. I didn't understand how much I cared about him in time. Not until...not until I saw him with another girl and realized I was in love with him. I ran away, and that's how I ended up at the park."

"And you're still in love with him," Hayden finishes, sounding defeated.

I nod quietly. "I'm so sorry, Hayden. I never meant to lead you on or use you. I just needed a friend, and I didn't have anyone else." I bite my bottom lip as tears start to threaten. "For a while, I thought maybe I could...maybe moving on was possible, but I can't. Not yet. I'm so sorry."

"Who is he?" Hayden asks. "I've never even seen you eat with anyone at lunch before Robin showed up." His eyebrows inch up slowly. Something seems to click in his mind, but I can't imagine what it is. "Is your friend, is it Robin?"

My eyes widen. "What? No! You think I'm into girls?"

Hayden looks trapped. "No, I mean, I didn't…no. It's just that she's the only person I've ever seen you hang out with. I didn't mean to suggest…I'm just a little lost right now."

"Robin has nothing to do with this. We're not even that good of friends, for crying out loud. The guy I'm talking about, he doesn't live here," I lie. "His parents are good friends with mine, but they're a military family. They live overseas right now. They came to visit, and all of this just kind of blew up in my face. I'm so sorry you got caught in the middle of it."

"So, the guy who attacked you, does he have something to do with this guy you like?" Hayden pinches the bridge of his nose.

I nearly choke on his question. "No," I lie again. "Too completely separate pieces of insanity."

A pained expression squeezes his features as he tries to piece together the lies and bits of truth I have just dumped on him. I say nothing as he attempts to process everything, not entirely sure how he's going to come out of it at the end.

"So, some lunatic stalker has attacked you twice, and your best friend turned almost boyfriend broke your heart?" he says. "Is that the main gist of all this?"

"Uh, basically."

Hayden pushes away from the wall and stares at me looking oddly determined. He takes a deep breath. "Okay. The stalker first. I still think you should go to the police, but regardless, I'm glued to your side for the foreseeable future at school and any other time I can manage. You have to tell your parents so they can watch for him, maybe get a security system if you don't already have one. Don't go anywhere by yourself," he demands.

"Secondly, whoever this guy is that chose someone else over you, he's an idiot. I get that you're not ready to start dating someone else, but that doesn't mean I'm going anywhere. You need a friend right now, and it's going to be awfully hard to stop me from being one."

Evidently out of words, he stares at me and waits for a response. My lips part, but I fear he may be standing there for a long while. It seems to take hours for my brain to kick start itself to life.

Finally, I say, "Hayden, I don't know what to say. None of this is your problem."

"I want it to be my problem," he says. "I want to know you're safe, and hopefully happy again."

How do I say no to that? I have no idea how to deal with this situation. Nothing comes to me before Hayden gently guides me back toward his truck. Before I know it, we're pulling into my driveway. I reach for the door handle, desperate for some quiet so I can think. Hayden is at my door by the time my feet touch the driveway. He walks me to the front door as his eyes scan the street for anything suspicious.

I unlock the door on autopilot and turn the handle. Before I step inside, I turn to Hayden.

"Hayden, I, um, thank you." It's all I can think to say.

He squeezes my shoulder gently. "I'm here, whatever you need."

I nod, because it's all I can manage, and step inside. I watch him turn away through the window and sigh. Maybe Evie can help me figure out what to do. I reach for the light switch, wondering for the first time why it's so dark. No way Evie went with Mom and Dad instead of staying here with Mason. She can't stand Ava Harper. I flick it up, but nothing happens. I start to call out for Evie and Mason, but something collides with the back of my head and everything winks out.

● ● ●

Chapter 33
Shatters

The sound of a familiar, yet repulsive voice echoes in my ears as I struggle to open my eyes. It's hard to focus with the awful pain pounding through my head. I try to reach up and touch the spot on the back of my head that seems to be the source of the pain, but my hand won't move. I try again, my head lolling to the side when the small, unsuccessful movement causes another wave of pain.

"The longer you wait, the worse their punishment will be," taunts the voice.

That voice. It isn't just familiar, I know it.

My eyes snap open to the sight of Alex the Sentinel pacing in front of me with a knife in his hand and a gun tucked into the waistband of his black cargo pants. Rage outweighs the fear and I lurch at him.

Except I don't leave the chair.

Ropes dig into my skin as I strain against them. My eyes burn as I take in his slinking form, walking back and forth with the knife held out menacingly.

"I know you're here, Mason. Come out and play or your friends are going to regret ever meeting you."

My body goes cold. He knows Mason's name! Weakness slides under my skin and wraps itself around my insides. They know who he is. They know he escaped them last time. I know they will not let him get away a second time. My eyes sweep the room for Mason, sure he is somewhere nearby.

Halfway through my sweep, I see Evie next to me. Seeing her trussed up next to me makes me want to cry. The thin stream of dried blood running down from behind her ear makes me furious. She had to have been attacked before I was, but she isn't awake yet. Why? I search her face desperately, trying to evaluate her coloring, see her chest rising and falling. Panic rises from the pit of my stomach because I'm not sure. I don't know.

I can't stand the idea of looking away from her, but I need to know where Mason is. I need to know he is safe. Maybe he can get to Evie and check to see if she's okay without the Sentinel knowing. The way my chest pulses in and out so rapidly brings black to the edges of my vision, but I can't slow it down.

"This is your last chance to save them," the Sentinel says. "I won't make the same mistake my predecessors made, Mason. You will die here

● ● ●

tonight. That is already decided. What is still to be seen is whether or not your pretty little girlfriend and her sister will die too."

It's so dark, it's nearly impossible to see anything more than three feet away, but the Sentinel's words do the trick. Mason stands up from behind the couch. The expression on his face is murderous. I can see it in his eyes that he has every intention of attacking the man holding Evie and me hostage.

My head starts shaking frantically, silently. He can't! The Sentinel will kill him if he reveals himself! I shake my head harder, trying to catch his attention, but the Sentinel is all he can see. I don't want to draw the Sentinel's attention to me and Evie any more than I want it drawn to Mason, but I have no choice.

"What do you want from us?" I scream at the Sentinel.

The quick turn he executes to face me is startling. I press myself into the chair, but refuse to look away. I have to keep his attention on me. I can't let him realize Mason is in the room. He stalks over to me. The knife stays held out in front of his body. It stops inches away from my throat as he towers over me. His amused expression makes me hate him even more than I already do, something I thought was impossible.

"Olivia, you're awake. How nice. It'll be more effective this way."

I only get a second to wonder *what* will be more effective before the knife digs into my arm. I don't want to cry out, but I have never felt pain like this. A scream tears out of my mouth. I can't smother it. I can't be strong and brave and silent even though it might mean keeping Mason safe. Tears pour down my cheeks as he yanks the blade from my shoulder. I bite my lip, drawing blood, and groan in agony.

Gulping in air, I try to fend off the pain and show Mason I can handle it. When I look up, Mason is barreling toward the Sentinel. The look in his eyes is utter chaos.

"No!" I scream at him.

But he doesn't hear me.

I watch as Mason's hands clamp onto the Sentinel's shoulders. There is no look of surprise in the Sentinel's eyes, only the triumph of success. Everything is stolen from me—air, speech, hearing—as the Sentinel's blade arcs through the air toward Mason. I am helpless, forced to watch the silent tableau, tied to a chair with no hope of saving him.

Evie's eyes flutter open slowly. The scene before her snaps her out of her haze. We both stare in horror as the blade jerks downward. Mason doesn't even seem to see it. His hands clamp around the Sentinel's neck as the knife touches his skin. I gasp in a breath, and everything happens at once.

Mason's body turns in the blink of an eye, wedging his elbow under the Sentinel's ribcage as the blade slides across his collar bone, drawing blood

● ● ●

along its way. Another blink and the Sentinel's body launches into the air. I am stunned by Mason's strength as he flips the Sentinel over his shoulder and slams his back into the ground. The Sentinel wheezes out a painful breath, but Mason does not give him even half a second's break before he spins and rams his knees into the Sentinel's chest.

"Nothing is decided," Mason growls, "except that *you* will be the one to die tonight."

The world inside the living room changes into something unfamiliar, something frightening and beautiful at the same time. There is no sound as the air in the room changes. What felt close and hot a moment ago now feels icy and swift, like air is being swept into the room at amazing speeds. But nothing moves. Not a single hair on my head is disturbed as the air compacts itself around Mason.

Evie whispers something to me, or maybe it just sounds like a whisper because I can't spare even a tiny portion of my attention to listen. I don't know what she says. All I can do is watch in amazement as the air solidifies around Mason's hand. It turns cloudy, then a brilliant white, flaring and becoming like glass.

What is even more startling is the shape it takes. A terrible mixture of fear and excitement rushes through me at the sight of a glassy dagger in Mason's hand. It points at the ceiling. Mason turns, his eyes drawn up to the blade. I expect surprise, unease, something, but he doesn't seem shaken at all to see what he has created. I watch in fascination as his fingers loosen and the knife begins to fall. For a moment, I think the shock has set in and he's going to drop the knife.

Then the tip of the blade spins downward. Mason's fingers tighten around the hilt when it is pointing at the Sentinel. His hand plunges down with the knife. It slams into the Sentinel's chest, sinking in to the hilt. Light flares as the blade shatters and throws everyone to the ground.

● ● ●

Chapter 34

The Line

Exhaustion fills my body. My mind stirs, telling me to wake up, but my body has no intention of doing as it says. Underneath my exhaustion is a sense of satisfaction, of rightness. Something feels different, like I have discovered something important. I can't pinpoint what it is, though, and my thoughts transfer to something more concrete. To Olivia.

The memory of her pressing herself against me in a desperate, apologetic hug before she left tonight stirs more memories. I remember Hayden then, and her leaving with him...her asking me to wait for her. The delight that request brings to mind is shoved away as images of what happened next assaults me.

Sitting with Evie on the couch, watching a movie, I should have known the volume was too loud to let me hear anyone approaching. We were too absorbed in the show to notice the quiet shuffle of his steps. I saw the butt of the gun too late to do anything to stop it.

Instinct I am not proud of sent me jumping away from her, protecting myself from being discovered instead of catching her as she slumped sideways to the cushions of the couch. I did no better in preventing Olivia from being hurt. The curtains were closed, opening one to signal her would have revealed myself to the Sentinel. Pain wells up inside my chest, tightening it nearly to the point of breaking as I relive my selfish actions.

"Olivia! I think he's waking up!" Evie yells.

I feel hands press on my face and arms, but I don't want to open my eyes. I don't know how to face them after failing them so blatantly.

"Mason," Olivia whispers, "please wake up. Please wake up."

It's her sob that finally pulls my eyes open. The pain in her eyes is overwhelming as she hovers over me. She is all I can see, all I can feel as her fingertips press gently against my cheek.

"Are you okay?"

I just stare up at her. No. My chest constricts as I bring my failure to the surface. "I didn't protect you," I say through the pain. "I'm so sorry, Olivia."

Her face scrunches as if she's confused about something. "What are you talking about? You saved me and Evie. We would be dead if it wasn't for you."

My head starts shaking back and forth. No, I let them both get hurt. I wasn't careful enough and he snuck up on Evie. I wasn't selfless enough to warn Olivia. I stood by and watched them both be attacked. My eyes dart

● ● ●

over to Evie and see the evidence of my betrayal, a trail of blood running own the side of her neck. I push myself up to sitting and shove Olivia's hands away from me.

"I should have stopped him from hurting you, but I protected myself instead," I argue.

Evie and Olivia share a look. They both shake their heads. Evie turns to look at me and asks, "Don't you remember what happened?"

"He snuck up on us and hit you, and then …"

"No," Evie interrupts, "after all that. After we woke up and he cut Olivia."

"What?" I demand.

Olivia turns away from me, just slightly. She speaks before I can do anything. "Mason, you attacked the Sentinel."

"I did?"

Evie nods. "Yeah. He's over there if you don't believe us."

I turn, not sure what I expect to see. The body of the Sentinel lies on the floor of the hallway. The dull sheen in his eyes makes it clear that he's dead. Confusion sets in as I scour his body for signs of what happened. There are no bruises or cuts on his exposed skin, no blood pooling under his body.

The front door slams open, stealing everyone's attention. My eyes widen as Robin comes barreling into the room with a frantic look in her eyes. She skids to a stop. Her mouth falls open at the sight of us on the floor next to the body of the Sentinel. Her already pale skin turns even whiter. Nobody says anything as she backtracks a few steps and shuts the front door. Her fingers turn the deadbolt as if acting independently from her brain.

"What happened?" she squeaks.

"What are you doing here?" I counter.

Robin swallows hard. "Olivia called me. She said you'd all been attacked and you weren't waking up after you did some crazy thing with the air and killed the Sentinel. She told me to get over here and I came."

There's more than one surprising bit of information in all of that, but I latch onto only one. "I did what?"

Olivia's fingers wrap around mine, something Robin notices. Olivia's other hand presses against my cheek and turns me to look at her. "Mason, you killed the Sentinel. You saved Evie and me from him."

"How?"

She shrugs. "I'm not sure I can explain it. You did something to the air. It got cold and the air in the room got all…dagger-like."

"What?" Robin and I ask at the same time.

Evie tries to explain. "Yeah. All the air swished over to your hand. It turned white at first, then it looked like glass, and it turned into a knife. A big

● ● ●

knife. You held up in your hand like this." She pauses to demonstrate. "Then we both thought you were going to drop it, but you didn't. You stabbed it right into that guy's heart, and when you did, the knife thing exploded, or turned back into air. I don't know. But it did the trick. That guy's totally dead. We checked."

My body slumps. I did what? I try to bring up the memories, to understand what Evie is talking about, but I come up blank. I remember him taunting me, telling me that if I didn't reveal myself to him he'd kill Olivia and Evie. I was on the verge of giving him what he wanted. I was so terrified of them being hurt, but I knew Olivia wanted me to stay put and wait it out as long as I could. I knew she would die to protect me, but I could never let her do that.

The memory of her scream shoots through my mind. My skin hums. The sound is etched into my mind. It wasn't a scream of fear. It was a sound of agony so rich it went straight to my bones. I remember standing, Olivia yelling at me, and me stepping forward.

My mind starts to twitch, an attempt to scatter my memories, but I refuse to surrender.

The air suddenly felt different after she screamed, like it wasn't just atoms and particles. It felt alive. It felt sentient. I can't explain how it happened, but my fury called the air too me once I had the Sentinel under my control. It pressed in close, like a second skin, familiar and right. I wanted to hurt him and the air gave me a way to do it.

As the memories crowd back into my mind, a strange sensation settles over me. The feeling that I have discovered something important returns, yet the *why* behind the feeling still escapes me.

"I...I don't know how I did that," I say quietly. My eyes are drawn to the body lying next to us. I half expect to shiver or feel something, but I don't.

Olivia turns to Robin. "Do you know how Mason did this?"

"I have no idea," Robin admits. She bites her bottom lip. Her eyes drop to the side.

That's all I need to see to know she's hiding something. My free hand grips her arm tightly. She doesn't look up until I yank her closer to me. Her eyes are wide behind her glasses, worn and scared. Robin licks her lips and takes a deep breath.

"You know...the special Aerlings I mentioned...I've been," she stammers, "uh, learning more about them."

"And?" Evie demands. "Spit it out Robin!"

"It's not just that their especially talented. They're important. More important than I realized. They're part of the ruling class of Aerlings." She gulps. "I've tried to find out more, but even Caretakers don't know very much about the Aerling world. I have no idea what it means to be a part of the ruling class, but I know it means that the Sentinels will do everything they can to kill those Aerlings. This won't stop. Another Sentinel will come. They'll keep coming until Mason is dead."

Nobody says anything. Olivia's fingers tighten around mine until our fingertips are beet red and throbbing with pain. "It won't happen," she finally whispers. "I won't let them take you away from me."

I squeeze her hand tighter, but I don't say anything. I can't. She's hiding what the Sentinel did to her, but it won't leave my mind. I can't shake off the guilt of knowing she was hurt because I am in her life. Robin's words echo in my mind. This won't be the last time we're attacked. How many more times can we escape the Sentinels' fury?

"What do we do about him?" Evie asks, pointing at the body.

Olivia's eyes drift over to the man who attacked her twice. "Maybe we should call Mom and Dad."

"No!" Robin yelps. "They can't tell the police. If the Caretakers in the police force find out, there's nothing my parents will be able to do to keep Mason here. They'll take him away. We have to take care of this ourselves."

"How?" Olivia asks. "What on earth are we supposed to do with a dead body?"

Robin's shoulders bob up and down in defeat. "I...don't know."

"I do," Evie says, surprising everyone.

All eyes turn to her expectantly. She doesn't disappoint.

"The new addition to the library," she says, "they're pouring the foundation tomorrow morning. Elizabeth's mom is the director and they have this big to-do planned tomorrow and Elizabeth has been trying to convince all her friends to volunteer. All we have to do is dig a hole big enough to fit him in and cover him up with dirt, and tomorrow he'll be gone. Forever."

Slowly, everyone else's heads begin to nod. I don't move. Not because I don't see the wisdom in Evie's plan, but because I can sense the line we are about to cross. Disposing of the body irrevocably draws Olivia and Evie into this world of Sentinels and Aerlings, Caretakers and laws we don't fully understand. There will be no going back. They were not born to this life, but it is about to become theirs.

I look into Evie's eyes. Her firm devotion won't back down no matter what I say. She nods when our eyes meet, and I turn to Olivia.

It isn't just strength I see in her eyes. It isn't determination alone. It's what I have spent twelve years hoping I would one day see in her eyes. Her unconditional love wraps around me and I know that if given the choice of

● ● ●

safety over being with me, she would even have to consider her answer. Olivia will walk with me to the end, no matter what.

The breath in my chest stutters, the depth of her love almost frightening because I understand what this may cost her. "Olivia …"

She shakes her head and pulls my forehead to hers. "Don't even think it," she whispers. There are tears in her eyes as she holds me. "Nothing will stop me from being with you. Nothing." She gasps in a breath and presses her lips forcefully to mine. "I love you, Mason. I love you and I'm not going anywhere."

Emotion renders me speechless. I could forget the air dagger, the body, the blood, everything in that moment. The strength it takes not to scoop her into my arms and run is almost more than I possess. Evie's quiet voice is the only thing that stops me.

"Mom and Dad will be home in an hour. We need to get rid of him now."

Chapter 35

Helpless

I am covered in dirt and sweat by the time I finish digging the hole. The girls wanted to help, so it would get done faster, but I didn't want to risk anyone seeing them. If someone spots a shovel hovering in the air, they'd likely just pass it off as a trick of the light or the late hour.

Exhausted, I toss the shovel aside and head back to the Jeep. Time to get the body.

Robin jumps out of the driver's side and rushes over to me. Olivia is a little slower, needing Evie's help. Is it just the moonlight that is making her look so pale? A tightness in my chest jolts me toward her. She said she was fine before we left the house, that the cut wasn't that bad. I stumble over to her, afraid she was lying.

"Are you okay? You look pale."

"I'm fine," she says.

Evie let's go of Olivia's elbow and crosses her arms over her chest as if daring me to contradict her sister. I want to, but I don't want to be caught standing around the construction site for too long. I grit my teeth and promise myself I will not let Olivia slip away from me later. Whatever that psychopath did to her, I *will* make it right.

"Mason," Robin says, "you're going to need help lugging this guy over there. He weighs a ton."

She says this as she tries to drag the plastic wrapped-taped up-heap toward the edge of the Jeep. The yellowish dome light casts heavy shadows across her face. For a moment, the effect gives me pause, because in the harsh light she looks more like a corpse than herself. I shake off the disturbing image and step up next to her.

"You guys stay here."

Robin and Olivia both try to object, claiming I'll need their help. No offense to them, but neither one would be much help right now. Olivia looks ready to pass out and Robin's slender arms don't give me much hope of her being able to heft this guy. Gripping the body under the shoulders, I yank him out of the bed and sling him over my shoulder.

Again, this would look really bizarre if someone spotted me, but I'm not as worried about that as I am getting this done and over with. I want Olivia back home and resting as soon as possible. All three girls troop back into the Jeep obediently as I carry the body over to the hole. There is no ceremony as I drop him into the ground. My aim isn't quite on and he lands half in and half out of the shallow grave.

* * *

I want to get out of here, but a sudden wave of white hot anger stabs at me. *He* is the reason Olivia is hurt. He's the reason Evie was tied to a chair. He's the reason my life is in danger. I can't contain my fury in that moment. My foot crashes into the body, kicking, shoving it toward the hole, hoping it will somehow take all the other Sentinels with him.

I already lost one family to these sickos. My heel snaps down on his skull. I don't care that one push would have been enough to get him into the grave. I don't care that he can't feel anything anymore. I don't care that none of this will stop the next Sentinel from coming after me. Every furious, pent up emotion clambering around inside of my head explodes out of me. My foot crashes down again and again. A primal scream rips out of my chest.

The body is in the hole, has been for a while, but I stomp on its chest one more time, letting everything go. Covering the body takes no time at all, but it steals what little strength I have left. I slump to the ground next to the grave and bury my head in my hands. How did our lives come to this? Why couldn't they just leave me alone?

"Mason," Robin says softly from behind me, "are you okay?"

I don't look up. My face stays buried in my hands. "I don't know how to fix this, stop this from happening again."

The night is quiet for a moment. A breeze rolls through the site and I notice for the first time that it is beginning to get cold.

"There is no way to stop it," Robin finally says, "not if you stay here with them."

My eyes spear her angrily. She holds her hands up in her defense, but doesn't back down.

"I know what I said earlier, but you aren't being realistic, Mason. Nothing is going to stop them from coming after you again. This douche bag disappearing will be all the confirmation the Sentinels need. They'll come after you, kill whoever they need to in order to make sure they get you this time." She touches my shoulder softly. "I know you don't want to hear this, but you know it's true."

I press the palms of my hands into my eyes sockets. The pain does nothing to block out the truth of her words. Still, I can't bring myself to admit it. "I just have to be more careful. I can hide. I can protect them. Whatever I did tonight, I'll do it again."

"You don't even know how you did it!" Robin argues. "You're going to bank on your ability to miraculously create some sort of air dagger the next time Olivia is in danger? We're talking about her *life*, Mason. You can't do that. There's only one way to protect her, and you know it."

"I'm not leaving!" I growl angrily.

Robin stares at me like I've lost it, which maybe I have. She stands up and crosses her arms over her chest. "You are leaving her, Mason, or did you forget that little tidbit of information. When February rolls around, you won't have a choice. Your birthday means going home, and yeah, maybe she'll get to go with you, but maybe she'll die trying. I have no idea. What are the chances of her making it to February to *get* you home if you stay with her? If she's not there on your birthday, bad things happen, Mason. You have to go home, or you die. Do you understand me?"

Her words pull me to my feet in a flash. My hands grip her shoulders and pin her against the edge of the temporary construction office. She winces as her head slams into the metal wall.

"What did you just say?" I demand. "I'll die?"

"If Olivia's not there to take you home on your birthday, you don't go home. You can't stay here either. You'll die, Mason."

My fingers dig into her shoulders. "When were you going to tell me this?" I yell angrily. "How many other answers are you hiding from me? What else have you lied about?"

"I haven't lied about anything!" Robin snaps. "I just found out about you dying if you don't go home. My grandma told me this afternoon when I went to see her. I was planning to tell you tomorrow."

She wedges her hands against my chest and shoves me back a step. Her glare matches mine. "I'm trying to help you, Mason, so how about you stop being such an idiot and listen to me."

"I'm not leaving Olivia," I snap.

Her eyes narrow. "Then you're going to watch her die."

Half a dozen angry retorts are waiting on the tip of my tongue, but none of them make it over the brink. The idea of walking away from Olivia makes me physically sick, but I don't know what else to do. Anger falls away from my body slowly. My shoulders sag. My stomach twists as I summon up the courage to form new words, frightening words.

"Maybe you're right."

Robin sighs, a certain level of satisfaction reflected in her eyes. I stare at her, not sure if there's something else, but before I can figure it out, Olivia steps out from behind the office. Wide, terrified eyes pierce me.

"What?" she shrieks. "What? You're leaving? What is she talking about? Your birthday? Dying? How long have you known? When ..." Her voice trails off, ending the string of half-formed thoughts. Her eyes turn glassy, reflecting the moonlight and intensifying the pain in her eyes. "Mason, you can't leave me, please."

The ache in my chest that has been tormenting me since Robin first explained what had to happen doubles, triples, until it nearly drops me under its terrible weight. I stumble over to Olivia and throw my arms around her. I expect her to do the same, but she yelps in pain and pulls back, tucking her left shoulder out of sight. She tries to hide the pain, but her left hand is trembling and a fresh trail of blood leaks out from under her sweatshirt.

Her hands try to fight me off as I yank at the zipper. Her one good arm bats at my hand, but I shove it away easily. She groans in agony as I slide her arm out of the black fabric. Weakness like I have never before experienced saps my energy entirely. One knee buckles at the sight of her torn flesh. *Cut* in no way describes what happened to Olivia. Her gaping biceps is swollen and inflamed, blood still seeping out from a nasty clot of half dried blood.

A sickening image forms in my mind as I picture the Sentinel stabbing his knife into her arm without remorse. My hands fall away in shock. My fingers look black in the moonlight with Olivia's blood covering them. Only then do I realize her sweatshirt is soaked through. How much blood has she lost? I knew she looked pale. I knew she was in pain, but I wanted to believe her when she said she was fine. Getting rid of the body blinded me to the truth.

"We need to get you to a hospital," I say shakily.

My whole body feels as cold as stone. Olivia is shaking her head. The way her pink lips stand out so starkly against her skin tightens my resolve. Olivia tries to protest as I scoop her into my arms and demand everyone get back in the Jeep. I ignore her voice and focus instead on her breathing. It seems too shallow, too labored as I get us both into the Jeep.

Robin speeds through town to the nearest hospital as Evie calls her parents and tries not to sound hysterical. We're halfway to the hospital when Olivia stops trying to change my mind. For the first five seconds, I feel relieved that she isn't arguing. It only takes that long before I understand that it wasn't her choice to stop arguing.

"Olivia!" My voice is high and tight as panic takes over every thought.

Evie snaps around from the passenger's seat, her wide eyes scouring her sister's body. "What happened? Why isn't she moving? Is she breathing?"

My head starts shaking back and forth. I don't know! Hastily, I lay her down on the seat with trembling hands. My blood is pounding in my ears as I lay my cheek next to her nose. I hold my breath, terrified.

Short, warm puffs of air pulse hesitantly out of her body and fall against my skin. I want to scream in relief, but they are too shallow and weak. Shaking so badly I can barely control my movements, I try to touch her face gently. My hand looks so dark against her skin!

"She's breathing," I manage to say, "but it's weak. Oh, Olivia, please hang on. It's going to be okay. Everything is going to be alright. Please, please."

Everyone lurches forward as Robin screeches to a halt in front of the Emergency Room. She and Evie leap out of the Jeep and rush around to my door. I try to push them back, unwilling to let Olivia out of my arms, but Robin yanks my hand away.

"You can't carry her in, Mason! What will that look like?" she demands.

I know she is right, but my hands stay clamped around Olivia's body.

"Please, Mason. Let us take her inside. You have to trust me. I'll keep her safe."

"Trust you?" I ask. How can I? I have no idea what else Robin has lied to me about. Can I really trust her?

Do I have any other choice?

Robin and Evie pull Olivia carefully out of my arms. I stumble out after them, leaving the Jeep door open. Together they lug Olivia into the ER while I trail behind, helpless, left alone to watch the blood drip from her fingertips.

Chapter 36
Stupid, Stupid Boy

Everything feels fuzzy. Opening my eyes seems more difficult than usual. There's a strange pressure around my arm. My fingers twitch as I try to reach the spot, but my arms don't want to move. A tired breath slips between my lips.

"Olivia?" Mason calls out. A second later his hands are pressed against my cheeks. "Olivia, are you awake?"

If I hadn't been already, I am now. My lips curl into a smile as I finally open my eyes and find him hovering over me. "Mason," I say softly.

I reach up and wrap my fingers around his shirt, pulling him closer. I can't pinpoint why, but I feel a strange longing for him, as if we've been apart for ages. As I look into his eyes, confusion plagues me. Why does he look so sad, so anguished?

"Mason, what's wrong?"

His shoulders jump as a pained breath shudders out of him. "I was so scared. I thought you were going to die, Olivia. I thought I had lost you."

Mason buries his face in my hair, squeezing me. His arm tightens around my shoulder and sends a sharp pain shooting down to my fingertips. I gasp. The fuzziness disappears. My eyes travel past Mason's shoulders to sterile looking walls that can only belong in a hospital. The sharp scent of antiseptic reaches my nose and the events that led me to this moment swim back into my mind.

Roughly, I shove Mason away from me. "Lost me!" I shriek. "Apparently that's what was going to happen all along! How could you not tell me that you had to go home on your birthday? How could you …"

My voice weakens and disappears as I realize I already know the answers to most of the questions running through my mind.

When did he find out? I clench my bottom lip between my teeth. He found out the morning he kissed me. After the kiss. Only something like this could have convinced him to do what he did.

Why didn't he tell me? Because he was afraid I'd spend the rest of our time together clinging to him, ignoring everything else, planning a way to get him home even if it meant my life was the price.

Why did he leave me for Robin? My chin starts to tremble. He didn't, not really. It was an act, a ploy to make me to forget him, to move on so his leaving wouldn't be so hard.

Was he really going to let me date Hayden when he knows I'm in love with him? Tears roll down my cheeks and my shoulders start shaking,

* * *

because I know the answer to that question too. Yes. If he thought it would protect me, he would have stood by and pushed me toward someone else.

"You stupid, stupid boy," I say through my tears. "What were you thinking?"

Mason's face crumbles. "I just…I didn't know how to protect you from everything. You've kept me safe for twelve years and I couldn't manage to do the same for you for even a few weeks!"

"No," I interrupt, "that's not what I'm talking about and you know it!"

"It was never about Robin," Mason says. His eyes drop, and his fingers find mine. "I love you, Olivia. That never changed. I'm so sorry I hurt you. It killed me to do it, but I honestly thought it was the right thing to do, at least until…until I saw the look on your face when I took Robin's hand. I didn't know …"

"You didn't know how much I loved you?"

Mason shakes his head slowly. "I didn't know you were *in* love with me."

It breaks my heart to hear him say that because it's my fault. Even after the kiss, despite the intoxicating passion we shared in that moment, I did nothing to make sure he knew. I don't make the same mistake twice.

The hands that shoved him away a moment ago curl around the fabric of his shirt. I pull his mouth down to mine. It hurts to strain my shoulder, but it's a hazy thought in the back of my mind as Mason's lips press hesitantly against mine. One of my hands releases his shirt and slips to the back of his neck. His hesitancy disappears with the tiniest amount of pressure.

Suddenly, Mason is pulling me into his arms. His lips crush against mine as his fingers burrow into my hair. I gasp at the force behind his grip, my breathing coming faster. My hand presses against his chest, but not to push him away, just to feel his heart racing beneath my touch. Mine easily matches his.

I can't breathe when Mason's lips leave mine and trail down the curve of my neck. His one hand slides down my body, tightening around my waist as he pulls me even closer. I feel dizzy as his mouth comes back up to meet mine, but that hardly stops me from lying back and pulling him along with me. The weight of his upper body pressing down on me is strangely reassuring. My breath sticks in my chest as I pull to close every last space between us.

Mason kisses me again, but this time it is less frantic. His mouth moves against mine slowly. His fingers which are nearly digging into my side soften and glide up my body slowly. Every inch they travel draws a strangled gasp from my lips. I didn't think my heart could beat any faster than it was a moment ago, but it is pounding so frantic it's the only sound I can hear.

● ● ●

A whimper escapes my lips as Mason pulls back slightly. My fingers curl around his shirt, begging him not to leave. "Mason, I love you," I whisper. "I love you so much and I can't stand the thought of being away from you. Not even for a moment."

I nearly groan in pain as Mason crushes me against him, but I bite my lip and hold it inside. Mason's hands slowly begin stroking my back. "I love you more than I can even tell you, Ollie, but ..."

I push him back roughly, shaking my head. "No buts, Mason, please. I can't lose you."

"You aren't safe with me here."

"I don't care. This," I say, gesturing at my bandaged arm, "is worth having you with me. I won't let them tear you away from me."

"I don't want to leave," Mason says, "but it's not just about us. It kills me to think of leaving you, but I can't stay here and watch the people I love get killed."

I shake my head at him. I won't accept this. "Nobody's going to kill us, Mason. We'll protect ourselves. I'll protect you, like I always have. You can't leave. I won't let you. Please, Mason."

"I know you would do anything in your power to protect me, Ollie," Mason says softly. "I have no doubts that you would sacrifice everything for me, but I won't let you."

"It's not your decision," I argue. He can't tell me what I can and can't sacrifice for him.

He shakes his head. "You're not thinking this through, Olivia." His voice is strained, almost harsh. "It's not just about what we want. Do you think I would ever choose to leave you if I had any other choice?"

My bottom lip begins to tremble. "You do have a choice. Stay with me."

"And watch Evie get hit and tied up again? Watch your blood soak into my jeans as I hold you, praying you aren't about to die? How can I stay when it might mean watching the only parents I have ever really known die at the hands of the Sentinels? I can stop all of this. I can make you all safe." Mason's jaw firms as his eyes turn glassy with unshed tears. "I can protect you, Olivia, all of you. All I have to do is leave."

"No!" I say it angrily, even though I know he is right. I know it's the only way to guarantee my family won't be killed. The guilt my selfishness inspires within me hurts almost as much as the Sentinel's blade slicing into my arm, but I can't let go of Mason. I can't give him up just to save myself.

"I'll come with you," I whisper, "wherever you have to go. I'll come with you."

Mason's stony stance melts. He falls back into the chair he must have been sitting in earlier. His head falls to his chest. "And leave your family? Leave school? Who will protect them in case the Sentinels come back, or don't believe I've really gone?"

His hands scrub against his face in frustration. "And it still leaves you with a bull's eye on your back," he growls. "If you leave, they'll know you came with me. They'll search for you...and they'll find you. You know they will."

"I ..." My voice falters. I want so badly to have the answer, to tell him it will be okay because I have a plan that will keep us safe and together. I want to believe that everything we have been through the past twelve years won't dwindle down to a goodbye that may last forever.

My brain scrambles to come up with something. I latch onto the only thought that gives me any hope. "What about being your Escort?" I demand. "I have to be with you when it's time for you to go home. Robin said so. We have to be together or you'll die here."

Mason's body goes strangely still. His hand crushes mine painfully. I'm not even sure he's breathing for a moment, until a breath lurches into his lungs like he's just come up from drowning.

"Didn't you listen to the rest of what she said?" Mason asks. His voice is heavy, harsh. The sound of it presses in on me. "She said helping me might kill you. The chance that you'll come with me may be nothing but fantasy!"

"It may be real!" I counter. "It may be the only way we can be together, Mason."

"Are you listening at all? Helping me get home could kill you!"

It hurts like hell for my shoulder to cross my arms over my chest, but I do it anyway. "Do you really think that will stop me?"

I expect Mason to admit defeat, but I am sorely disappointed. He stands next to my hospital bed and leans in with a deadly serious expression. "I will not put you in harm's way again, Olivia. I love you too much to watch you die. All I have to do to stop you is leave."

The pain in my arm is forgotten entirely. The dead body we just buried disappears from my mind. Everything but the sickening thought of living without Mason vanishes. All of the air is sucked out of my lungs like I have just been punched in the stomach. My shoulders curl in as my arms squeeze my body nearly in half.

"You can't!" I cry. "You can't leave me, Mason. Please. Please don't go. I can't stay here without you, not knowing whether you're safe. I can't. You can't. Please, Mason, please."

My body is jostled as Mason climbs up on the bed and sits next to me, his arms encircling me in an instant. His lips press against my temple, but he doesn't say what I need him to say. I sag in defeat as Mason cradles me against his chest. The gentle stroke of his hands along my back as he whispers that everything will be okay are not enough to break through the agony building up inside of me.

"Please don't leave," I beg.

His tears splash down on my skin as he says, "I can't stay, Olivia. I have to go."

"Where? Where can you go that will be safer than staying with me?"

The sound of a door opening sends me cringing against Mason's chest. I don't know what I expect. Sentinels? Police come to arrest us? Some new threat I haven't even considered? I would have welcomed any of those over what I really see.

Chapter 37
This Gift of Joy

I have never met Robin's parents, but I know who they are the moment they step into the room. Her mother has the same wispy brown hair that is constantly escaping clips and bobby pins. Her father has her same pale skin and bright eyes. Robin stands between them, with my own family a step behind.

They already know, I realize. Evie's red eyes betray her. Mom and Dad share a look half relieved that I am awake, half agonized because they too have already agreed to let Mason slip out of our lives, maybe for good. Robin and her family are the worst. Her parents' calm, pleased expressions make me want to scream.

I don't want to show them any weakness. I want to prove that I am strong enough to protect Mason, better suited to keep him safe than they are. Every ounce of strength I have goes into not breaking down. I pull my head up off Mason's shoulder and meet eyes with Robin's mother.

"You're taking Mason?" I ask.

"He asked us to help him hide," she corrects, "until his birthday when…if you take him home."

Gritting my teeth, I stare her and Mason down. "When. When I take him home. That's not up for debate."

Mason's mouth opens, but a scathing glare from me shuts him up. I turn back to Robin's mom. "How exactly do you intend to keep him safe? We've been protecting him for twelve years, and we were doing a pretty good job of it until *your daughter* stumbled into our lives and set the Sentinels on our trail."

I don't even try to hide the vile look I shoot directly at Robin's head. The look of shame I see in Robin's eyes is only a tiny spark compared to what I think it should be. She's the one who knew all the rules. She broke them once and it cost Eliana her life. Why didn't she learn? Why did she egg on her relationship with Mason, putting him in danger and nearly getting us killed? It is almost painful to tear my eyes away from her and put aside my anger.

Looking back to Robin's parents, I see my own anger reflected in their eyes. At first, I expect them to lash out at me for blaming their daughter, but they don't. Robin's father glances down at his daughter in disgust before looking back at me with a tight expression.

"Robin's actions will be dealt with at a later time, and I can promise they will be appropriately harsh. Right now, Mason is our main concern. If

* * *

he is indeed one of the Aerling ruling class as Robin has speculated—which we are inclined to agree with—it is imperative that we send him into hiding as soon as possible. Tonight, in fact. Arrangements have already been made."

He stares down at me as if every word that just came out of his mouth didn't stab me in the heart. "Tonight?" I squeak.

Robin's mom nods. "You were smart to get rid of the body of Sentinel that attacked you, but it won't be long before he's missed. They'll come back for Mason if they believe he is still with you, and they won't stop with just *his* life."

"How …" I gulp in a painful breath. "How will they know he won't be there? They can't see him. They won't be able to tell he's gone. Won't they just come looking regardless and…and kill us?"

Mom and Dad glance at each other worriedly. Mom pulls Evie in under her arm and tries to squeeze away the fear in her eyes. I feel weak and wobbly as Mason's arm tightens around my shoulder. Is this all for nothing? Will we die no matter what we do? A flash of selfishness says that if we're all going to die, I'd rather spend my last few hours in Mason's arms than waiting alone for news that the Sentinels have found him.

The cruelty of such a thought slaps against my love for him. I told Mason already that I was ready to give my life in exchange for his, that I could never stand by and let him die when I could have prevented it no matter what the cost might be. Was I lying when I said that?

An ache starts deep in my chest and quickly swells to my fingertips and toes. I want so much to be with Mason. I want to be swallowed in his love and lose myself completely in his touch. I want my world to begin and end with him, but I can't lie to myself. I have to face reality, and that means giving in when it's the last thing I want to do.

I look back up at Robin's mom and she sees the acceptance in my eyes. It spurs her to answer my question. "Robin has mentioned to you that we have Caretakers serving in the police force. They will be stationed outside your house. Not only will this protect your family from the Sentinels, it serves as a message to them. They will understand that we are aware of their interest in Mason. The Sentinels know we would never leave an Aerling within their reach. It should be enough to turn their search elsewhere."

"Should be?" I snap. Maybe she doesn't care all that much about my family given that they aren't Caretakers, but I am not about to kick up my heels on *maybe*.

"We have every confidence that they will back off," Robin's dad says, "but if they continue their interest, the Caretaker officers will be there to protect you."

"And my family, right?" My eyes narrow at the both of them. "I may be Mason's Escort, but you all are going to protect every member of my family."

It's not a question. In the back of my mind I admit that I have absolutely nothing to bargain with, but either they don't realize that, or they think I have some way of thwarting their plans. They share a look that doesn't seem entirely pleased, and then nod curtly.

"Of course your entire family will be protected."

My eyes bounce between theirs and I get the twisted feeling that making a deal with them is something akin to selling my soul. I don't know what else to do, though. Hiding the growing sense of panic, I fix my gaze on Robin's mother.

"You never answered my original question. How exactly are you planning to keep Mason safe?"

Her lips stretch tight into a smug smile. "You act like this is the first time Caretakers have ever had to hide an Aerling. We know how to protect them better than anyone."

"Is that why Mason's in danger now?" I snap. "Because you're all so great at keeping secrets and protecting people?"

The skin around her eyes crinkles as she narrows her glare.

"Answer the question," I demand.

"Mason will be moved every two weeks from one Caretaker family to the next. Only the Caretakers he is with will know his location. He will be kept indoors at all times once he is transferred so there is no chance of a Sentinel spotting a door opening by itself or other strange occurrences. He will be monitored closely and allowed no contact with anyone outside the family he is with, ensuring he remains safe," she says. "This will continue until his eighteenth birthday when the Caretakers he is with will contact us and makes arrangements for you to join Mason and escort him home."

My family has been silent throughout this exchange, but now my dad unravels himself from Mom and Evie and storms up next to my bed. His hand slips into mine as his gaze travels to Robin's parents. "What exactly happens then?" he demands. "You expect Olivia to waltz in to be Mason's Escort, but no one has bothered to explain what will happen when she does. We need to know that our daughter will be safe before we agree to any of this."

Robin's father, who should understand better than anyone a father's love for his daughter, tightens his jaw angrily. The expression on his face makes me shiver. "Your daughter was born into this world to serve a purpose. What right do you have to deny her the opportunity to fulfill her purpose? If she is destined to die helping Mason return to his world, then she will die knowing she has done the right thing. It is not your place to determine her future."

Dad goes rigid next to me. "Not my place?" he growls. "I am her father! It is my *purpose* to love and protect her, from the Caretakers if necessary. You are fooling yourselves if you think we'll hand her over to you blindly."

It is like an old western showdown between them. Robin's parents look furious that my dad would question them, let alone threaten them. Dad looks ready to throw a punch. I love him for standing up for me, for loving me enough to stand up to these nutjobs, but he's wrong about this. Robin's parents are right about one thing. It isn't his choice whether or not I will help Mason and possibly die in the process. I will save Mason's life and take him home. That is not up for debate.

"Dad," I say quietly as I touch his arm, "it's okay."

He peers down at me, confused.

"Nothing has to be decided right now," I lie. "Let's just hear them out, okay?"

Dad clenches his jaw. Mom looks like she is on the verge of tears while I fear Evie is about to tear into Robin and her parents. The room stays quiet, neither agreement nor dissent passing between us. It's the best I can hope for right now. I look back at Robin's parents and study them for a moment.

I'm sure they are very dedicated Caretakers. Clearly, that's their main priority, even over their own daughter. I get the impression that they only had a child to pass on their *purpose*. And she stripped them of that. Robin's head dips down when her father deigns to glace in her direction. The look in his eyes echoes my own anger and frustration I feel toward Robin because of the problems she has caused us, but there is something even more intense in his expression. Hatred.

I never thought I would pity Robin. I've been too busy despising her for that, but in this moment I feel sorry for her. My parents are standing beside me, protecting me because they love me. Robin's parents would throw her to the wolves if they thought it would win them another chance to care for an Aerling and fulfill their purpose.

A strange mixture of emotions crowds in on me, but I push them all back and refocus on Robin's scary mother. "What happens to Escorts after they help their Aerlings return home?"

"Their fate is…uncertain."

"What is that supposed to mean?" Mason demands, speaking up for the first time. His body is tight beside me and his fingers are strangling mine.

"It means we don't know," she snaps. "Most Escorts never return. We have no idea whether they are able to cross into the Aerling world with their charge, or if their lives are the cost of sending the Aerling home. There is no way for us to know for sure."

"What about the ones who do return?" Dad asks. "Surely they have given the Caretakers some insight."

Robin's father shakes his head. "The ones who do come back...they aren't the same."

"What do you mean?" Evie demands, nearly yelling out her question. "Like she'll be crazy? What kind of jacked up system is this?"

Neither of Robin's parents seems interested in answering. Their hard expressions stay fixed on me. I suppose to their minds, it shouldn't matter what might happen to me. It's my *purpose*. Surprisingly, it is Robin who answers.

"The Escorts that have come back, they aren't crazy, but there's something wrong with them. Guilt maybe. None of them will ever talk about what happened. Most Caretakers believe they either failed to return their Aerlings and witnessed their deaths, or were too cowardly to follow through and abandoned their Aerling." Robin twists her fingers around each other. "Not fulfilling our purpose is like treason to Caretakers. Escorts who come home are ostracized."

"Wait," I say, "are most Escorts Caretakers?"

The look that passes between Robin's parents is irritating, like they're debating whether or not I am worthy enough to receive whatever information they're hoarding. Robin's mother tilts her chin up snobbishly before speaking, "Yes, most Escorts are Caretakers. Only rarely do we find an Escort among the lay people."

Evie snorts, and I have the urge to do the same. Lay people? Like they're better than everyone else just because they're Caretakers? Mason shakes his head, which only serves to irritate Robin's parents. Like I care at this point.

"Escorts who are not Caretakers," Robin's mom continues, "are rare, and usually a sign of ..."

When her voice trails off, it's not easy to resist the urge to grab her and shake the answer, all the answers, out of her skinny little body.

"It means," Robin says as she steps forward, "that Mason is very important."

Evie laughs out loud. The mocking lilt to her laughter grates on Robin's parents. My own smile is vicious as well, because I know why Evie is laughing. "So, the most important Aerlings can't be trusted to the Caretakers."

* * *

"That's not true," Robin's mother snaps.

"Of course it's true, yet you still want us to trust you to protect Mason until his birthday." If both of my hands weren't occupied holding onto Mason and my dad, I would throw something at her.

Mason's hand tightens around mine, and at first I think he is doing it to show his agreement. When he looks down at me I know I am wrong. My heart aches because it is the same look I gave my dad just a few minutes ago. Mason's thumb grazes my knuckles lightly.

"I know you don't want to agree, Olivia, but it's the only way I can be sure you'll be safe. I have to go with them."

"No," I beg. Tears spring to my eyes and begin rolling down my cheeks. The pain in my chest spreads to every part of me. "Please don't go."

The agony in his expression kills me. His head shakes back and forth, breaking my heart. "I can't stay. I have to leave. You know this is the only way."

"I don't know, and neither do you! Please, Mason, don't go," I beg.

His fingers brush away my tears. Dad's hand slips out of mine as he steps back and let's Mason take me in his arms. Everyone else disappears from my mind as I look up at Mason through tear-filled eyes. He blinks away tears, but they roll down his cheeks anyway. I shake my head back and forth, refusing to believe our time together is over. I can't do this without him. I can't sit back wondering and waiting, not knowing where he is or if he's safe. I can't wake up every morning knowing he won't be there.

"Let me come with you," I beg one last time.

Mason crushes me against his chest. The pain in my shoulder flares, but I only grip him tighter. My frightened tears explode into a torrent. I only cry harder when Mason's tears splash down on my skin.

"I love you, Ollie," Mason whispers. "This won't be forever, I promise. We'll be together again soon."

Squeezing my eyes shut tightly, I press my forehead into his chest. I can't face him. I can't say goodbye, even if it's only for a few months. I can't, because I don't trust Robin's parents. I am terrified that this will be the last time I ever see him. My head shakes back and forth until Mason forces my chin up so I have no choice but to meet his gaze. His red, swollen eyes send another shot of agony through me.

"Ollie, please. Don't make me leave you like this. You know I don't want to go. I would never leave you if I had any choice." His expression is pleading, begging me to tell him this is okay.

I don't want to, because it's not. It's not okay! But the pain in his eyes is too much. "I know," I whisper hoarsely. "I know you don't want to leave.

I'm sorry, Mason. I want to be strong for you, but I don't know if I can. I love you so much. I can't imagine not being with you every day."

"I know," he whispers, "I know."

His arms curl around me and we hold each other in silence. There is so much to say, but I am out of words. I lean up and pull Mason's lips to mine. I don't care who is watching or what my dad may think. Every ounce of my love flows into this one kiss. My fingers slide back into Mason's hair as he cradles me against him. Heat grows between our bodies as our souls irrevocably connect, mixing in a way that will never let us drift apart. In the midst of this terrible pain, we are sheltered by this gift of joy. Mason is mine, and I am his, no matter what we are forced to face.

Chapter 38
Join the Club

Sitting on Mason's bed, alone, I stare out the window at the Caretaker cop parked outside our house. The Dewalts give it a strange look as they carry their luggage back into their house. One corner of my mouth turns up faintly at the sight of them. It's the best I can manage, even though I am extremely relieved that they were in Florida visiting friends while the Sentinels invaded their house and are not actually dead, rotting in the basement.

My phone buzzes, but I ignore it. No doubt it's Haden again. It didn't take long for him to hear the story Evie spread about what happened to me. Not the truth, of course, but part of our plan to make sure the Sentinels know Mason is gone. Evie told a few of her most gossip hungry friends about a creepy guy with a scar who has been stalking me. We blamed him for the knife attack and made sure everyone knew what he looked like. The school is even going to post pictures of the sketch the police did all around the school.

It's a good plan, but I refuse to give Robin's parents any credit. They took Mason away from me, and I will never forgive them for that.

A knock sounds at my door, and I look up expecting Evie, but finding Robin instead. A heavy breath flows out of me. I think this is the first time I have ever been relieved to see Robin. Not that I will admit it, but I turn around eagerly to face her.

"He's safe?" I ask desperately.

She nods as she sits down on the bed with me. Part of me wants to push her off, but the other part clings to the pity I felt when I realized how badly her parents treat her. I know she's made mistakes, but she doesn't deserve to be hated by her own family.

"How much can you tell me?" I ask.

"Not much." Her eyes stare at the blanket beneath her legs. She bites at her bottom lip as she squeezes her hands together. "All I know is that a Caretaker family met us out in the middle of nowhere late last night and hustled him into their car. They told my parents they'd pass my mom and dad's contact info onto the next family so whoever has him in February will be able to get in touch with us and set up the meeting."

I nod, treasuring even this tiny amount of information. At this point, I think I hate the Caretakers just as much as I hate the Sentinels, but I know they'll protect Mason. From what Robin managed to tell me before they left last night, her parents aren't even the worst of the Caretakers when it comes to their fanaticism with fulfilling their purpose. They'll keep him safe.

● ● ●

"Did Mason say anything before…before they took him?" I ask quietly.

Robin's mouth turns down at the corners. "He said he'd find a way to let you know he's safe."

"How?" I ask.

She shakes her head. "I don't know, but I've learned not to doubt him."

I don't doubt Mason either, but I don't know how long it will take him to find a way to contact me. I don't know how long I can bear waiting. The air in Mason's bedroom seems thick. It's almost claustrophobic, but I can't bring myself to get up and leave it. An irrational part of me fears it will all disappear if I step out of his room, that every reminder I have of him will be stolen away like he was.

"I hate your parents."

The words slip out of my mouth before I can stop them. I wasn't planning to say them, but once they are out, I don't regret them even a little.

Robin snorts. "Join the club."

"It's not just about Mason," I say. "Whatever you've done, it isn't right that they treated you the way they did."

She shrugs slowly. "I don't know. Maybe they're right. I should have been able to live up to their expectations, but I haven't."

"They shouldn't hate you for that."

"But they do," she says stiffly.

A strange silence falls over us. It's not awkward, because we are beyond that, but it isn't comfortable. It feels charged, like we are both on the edge of doing something drastic, but don't know where to start. We need each other's help, I realize. I know what I want. I want to save Mason's life, hopefully without losing mine if at all possible. To do that, I need to know as much about being an Escort as I can. I need Robin's help.

But what does she want? And why does she need my help? I stare at her, trying to figure it out, but everything about her is closed down right now. Robin is a Caretaker, and I have already decided that they are a group I should be wary to trust. I have no one else, though. Whatever Robin is after, I have no choice but to hope it is the same thing I want, or at the very least, that it won't stop me from saving Mason.

"Robin," I say hesitantly, "how would you like to know the truth?"

"The truth?" she asks. She voices the question, but I can see in her eyes that she knows exactly what I'm talking about. Her feigned ignorance only lasts a second longer before her hands tighten into fists. "You don't believe them either?"

I shake my head. "If there's one thing Caretakers are good at, it's keeping secrets."

"I knew they were lying when they said they didn't know what happens to Escorts," Robin says, "but I don't know how to prove it. I know they're lying about other things too, but where do I start trying to find the truth?"

It's a good question, one I don't really have the answer to. I can only choose a direction and hope it is the right one. "They said that some Escorts have returned, right?"

Robin nods.

"Then we need to locate one of them and find out what really happened."

"How?" Robin asks.

Another good question. Another answer I don't have. "We'll find a way."

For a moment, Robin looks skeptical, but then her resolve tightens. She nods and the beaten down look in her eyes disappears. Robin might be the last person I want to form a secret alliance with, but Mason's life is worth putting aside petty jealousy and anger. She's my only way into the secretive world of the Caretakers. Trusting her is still a huge risk, but doing nothing will cost Mason his life.

Robin and I turn when Evie walks into the room. I know she has taken Mason's leaving hard, but there is no evidence of weakness in her stance as she stops in front of the bed. Her hard eyes dart between the two of us. For a moment, I wonder where my silly, girly, jabbering little sister has gone. It's a fleeting thought, though, because I have always known that under her prissy exterior is the kind of strength you never have to doubt.

"So, have you two come up with a plan yet, or what?" Evie asks.

"Are you offering to help?" Robin asks skeptically.

I stand up and put my arm around Evie's shoulder. "Did you ever doubt she would?"

Robin doesn't look entirely convinced of Evie, but she sighs and shakes her head. "We can start with my grandma. I don't know if she'll know where we can find an Escort who returned, but I don't know who else to turn to. My parents are obviously out."

"Obviously," Evie snaps.

Gently, I push Evie back before she starts clawing Robin's eyes out. "Why are you doing this?" I ask Robin.

"Because I care about Mason," she says, as if the answer should be obvious.

I shake my head at her. "It's more than that. If you want us to trust you, I want the real answer."

Robin pushes herself up from the bed slowly. Every movement is hard and jerky. There is a flame of determination in her eyes that startles me. "The real answer?" Her teeth grind together. "If you had to live every day with two people who despise you, wouldn't you want to escape? Wouldn't you do anything to get out from under their hateful eyes? I can't spend the rest of my life with them."

"The rest of your life?" Evie snorts. "You're almost eighteen. You'll get to move out soon, and then you never have to see them again if you don't want to."

Robin's head starts shaking halfway through Evie's comment. "I can never leave. It's my punishment for breaking my covenants to protect Eliana. Among Caretakers, I am a prisoner. Even if I try to run, they'll find me. Believe me, I've tried."

"What?" I ask slowly. "You've run away before?"

"And they drug me back, every time."

Evie stares at Robin as if seeing her for the first time. "How many times have you run away?"

"At least ten, maybe more. I've lost track."

Pressing my hand to my forehead, I try to understand what she's telling me. "So, you want Mason to...take you with him?"

Her bottom lip begins to tremble. "It's the only place they won't be able to find me."

"Is that even possible?" I ask.

Robin shrugs. "Probably not, but I have to try." She wipes away a tear before it can slither down her cheek. "I know you have every reason not to trust me, but I'm begging you to give me a chance."

Evie and I look over at each other with the same question in our eyes. She could be lying. She's a Caretaker after all. But if she is, I can't figure out what benefit she would get out of it. Even if she reported everything to her parents, they want the same thing we do—to see Mason get home safely.

I look away from my sister and turn back to Robin, still unsure. It's clear from Robin's expression that she knows we are not convinced. A strange look of resolve mixed with shame settles over her. I watch as her fingers grip the bottom of her t-shirt. She only has to lift it an inch or two before Evie and I both gasp, but she pulls her shirt up to just beneath her bra so we can see the full extent of what living with her parents has cost her. The collection of mottled bruises covering her abdomen is staggering.

"I am well aware that trying to cross into the Aerling world might kill me," Robin says, "but at this point, it's a risk I'm willing to take."

Evie and I don't need to look at each other. We both nod, accepting Robin's help and making the decision to trust her. There is still no guarantee that we are making the right choice, but when does life ever guarantee anything?

The three of us sit back down on Mason's bed. The room is quiet until I speak. "If I'm supposed to be able to take Mason home, it must mean that either I have some kind of power capable of doing that, or something about me is inherently different. We need to find out everything we can about Escorts and how they cross between worlds. Whatever the Caretakers are lying about, we need to be prepared for it."

"We will be," Evie says. Her hand slips into mine and squeezes. "We aren't going to let anything bad happen to Mason, or to you. We'll figure this out, Olivia."

We spend the next hour tossing out ideas and brainstorming for even the most outrageous possibilities. I think all three of us could have gone on for hours longer, but a call from Robin's parents cuts it short. It is an odd experience to hug Robin before she leaves. I am careful not to hurt her, but I am not prepared for the feeling of responsibility I feel toward her when I pull back.

"Thank you," she says quietly, before turning and walking out to her car.

Evie asks me if I want to talk, but I am too exhausted to do anything but collapse into bed. Night is still hours away, but I can't keep my eyes open more than twenty seconds after my head touches the pillow. I wake hours later to my phone vibrating under my face.

My first instinct is to push it aside and go back to sleep, but the preview of a text message from a number I don't recognize flashes on the screen and yanks me up to sitting. I slide my finger across the screen in a panic, an irrational fear that it will disappear before I can read it plaguing me. I bring up the message, holding my breath.

I am safe. I love U, Ollie. We'll be 2gether soon. I promise.

The End

...

Chapter 1

A Dangerous Idea

Being invisible once seemed like a curse. After the last few days of constant supervision, I wish I could go back to being the guy nobody even knew existed. I never realized how much I valued my privacy until it was gone. Losing it to complete strangers makes it even worse. Losing it because there is a whole society of killers out to murder me makes it unbearable.

"You're not listening," Molly complains.

"Huh?"

She sighs and shakes her head. "Mason," she whines, "you have to learn how to harness you're power or you won't have a chance against the Sentinels when they find you."

"When?" I question. "What happened to if?"

Molly screws up her cute little nose at me. A sudden pang shoots through my chest as her innocent expression reminds me of Olivia. It's been three days, only three days, since we were separated from each other, but the hole in my chest only seems to get bigger every second I can't see her or touch her.

Small, seven-year-old fingers wrap around my larger hand. Molly squeezes, but I can feel a slight tremble in her hand. It surprises me and causes me to look at her. The pleading look in her eyes captures my attention.

"Mason, please focus, okay? They're expecting me to teach you while you're here. You have to learn to access your power and control it. You're important to them, to all the Caretakers. You have to try harder," she begs.

"Why? What makes me so important to them?"

Molly bites her bottom lip. "You know you're one of the ruling class. You're stronger than the rest of us. It's been a long time since the Caretakers were responsible for someone like you. They have to succeed this time."

Something about her voice piques my attention. She sounds nervous, anxious, more so than seems justified. "What do you mean *this time*?"

"Um, just...just that it's, uh, important that you make it back. They want all the Aerlings to get home, of course, but people like you are more important than people like me."

"How would they know?" I ask. "They don't know what happens after Aerlings go home, right?"

Molly shakes her head, brunette ringlets bouncing into her eyes.

"Then how do they know?"

"I…don't know," she says. "I just know that they told me I *had* to teach you."

Feeling the trembling in her hands increase, I decide not to push her anymore about what she thinks will happen if she doesn't succeed in teaching me. The Brittons are not Molly's biological family, of course. She's an Aerling like I am. They are the only family she has ever known, though, and they remind me more of Robin's harsh, unbending parents than Olivia's loving family. I have no doubt that failure will mean punishment for Molly.

I'm not giving up on this topic, though. Attempting to steer the conversation in a less threatening direction, I ask, "What happened the last time there was a ruling Aerling, like me?"

Still visibly upset, Molly relaxes somewhat and answers the question. "Usually, ruling Aerlings are identified at a young age. They show special talents right away. As soon as they're identified, they start intensive training. The Caretakers are afraid of failing."

"Why? What does it matter?" I ask. "Aerlings go home when they turn eighteen and never come back. Who cares if they aren't at their full potential when they leave?"

"It's not about the Aerling," Molly says quietly.

Her eyes are downcast. I am tempted to pull her chin up and make her face me, but I don't want to scare her. The Brittons are intimidating and borderline unkind. I like Molly, though. She is a sweet little girl, and the only friend I have in this strange place. I feel a sense of responsibility for her as well.

Turning so I can put one arm around her small shoulders, I hug her against my side. "If it's not about the Aerlings, what is it about?"

"The last time the Caretakers found someone like you, their training didn't work. They blamed the Aerling, I guess. They said he wasn't quite right and couldn't learn to control his power. When he tried to use his talents, things got scary. When he turned eighteen, they were more than happy to send him on his way, but the bad things didn't stop when he left."

"What happened?"

Molly doesn't answer right away. Her lips press together, probably to stop them from trembling. She tucks her body more tightly against mine. "The first time it happened was the day he went home, not an hour after the Aerling and his Escort vanished. It was one of the Caretaker children, the ones closest to his age that was first. Nobody could explain why she just

● ● ●

222

stopped breathing. Nobody connected the dots at first. It took two more of the family members dying for them to realize what was happening. And it didn't stop with the family. Everyone who tried to teach the Aerling was dead within weeks of him leaving."

Finding a response to what she's just told me is impossible. If I don't learn to control my power before my eighteenth birthday, it could kill everyone who has tried to train me. Does that extend to non-Caretakers? Could Olivia's family be in danger? Robin for sure would be held responsible. I don't know if Molly would, as she's an Aerling, but I can only imagine the way she would be treated if the Brittons were affected because she failed to teach me control.

I am supposed to be moved every two weeks until my birthday. That's five months away. That is ten different families I will live with before then who will all be responsible for training me. Ten families could be dead because I can't stop thinking about how much I miss Olivia long enough to train.

"Molly, I'm sorry."

She shakes her head, almost angrily. "I'm not trying to blame you," she says. "It won't hurt me. I'm an Aerling. And even if it hurts the Brittons …"

Molly doesn't finish her thought, but she really doesn't need to. I felt the coldness of this house the moment I stepped through the door three days ago.

"You're scared, though," I say quietly.

She nods.

"Why?"

It takes a moment before Molly pulls away from me enough to meet my gaze. Her tiny frame looks so small sitting in front of me, vulnerable and fragile. I stay silent as she gathers her courage.

"What will happen to me if there isn't enough time to train you?"

Before Robin's parents handed me over to the Brittons, they gave me strict instructions not to discuss any of the details that brought me to that moment. I was forbidden to tell anyone that my original Caretakers were murdered in front of me when I was five years old. I was definitely not allowed to tell anyone that Olivia found me a few days later, wandering lost and alone and I have been living with her family for the last twelve years.

The only information exchanged between Robin's family and the Brittons was that the Sentinels had found me and I had to be kept on the move until my birthday.

To myself, I added that I should never tell anyone that Olivia was my Escort, the person meant to guide me from Earth back to the world of the Aerlings on my eighteenth birthday. Not that either myself or Olivia knows how that is supposed to work. I also didn't need to be told that I should keep the fact that I can choose to reveal myself to people, both visually an audibly. That is not something Aerlings are supposed to be able to do. Robin's parents do not know about that certain ability, and I intend to keep it that way.

I pull Molly into my lap. She is so light, it takes hardly any effort. She snuggles against me immediately, and I can guess she rarely gets this much affection. It saddens me and makes me wonder if my memories of my Caretakers those first five years of life are tinted as if being seen through rose colored glasses. I remember being happy with them, but the only other Caretakers I have met have not been like that at all. I want Molly to be happy like I was up until three days ago.

"Molly," I say, "how good are you at memorizing?"

Not prepared for this seemingly random question, Molly looks up at me oddly for a moment before answering. "Good. It's one of the things I'm best at."

I nod, pleased. "I want you to remember what I'm about to tell you. If you're ever in trouble, I know someone who will help you and take care of you."

Molly's eyes widen. "Other Caretakers?"

When I shake my head, her eyes widen even more. "No, they aren't Caretakers, Molly. This is the first time I've lived with Caretakers since I was five years old."

The way Molly's eyes dart around fearfully puts me on edge as well. I scan the living room carefully. When we are both convinced that we're truly alone, I lower my voice and tell Molly what I was told never to tell anyone. I repeat Olivia's address and her home phone number until Molly has it memorized. She proves her superior memorization abilities when she has the information stowed away in only a few minutes.

I can see the hope filling her eyes, but she isn't convinced yet. "But, how will they know I'm there? They won't be able to see or hear me."

"Don't worry, they'll find a way to make it work." I hesitate, not sure how much I can tell her. No doubt it is a risk, but I feel connected to Molly and I refuse to leave her alone and scared. "Maybe…maybe I can teach you a few things before I leave, too."

Molly looks at me sideways, not sure if I'm playing with her. Her eyes glint with the desire to believe me. The corner of my mouth turns up, and suddenly I want to teach her. I don't even know if I can, but I am determined to try.

Mrs. Britton walks in from the front yard where she was preparing flower beds for the quickly approaching winter months. Her eyes narrow at the sight of me holding Molly on my lap. She stops in the hallway. "Are you two working?"

"Yes, ma'am," Molly says quickly as she scoots away from me and crosses her legs.

"I should hope so," Mrs. Britton says. "You have very little time, Molly. Don't waste it."

"I won't," Molly says quietly.

Mrs. Britton nods and continues on her way.

Disturbed by Mrs. Britton's words, I turn to Molly and say, "Olivia's family will take you in, no matter why you show up on their doorstep."

Molly blinks quickly, but a tear escapes and rolls down her cheek. "They sound like a wonderful family. No wonder you can't focus. If I had a family like that, I'd never want to be away from them either."

I smile at her, but it is stretched thin.

"Will you tell me about them?" Molly asks quietly.

This time it is much easier to smile. "Of course."

As I quietly regale Molly with stories of Olivia, Evie, and my life with their family, the ache in my chest returns worse than ever. I can't talk about Olivia without picturing her beautiful face, her soft lips and sweet smile. Images of the last moments we were together swim in my mind, making me lose focus and falter.

Suddenly, it's difficult to breathe. I want her so badly. I hate being away from her. There is no way I can spend the next five months away from her. I know I should not even entertain such a dangerous idea, but dreams of grabbing Molly and running back to Olivia fill my mind to overflowing.

About the Author

DelSheree Gladden lives in New Mexico with her husband and two children. The Southwest is a big influence in her writing because of its culture, beauty, and mythology. Local folk lore is strongly rooted in her writing, particularly ideas of prophecy, destiny, and talents born from natural abilities. When she is not writing, DelSheree is usually reading, painting, sewing, or working as a Dental Hygienist. Her works include *Escaping Fate, Twin Souls Saga, The Destroyer Trilogy*, and *Invisible*. Look for, *Wicked Power*, the next book in the *SomeOne Wicked This Way Comes Series*, and *Soul Stone*, book two in the *Escaping Fate Series*, coming 2014.

Connect with DelSheree online at:

http://www.delshereegladden.com

http://delshereegladden.blogspot.com/

Smashwords:
https://www.smashwords.com/profile/view/DelShereeG

Facebook:
https://www.facebook.com/AuthorDelShereeGladden

Book Blog:
http://theediblebookshelf.blogspot.com/

Goodreads:
http://www.goodreads.com/author/show/4305414.DelSheree_Gladden

9436919R00134

Made in the USA
San Bernardino, CA
16 March 2014